WITHDRAWN
UTSA LIBRARIES

GREEK WEDDING

*Books by Jane Aiken Hodge*

Greek Wedding
Marry in Haste
The Winding Stair
Here Comes a Candle
Watch the Wall, My Darling
The Adventurers
Maulever Hall

# GREEK WEDDING

JANE AIKEN HODGE

Doubleday & Company, Inc.
Garden City, New York 1970

*All of the characters in this book are fictitious, and any resemblance to actual persons, living or dead, is purely coincidental.*

*Library of Congress Catalog Card Number 79–116214*
*Copyright © 1970 by Jane Aiken Hodge*
*All Rights Reserved*
*Printed in the United States of America*
*First Edition in the United States of America*

# GREEK WEDDING

Historical Note: *The War of Greek Independence began in 1821, and ended, to all intents and purposes, with the intervention of the Great Powers (Great Britain, France and Russia), and the Battle of Navarino in 1827. I am not rash enough even to try and summarise the events between these two dates, but it is important, for the purposes of my story, to remember that neither Turks nor Greeks were internally united. The Sultan of Turkey was threatened both by the power of his own army élite, the Janissaries, and by the increasing strength and independence of his Egyptian vassals. The Greeks, for their part, passionately united, immensely brave (and cruel) when danger threatened, fought just as bitterly among themselves when the outside pressure slackened.*

*Meanwhile the first concern of the Great Powers was to maintain the European balance so precariously achieved in 1815. There was immense popular support for the Greek cause, partly owing to the romantic involvement of Lord Byron, but at the diplomatic level the case was quite different. Allied intervention was late, reluctant and tentative. The Battle of Navarino itself, a kind of inspired accident, was described in Parliament as 'this untoward event', and Sir Edward Codrington, who commanded the Allied Fleet, was first given the GCB and then recalled for having exceeded his instructions. But by destroying the Turkish fleet, he had ensured Greek liberty*

*I am overwhelmingly indebted to C. M. Woodhouse, whose three books,* The Greek War of Independence, The Battle of Navarino, *and* The Story of Modern Greece, *have helped me steer my course through the remarkable number of conflicting contemporary records of this war. A bibliography of the histories, memoirs and travel books I have read would be long enough, I think, to seem ostentatious in connection with a romantic work like this. I can only urge any reader who wants to know more about this war, with its fascinating implications for the situation of modern Greece, to begin with C. M. Woodhouse and go on from there.*

# 1

The last glow of sunset faded from the still water of the Golden Horn. As quick night fell over Constantinople, the sounds of fighting began to die away. Merciful darkness hid the mangled bodies of the Janissaries that hung in clusters from the trees of the old city, but red light in the direction of the Et Meidan Square showed where their barracks were still burning. An occasional hoarse cry, a volley of shots echoing out over the water of the harbour meant that another of them had been hunted to his death by the Sultan's men.

On the deck of his steam-yacht *Helena,* Brett Renshaw lifted a skull-shaped goblet to drink a toast: 'It's the end of an era.'

'Or the beginning.' Captain Barlow moved restlessly across the deck to stare up at the lighted buildings on Seraglio Point. 'We've got steam up, sir. I wish you'd let me give the order to sail. I'll be glad to be safe away from these murdering Turks.'

'And miss the end of the massacre? I think not. We came to the Mediterranean to find adventure and, by God, we've found it.' He was a little drunk, not seriously so yet. 'You want to drag me away from the first real distraction I've had since we left England?' He drank again from the sinister goblet. 'Here's to Sultan Mahmoud the Second! And may this year of grace, eighteen twenty-six, bring him victory over the Greek rebels as it has over his mutinous Janissaries.'

'How can you, sir?' Now Barlow was shocked. 'Those poor Greeks are only fighting for their freedom.'

' "Poor Greeks," indeed! A mob of piratical Jacobins! They're no more fit for freedom than the French ones were. I tell you.' He spoke with the careful emphasis of the slightly tipsy. 'Now Mahmoud's dealt with the threat of the Janissaries at home, he'll give his rebel subjects in Greece short shrift, you see if he doesn't.'

'It's what he'll do to us bothers me. Tyrants don't much

like witnesses to their tyranny, Mr. Renshaw. I wish you'd let me give the order to sail.'

'To steam, you mean! You're forgetting, Captain. With our engines, we can show the Turks a clean pair of heels any time we want to.'

'So long as the engines don't fail.'

'Oh, for God's sake, get below, you old Jonah. I'll let you know when I'm ready to sail, and it will be when I *am* ready, and not a moment before.'

'Very good, sir.' On the long voyage out from England, Captain Barlow had learned to like his difficult employer, and to modulate from friend to employee as his moods required.

Left alone, Brett stared unseeing for a while at the fringe of mosque and minaret outlined against the afterglow in the western sky. He was looking into himself, and disliking what he saw. ' "Distraction." ' He quoted himself with disgust. 'A massacre. The first real distraction. It's true, too.' He moved over to a table on the foredeck and refilled the skull goblet. 'Congratulations, Helena, you've made me the monster you wanted. And still your slave–like those "poor Greeks" Barlow talks about. Freedom.' He savoured the word. 'Why not?' Suddenly resolute, he shook something out of a paper into the dark wine. 'Freedom.' And then: 'Helena, this draft I drink to thee!'

But he lowered the goblet, untasted, at the sound of muffled oars from the direction of Seraglio Point. Since he had sent both Captain Barlow and the lookout below, he was alone on deck, responsible for the *Helena* and her crew. Well, what of that? He raised the goblet again. Drink this, and it was no affair of his.

He shrugged irritably in the darkness. No use. Brought up in the tradition of responsibility, he found he simply could not bow out, drink his poisoned draft and leave Barlow and the crew exposed to whatever danger was approaching, stealthily, with muffled oars. Besides, suddenly cheerful, he put down the goblet: he had wanted distraction and here it was. A fleeing Janissary perhaps? Would it be amusing to help him escape? He leant his elbows on the rail and peered down into darkness.

He could see nothing. The boat must be without lights.

So—either a fugitive or a secret attack of some kind. Tyrants don't like witnesses to their tyranny. He ought to do something; call Captain Barlow; have him rouse the crew; prepare to defend the yacht . . . He stayed, leaning on the rail, staring into the darkness, listening to the furtive beat of the oars. Only one pair. Nothing, surely, very formidable about that.

Now, he could hear whispering voices. And at last the shape of a small boat loomed, a darker shadow in the darkness, not more than a hundred yards from the *Helena.*

Stupid! In the still night, a lantern burned on the deck behind him. He must be clearly illuminated, a standing target to the rowers in the boat. He was across the deck in a bound, to blow out the light, and wait, motionless, till his eyes got used to the darkness. Back at the rail, he thought the little boat had lost way. Yes, the oars were silent: only the sound of whispering came across the water.

He really ought to summon Barlow. Still he did nothing. Darkness and silence stretched out round him. Then, suddenly, an outburst of shouting drew his eyes up to the lights of Seraglio Point. Something was happening in the palace. Torches flared here and there among the hanging gardens he had admired when they sailed into the Golden Horn the week before. Trouble in the harem? He smiled to himself, suddenly sorry for Sultan Mahmoud. Women! he thought, and was distracted once more by the sound of oars. The boat was approaching again, quickly now, sacrificing silence to speed. And then, astonishing, a woman's voice, low, cautious, from across the water: 'Ahoy there, *Helena,* can you hear me?'

Women! A woman at least. The sex he had left England to escape. Memories flooded back, bitter as Acheron. Helena. An angel with hair *à la grecque*; her laugh; the perfume she used; the butterfly caresses she sometimes allowed. And her last words to him: the ruthless dismissal . . .

'Are you there, *Helena*? Can you hear me?' The boat was nearer now and he could sense panic in the strained whisper. Well, serve her right, whoever she was. An adventuress, of course. What else could she be? What else were any of them?

The boat was very close. The shadowy figure of the

rower backed water to hold her steady beside the yacht. A second figure sat huddled in the bows. It was most unlikely that they could see him, as he stood black against the blackness of the *Helena*'s huge, boxed-in paddle wheel. Another burst of shouting from the shore drew his eyes once more to Seraglio Point, where torches flashed among the hanging gardens as if in some mad game of hide-and-seek.

'*Hélène*!' Now the woman spoke in French. 'For the love of God let us come on board. It's death if we're caught. You'd not leave two women to the vengeance of the Turk?'

Two women! As if one was not enough. Her French was almost as good as her English but both were spoken with a curious, rather attractive accent. If one could imagine anything about a woman as being attractive. Whatever vengeance these two were fleeing had doubtless been richly earned. He had nothing to say to them, and stayed in the shadows, watching, as the rower took the little boat slowly down the *Helena*'s length, obviously looking for some way to board her. She was out of luck, he thought savagely, and surprised himself with the realisation that he was imagining Helena herself down there, helpless and panic-stricken in the dark.

Panic-stricken? The little boat had reached the anchor cable and he could see a flurry of activity on board. Yes, they had tied up to the cable. He moved quietly down the deck to see what would happen next. Behind him, the poisoned goblet stood untasted on the table.

'Mr. Renshaw! What's happening?' Captain Barlow stood, lantern in hand, at the entrance to the companionway, straining to see beyond its light.

'A couple of women in a boat.' Carelessly. 'They say they want to come on board. God knows why. They're not going to, that's certain.' Brett spoke loud enough for them to hear.

'For pity's sake, help us!' From her tone, the woman had indeed heard him. 'You'd not leave a dog to the fate we shall suffer if we're caught. We've fled from the Sultan's harem.'

'Good gracious!' Barlow was a mild-spoken man. 'Then we must lose no time in getting you safe on board.'

'Two of the Sultan's whores? What are you thinking of?' Brett exploded. 'I'll not have them on my ship.'

'It may be your ship, Mr. Renshaw, but I'm its captain. And after what we've seen and heard today, I'd not leave a mad dog to the mercy of the Turks.' He leaned over the rail and gave a series of quick instructions to the women in the boat. 'And the last one out had better sink her,' he concluded. 'Then there's a chance they'll think you're drowned. Can you do it?'

'No trouble at all.' Incredibly, there was a hint of laughter. 'The problem's been to keep her afloat. But you'll need to give my aunt a hand on board, sir. She's not so young as she was, and not well either.' And then, to her companion: 'Of course you can, Aunt Cass. You can't fail me now.'

Vowing vengeance (back in England he would see to it that Captain Barlow never got another ship), Brett Renshaw found himself actually helping get the two women on board. The silent one came first and it took all their strength and ingenuity to get her up. Safe on deck, she spoke at last. 'Oh, God bless you, sir, but, please, don't waste a minute. Miss Vannick! Help her!'

Brett could hardly believe his eyes or ears. This fugitive from the Sultan's harem was speaking to him, like an equal, in the voice of an English gentlewoman. Less irritating, if more surprising, she was revealed in the lamplight as a little, colourless, dried-up spinster, somewhere in the no-woman's land between forty and sixty. 'Please,' she went on, 'don't trouble about me. Help your friend with Miss Vannick.'

But no help was needed. Already, the little boat was settling in the water, as the second woman came agilely, hand over hand, up on deck, to be silhouetted, dripping wet, against the light of the lantern Barlow had hung at the foremast. Her Turkish costume of flowing tunic and full trousers clung revealingly to the figure of a Diana, but all her thought was for her companion. 'Cass! You're not hurt?' And then, reassured by a murmured reply, 'God bless you, sir.' To Barlow. 'But we must lose no time. They're still searching the palace gardens, but any minute now they'll find how we got out. And then–'

'Yes.' Barlow turned to Brett. 'With your permission, sir, I'll give the order to sail at once.'

'I'm surprised you trouble to ask me.' Brett was in a cold rage and did not try to hide it. 'But, yes, since you have risked all our lives for a couple of the Turks' whores, I suppose we had best turn tail and run for it.'

'I don't know who you are, sir!' The older woman turned on him like a fury. 'And I don't much care, but if you were King George the Fourth you'd have no right to speak of Miss Vannick like that. Apologise, please, this instant.'

The younger woman went into a peal of laughter; then, quickly, put her hand over her mouth to stifle it. 'Or we'll jump back into the harbour, Aunt Cass? Be reasonable. This gentleman seems to own the yacht, and frankly I don't much care what he calls us so long as he gets us out of here alive. And himself, too.' She turned to Barlow. 'I do recommend you lose no time, sir. Sultan Mahmoud's a bad man to cross. I'm ashamed to have involved you in this trouble . . .'

'That's all right, miss. Luckily we've got our clearance already, and steam up, too. They're not to know our sailing has anything to do with you.'

'I hope not.' But he had turned away to rouse the crew.

Left alone with her reluctant host, Miss Vannick took charge of the situation. 'I'm sorry, Mr.—' She paused hopefully.

'Renshaw. Brett Renshaw. At your service, it seems.' He said it without pleasure.

'I *am* sorry.' She answered tone rather than words. 'But let me introduce my aunt, Miss Cassandra Knight. And I'm Phyllida Vannick, from New York.' She said it, he thought irritably, almost as if she expected him to have heard of her.

'Welcome on board the *Helena*.' His tone belied the hospitable words. He crossed the deck to where his poisoned goblet still stood untasted on the table. 'Captain Barlow will take good care of you, I am sure, as soon as we are under way.' His hand went out to the goblet. Why not? It was the obvious escape.

'Oh, how kind!' Phyllida Vannick had followed him. 'It's just what Aunt Cass needs.'

He might poison himself, but he could not murder—even a woman. He looked for a distraction, and found it easily. 'There they come.' He upset the goblet as he pointed back to Seraglio Point. 'You'd best get below, Miss Vannick. I'll take you to my cabin.' It was merely the last straw to find himself compelled to give it up to them.

'I'm sorry,' the girl said again. 'We won't impose on you a minute longer than we must. And we are *grateful,* aren't we Aunt Cass?'

'To the captain. Yes.' Miss Knight had not moved from her original position by the rail. 'As for you, Mr. Renshaw, I am still awaiting your apology.'

'Oh, Aunt, be reasonable.' There was laughter in the girl's voice again. 'What do you expect Mr. Renshaw to think of us, arriving as we did?'

'I don't care what he thinks,' said Miss Knight. 'It's what he said that we're discussing. I'm English myself, Mr. Renshaw. I thought a gentleman–you *sound* like a gentleman–was raised to a certain code of good manners. I can tell you one thing, if any of my brothers had spoken to two ladies as you did, he'd have had his mouth washed out with soap, and quickly, too.'

Phyllida Vannick was laughing again. 'Dear Aunt,' she said, 'I'd like to have seen you do it to Father.' And then, disconcertingly, on a sob, 'Oh, poor Father–'

'Now look what you've done.' Once more, Miss Knight turned on Brett. 'You've reminded her of her father, that she saw cut down before her eyes.'

'Cut down? I'm afraid I don't understand–'

'Well,' said Miss Knight, 'you didn't, surely, think we were in the Sultan's harem for the pleasure of it, did you?'

'Of course he did.' Miss Vannick had herself in control again. 'And we won't burden him with our affairs, Aunt.' It was, unmistakably, an order. 'All we ask, Mr. Renshaw, is asylum on your ship until we are out of reach of the Turks. We will take care to be as little trouble to you, or your crew, as possible. And, of course, we will pay you for our accommodation.'

'Pay?' As she spoke she had moved forward between him and the lantern, so that every detail of her admirable figure was outlined against its light. 'With your diamonds, I suppose?'

'If you like. Though it would mean waiting while I get them out of store in New York.' And then, suddenly understanding, she whisked herself into the shadow and changed to a tone of steel. 'Now I will have that apology, Mr. Renshaw. Your first insult was understandable. I don't blame you for the misapprehension. But now, Aunt Cass is right. If you are an English gentleman, as she seems to think?' She made it a question. 'You have had time to recognise us as ladies in distress, though it's true that I am an American one. Look!' In her turn she pointed to the shore, where they could see frenzied activity at sea level. 'They're getting the boats out. Shall I call and tell them we're here? It will mean a slow and subtle death for us all. Or shall I have your apology?' She paused. 'It seems a little hard on Captain Barlow and your crew.'

'Yes.' He was angrier than ever, but quite helpless. 'And on your aunt, Miss Vannick.' If only he had not spilled that wine. He caricatured a ceremonious bow. 'Accept my humble apologies, ma'am, for anything I may have said to offend you. And you, too, Miss Knight.' His tone warmed a little as he spoke to the older lady.

'Well, thank goodness for that,' said Cassandra Knight. At last she abandoned her station by the rail and came across the deck to the lighted opening of the companionway. 'I take it you're one of the Renshaws of Sarum, sir.'

If it was meant for an olive branch, it was an unlucky one. 'A cousin.' His voice was cold again. 'And now, perhaps, you will do me the honour of coming down to my cabin.'

'We'll make it very wet, I'm afraid.' Phyllida Vannick had recovered her temper. 'Cass is not so bad, but I had to swim out to the boat.'

He suddenly realised that she was shivering in the warm June air, and fighting to hide it. It put him, finally, irretrievably in the wrong. And, to make matters worse, he was aware of curious glances from the members of the crew, who were now busy on deck, making ready to sail. 'We'd best get out of the way,' he said. 'Down here, Miss Vannick–Miss Knight.' He ushered them down the companionway to the large saloon in the stern of the ship that served him as dining and living room. 'My cabin's through there. Do, please, make yourselves quite at home.' Once again his tone made nonsense of the hospitable words.

Left alone, the two women stood for a minute, looking at each other in silence. Then, 'He doesn't much like us,' said Phyllida Vannick. 'Poor man.'

'"Poor man!"' Miss Knight crossed to the half-open

door of the cabin. 'I wouldn't waste my sympathy on him if I were you. If it weren't for the captain, we'd be in the Turks' hands by now. Listen!'

Phyllida was making sure that the curtains at the cabin portholes were closely drawn. 'He likes his comforts, doesn't he?' She fingered the soft black velvet, then stopped to listen to shouting outside.

'What are they saying, Phyllida?'

'What you'd expect. The Turks began by asking if we'd been seen. Mr. Renshaw's doing it well, to give the devil his due. He's playing for time. First he pretended not to hear, then not to understand. Now he's telling them he's seen no one. They sound very near. No! Don't look, Aunt. I just hope Captain Barlow really had got steam up. I wish I knew more about these steamboats. The ones on the Hudson work well enough, I know, but whether the English can manage them–'

'What is it now?' Her aunt had seen the change in her face.

'The Turks want to come on board and search. They were bound to, I suppose. In case we have stowed away. That's how they put it. Clever of them: it gives him a way out, if he wants to take it.'

'Phyl! He wouldn't?' But it was a question.

'We must hope not. He'd be crazy, of course. The state the Turks are in tonight, they won't care two cents for the chance of an international incident. If they find us, they'll kill everyone on board, and call it a regrettable mistake afterwards. I just hope Mr. Renshaw has the sense to realise that. No use hiding, if they do come. Would you say the engine was making a different noise?'

'Yes. Is that good, do you think?'

'We might as well hope so.' She came back from Brett's cabin with a silver-mounted pistol. 'Loaded,' she said. 'Obliging of him. You won't mind, Aunt?'

'Of course I shall mind,' said Cassandra Knight. 'Who wants to be dead? But, yes please, Phyl.'

'That's settled then. But not till the last moment. He's not doing so badly up there. He's asking them why in the world he should let them on board after what he's seen and heard today. How does he know, he says, that they're not fugitive Janissaries themselves, who will take over the ship the moment they get aboard. He's a true friend of Sultan Mahmoud's. He must have proof that they really are his officers. I don't know how they are going to set about proving it out there in the dark.'

'I don't suppose they'll try,' said Cassandra. 'They sound awfully angry, Phyl.'

'Yes. They're insisting on coming on board. They'll show him their credentials then. They say.'

'Are there many of them?'

'Hard to tell. But if it should come to a fight, we're lost anyway. It will alert the harbour guard. We'll never get past the point alive. I'm sorry, Aunt. It's all my fault. I should never have brought you.'

'Dear Phyl, you know perfectly well you had no choice. I told your father I'd look after you, and I shall. Besides, I love you, child. You're all the family I'll ever have, and if you're going to die, I want to be right here along with you. What's that? Are they coming aboard?'

'No, I don't think so. Aunt Cass, I rather think it was the anchor coming up. My God, I believe we're moving.'

'Phyllida,' said her aunt, 'I don't like to hear you take your Maker's name in vain.'

# 2

Half an hour later, Brett Renshaw was irritated to find himself knocking tentatively on the door of his own saloon. It opened at once. 'Congratulations,' said Phyllida Vannick.

'Thank you. Yes. We're well out into the Bosphorus by now. Our troubles are over—at least until we reach the Dardanelles.' And then, to Cassandra Knight, who was hovering anxiously in the background, 'There's no wind. They can't follow by sea. With luck, they won't try by land.'

'No?' Phyllida sounded unconvinced.

'How well do you know the Turks, Miss Vannick? For them, failure in the service of the Sultan means death. So, if they fail, they are apt not to admit it. I'll be surprised if the officers who tried to stop us don't report that we left the harbour before your escape. Don't you see? That way they are safe.'

'And so are we.'

'Precisely. Though of course we'll take no chances at the Dardanelles. I'm glad, by the way, to see that you have contrived to find yourself some dry clothes.'

Phyllida was wearing the sumptuous frogged dressing gown he had had made for his honeymoon. It made him sick to see it, and yet he could not keep his eyes off her. She had belted the fine crimson alpaca tightly round her slim waist, and tied a black silk scarf as a cravat at the neck. Above it, her face looked ivory white, her short hair, drying in curls, blacker than the scarf. Her eyes, dark too, had huge violet circles round them and the mobile lips showed pale above the red robe.

How could he help remembering Helena? That deep red was to have been the foil for her blond, ethereal beauty. He wrenched his eyes away to Miss Knight, whose question had hung anxiously in the air. 'You don't mind?' she had asked, apologetically.

'Mind? Why should I?' She had confined herself, he saw, to purloining a pair of his Turkish slippers in exchange for her own wet shoes. Her voluminous black skirts, which had been kilted to her knees when she came on board, were in place once more round her ankles; her mouse-coloured hair was neatly braided round her head; she was every inch a maiden aunt.

'You looked so angry,' she said.

It was the last straw. Bad enough to have to act host to this pair of unwelcome women, but if he must suit even his looks to their pleasure . . . He drew a deep breath.

'Don't,' said Phyllida Vannick. And then, to Miss Knight, 'You can hardly expect Mr. Renshaw to welcome us with open arms, Aunt Cass. But, I promise you, sir, we won't trespass on your hospitality a day longer than we must.'

'No?' He did not try to keep the scepticism out of his voice. There she stood, penniless, a fugitive, wearing his dressing gown, beholden to him for her life, and dared to look him in the eye and speak to him as an equal.

'No. We owe you more than we can repay already. But may I ask where we are headed after the Dardanelles?'

'Wherever you please, Miss Vannick.' What else could he say?

'Generous!' Could there really be a hint of laughter in those unfathomable dark eyes? 'Suppose I should say, "New York"?'

He had asked for it. 'I should give the order to Captain Barlow.'

'More than generous. But I won't put your ship–or your hospitality–to such a test. You're cruising here for pleasure, I take it?'

For pleasure! 'Naturally,' he said. The knowledge that if she had, in fact, taken him up on his rash offer, he probably could not have afforded to take her so far as New York merely added to his rage.

'Then you wouldn't mind taking us to Zante?'

'Why not?' He had meant to go there anyway. There should be letters there that would confirm–or, please God, deny–the bad news he had received at Constantinople. 'Then, with your permission,' he went on, 'I'll suggest that Captain Barlow dine with us as soon as he thinks it safe to come below. He'll know whether we can make the trip without stopping, or, if not, where we can most safely stop.'

'Yes,' said Miss Vannick. 'I was wondering about that. But you took on coal at Constantinople, did you not? I watched from the palace garden. It gave me my first glimmer of hope for six months. Tell me, Mr. Renshaw, what does she do to the ton, this remarkable yacht of yours?'

'Well over a hundred miles.' He would not let himself show surprise at the knowledgeable question.

'That's better than our Hudson River steamboats–but then of course they're larger. I expect your *Helena* is faster too.'

'You really were in the Sultan's harem?' He shocked himself by the abruptness of the question.

'Why, yes, I told you so.' And then, taking pity on him,

'I expect you do not rightly understand what it means, Mr. Renshaw. But you speak Turkish?'

'My father was here in the diplomatic service when I was a boy. But as to the harem–' How could she speak about it so casually? 'I don't suppose any European knows much about that.'

'No.' She had seated herself at the saloon table and stared down thoughtfully at her thin white hands. 'Will it make you feel happier, Mr. Renshaw, to know that I was merely in training for the Sultan's favours? I was really beginning to hope that I was, simply, too old for him.'

'Nothing of the kind,' said Cassandra Knight. 'Remember what happened last week, when the golden bell rang. If it hadn't been for the Janissaries, you'd be a Guzdeh by now.'

'Darling Cass! You wouldn't want me to take second place even in the harem! But poor Mr. Renshaw is looking more perplexed than ever. It's all Greek to him. You should explain–if you really wish to trumpet my success–that the ladies of the Sultan's harem are as strictly regimented as the soldiers in his Army –more successfully so, you might say, than those wretched Janissaries. We had our ranks, with their duties and privileges–' The savage irony of her tone belied the word. 'First, the Odalisque, trained by her preceptors in a thousand arts of seduction to please her royal master.' Her laugh was harsh. 'Don't look so alarmed, Mr. Renshaw. I won't go into details, nor was I at all an apt pupil. Mere bad luck made me catch the Sultan's eye on his latest visit to the harem. I thought I'd be safe if I only looked sullen enough while the others sighed and ogled. It worked just the other way. When I was summoned out of that twittering crowd and met the royal eye for the first time I knew my mistake. Sullen himself, Sultan Mahmoud was bored with his bevy of adoring houris. It was to me that he threw the handkerchief. I was to be a Guzdeh–marked for his pleasure. I knew then that I must escape or die.' She laughed again, showing perfect white teeth. 'I had pretended toothache off and on ever since I reached Constantinople. They're lavish with their opium in the harem: I had enough saved to dispose of half my furious rivals let alone the two of us. But the air was already full of rumours about trouble with the Janissaries. I was not much enamoured of death. Time enough for that when the summons came. I had made friends with a Kadine, the mother of one of the Sultan's sons–in so far as friendship was possible in that place. Of course she wanted me out of the way–but she risked her life to help me. She knew, you see, that the Sultan intended to make an end of the Janissaries next time they beat their kettledrums and went on the rampage. That would be our chance, she said. In the general chaos. She was right. And when I saw the *Helena* come steaming into the Golden Horn last week, it seemed like a direct intervention of Providence. Have you ever thought of yourself as the answer to prayer, Mr. Renshaw?'

'Hardly.' It jolted him extraordinarily to hear her talk, so casually, of the suicide's death he had planned for himself. Had planned? Nothing was changed. It was merely to wait until he had got rid of these two women. 'What I don't understand,' he said now, 'is how it happened. How in the world did you come to find yourselves in the Sultan's power?'

'Algerian pirates.' Her hands, so still before, writhed for a moment on the table. 'They boarded us at night–just this side of the Straits of Gibraltar. We hadn't a chance–a merchant ship–taken unawares. If Father had been captain instead of merely a passenger, it would have been another story. As it was'–a long shudder shook her–'he was cut down, in front of our cabin door. I don't know what happened to the others. Aunt Cass and I were set apart, right from the beginning. We were–lucky, I suppose. Flattering, wasn't it? A gift from the Dey of Algiers to his master the Sultan. And never a chance of escape, till today. Oh, they treated us well enough–they wanted me in looks!' She rose, suddenly, furiously, to her feet and prowled across the room to the gold-framed looking-glass Brett had hung for Helena. 'How I hate this white face, these useless hands–' She turned them over. 'I actually blistered them rowing out here.'

'Good gracious, so you did.' Her aunt was on her feet in a flash.

'Oh, don't fuss, Aunt Cass.' And then, as the door opened to reveal a servant with a loaded tray: 'Look, food! Real Western food, and forks to eat it with. Will it shock you, Mr. Renshaw, if I admit to being most vulgarly famished?'

'Of course not.' But it did shock him. Even at the best

of times, frail Helena had been above such mundane pleasures as food. He remembered her so well, sitting, gracefully drooped, like a snowdrop, a lily, through course after course of a London dinner, taking only a bite or two, here and there, of some specially favoured dish. He remembered, too, how he had studied her tastes in those happy weeks before their marriage, and urged the *Helena*'s chef to lay in ample supplies of the fragile delicacies she liked best. Merely to have heard a story like Miss Vannick's must have brought on one of Helena's nervous spasms. And here was this extraordinary young woman proclaiming herself 'vulgarly famished'.

He welcomed Captain Barlow's appearance with heartfelt relief and began at once to question him about the voyage to Zante.

'One thing at a time.' Barlow was a hard man to hurry. 'Let's get clear of the Dardanelles first. I wish I knew what kind of a posting system the Turks have along the shore. If any word of this affair gets to the narrows before we do, we're as good as dead, the lot of us. I've been thinking about it up there on deck. On engines alone, we should get there tomorrow evening sometime. I mean to see to it that we don't enter the straits until after dark—you remember the nine days' wonder we were coming up? This time, with your permission, sir, I propose to burn enough kitchen waste on the boiler to give an even greater volume of smoke than usual. If they think we're on fire, they won't want to stop us. They're terrified of fire, the Turks.' He turned to explain this to Miss Vannick. 'That's how the Greeks have managed to keep their fleet at bay—they send in fire-ships and panic them.'

Phyllida Vannick leaned forward eagerly. 'What is the news of the Greek war? It didn't sound good, what we heard in the harem. Are the Turks really winning again?'

'Why should they not?' Brett Renshaw broke in angrily. 'I suppose it's understandable that you, Miss Vannick, as an American, may find yourself in sympathy with the Greek rebels, but it's more than I do. They're murderers, truce-breakers, pirates . . . why, they can't even agree among themselves. Was it two governments or three they had going at once, Barlow, when we were there? It's no wonder if they've lost Missolonghi at last. I'm just surprised they managed to hold it for so long.'

'Lost Missolonghi?' If possible, Phyllida was whiter than ever, and her hand clenched convulsively on the stem of her wine glass. 'Are you sure?'

'I wouldn't say so otherwise. We stopped for water at Nauplia two weeks ago. They'd just had the news. As bad as it could be: the whole town was in mourning. Just like the Greeks: cut each other's throat one day; celebrate the funeral with pomp and circumstance the next. If their sailors had stood to their post, the Egyptian, Ibrahim Pasha, would never have been able to join the siege.'

'He was there, too?'

'Yes. By all reports he's pretty well subdued the Morea. I suppose he thought he'd share the glory of Missolonghi with Reshid Pasha. The defenders saw the writing on the wall when he got there. They planned a breakout, the whole lot of them, women, children and all. Let me give you some more wine, Miss Vannick.'

'But what happened?'

'They were betrayed. By a Bulgarian, it's said. It might just as well have been a Greek. You can't trust them further than you can see them. Look what happened to that leader of theirs, Odysseus. "Killed trying to escape". I fancy I've heard that one before.'

'Mr. Renshaw!' Was he pleased to detect a tremor in her voice? 'Will you please tell me just what happened at Missolonghi?'

'But I did. They planned a breakout, and were betrayed. The Turks were waiting for them. And that was that. Lucky for Lord Byron he didn't live to see that day.'

'They were all killed?'

'Of course they were. After all, they set the style. Look what happened to the Turkish garrisons at the beginning of the rebellion, when they surrendered under promise of "safety". And here there was no question of a surrender. A terrible business, of course.' It was a belated acknowledgement of her white, still attention. 'The women and children . . . Mr. Meyer, who edited the *Missolonghi Chronicle* . . . and I don't know how many Philhellenes, poor crazy fools.'

'Crazy?' She had given up any pretence at eating. 'Mr.

Renshaw, you have not asked me why we came to the Mediterranean, my father, Aunt Cass and I.'

'No. I thought it no affair of mine.'

'Nor is it. But I shall tell you just the same. We came to look for my younger brother, who ran away from home four years ago. A "crazy Philhellene", Mr. Renshaw, and the last news we had of him was from Missolonghi.'

'But that was a year ago, Phyl.' Miss Knight leaned forward to break the shocked silence. 'He may have left long since.'

'A year of siege and danger. Can you imagine that Peter would have considered leaving at such a time? Deserting his friends?'

'Miss Vannick.' This was Captain Barlow. 'Mr. Renshaw's not quite right, you know. I don't want to raise false hopes, but a few of the defenders did manage to escape and join the brigand leader Karaiskakis in the mountains. But only a very few, mind.'

'Oh, thank you! No–I'll try not to hope too much, but how can I help . . .' She turned to Brett. 'Mr. Renshaw, would it be too much to ask? Do you think we could stop at Nauplia and find out if there is any more news? They'll know there, won't they, if anywhere?'

'I suppose we could.' It sounded grudging, even to him.

'We'll have to stop somewhere for water,' said Barlow. 'And to scour out the boilers. I'd thought of Smyrna, but with things as they are, I think we'd do well to keep right away from the Turks. And that reminds me: I'm afraid you and your aunt had best keep below decks tomorrow, Miss Vannick. We don't want to set tongues on shore wagging by the sight of women on board, and we'll be close in to land most of the day.'

'Of course. God knows, we don't want to put you in any more danger than we already have. I've not begun to thank you properly.' She was speaking more to Barlow than Renshaw. 'I don't see how I can. As for tomorrow, now I'm safe, I feel as if I could sleep all day. I'm only sorry it has to be in your cabin, Mr. Renshaw.' His man had been busy moving his effects into Captain Barlow's cabin. 'And poor Captain Barlow, too.'

'That's all right, miss.' Aware of Brett's brooding silence, the captain answered for them both. 'There are worse things happen at sea. I just hope you and your aunt will be comfortable. I'm afraid we've not much to offer you ladies–' And then, struck by a sudden thought: 'Mr. Renshaw, would you think it presuming if I reminded you of the boxful of things in the hold?'

'Yes!' He was on his feet as if a spring had snapped inside him. And then, with an effort: 'I mean, no. Do whatever you please, Captain. It's your ship. Good night.'

'Oh dear,' said Phyllida as the saloon door shut behind him.

'What's the matter with the poor man?' asked Miss Knight.

'You must bear with him, ma'am.' Captain Barlow was glad of the chance to explain. 'He doesn't mean a word of it: not really. I know he must have seemed unwelcoming, harsh even, to you two ladies, but, you see, it's like this: he had the *Helena* specially built for his honeymoon. There wasn't anything good enough for his lady–for Miss Helena–not by his way of thinking. Planned and replanned, this boat was; designed and redesigned till I thought she never would be launched. Poor Mr. Renshaw. It took years . . . I never did know whether it was his idea to delay the wedding till the ship was ready, or hers. Though, mind you, I'd venture a guess. It was a bad idea for Mr. Renshaw; that's for sure. The ship was ready at last, and the day set for the wedding. We'd champagne on board, and quails in aspic and potted grouse and a lot of other knickknacks and kickshaws, and then, a week before the wedding, comes the news that the Duchess has had a son. Mr. Renshaw was the heir, you know. They'd been out of England, see, her and the Duke, and anyway, what with one thing and another–the old Duke being the age he was, and the state he was in–no one reckoned there was a chance. Except Miss Helena, if you ask me. Sharp, she was, though poor Mr. Renshaw never saw it. I always thought she was glad the ship took so long a-building. It gave her a chance to hedge her bets, don't you see? She certainly changed her mind times enough and set things back. She said her say pretty quick when the bad news came. No dukedom, no marriage. Just like that. I never saw anything so downright cruel in my life, ma'am.' He had been addressing himself throughout to Cassandra Knight. 'Mr. Renshaw, he was brought up to be a Duke; it's what he's trained for, knows how to do, could do well, though I admit you might not think so after seeing him today. But to have that taken away from him, so sudden, and the woman he loved, all in one breath like. Well, no wonder he's in a state. And you know what she did? Miss Helena?'

'No?' Cassandra Knight leaned forward with gratifying interest.

'She made him take the blame. With his heart breaking, he had to jilt her. She showed up in church, see, on the day, and told him to stay away. Get drunk, she said. Do what you like. Just, don't come. If you do, she said, I'll refuse you, there in the church. And then she cut a lot of wheedling stuff about her broken heart and a woman's reputation–oh, it would make you sick. And if you're wondering how I came to hear it, ma'am, you're quite right, I listened. It all happened right here on the *Helena* and I heard every word of it, and glad I did. If I hadn't, I doubt I could have borne with Mr. Renshaw these last months. As it is, I'm right down sorry for him and so would you be if you knew the half of it.'

'I thought he didn't much like women.' Phyllida absent-mindedly drank out of the glass Brett had filled for her. 'Now I can see his point. But I don't quite understand about this Duchess.'

'No, you wouldn't,' said her aunt. 'You never did pay much attention to the English aristocracy. It's Sarum, isn't it, Mr. Barlow?'

'That's right, ma'am. "The oldest Duke in the world," they used to call him. He was in corsets before Trafalgar. Long-lived they are, the Renshaws. No one ever thought the old Duke would marry, that's certain. Everything else–oh yes, excusing me, ma'am, but not that. And when he did, he was past seventy. That was five years ago. Well, you can't really blame Mr. Renshaw for expecting the dukedom, can you?'

'Waiting for dead men's shoes?' Phyllida said. 'We don't think much of that in America.'

'But you don't understand, miss. Mr. Renshaw didn't need to wait. He's to be rich as Croesus on the distaff side–his mother's side. His uncle could buy up Sarum twice over and never notice the difference. You don't think he'd have had the *Helena* built on expectations, do you? Shipwrights work for cash down and no nonsense. But money alone wasn't enough for an accredited beauty like Miss Helena. Poor Mr. Renshaw, I've been hoping and hoping he'd come to see the whole thing as a merciful release. And I did think he was a little easier in his mind these last few weeks. But something happened at Constantinople that changed all that. Something he got in his mail, I reckon. I tell you, ladies, I was frightened for him tonight. He'd sent me below–and the lookout–which I shouldn't have agreed to, only I was afraid of what would happen if I didn't. I could hear him from below decks, prowling up and down, talking to himself. I didn't much like the sound of it. I was right down grateful to you two ladies when you gave me an excuse to come back up.'

Phyllida Vannick laughed. 'Well, I'm glad someone was pleased to see us. It was more than Mr. Renshaw was. If you'd not intervened, I really think he'd have left us to our fate.'

'Oh, no, miss. He'd have come round in a minute or so. He wouldn't hurt a fly, Mr. Renshaw. It's just that he's not very fond of women just now. He'll get over it. Just bear with him in the meantime.'

'That's the least we can do, considering we're accepting his hospitality and risking all your lives in the process.'

'Oh, I wouldn't worry too much about that,' he said comfortably. 'The Turks are going to have problems enough without troubling about two runaway women. The Sultan really does intend to make an end of the corps of Janissaries, you say?'

'That was certainly his plan. And he'll have to now, won't he? The ones in the rest of the country will never stand for what's happened in Constantinople today. They were killing them like flies. My aunt and I had to walk through their blood when we escaped. They were lying everywhere. Not just killed–mutilated . . . savaged . . .'

'Don't, Phyl,' said her aunt. 'Don't think about it.'

'Or rather, do think,' said Captain Barlow, 'that the worse the massacre, the worse the revenge. The Sultan is going to be busy for a while. It's not just you two who should be the gainers. I think this is the first ray of hope for the Greeks, too. The whole Turkish Army is going to be disorganised by this day's work. It may give the Greeks the breathing space they need.'

'I certainly hope it does,' said Phyllida. 'Things are really so bad with the Greeks, Captain?'

'They're pretty bad. Well, you'll hear for yourself, when we get to Nauplia. Poor things, you can't even blame them, that I can see. They've been slaves for going on four hundred years, it's no wonder if they don't rightly know how to behave as free men. Just because they were statesmen and heroes and artists and so forth more than a thousand years ago, they're supposed to come right out of slavery and behave—well, like statesmen and heroes. Of course they don't. Why should they? The miracle is that they've shaken off their chains at all.'

'You might be right at that,' said Cassandra Knight. 'But, Captain, you said something earlier about a box in the hold. Would it be too much to hope that it contained feminine knick-knacks and kickshaws?'

'That's just exactly what it does contain, ma'am, and I'll have it fetched up for you at once, and wish you a very peaceful night. You'll be safe as houses in there in Mr. Renshaw's cabin. Leave your wet things in the saloon, miss, and I'll have Price—Mr. Renshaw's man—see to them.'

'But you mustn't give up both these rooms to us,' Phyllida protested.

'It's no trouble, miss. My cabin—Mr. Renshaw's now—opens outside onto the gangway, you see. And I'll be right as rain down in the crew's quarters. As for the saloon, we'll sort things out in the morning; don't you worry. And I'll have that box sent up right away.'

'Full of the things Mr. Renshaw bought for his fiancée?' Phyllida asked after Barlow had left them. 'Do you think we really want them, Aunt?'

'It depends what they are, doesn't it? Captain Barlow strikes me as a remarkably sensible man, by and large, but what he dismisses as female kickshaws might be just the things I've been longing for. Just imagine, Phyl, a proper toothbrush, for instance? I suppose it would be too much to hope for a nightgown!' And then, reading her thoughts: 'Don't worry too much, love. He may not have been at Missolonghi at all.'

'I think I'd rather face it, Aunt, than pretend. But I

promise I'll do my best not to let it show. Mr. Renshaw shan't have the satisfaction of thinking me an hysterical female.'

'Poor Mr. Renshaw.' But Cassandra was interrupted by the arrival of two beaming, frankly curious seamen with a large sea chest.

'Do you think we ought to?' Phyllida watched with distaste as her aunt threw open the lid to reveal a jumbled pile of feminine accessories. Brett Renshaw must have scoured London to collect this curious, touching gallimaufry of the needs of a lady of high fashion. And then, ruthlessly jilted, he had hurled it all into the box. A hare's foot stuck oddly out of a pile of French gloves; a box of powder had come open, and a strong smell of perfume filled the air. 'It's not decent.' Phyllida turned away. 'It's like robbing a corpse.'

'Nonsense,' said her aunt. 'Look, Phyl, a whole packet of toothbrushes! And if these aren't nightgowns!'

'Poor Mr. Renshaw,' said Phyllida at last.

# 3

Waking early, Phyllida sat up to peer out from behind the black velvet curtains of the luxurious cabin Brett Renshaw had planned to share with his bride. She could see land quite near, green hills rising from the quiet water of the Bosphorus, with here and there a windmill, its white sails motionless. There was no wind at all, and the only sound was the soothing splash and flutter of the ship's huge paddle wheels and the erratic thump of her engine.

Except for a flock of grazing sheep, the hills seemed deserted in early morning sunshine. Then looking ahead, she saw a solitary figure on the stony track that ran along the shore, a rider, pressing his horse hard, going their way, and faster. One good look, and Phyllida picked up the crimson dressing gown she had worn the night before. Belting it tightly round her, she opened the cabin door quietly, so as not to wake her aunt. Outside, the main saloon was empty, with black curtains still drawn at the stern windows. Someone had been in, just the same. The Turkish costume she had worn the day before lay dried and neatly pressed on a chair. She looked at it, for a moment, with revulsion, then moved nearer and saw that it had been washed. The bloodstains were gone from the ankles of the loose trousers. She gathered it up with a sigh of relief and retired to the cabin to put it on. She had not missed Brett Renshaw's look of dislike–no, that was too weak a word–his look of disgust when she had appeared, the night before, in his dressing gown. No doubt, like the hare's foot and all those bottles of sal volatile, this had been bought with his bride in mind. She would not irritate him by appearing in it again. Besides–she adjusted the straight tunic over her loose trousers–she had grown to like the cool, comfortable Turkish costume.

When she opened the door of the saloon the rhythmical banging of the engine sounded much louder, almost drowning out the whoosh of the paddle wheels. Someone must have worked hard to cut out so much of the engine noise from the saloon. She felt, for the first time, genuinely sorry for Brett Renshaw. It might be faintly absurd to have let himself be jilted by a designing female, whose schemes had apparently been perspicuous even to Captain Barlow, but there was still something touching about the devotion that had built this ship–designed that cabin–combed London for those–she smiled to herself at memory of Barlow's phrase–those 'female knickknacks and kickshaws.'

The saloon door opened into a passageway that looked as if it might run the length of the ship. To her left must be the door of Captain Barlow's cabin, which Brett Renshaw had occupied the night before. There was no one in sight, and no noise but the steady pounding of the ship's engines. But Barlow or Renshaw ought to be told, at once, about the hard-riding messenger on shore. Nothing would induce her to knock on Renshaw's cabin door and rouse him. The only alternative seemed to be to go up on deck and ask the lookout to summon Barlow, unless, indeed, she found him already there. He had asked them to keep out of sight today, but the rider was well ahead of them by now, and, save for him, there was no sign of life on shore. Besides, she badly wanted a breath of fresh air. She hurried up the companionway before Brett Renshaw could appear to prevent her, and ran slap into him on deck.

'Miss Vannick!' He had abandoned last night's formal attire for a casual outfit similar to the loose shirts and bell-bottomed duck trousers worn by the crew. Black hair, cut rather long, ruffled round his brown, aquiline face. 'I thought Captain Barlow asked you and your aunt to stay below today.' Black eyes blazed furiously in the gaunt face. 'Do you actually want to get us all killed?'

'I'm sorry.' She was in the wrong, and knew it. 'I thought since there was no one about . . .'

'Sorry!' He took her arm in a grip that hurt and pushed her back into the entrance to the companionway, then let her go so suddenly that she had to grasp the door to prevent herself from falling down the steep flight of steps. 'And I suppose you'll be "sorry" when they open fire on us from the guns along the Dardanelles? Do you think of no one but yourself, Miss Vannick?'

'But that's just it.' She fought down fury. 'That's why I came to find you, or the captain. Did you see the Sultan's messenger on the shore just now?'

'The rider? Of course I did. And he's still in sight, too. You didn't pause to think he might turn round and see you?'

'Do you take me for a fool, Mr. Renshaw?' She lost her temper as completely as he had his. 'Are you seriously suggesting that a man, riding hard, several miles ahead of us, could make me out for a woman in this costume?'

He had moved away from her, out onto the deck, as if, she thought angrily, he found her very proximity distasteful. Now he favoured her with a withering, comprehensive scrutiny. 'It's true enough,' he conceded, 'that there is nothing particularly feminine about your appearance this morning. In fact, I'm surprised that you wish to expose yourself in such a guise. But that is nothing to the purpose, nor is the question of how many miles ahead of us that Turk may be. What we are discussing, and I would like to have it settled once and for all, is your position as an unexpected guest on my ship.'

'Pray don't spare my feelings,' she interrupted him furiously. 'Say, "uninvited". It's what you mean.'

'Of course it is. And, since you are here, at considerable

risk to the rest of us, it strikes me that at least you might obey the captain's orders, particularly when they concern the safety of us all. Including yours, Miss Vannick.'

'I *am* sorry.' She meant it. 'You're perfectly right. It was inexcusable of me. My father would have beaten me for less. Only, what was I to do? I really did want to talk to you or the captain. I wasn't sure whether you'd know that that's one of the Sultan's messengers, ahead there.'

'You're sure?'

'Oh, yes. I know the costume well enough. And, besides: I must speak to you, Mr. Renshaw, up here where my aunt can't hear. Because it's true: everything you say. I have put you all at risk: appallingly so. But I think I see the way out. If they do stop us in the Dardanelles, you must give me up at once. Just me, don't you see? Tell them I stowed away; you didn't find me till this morning. Be as furious as you please: you'll find it easy enough to make it convincing. And say nothing about Aunt Cassandra. If they've got me, they won't bother about her. And if you give me up, freely like that, I doubt if they'll harm you. You're English; I'm American. The Sultan cares nothing for us. He thinks we're a pack of low rebels and won't even receive our ministers.' She laughed, surprisingly. 'Rather the way you feel about the Greeks. But it will make it easier for you. Just wash your hands of me, as an American interloper, and hand me over. They'll be grateful for an excuse not to embroil themselves with the English by harming you or the *Helena.*'

'But what will happen to you?' He could not help thinking there was a good deal of sense in what she said.

'That's my affair.'

'I can't let you do it.' The words seemed to speak themselves. 'It's generous of you, Miss Vannick, but I can't let you. We must think of a better plan. Ah'—with relief—'here's the captain. Miss Vannick confirms that it was a Sultan's messenger, Barlow.'

'I was afraid so. Morning, Miss Vannick. I'm glad to see you none the worse for your adventure.'

'Not so far, thank you. Captain Barlow, you must help me persuade Mr. Renshaw that if the Turks do stop us in the Dardanelles, you should give me up as a stowaway, for all your sakes.

Or, if that doesn't convince you, for my aunt's. She's suffered enough already on my account.'

'Nonsense,' said Captain Barlow. 'I'd shoot you, rather than give you up, Miss Vannick. But don't you think you are being unnecessarily gloomy? Of course Sultan Mahmoud's got his messengers out today. I expect they've been riding all night, on every road from Constantinople. But surely they must have more urgent affairs than the question of two women? The Sultan declared war on the better part of his Army yesterday. The corps of Janissaries are spread throughout his empire. Naturally, he'll want to send first news of their dissolution, to arrange, I suppose, a series of murderous scenes like yesterday's. I'm not sure the messenger you saw isn't a good omen for us. Don't you see? By the time we get to the Dardanelles, the news will be out. If there are Janissaries on guard duty there–which I should think there are bound to be–they'll have other things to think of than stopping one private yacht. And it apparently on fire, too.'

'I do hope you're right,' she said. 'But you must promise me, both of you, that if it should come to that, you will give me up as I suggest.'

'We'll promise nothing,' said Renshaw. 'Naturally, in a crisis, Captain Barlow must do what he thinks best for the safety of his ship and crew. He's got more sense than to bind himself with promises.'

Just because it was so reasonable, she found his answer infuriating. 'I must see if my aunt is awake.' She met Renshaw's man, Price, at the foot of the companionway, and stopped to thank him for the trouble he had taken over her clothes.

'That's all right, miss. I was sure you wouldn't want to be wearing Mr. Renshaw's any longer than you must.' His eyes met hers with a look that spoke respectful volumes. 'And, besides, that's a very practical rig-out for a young lady on board ship, if you'll excuse my saying so. Skirts is all very fine on dry land, but there's nothing like–ahem–gentlemen's wear when it comes to the sea breezes. In fact, I hope you won't take it amiss, but I've made so bold as to ask around among the crew. We was on shore at Hydra, see, just for half a day and I reckoned some of them would have come back with souvenirs like. And sure enough Mr. Brown–him as minds the engines–had bought an outfit for his daughter. It's much like what you have on, miss, only a very becoming shade of dark blue. Mr. Brown said he'd be honoured if you'd accept of it, to make a change like. And you won't mind me valeting you, till the master can arrange something more suitable?'

She had faced death dry-eyed, but this unforced kindness overset her completely. 'Mr. Price, you're an angel.' Her eyes were aswim with tears. 'Please thank Mr. Brown a thousand times for me and tell him I'll be proud to wear his daughter's costume–and will replace it as soon as I am able. As for valeting–' She smiled at him mistily. 'It's wonderfully kind of you, but I'm an American, you know. I've never had a maid. I can look after myself, thank you just the same–and my aunt, too.'

'I'm sure you *can*, miss, but not on this ship, you mustn't. If you'll excuse the liberty. It'd be much easier, all round, if I was to look after you, see?' His pale, intelligent face was telling her much more than he could say.

'"When in Rome, do as do the Romans", you mean? Thank you, Mr. Price. I think I understand. Only, it will be so much trouble for you–'

'Nonsense, miss.' It was what everyone seemed to say to her this morning. 'It will be a pleasure. Only–you'll not mind my telling you–not "Mr. Price"–just "Price".'

'Oh dear!' And then, the tears suddenly too much for her, 'Price! Could you possible lend me your pocket handkerchief?'

'I'd be honoured.' It was perfectly clean, and both whiter and softer than any linen she had ever felt, so that she found herself wildly wondering whether he carried a special one (doubtless Brett Renshaw's) for the succouring of damsels in distress. But he had another question for her. 'And now, about the saloon, and meals?'

'Oh, yes!' She was delighted to have this point raised. 'You must go on just as usual, Price. Mr. Renshaw and Captain Barlow eat in the saloon, do they?'

'Mostly, miss, except when Mr. Renshaw is in the glooms, if you understand me. Then the captain's been eating with Mr. Brown. It's a bit difficult, on a small boat like this, you understand, to keep things as they should be, but I hope I do my best.'

'I'm sure you do.' She was suddenly aware of a delicious aroma of coffee mingling with the familiar, indefinable smell of ship. 'Is it breakfast time now?'

'Just on, miss.'

'Then come right in and get on with it. I'm sure my aunt will be up by now, and anyway you mustn't let us make any difference to the way you run things. We've our own cabin, when we want it–or rather poor Mr. Renshaw's.'

'Don't you trouble yourself about him,' said Price comfortably. 'A bit of distraction was just what he needed. But if I could come and lay the table?'

'Of course.' Opening the saloon door, she found her aunt up and dressed in her durable black. She had drawn the curtains at the stern windows so that morning sunshine flooded the big, untidy room, and was looking with disapproval at the dust it revealed.

'Mr. Price!' She greeted him with enthusiasm. 'The very person. I'm sure you could find me a duster?'

'Presently, ma'am. I'm afraid things ain't quite as shipshape as I could have wished in here, but maybe Mr. Renshaw won't mind if *you* do a bit of tidying.' It was both apology and warning.

What an admirable creature he was, Phyllida thought. 'Who cares about a little dust?' she said cheerfully. 'Frankly, breakfast is my main consideration. Would it be right, do you think, Price, if I were to ask you to invite Mr. Renshaw and the captain to do us the honour of joining us for it?'

'It would be quite right, miss.' He looked at her, now, with approval. 'I'll pass the word to the cook, right away, and then deliver your message.'

That day seemed endless. Confined to the saloon, Phyllida pretended a calm cheerfulness she was very far from feeling, and racked her brain for some expedient that might save them all. It was no use. If she were to slip over the side, and swim for it, her aunt's presence would still condemn the others if a search were made. And what foolishness to have swum for it, and very likely drowned, if Captain Barlow was right, and there was no search.

Her bitterest regret was that she had lost her carefully hoarded stock of opium while escaping from the seraglio. It had got wet when she waded out to the boat she had stolen, disintegrated into a sodden mess in the pocket of her trousers, and been carefully washed out by Price. Whatever happened, the Turks must not catch her alive. What had Barlow said? 'I'd shoot you myself.' So that was all right . . .

She was distracted by her aunt's voice. 'Look! There's someone riding along the shore. Isn't it one of the Sultan's men?'

Another messenger. 'I believe so.' She made her voice casual. 'Captain Barlow says the Sultan will be sending in all directions today, to order the murder of the rest of the Janissaries.'

'You don't think it's about us?'

'I hope not.'

This messenger, too, was pulling slowly ahead of the ship, and she could not help wondering whether Captain Barlow's plan of waiting till dusk to approach the Dardanelles was wise. Suppose it merely gave the Turks time to prepare for their capture? No use thinking like that. She concentrated on the view of undulating green hills from the cabin window, with here and there a mountainous island, rising sharply from the still water. The light was beginning to change at last, and the hills were closing in on the ship. The moment of crisis must be very near. Last time they came through the Dardanelles, she had been a helpless prisoner, locked in her cabin, so that though she could remember the ship's being stopped, she had no idea where the Turkish strong-points actually were.

'I'm sorry, Aunt, what did you say?' She dragged her attention back to Cassandra.

'I was wondering if they have check-points at both ends of the straits. I was asleep last time. It seems extraordinary, doesn't it?'

'Yes.' What was there to say? 'Aunt Cass, if we are stopped, tell them at once that you are English. It might make a difference.'

'If we are stopped, child, I don't think anything will make much difference.'

# 4

'If we could only *do* something!' Phyllida stopped short at the sound of rushing feet on the deck above them. 'What's going on up there?'

Miss Knight was reading a Bible Price had produced for her. She put in a careful finger to mark her place. 'I expect we'll know soon enough.'

'It sounds as if something were wrong.' Phyllida opened the saloon door and peered out into the empty passageway, now lit by hanging lanterns. The engine's clanking sounded louder than usual and there was a strong smell of hot metal. 'Thank goodness, here's Price.' She moved aside to let him enter with a loaded tea tray. 'What's going on, Price?'

'Nothing to fret you ladies.' But there were black smudges on his usually immaculate white jacket. 'I thought you might like a cup of tea to pass the time.' He set the ornate silver pot on the table in front of Miss Knight. 'Mr. Renshaw and the captain are staying on deck. They send their excuses.'

It seemed unlikely to Phyllida, but she was grateful for the intention of his lie. 'Where are we, Price?'

'Pretty close now, miss.' He did not pretend not to understand her. 'We'll be under their guns any minute. Terrible poor shots, they are, the Turks, by all reports. If you ask me, our greatest danger is that they'll hit us by accident. *If* they try to stop us at all, which I doubt. You never saw such a head of smoke as we're making, and sparks flying in all directions. Captain Barlow's got all the crew that can be spared from the engines out on deck damping down.'

'I wish we could help,' said Phyllida impulsively.

'Don't think of it, miss.' It was a warning. 'You just stay here and drink your tea and don't fret. A few hours now and we'll be out in the Aegean, laughing at the Turks.' He moved over to the stern windows. 'Captain Barlow said I was to make sure you had the curtains drawn nice and tight.'

Phyllida smiled at him. 'Don't worry, Price, we won't try to look out.'

'There's nothing to see anyway. Not yet.' He lifted his head at the sound of another rush of feet on the deck above. 'I think I'd best be going, if you'll excuse me, ladies. The sparks is flying pretty free up there. But nothing to worry about, of course. Captain Barlow is a gentleman it's a pleasure to sail with.'

'Just so long as the boilers don't burst,' said Phyllida.

'That's what Mr. Brown says—' He stopped short, looking at her with respect. 'You know about these steam engines, miss?'

'Enough to know ours oughtn't to smell the way it does right now.'

'But look at the pretty turn of speed we're doing. Mr. Brown says he reckons we're beating every record. He was on the *Rising Star,* you know, before she left for Chile. She could do twelve knots on a good day, but he says we've got her beaten to a fare-thee-well. They'll need wings to catch us, and pretty sharp shooting to hit us, so you drink your tea, ladies, and count on me to let you know if there's anything you *need* to know.'

And with that they had to be content. Miss Knight lifted the heavy teapot. 'Cream and sugar, Phyl?'

Phyllida was studying the meal Price had provided. 'What a man, Aunt! Any minute now, we're going to be sunk by gunfire, or blown up by a bursting boiler, and he's brought us cucumber sandwiches and three kinds of cake. I wish the English were all like him.'

'Poor Mr. Renshaw,' said Cassandra.

But up on deck, Brett was enjoying himself. 'This is more like living,' he shouted to Barlow as the *Helena* surged through the darkness, sparks flying in all directions, and the deck hot underfoot near the funnel. 'Price!' He saw his man emerge from the companionway. 'Fetch a bucket and damp the deck round the funnel here.' And then. 'Are your charges behaving themselves?'

'Good as gold, sir. Drinking tea like the ladies they are.' If it was a rebuke, it was delicately administered.

'Good.' He turned away to help fight a fresh shower of sparks on the afterdeck. 'We don't want them burned to death in the saloon.' A quick glance at the belching funnel. 'You don't think Brown is overdoing it, Barlow?'

'I hope not, sir. Look! Here they come!'

The Turkish boat was putting out from where a cluster of lights showed ahead. Lanterns at prow and stern showed the banks of rowers bending to their oars. 'Give me the trumpet,' said Brett. 'I'm going to speak first.'

'First?' Puzzled, Barlow handed him the speaking trumpet.

'Yes.' The two ships were closing swiftly now. 'Attack is the best mode of defence.' And then, in stentorian Turkish, through the trumpet: 'Help, there! We're on fire! We're going to blow up any minute. Throw us a line, for pity's sake, and help us slow down.'

A quick order in Turkish and the rowers backed water, holding the galley a little way off. 'What ship?'

'English. Stop us, for God's sake; we're out of control. Here, you,' to Barlow, 'get ready to throw them a line. It might just save us.' A fresh shower of sparks gave point to his words.

It also seemed to make up the Turks' minds. Another order, and then a shouted command. 'Keep off!'

It was hardly necessary. In the short time they had talked, the *Helena* had surged forward through the straits. The Turkish galley was already well astern when they saw her turn and head back for the lights on shore.

'Oh, well done, sir,' said Barlow.

Brett laughed. 'A lively scene for *Childe Renshaw's Pilgrimage*! With an apology to Lord Byron, of course. If only life could be all action, Barlow, I might be a happy man.'

'We've got action aplenty now, sir, if you ask me. Just look at those sparks! Shall I send below and tell Brown to damp down his engines?'

'No! Not till we're through the straits.' He laughed, and quoted: ' "Pleasure and action make the hours seem short".'

Down in the cabin, time passed more slowly. 'Oh, God, who'd be a woman!' said Phyllida. 'Always waiting . . .' And then, 'I know.' She crossed the saloon quickly and for one horrified moment her aunt was afraid she was going to draw the curtains and look out. But she was merely looking for something in the shelves under the stern windows. 'Here! I noticed it this morning.' She came back with a chessboard and a box containing an elaborate carved set. 'Black or white, Aunt?' she laughed. 'Can you really believe that Helena played chess? Or do you think that poor man intended to teach her?'

'I'm sure I don't know.' Disapprovingly. 'And I'm sure you ought not to speak of her like that.'

'Of Helena? But we don't know any other name for her, do we? Would you like me to ask Price?'

'No, Phyllida, I would not. Nor am I at all sure whether Mr. Renshaw would like us to be playing with his chessmen.'

'Then he should be down here entertaining us,' said Phyllida, arranging pawns. 'Aren't they beauties, Aunt? Do you think he had them specially made for her?'

'Probably,' said her aunt repressively. 'And all the more reason why he should not find us amusing ourselves with them.'

'Amusing ourselves! Aunt Cass, do you happen to remember that two days ago we were slaves in the Sultan's harem? That I was expected momently to have to kill myself rather than submit to his "passion"? And that, right now, we are careering down the Dardanelles so fast that if there are islands in the way we will probably run into one of them—if the boiler doesn't settle our business by blowing up first? Don't you mind the idea of death? I hate it. I've so much living to do. How can I bear the idea of ending here, in the dark, with so much that I've never seen, never thought, never done? Do you know, sometimes, in the harem, I wondered if it might not to be better to live, whatever happened, to be the Sultan's toy, his amusement, his drab—Oh, I'm sorry—' She answered her aunt's horrified expression. 'But don't you see, here I am, twenty-seven and never lived. To die would be so wasteful.'

'I don't know what you mean, child.' Her aunt chose the easiest point to answer. 'Never lived? What in the world would your poor father say?'

'Father?' She thought about it for a moment, then smiled. 'I think he would understand. Why do you think he brought me? He saw there was no way I could really live at home. A woman? A thing! For a man to play with, and get children by: never, never to talk to.' She laughed, suddenly. 'I suppose one should give the devil his due, after all. Can you imagine an American husband planning to teach his bride chess? I just wish I knew whether Mr. Renshaw had consulted Helena. Oh!' The saloon door had opened behind her, and she was aware, just too late, of Brett Renshaw himself. 'Mr. Renshaw! You startled me. I do hope you don't mind my appropriating your beautiful chess set to help us pass the time.' She was babbling, and knew it, but in face of his white and, momentarily, silent rage what else was there to do? 'I beg your pardon,' she went on, absurdly, and, her aunt thought, almost pitifully.

'I beg yours, Miss Vannick, for intruding on your privacy. I merely came to tell you we are out of danger for the time being, but from your tone I collect you were already aware of it. I won't intrude on you further. Your servant, ma'am.' His bow, formal, and oddly final, was for Miss Knight.

'Oh dear!' Phyllida moved a pawn at random. 'He's very angry.'

'And I don't blame him,' said her aunt roundly. 'I hope you're ashamed of yourself, Phyl, because I certainly am.' And then, as Phyllida dissolved, suddenly, into tears, 'Oh, darling, I'm sorry!'

'So am I. How could I be so stupid, so heartless . . . ?' She delved into the pocket of her tunic, produced the handkerchief Price had lent her earlier in the day and blew her nose. Then, looking at it: 'It's even his handkerchief! I wish I was dead.'

'Nonsense,' said Cassandra. 'Think what you were saying a few minutes ago. Besides, you may still get your wish. We're not out of the woods yet—or the Dardanelles—and if the Turks don't get us, the boiler may. So no need to *wish* yourself dead, child.'

'I'm sorry. For everything. But what can I do about Mr. Renshaw?'

'Nothing, I'm afraid. I doubt if you'll get the chance.'

'What do you mean?'

'Didn't he sound rather final to you? I think we're going to find ourselves in a kind of Coventry from now on.'

Price proved her right when he appeared a little while later. 'May I lay supper, ma'am? For the two of you?'

'The two of us, Price? What do you mean?' Phyllida was grateful to her aunt for asking the question.

'Those are my orders, ma'am.' Price kept his face wooden. 'Mr. Renshaw and the captain are to eat with Mr. Brown.'

They made a brief and silent meal. Cassandra Knight felt at once sorry for her niece and impatient with her. They were Brett Renshaw's guests: she should have been more careful. Now they were in Europe she must learn to restrain her casual American habit of coming right out with things. If only she had got to America sooner to take charge of Phyllida and Peter. But when their English mother had died, in 1812, America and England had just gone to war. Cassandra had not even heard the news for nearly a year, and then it had been impossible to follow her first instinct and cross the Atlantic to look after her favourite sister's children. When she finally reached New York late in 1815, she had found them a formidable enough pair. Their father had been at sea throughout the war, running the British blockade and doubling his fortune. At fourteen, Phyllida had taken charge of the big house outside New York and of her eight-year-old brother. There had been no one to intervene. Her father's nearest relative, a cousin, was with the Army on the Canadian frontier. The neighbours had problems of their own. And Phyllida had a sharp tongue, a driving temper and a way with her that servants respected. Her aunt, who arrived expecting to find a household in chaos, had been surprised and a little daunted to find everything in apple-pie order and the niece she had planned to mother a grown-up young woman, at seventeen, who welcomed her, with enthusiasm, but as a guest.

Cassandra sighed. Should she have made more of an effort to take control of the situation ten years ago? And, if she had, would it have done any good? Might it not simply have meant the final quarrel with her niece she had managed to avoid? Used to the strict British code of chaperonage, she had been appalled at the freedom of Phyllida's behaviour, but had had the good sense to see both that it was less shocking to other Americans than to herself and that it was too late to do much about it.

What really saddened her, as she grew increasingly found of her wilful niece, was Phyllida's attitude to men. An old maid herself, Cassandra knew she would have been a much happier woman if her fiancé had not been killed at the Battle of Aboukir Bay. She did not like being a spinster, and hated to see her niece repel one possible suitor after another. 'But they're all such bores,' Phyllida had explained. 'They think of nothing but making money, and they talk to me as if I was a fool.'

Peter had been a problem too, and Cassandra had hoped in vain that life at Harvard College would suit him and help him to settle down. Instead, he had flung off to Greece, where he had been taken up by Lord Byron just in time to help nurse him through his last illness. The whole business had infuriated his hard-headed father, who had decided, at last, to go to Europe and bring him home 'by the scruff of his neck.' When he half-seriously suggested that Phyllida and her aunt go too, Cassandra had welcomed the idea. If it was a chance for Peter, it was also, she let herself hope, one for Phyllida. Twenty-seven, and heiress to at least half her father's immense wealth, she had still not found a man who did not bore her. Soon it would be too late. But, perhaps, in Europe?

Miss Knight was too sensible a woman to blame herself for the disastrous outcome of their European voyage. It had been no part of her plan that her brother-in-law should be killed, and her niece immured in the Sultan's harem. But now? It had been impossible not to feel a small, guilty spurt of hope at being rescued by so eligible a young man as Brett Renshaw. And look what had happened. She sighed, and reopened her Bible.

'I'm truly sorry, Aunt.' Phyllida answered the sigh. 'And you're an angel not to give me the scold I deserve.'

'I learned better than to scold you ten years ago, love. Besides, there's no need, is there?'

'You certainly couldn't call me worse names than I've been calling myself. But, Aunt Cass, what are we to do?'

'I don't think there's much we can do. Except wait for him to come about. His manners are so good, basically, that I expect he will.'

'Unlike mine!'

'I didn't say it, but I'm glad you did. Manners are important, you know. Manners of the heart, at any rate.'

'Of the heart? You never put it like that before. I wish you had.'

'So do I.' By tacit consent they left it at that, but Price, coming to clear the table, thought he saw the shine of tears in Miss Vannick's eyes. And a good thing, too.

'Where are we, Price?' she asked.

'Getting along nicely, miss, and the boilers cooler. Captain Barlow says you ladies are to go to bed and not to worry.'

'And Mr. Renshaw?'

'Says nothing, miss.'

Left alone, the two women looked at each other. ' "Go to bed and don't worry"!' quoted Phyllida furiously. 'And get hauled out in our nightgowns when the Turks board us. I don't think so!'

'Perhaps not,' said Miss Knight. 'But we will most certainly retire to our cabin and put out the light.' For a moment she thought Phyllida was going to rebel, but then she sighed, and smiled, and crossed the saloon to give her a quick, conscience-stricken kiss.

'You're quite right,' she said. 'It's the least we can do. And besides'–incorrigibly–'once the light is out there's nothing to stop us looking out the windows.'

But there was not much to see. Lights here and there along the shore looked alarmingly close. 'Do you think there are guns all along?' asked Phyllida. And then: 'Aunt Cassandra–'

'Yes?'

'Do you really think there's a chance Peter might have left Missolonghi?'

'My love, I doubt it.' One of Miss Knight's virtues was an unswerving, almost ruthless honesty. 'You remember how he felt about Lord Byron, and the place as connected with him. No, our hope, I think, must be that he might be one of the group who fought their way out. After all, he was young and strong . . .'

'Was?' She was crying quietly now in the darkness.

'I'm sorry. But I think it would be wrong to encourage you in much hope.'

'Yes.' She swallowed a sob. 'Aunt, do you think it was my fault he went to Greece?'

'Your fault?' Pretending amazement, Cassandra racked her brain for an answer that would satisfy her own high standards of truthfulness.

'You know perfectly well what I mean. Don't pretend, please. After all, I brought him up, all those early years.'

'And then, so did I. But I'm not blaming myself, Phyl, and nor should you. What's the use? Besides, think how he enjoyed himself at first–' Again that fatal past tense. She hurried on. 'Remember his letters; he sounded alive as he never did at Harvard College.'

'And now he's probably dead.' Phyllida was crying unashamedly now. Presently she gave a loud sniff and sat up in the creaking berth. 'Poor Mr. Renshaw,' she said surprisingly. 'How am I going to apologise, Aunt?'

'God knows.' Once again, she would not pretend a comfort she did not feel. 'We'll think of something in the morning. I hope.'

'If we live till morning.' But she spoke sleepily now. It had been a long day.

They were waked by Price with a welcome offer of hot water. 'I hope you ladies slept well.' He was splendidly matter-of-fact as he drew the black velvet curtains to let in a flood of daylight.

'Where are we, Price?' Phyllida sat up and pulled down her tunic all in one movement.

'Well out in the Aegean, miss, just like I said. They never even stopped us at the bottom of the Dardanelles. Fast asleep in bed, I reckon they were.' He was arranging his hot-water cans on the cabin's wash-stand, whose Dresden china basin and ewer had filled Phyllida with awed amusement. 'What time shall I serve your breakfast, ma'am?' He turned to Cassandra.

'In half an hour?' She exchanged glances with Phyllida. 'And Mr. Renshaw?'

'Had his some time ago. With Mr. Brown.'

'Price, what shall I do?' Phyllida leaned forward impulsively to ask it.

'Nothing, miss. If you'll take my advice. Just leave it. He'll come about.' And with this bleak encouragement, he left them.

'May we go up on deck?' Cassandra felt positively sorry for her niece when she heard her put it to Price as he poured her second cup of coffee.

'I don't know, miss, I'm sure. Would you like me to find out?'

'Oh, yes, please! And, Price—'

'Yes, miss?'

'Say we'll be quiet as mice. Tell Captain Barlow—'

'Yes, miss.' He understood her perfectly.

# 5

The message Price brought back was not encouraging. 'Could you wait until this afternoon to take the air, miss? The captain says there's less chance then of our meeting a Turkish ship.' His tone quite failed to carry conviction. Cassandra wondered whether he even intended it to. She was not at all surprised, when she and Phyllida emerged into brilliant afternoon sunshine, to find the deck empty save for the lookout.

But a canvas shelter had been rigged up just forward of the ship's tall, slender funnel. Two chairs and a table stood in its shade, and she was glad enough to settle at once in one of them and watch as her niece took a quick turn to the ship's rail and back. 'I feel like a prisoner out at exercise! Do you think Mr. Renshaw has told the captain he's not to associate with us either?'

'Well, it is Mr. Renshaw's ship,' said Cassandra mildly,

but was relieved, just the same, to have Phyllida's conjecture refuted by the appearance of Captain Barlow himself.

He looked, poor man, hideously embarrassed as he made his enquiries as to their well-being, and received their congratulations on last night's escape. 'Mr. Renshaw begs that you will excuse him,' he said at last. 'He's not feeling quite the thing today.'

'Kind of you, Captain,' said Phyllida dryly. 'But this is too small a ship for pretences. He won't meet me, is that it?'

Cassandra thought Barlow looked relieved. 'That's precisely it, miss. It will make it much easier for all of us if we just admit it. Of course,' he hurried on, 'Mr. Renshaw said nothing about his reasons. Some misunderstanding, I'm sure–'

'Not at all,' said Phyllida. 'It was my fault entirely. But–it's awkward, isn't it?'

'Deuced awkward, miss. Excusing me, ma'am. It's too small a ship–'

'We'll leave it at Nauplia,' Phyllida interrupted him. 'I shall want to spend some time there anyway, making enquiries about my brother.'

'But, Phyllida,' interposed her aunt, then hesitated. How could she point out to her niece, in front of the captain, that they were, for the moment, penniless?

'You're thinking of funds?' Phyllida did not share her scruples. 'Surely Nauplia is as much of a capital as Greece has got right now? There must be an American representative of some kind there, who will make us an advance until we can get in touch with Mr. Biddock, my father's agent on Zante. We can do that just as well overland as by sea.'

'I don't know about that, miss.' Captain Barlow looked unhappier than ever. 'You can't rightly know what's been going on in Greece. The news is terrible. I doubt if it would be possible to get a message across by land.'

'Things are so bad?'

'I'm afraid so. It all seemed to be going so well for the Greeks until Ibrahim Pasha arrived from Egypt. Since then, it's bad. He's got Modon, and Navarino, and Tripolitsa, which gives him pretty well full control of the Morea. He could have had Nauplia last year, by all I hear, if it hadn't been for a gallant stand by one of those Greek brigand captains, someone called Makriyiannis. But, don't you see, that was a kind of miracle. It won't happen every time. You know how divided those poor devils of Greeks are among themselves? Half the time they've got two governments going at once. *If* not three. And, meanwhile, who knows what Ibrahim will do now Missolonghi's fallen? The word, when we were at Nauplia, was that they were afraid he'd be back there soon, while Reshid Pasha, who's responsible for mainland Greece, had a go at Athens. Well: what's to stop him? And what's to stop Ibrahim taking Nauplia any time he really sets his mind to it? I don't think you ladies ought to leave us there, I truly don't. Let us take you on to Zante—to the Ionian Islands—where you'll be safe on British soil. Please?'

'And make poor Mr. Renshaw spend half the day in his cabin to avoid me? On his own ship! Not on your life, Captain.'

It looked, for the moment, like deadlock. 'When shall we reach Nauplia?' asked Cassandra.

'All going well, sometime tomorrow. The wind's freshening; we're going to put on some sail and take advantage of it. If it holds, we might be there quite early. Mind you, I'm not going in there until I've spoken a Greek ship and made sure all's well.'

'It's as bad as that?'

'Quite as bad. I didn't save you ladies from the Turk at Constantinople to hand you over to him at Nauplia. I do beg you'll be considering your position before we arrive. It shouldn't take more than a few days to round the Morea and deliver you safe and sound on Zante. And now, if you'll excuse me—' He turned away to shout an order and the two women watched as the square sail was run up on the funnel.

'You'd think it would catch fire,' said Cassandra.

'Yes, it does look risky. Father said the *Savannah* had an adjustable elbow to her funnel so they could direct the smoke and sparks away from the sails. I see Captain Barlow just relies on extra lookouts.'

'And tubs of water,' said her aunt approvingly. 'He's a very sensible man.'

'Yes. But if you think I'm going to take his advice and stay on board all the way to Zante, you're crazy.'

'Let's wait and see.' Cassandra never believed in rushing her fences. 'We can't decide till we know how things are at Nauplia. Even you will hardly insist on going ashore if it's in the hands of the Turks. Nor would Captain Barlow let you. They've risked enough for us already.'

'Yes. I wish I knew how much coal their bunkers hold. If we can't put in to Nauplia, I suppose we'll have to go clear round to Zante before coaling up. Look at that miserable little bit of sail, and think what it will be like, cooped up here, out of coal, while we wait for a wind to take us round Cape Matapan.' And without waiting for an answer, she resumed her restless promenade up and down and to and fro on the deck.

Cassandra watched her anxiously and actually found herself hoping that Nauplia would turn out to be in the hands of the Turks, so that the question of going ashore there would not arise. No good pretending that she could influence Phyllida's decision. She folded her hands tightly in her lap and found herself wishing for that beloved and soothing stand-by, her embroidery. A shadow fell across her and she looked up to see Price.

'Will you be taking your tea on deck, ma'am? You and Miss Vannick?'

'If it's no trouble.' A quick look established that Phyllida had vanished from the deck. Was it also, visibly, an anxious one?

Apparently it was. 'It's all right, ma'am,' said Price. 'She's in the cabin. Crying, I rather think. I'll fetch her when tea's ready. No—' He had seen Cassandra's instinctive movement. 'I'd leave her, if I were you. She needs it, don't you think?'

'Price, you're extraordinary.'

'Thank you, ma'am.' He seemed, for once, to hesitate. 'There's one thing, if I might make so bold as to ask it?'

'Anything, Price.' What could be coming now?

'Thank you. It's Mr. Renshaw's linen,' he said, suddenly confidential. 'I can manage—ahem—everything else, but I'd counted on Miss Helena's woman to do the fine work on the linen. I don't know what the master will say if he finds he's not got a shirt fit to dine with the High Commissioner, when we get to the

Ionian Islands. That was the last one he put on yesterday, of the evening ones, that is, and full of burns now. Little holes, you know. I wouldn't know how to set about them.'

'Price!' She sounded like a war-horse hearing trumpets. 'Do you mean they need mending?'

'That's just exactly it, ma'am.'

She smiled up at him a little mistily, and he thought, what an unusually pleasant lady she was. 'And I was just missing my embroidery. I hate to sit idle. Price, I saw a needlebook in that box–' She paused, at a loss how to describe that heart-rending collection of offerings for Helena.

'In the saloon,' he finished for her. 'I'll fetch it, ma'am, and the shirts, before I make the tea.'

So Phyllida, emerging from the companionway red of eye but apparently calm, found her aunt busy sewing. 'Do look, love,' Cassandra said cheerfully. 'Did you ever see such fine linen?'

'What on earth are you doing?'

'Mending Mr. Renshaw's shirts,' said her aunt, blandly ignoring storm signals. 'And high time, too. Poor Price had counted on the abigail to do it.'

'Abigail? What do you mean?'

'Of course, you don't have them in America. The lady's maid. Helena's. Price thought she would do the fine mending.' She laughed. 'He said he could manage–"ahem, everything else".' She found herself waiting anxiously for Phyllida's reaction.

When it came, it was a reassuring peal of laughter. 'God bless Price,' said Phyllida. 'Hand me a shirt, Aunt. Maybe we can earn our keep on this ship after all.'

'You'd better do the cravats,' said Cassandra nobly. 'They're finer still. I was really wondering how I would manage.'

They spoke a Greek ship later that evening, and Price brought news with supper for two to the saloon. 'They were fresh out from Nauplia,' he said. 'All's well there, so far. Captain Barlow hopes to arrive towards midday tomorrow. We don't use sail at night, of course, for fear of sparks from the funnel.'

'Yes.' Phyllida was thinking about something else. 'Price, do you think you could persuade one of the crew to let us have his kit bag? I promise to pay for it, handsomely, as soon as I'm in funds.' She turned to Cassandra. 'I hate to take so much as a toothbrush off this ship, but I don't see much alternative, do you? Besides, I expect Mr. Renshaw will think it cheap as the price of getting rid of us.'

'There'll be no need, miss.' Price spoke a shade repressively. 'I'm speaking out of turn, I know, but it's only what the captain will tell you after supper. Mr. Renshaw plans to leave the ship at Nauplia and make the journey by land. He says he'll enjoy it, specially if it's dangerous. And of course, he's quite right. As an Englishman–and not unknown–he'll be a deal safer from Turks *or* Greeks than you two ladies. He's planning to see the ruins at Argos and all kinds of other antiquities on the way.' He paused for a moment and Cassandra was increasingly aware that this was the most calculated of indiscretions. 'I think it will do him good,' he went on. 'There's been something on his mind since Constantinople–'

'There has indeed,' said Phyllida angrily. 'Us.'

'No, miss, not that, excusing me. There was something he got in his mail there. Bless you, miss, I've served Mr. Brett since he was in short coats. I know when things go wrong with him, and they was worse than wrong before you ever put in an appearance. And not just on account of Miss Helena either. There was something new. So what I'm trying to say is, if you ladies are halfway grateful for what he's done for you, you'll let him go ashore and make the land trip, without–excuse me–making a potheration over it?' He ended on a note of question, and looked relieved when Phyllida burst out laughing.

'You're a fiend, Price,' she said. 'As if I wasn't far enough in the wrong already, I have to accept this sacrifice too?'

'That's about it.' He was pleased with her. 'And–there's another thing. You ladies will be able to manage without me? I thought we might try and find you a girl in Nauplia, but I won't say I'm hopeful.'

'You go with Mr. Renshaw?'

'I always go with Mr. Renshaw.'

'Do you know,' said Phyllida, drinking the wine Price had poured before he left them, 'I actually think he's fond of Mr. Renshaw.'

'Fond of him! My good child, he adores him. You might think of that a little, next time you feel like losing your temper with Mr. Renshaw. He and Price seem to disprove the saying about no man being a hero to his valet. And–did you notice–Price has been with him for ever.'

'"*Fidus Achates*",' said Phyllida crossly. 'Aunt, I do beg that you won't make me feel any worse than I do already. How can I accept such a sacrifice from someone who detests me?'

'How can you not?' said her aunt.

So Captain Barlow, arriving nervously with the coffee, found his mission a good deal easier than he had feared. When he left them it had been agreed that they would make the journey round the south of the Morea on the *Helena,* while Brett Renshaw and Price travelled overland. 'The government at Nauplia will provide them with a bodyguard,' said Barlow. 'I think Mr. Renshaw is looking forward to the trip.'

'And if he's killed by the Turks, it will be my fault,' said Phyllida.

'But why should he be? He has his *laissez-passer*– it's not as if he was a Philhellene.'

'It certainly isn't,' said Phyllida. 'Captain Barlow, will it be possible for me to go ashore at Nauplia and make enquiries about my brother?'

'I'd be relieved if you'd let me do it for you, miss. I've thought about it a good deal. You know–or maybe you don't– what these Greeks are like. They're great ones for the main chance. If they know what store you set by hearing of your brother, they may be tempted to make up all kinds of tales–for what it's worth to them, do you understand? I think it would be better if I made the enquiries, casual-like. And I'll have plenty of time'–he anticipated her objection–'while we're coaling. If there is any coal at Nauplia.'

'It's very good of you, Captain.' Cassandra was delighted to hear her niece so reasonable. 'Just one more thing,' Phyllida went on. 'Do you think Mr. Renshaw could be persuaded to let us say good-bye, and thank him?'

'I don't know, but I'll certainly ask.' And with that, looking dubious, he took his leave.

Alone with her aunt, Phyllida pushed back her chair

and surged to her feet. 'It's intolerable.' She was across the saloon, looking out through the stern window at darkness. And then, as her aunt watched her anxiously, 'To be so out-generalled,' she went on. 'How could the wretched man behave so well?'

Phyllida woke suddenly. Could they have reached Nauplia already? The *Helena* was lying to, wallowing disagreeably in the waves. Now something grated along the side, sounding disconcertingly loud through the thin planking. It woke her aunt, who sat up and drew back the curtains to let in a flood of grey light. It must be very early still.

They could hear shouting now. Phyllida put her finger to her lips and listened intently. 'Thank God,' she said at last. 'They're Greeks, not Turks.'

'That's all right then,' said Cassandra. 'I was afraid, just for a moment. Can you see anything, Phyl?'

'No. They must have tied up forward. I wonder why they've stopped us. I hope it's not bad news from Nauplia after all. Hush!' She was listening again. Then: 'I don't like the sound of it.'

'You can understand?' On the long voyage from New York, Phyllida had persuaded a Greek member of their ship's crew to teach her his language and had amazed him by the progress she made.

'What I can hear, which isn't much. I don't like the tone of it. We'd better get dressed.'

So they were ready when Price knocked on the door ten minutes later. He, too, looked as if he had dressed in haste. 'Thank God you're up, ladies. You're wanted on deck. At once.'

'What's the matter, Price?'

'I don't rightly know, not understanding their lingo. They're Greeks, not Turks,' he hurried to reassure them. 'But something seems to be wrong just the same. Mr. Renshaw and their captain are talking nineteen to the dozen, and very angry they sound. The only word I've understood so far is "Constantinople". I don't much like it.'

'No.' Phyllida needed no further explanation. If the Greeks knew (but how could they?) that the *Helena* had just come from Turkish territory, they might consider themselves entitled to stop and search her. Her father had told her that neutral ships, supplying the Turkish Army, had frequently been stopped and impounded by the Greeks. 'But anyone can see we're just a private yacht,' she objected.

'Yes, miss, but a steam yacht! Think of the advantage they'd have over the Turks if they had a steamship to tow their *brûlots*–those fire-ships of theirs–into the heart of the Turkish fleet.'

'They'd never dare–'

'I hope not. But I don't like the look of them above half. If they're not pirates, they're the next best thing.'

Phyllida had heard enough about the unorthodox Greek Navy to know that he was all too probably right. But there was no need to frighten her aunt. 'Well,' she said cheerfully, 'if we're wanted on deck, let's go up and have a look at them. One thing I do know about the Greeks is that they don't molest women.'

'Except Turkish ones,' said her aunt.

'Which, thank the Lord, no one could think us.'

There was nothing reassuring about the scene on deck. The rails were lined with piratical-looking Greek sailors in the tight jacket and typical full trousers, oddly drooping behind, of the islanders. They were armed to the teeth, and their lank hair and long mustaches did nothing to improve their appearance. Their ship lay a few cable lengths away, her guns covering the *Helena*, and another swarm of brigandish figures visible on her high, curving deck.

Brett Renshaw was arguing furiously in a mixture of ancient and modern Greek with one of the pirates, whose silver-mounted pistols and yataghan proclaimed him the leader. Phyllida did not think he understood much of what Brett was saying, and was not surprised. He did not seem to care either, but merely said, over and over again, cheerfully, in broken English, 'You come from Constantinople; you are lawful prize.' He broke off, at sight of the ladies, gave Phyllida a look of unqualified admiration and a sweeping bow, and broke into rapid Greek. 'You have ladies aboard! Have no fear. We are not Turks. You shall all be landed safely at Hydra.'

'I should hope so, too,' said Phyllida in her fluent, ungrammatical modern Greek. 'But this is a private ship, Captain, you cannot possibly intend to treat it as a prize.'

'You speak our language.' He showed white teeth in a flashing smile. 'Miraculous. You can explain to this angry milord that the very fact of visiting Constantinople makes him our enemy.'

'I'll explain no such thing,' said Phyllida tartly. 'And you certainly will have enemies, Captain, if you set about seizing innocent private vessels.'

'Exactly.' Brett Renshaw could understand modern Greek better than he spoke it. 'Tell him I have powerful friends, Miss Vannick. He'd best let us go at once if he doesn't want the English Navy down on him like a nest of hornets. I don't know where Hamilton and the *Cambrian* are, but I'll find out soon enough.'

'Hamilton?' This was a name to be reckoned with. Then he spat on the deck. '*Po, po, po*; the milord wants to frighten me. But we don't frighten easy, we Greeks. With this beautiful ship we can show even the *Cambrian* a clean pair of heels. Tell the milord'–he turned back to Phyllida–'that I've not waited here since he left Nauplia to lose my prize for a few big words.'

'You've waited?'

'Of course. Since we heard she was going to Constantinople.' He patted the *Helena*'s rail affectionately. 'This is a great day for the Greek Navy. As for you.' Another sweeping bow for Phyllida and Cassandra. 'You are our honoured guests. You would prefer, no doubt, to remain on board your ship till we reach Hydra. Tell your captain–and the milord–that if we have their promise of good behaviour, you may all do so. I know that the word of an Englishmen is not like the word of the other Franks, but almost as good as that of a Greek. Speak to them, *kyria;* explain.'

There was nothing for it but to do so. 'Hydra?' said Brett Renshaw. 'With any luck there'll be a British ship in port, or at least a French one. Tell him we give our word, Miss Vannick.'

'You are wise,' said the pirate captain. 'It will be better for us all, so. You may tell your crew to return to their duties; one of my men will accompany each of them, not because I do not trust you, milord, but so that they can learn to handle this beautiful ship. I myself will join the man you have left below to mind the machine–you will be so good as to make me known to him and explain that he must teach me how it works.' He turned to shout a series of orders to his savage-looking second-in-command. 'My *Hera* will lead the way. You have noticed, of course, that we have guns both fore and aft. There will be no trouble.'

'Of course not,' said Brett angrily. 'You have my word. But under protest, I warn you.' And then, seeing that the captain had not understood him, 'Explain to him, Miss Vannick?'

'Best not, I think.' The only good thing about this ominous situation was that Brett Renshaw had forgotten his fury and was consulting her as ally and adviser. 'I doubt if he'd understand the idea, even if he did the words. Time enough, don't you think, when we reach Hydra?'

'Yes. We're bound to get help there.'

'I'm not so sure,' said Captain Barlow gloomily. 'The trouble is, there are more ports than the main one on Hydra.'

# 6

It was a long, gloomy day. The pirate captain had shepherded Brett and the ladies down to the saloon with every appearance of courtesy, and urged that they remain there. 'We do not want an incident with my men,' and had then retired to the engine room to watch Brown at work. Price, serving dinner as imperturbably as ever, reported that a close watch was being kept on the crew. Only the men who were actually working the ship were allowed on deck, and each of them had his Greek shadow. 'They've brought their own food,' Price said. 'They're picnicking all over the deck, on bread and onions. At least they seem civil enough.'

'Yes, thank God.' Captain Barlow had joined them for dinner. 'I've heard some pretty blood-curdling stories of the

Maniote pirates down in the south of Greece, but these seem a good enough sort of men despite their savage appearance.'

'Polite as you please!' Phyllida, too, had heard about the Maniote pirates and did not want her aunt to learn too much about them. 'But it's dreadful about your ship, Mr. Renshaw. Only, surely, Captain Hamilton will make them give her back?'

'If he can find her,' said Brett gloomily. 'Think of the inlets and harbours of all these islands–and the mainland, too, where the Turks aren't in control. We don't know whether these brigands really intend to use the *Helena* to fight the Turks at all. If they do, I'll doubtless get her back, sooner or later, but if they plan to use her for more piracy . . . ? Oh well, she's been an unlucky ship to me from start to finish, maybe it's all for the best.' He pushed back his chair. 'Yes, you may clear, Price.'

Captain Barlow rose too. 'If you'll excuse me, I'll get back to the engine room. It's one thing to confuse that Greek brigand and burn up our coal, but I don't want him damaging my engines, in case we do get the *Helena* back. Which, please God, we will.'

The saloon seemed oddly small with the three of them in it. Brett took a restless turn across to look out the window. 'Not a sign of a ship,' he said, and then: 'Good God, ma'am, what are you doing?'

'Mending your shirts,' said Cassandra placidly. 'And enjoying it more than anything I've done since I left New York, so I hope you won't object. Mr. Price suggested it . . .'

Brett laughed. 'Trust Price! And what has he found for you to do, Miss Vannick?'

'Your cravats. I find it quite remarkably soothing.' She looked at him speculatively. 'What does a man do when confined to quarters, Mr. Renshaw?'

'God knows. Take to drink, perhaps, but it would incommode you ladies too much.'

'Good of you. Besides, if you drink yourself into a coma, who is to take our decisions for us when we reach land?'

Now he positively smiled at her. 'I think you amply capable of taking your own decisions, Miss Vannick. My only regret is that I have made such a botch of things for you.'

'A botch! By rescuing us from certain death? What are a few Greek pirates compared to the Turks? As far as I can see, the worst that can happen to us now is an awkward journey across Hydra, which cannot, surely, be a very large island? There's bound to be an American representative of some kind there, and then, I hope, my aunt's and my troubles will be over.' She paused a moment. 'If only we can get some news of my brother.'

'Miss Vannick—' But why depress her with his certainty that her brother must have been killed in the disastrous breakout from Missolonghi? He changed his sentence: 'Take pity on me, and play me a game of chess?'

Here was an olive branch indeed. 'I should love to,' said Phyllida with enthusiasm. 'I can't think of any better distraction than a good beating!'

In fact, having played often with her father, she made him work for his victory, and they were still at it when Price appeared to serve tea and pass on a report, brought below by one of the crew, that there was an island in sight dead ahead, and the mainland beyond. 'I wish one of us understood their lingo, the way you and Miss Vannick do, sir. The pirates are jabbering away nineteen to the dozen up there, and laughing fit to bust, too, which I don't altogether like the sound of.'

Neither did Brett, but he did his best to shrug it off. 'I expect it's nothing to do with us. At least they seem a cheerful enough set of savages.'

'Smile all over their faces and cut your throat,' said Price, arranging tea things. 'Just my joke, of course,' he went on hurriedly, quelled by Brett's furious glance. 'There's been no trouble of any kind up top, that I *do* know. All's going merry as a marriage bell.' And then, aware that this, too, was an unlucky phrase, he plumped the teapot in front of Cassandra and hurried away.

'Something's shaken Price,' said Phyllida thoughtfully. 'I wonder what.'

Brett had thought the same, but hurried to deny it. 'The man's a fool, that's all.' He drank his tea quickly, then rose, with an apology and an imprecise explanation about fetching something from his cabin. As he had hoped, he found Price there, pretending to tidy immaculate drawers. 'What's the matter?' The Greek on duty at the bottom of the companionway was near enough to hear, but could not possibly understand.

'I don't know, sir, and that's a fact.' Price sounded both anxious and apologetic. 'It all seems smooth sailing enough–I mean aside from losing the *Helena,* and, between you and me, sir, will that be such a disaster? But there's something else. I've just heard that the Greeks spoke another of their damned *mystics* earlier on and there was a lot of wig-wagging of turbans between us and them. Like as if they had a code of signals, sir, you know, such as Lord Nelson used? And it's since then that the prize crew have been so uncommon jolly. I don't like it, sir, not above half.'

'Nor do I, Price, but for God's sake don't frighten the ladies.'

'I'm sorry, sir. It just slipped out. And mind you, those two would take quite some frightening. As right a pair of ladies as it's ever been my pleasure to serve. I just hope–'

'I know.' He, too, was thinking of all the unpleasant possibilities. 'When I leave, shut the door and see to the priming of my pistols, Price.'

'I'm sorry, sir. They made a search, right through the ship, while you were having dinner. They've got the lot.'

'You should have told me.'

'What difference would it have made, sir?' And then, 'Look out, here comes that captain.'

'Is there anything I can do for you?' As before, the pirate captain was all smiles, but Brett liked the look of him less than ever.

'Yes,' he said at once. 'You can return the arms my man tells me you have impounded.'

'But of course.' He reached negligently into his broad red sash, pulled out his yataghan and made a little business of picking his teeth with the sharp point. 'When we land, milord, you shall have your arms back. But in the meantime, we none of us want trouble, do we? My men are quick on the draw.' He illustrated this by replacing the dagger in its sheath, then whipping it out again at electric speed. 'We don't want to start anything we might not be able to stop.' It was the most smiling of threats. 'But I have good news for you, milord. We are in sight of land. You wish to come on deck and see?'

'If I may bring the ladies?'

'But of course. They too must enjoy the sight of free Greek soil. Bring them by all means, milord.'

'I don't like it,' said Price in English.

'Nor do I.' Brett turned away to summon the two women from the saloon.

'At last,' said Phyllida. 'I'm sorry to say it, Mr. Renshaw, but as a gaol, your fine ship is even worse than Mahmoud's harem. At least, there, we had free access to our own walled garden.'

On deck, they found the pirate captain. 'So this is Hydra?' Brett looked at the rugged island ahead.

'No, Spetsai.' The Greek grinned broadly. 'My own island. We thought it time we came home.'

'I don't understand.' Brett gazed at the barren-looking island, where the *Hera* was already furling her sails in a small harbour from which a tumble of white houses climbed steeply uphill. 'Surely the entire population here can't be given to piracy? Do you think we have misjudged the situation completely?'

'I doubt it,' said Cassandra. 'But it is odd, I agree. In a town that size, there must be some foreigners—or at least foreign representatives who would be compelled to take our side. Perhaps they have had good news of some kind that has changed all their plans.'

'Let us devoutly hope so,' said Phyllida. 'If it means the *Helena* is safe.' They were very close in now, and Greek and English sailors, working together in apparent amity, had got down the sail, so that they glided slowly on under engine power only. 'Something's very odd,' she went on. 'Can you see anyone in the town? At a little place like this, the arrival of two ships should bring the whole population helter-skelter down to the harbour.'

'You're quite right.' Brett had been surveying the town through his pocket glass. 'There's not a soul in sight except the crew of the *Hera*.'

'And no washing hanging from the houses. Or nets,

drying in the sun. Or ships, come to that.' She looked from Brett to her aunt. 'Am I being stupid? Is there some simple explanation?'

'Just so long as it's not the plague,' said Cassandra.

'That would hardly have made our captors so happy.' Brett turned to the pirate captain. 'What's happened to all the people?'

'Extraordinary, isn't it.' The captain's teeth flashed in his mechanical smile. 'A ghost town, milord. To stay here will be an experience you are not likely to repeat. We learned of the evacuation only this afternoon, and thought we had best come home and see that our wives left all tidy before they went.'

'Evacuation? What do you mean?'

'That the Turkish fleet is out of the Dardanelles, may they rot in hell. Spetsai is as you see–almost indefensible. We don't want another massacre like the one on Chios . . . So our brothers on Hydra sent inviting the entire population of Spetsai to move over there. What do you think of that, milord? Does it not give the lie to the tales you Franks like to tell about internal dissension among us Greeks?'

'The whole town is empty?'

'Just so. You can have the choice of any house in the place. You and your beautiful ladies. And your crew, of course, unless any of them wish to throw in their lot with us.'

'You propose to leave us here? Alone on an island that may be attacked by the Turks at any moment?'

He spread his hands in a gesture of disengagement. 'What's that to you? As Franks, you will be safe enough with the Turks. Anyway, very likely it's all a false alarm, like so many others. You have only to wait awhile . . . I expect your *Cambrian* will call here sooner or later; or the French admiral, De Rigny. What a fine tale you will have to tell, will you not? A regular romance–' A flashing glance between Brett and Phyllida underlined his point.

'It's monstrous,' began Brett. 'How do we know there is food and water on the island?'

'Oh, there's bound to be. Our wives are good women, but not capable, like the *kyria* here. They will have left plenty behind. And as for the cisterns, they would hardly have emptied them.'

Brett and Phyllida exchanged a speaking glance. 'I suppose it might be worse,' she said.

'Not much. He may honestly think there will be enough food for all of us, but I wonder.'

'Surely he'll tell someone about us?'

'Why should he? It would merely endanger him.'

It was all too obviously true. They were a very silent party as they were landed by the *Helena*'s boat. Brett had made one last protest, which had been received with another of the captain's flashing smiles. 'Time for such talk,' he said, 'when we have beaten the Turks. Your baggage will come next, and then your crew. In the meantime, perhaps you would like to choose your house —or houses—' Another look of extreme roguishness flashed to Phyllida and back. 'Then your men will know where to take your baggage. Doubtless they will find their own quarters.'

The crew of the *Hera* had already dispersed, shouting to one another, among the narrow lanes and whitewashed houses on the steep hillside. Now the pirate captain turned away from Brett to shout angrily as the Greeks on board the *Helena* also began to leap ashore one by one. They took no notice of his furious commands, but disappeared up the hill after their comrades from the *Hera*.

'They're looting their own houses!' Phyllida exclaimed.

'Or each other's,' said Brett. 'I hope to God it doesn't end in fighting.'

'It might be our best chance.' Like him, Phyllida was looking thoughtfully back to where the *Helena* lay quiet in evening sunlight. But if there had been a momentary chance of repossessing her, it was already gone. By furious shouting, the pirate captain had managed to collect a small group of his men to guard her. Now he returned to the three of them on the dock. 'We've not been home in months,' he said as if in extenuation. 'But my men will see that all is safe on the *Helena*. See, your people are beginning to come ashore already. I had best make sure they are bringing nothing they should not.' And he turned away once more to join Captain Barlow, who had stayed to supervise the unloading. The pirates had stipulated that only personal effects might be brought ashore and were now examining the crew's small bundles as they allowed them to land one by one.

'I told Barlow to see to it that each man carried food for at least twenty-four hours,' Brett told Phyllida. 'It looks as if they are getting through with that.'

'Thank God. But–' She looked at the bleak hillside above the houses. 'Twenty-four hours?'

'I know. I've heard that Spetsai and Hydra are the most desolate of all the inhabited islands. We must pray for a quick rescue. And see to it that the men husband their provisions.' He moved forward as the first of the crew approached them, retying his bundle and swearing under his breath. 'What is it, Jem?'

'They've taken all my pay, sir. They laughed and said I'd have no need for money here. All's free, they said. Every penny they took, and laughed.'

'I'll make it up to you, Jem, when we get out of here.' Passionately he hoped he could. 'But they left you the food?'

'Yes, sir. Biscuit and salt beef, like the captain said. I don't think they reckon much of our salt beef.' He looked up at the bare hillside. 'Just as well, by the look of things. What's to do, sir?'

'We'll all stay together for the moment. Till the Greeks are back on board. Pass the word, Jem.' And then, to Phyllida: 'I'll feel a great deal safer when their captain's got them rounded up.'

'So shall I. Goodness, what's Price doing?' On the deck of the *Helena,* Price seemed to be signalling to her and at the same time pointing to something heavy carried by two of the crew. 'What can he mean?' Now she recognised Helena's box. 'Oh!' Suddenly she understood. 'Forgive me?' To Brett. 'Aunt, come and help me.' She hurried forward just as the two men brought the big sea chest across the deck towards the check-point the Greeks had established. 'Captain!' She put a pleading hand on the pirate's arm. 'Those are our things, mine and my aunt's. You Greeks are known for your gallantry. You'll never let your men examine them? Out here, in full view? It's not possible!' She cast an anguished glance back towards Brett as if to suggest that it was his inspection of her intimate effects that she minded most.

For once she was pleased to see the pirate captain's grin. 'Only one box for two ladies?' he said. And then, as she held her breath, 'Very well, *kyria,* you shall not be shamed in front of the milord.' He shouted an order to his men, then smiled broadly at her again. 'You should bless me, lady. No doubt you do. To spend the night with him here on shore—one night and many more, perhaps? I congratulate you, milady?' He put just enough question into his voice to make the insult unmistakable.

Or rather, she thought, not an insult but simply a statement of fact, as he saw it. Naturally, he assumed her to be Brett's mistress. Furious colour stained her cheeks. But, thank God, no one else had understood.

But she actually found herself sorry for Brett as the Greeks held up shirt after shirt with amused comment on milord's luxurious tastes. The crimson dressing gown raised a small cheer and was instantly appropriated by the pirate captain. Behind her, she heard Brett swear under his breath and turned quickly to comfort him. 'Don't mind it,' she said. 'Just let's wonder what Price has put in—' She paused.

'Helena's box?' He supplied the phrase. 'Food and warm clothing, I hope. You're wonderfully quick, Miss Vannick. That's the second time today we've all had cause to be grateful to you.'

'And to Price.' She coloured with pleasure at his praise.

'And here he comes. You're all ashore?' Price and Barlow had come ashore together.

'Yes.' Barlow was still red with anger from having his own effects examined and his money appropriated. 'Set of thieving pirates! But we've got some food ashore, sir, like you said.'

'Thank God for that. And the box?' To Price.

'Food and warm clothes, sir. Mostly food. And a few things I thought the ladies might need on top. Thanks to you, miss.'

'Yes, we'll all be blessing you both if we have to stay here any length of time.' He looked thoughtfully at the shadows that were lengthening round them. 'It will be dark soon. We must find ourselves quarters. Brown, you and Price stay here with the crew and the ladies. The captain and I will explore the town.'

'You'll be careful?'

'Of course. And you'll stay here, all together, on the quay. At least, here, you're under the Greek captain's eye.'

'For what that's worth,' said Phyllida. And then, suddenly: 'Look!'

Turning, they heard shouts from the men on lookout duty on the *Helena* and *Hera,* and saw an island brig just rounding the point, all sails set to catch the evening breeze.

'He'll never make it!' Phyllida was amazed at the daring of this swift entry into the harbour.

'Oh yes he will.' She had spoken in Greek, and the pirate captain answered her. 'That's Alexandros in the *Philip.* He can do anything. Watch!'

As he spoke, the sails of the new ship came rattling down, and, suddenly, amazingly, she was sliding to a halt exactly behind the *Helena.* 'And he not even a Spetsiot,' said the pirate captain with reluctant admiration as he went forward to greet the tall young man who had leapt ashore.

'They're friends, worse luck.' Brett watched gloomily as the two men embraced each other.

'I'm afraid so,' agreed Phyllida. 'I wish we could hear what they're saying.' It was obvious from the two men's gestures that they were talking about the *Helena.* Now they turned and approached along the quay, apparently arguing.

'They understand Greek,' were the first words Phyllida caught, spoken in warning by their captor.

'Do they indeed?' The newcomer was the most handsome man she had ever seen. His tanned face was a Greek god's from an antique coin, his dark hair curled, his brilliant smile had a warmth the other man's lacked. On him, even the curious baggy trousers of the Greek sailors contrived to look elegant. Now, approaching, his flashing smile was for them. 'Welcome to Spetsai!' A graceful bow for Phyllida. 'I have been telling my friend here that he cannot possibly abandon a beautiful lady on this desolate island. You Franks are our friends. We may need your ships, but we will never willingly expose you to harm.'

'I'm more than relieved to hear you say so,' said Brett. 'It's not so much for myself that I'm anxious, as for Miss Vannick here, and her aunt.'

'Vannick!' The young Greek's eyes flashed suddenly into fire. 'You are Miss Vannick?' He turned his brilliant gaze searchingly on her and spoke in quick English with an accent that she recognised, with surprise, as like her own.

'Yes? Why?' Wild, unreasonable hope surged up in her.

'You have a brother, Petros? Peter, I should say?'

Now it was more than hope. 'Yes?' Eagerly.

But his face had changed. 'I spoke too rashly. One should not tempt the fates. But some of them escaped from Missolonghi. So why not Petros? He was a fine fighter; a brave man; my friend. And you are his sister.' Surprisingly, he kissed her lightly on the cheek. 'Welcome to Greece, sister of my Brother Petros.'

'You know him well?' She would not use the past tense.

'Well! He sailed with me when he first came to Greece. He taught me your language–' He laughed. 'And I did my best to teach him ours. A brilliant teacher, your Brother Petros, and a fine man. If only he had not fallen under the spell of that mad Lord Byron–but nothing would do but he must serve him. When the mad lord died, I hoped Petros would come back to me and the *Philip,* but he said he must stay in Missolonghi. Always, when we took supplies in, I urged him to come away, but each time their situation was worse. I knew he was right to stay. Don't look so sad, sister of my friend. We will pray, together, that he is safe.'

'Yes, indeed.' Brett had listened with increasing hope. 'And, in the meanwhile, perhaps you, sir, will speak for us to your friend the captain here. I was taking Miss Vannick to Nauplia to make enquiries about her brother. Your friend seems to think us a lawful prize, merely because we have come from Constantinople.'

'Where Mr. Renshaw had, in fact, rescued us–my aunt and me–from the Turks,' interposed Phyllida.

'From the Turks?'

'Yes.' Phyllida was grateful to Brett for intervening. 'That is why it is so dangerous for them to remain here, where, I understand, the Turks are expected momently.'

'Oh well, as to that–' His smile flashed out. 'I only believe in the Turkish fleet when I actually see it. I think the Spetsiots have let themselves be panicked too easily. But never mind that. Of course you must not be left here. I will explain to my friend that your mission to Constantinople was one of purest gallantry.' This time the lightning smile was for Phyllida alone. 'You see how well your brother taught me to speak your language. I am glad, now, that I paid attention to him, since it makes it easier for me to serve you.' He turned away to embark on a furious argument with the pirate captain.

Brett and Phyllida watched and listened anxiously, but it was difficult to catch more than an angry phrase here and there. For a moment it seemed that they would come to blows; then their rescuer used one quick, venomous phrase and it was over.

'What did he say?' Phyllida had missed it.

'Something about the Mavromikhalis,' Brett told her. 'I've heard of them. They're the ruling family down in that wild southern part of Greece, the Mani. Not even the Turks dared meddle much with them; they used merely to name the head of the family their representative and make do with a token tribute from him. I don't suppose our captor there would much want to make enemies of them.'

'No.' She turned to greet their rescuer.

'All's well,' he said. 'My friend there understands his mistake at last. Your ship is yours again, milord–'

'Just plain "Mr.",' said Brett. 'Brett Renshaw, and your debtor for life. And you?'

'Alexandros.' Again his smile was for Phyllida. 'My friends call me Alex. And you are no debtor of mine, Mr. Renshaw. It is for Miss Vannick that I have annoyed my friend over there. Who knows? If it had not been for her, and her brother, I too might have found that beautiful *Helena* of yours irresistible. A steam-yacht, here in Greece. Do you not understand what a temptation she represents?'

'I think I am beginning to,' said Brett dryly.

# 7

It seemed too good to be true, but an hour later they were all back on board the *Helena*, with the greater part of their possessions safely restored. 'That's a most remarkable young man,' said Brett.

'Isn't he?' Phyllida's cheeks glowed as if the praise had been for her.

'I'm more in debt to you than ever,' he went on. 'I begin to think it was the luckiest day of my life when you rowed out to the *Helena*.'

She laughed. 'Just don't try to pretend you were glad to see us at the time.' And then, seeing his face change. 'I'm sorry. That was a bad night for you, was it not?'

'One day, perhaps, I'll tell you just how bad. But now, if you will excuse me, I must find Barlow. It's time to think about sailing. Thank God.'

'But not before we thank–' She hesitated. It was disconcerting not to know their rescuer's surname.

'Yes, indeed we must thank him. But in fact he promised to come aboard for a demonstration of our engine.'

'Oh, I'm glad.' Disconcerting to recognise just how glad she was.

But the demonstration was not a success. Mr. Brown, sweating and cursing, was beginning to discover just how much damage the pirates had done to his beloved engines. 'As much wear and tear as on the whole voyage out,' he summed it up gloomily. 'It's going to take me every spare part I've got to fix it. I think I can, but once anything else gives way, we're done. Oh, no,' he answered Brett's question. 'Nothing wilful about it, I shouldn't think. They just couldn't resist playing with it.'

'Of course not.' Alex said. 'My countrymen are like that, I'm afraid. No malice, and not much sense. How long do you think before you can get her going?'

'Tomorrow sometime.' Brown was wiping his hands on a bit of cotton waste. 'We should make Nauplia by night.'

'If it's safe to go there,' said Brett.

'Safe?' asked the young Greek. 'Oh, you mean the Turks? No need to trouble yourself about them. I was in Nauplia yesterday. All's quiet, or at least as quiet as we Greeks know how to be. But just the same I think I shall give myself the pleasure of waiting and escorting you to Nauplia. My friend in the *Hera* is an obstinate man.'

'But if you were in Nauplia yesterday,' Phyllida pounced on it. 'You'd know if there was news of Peter.'

'I'm afraid I probably would.' He was too honest, she thought, to spare her. 'But we will set further enquiries on foot. The refugees I talked to yesterday were in no state to think of much beyond their own troubles. But tomorrow, while the engine is repairing, will you let me be your guide round Spetsai, *kyria*? There are none of the Greek antiquities you Franks set such store by, but some chapels, I believe, that are worth the visit.'

When they reached the quay next morning, the *Hera* was ready to sail, and they paused to watch her go. 'I'd as soon not leave your *Helena* till she's well away,' Alex told Brett. 'I wouldn't want to put temptation in my friend's way. Even without her engines, yours is a splendid ship, milord.'

'Yes, but she's intolerably slow under sail alone. It was one of my major disappointments in her design.'

'That wretched little square sail on the funnel? I was thinking about that. It seems to me, that with a little of our Greek ingenuity, we could rig you something much better. You'll let me experiment, when we have tired Miss Vannick out with chapels?'

'If Captain Barlow agrees.' Barlow and Miss Knight had both stayed on board, Barlow to help Brown, and Miss Knight for a badly needed rest.

Phyllida, finding one faded Byzantine fresco very like another, was almost tempted to envy her aunt as the sun grew hotter and the odours of peasant living stronger. She was tired of picking her way through filthy alleys, tired even of listening to Alex and Brett talk about the course of the war. Her head was beginning to ache.

'You're tired.' Brett took her arm to guide her round a particularly unsavoury pile of rubbish. 'We've brought you too far. It was monstrous of me to forget all you've been through.'

'Not at all.' She was beginning the polite, necessary lie, when Alex, who had gone on a little ahead, came back to meet them.

'I've a surprise for you.' She wished he would go on calling her 'sister of my friend,' but this time he made do with a warm, admiring smile. 'I hope you'll agree that I've not brought you all this way for nothing. You'll let me–' Somehow he had removed her from Brett's supporting arm and was guiding her forward to a hilly corner beyond the houses. 'There!' He smiled with pleasure at her exclamation of surprised delight. 'You see, your brother taught me how you Franks like a–what do you call it?–a prospect?'

He had brought them out onto a small, cleared plateau. In front, the ground dropped away sharply to the wine-dark sea. Ahead, clear in the extraordinary pellucid light, lay the mainland, Greece itself, the fabled shore she had longed to see. Those purple mountains, ranging away to the south, might once have harboured Zeus himself. She smiled at her own nonsense, and turned back to Alex, who was speaking again.

'I have another surprise for you, *kyria,* one that I hope will please you too.' He led the way across the open space to where a group of Greek sailors were busy under the shade of a huge mulberry tree. 'We are to have a picnic here.' And then, with a flash of white teeth, 'I little knew how grateful I should be to Petros for teaching me his language–and yours.'

Resting in the grateful shade of the mulberry tree, Phyllida was glad to drink the light white wine that Alex's men had brought, to eat highly seasoned cold lamb in her fingers and listen to the two men talk. They seemed to have established, from the first, a surprisingly easy understanding. It pleased her enormously, and puzzled her at the same time, but as she listened and gazed out at the splendid sweep of sea and shore she thought she began to understand. In his own way, each was that extraordinary phenomenon to an American, an aristocrat. She had never heard of the Mavromikhalis, but listening to Alex talk of his home down south in the Mani she felt something of the power his family must wield there. And Brett? He, too, behaved with the calm confidence of one who had always been exempt from the minor problems of every day. Just the same, as Alex began to question him about life in England she saw a shadow cross his face and remembered what he had said to her: 'One day I'll tell you perhaps how bad.' She was sure, now, that there was more wrong in his life than Helena's rejection.

'You have great estates in England?' Alex was asking.

Brett's face closed. 'No. None at all. The *Helena* is my estate.'

'Then I'm glad you didn't lose her.' Alex rose gracefully to his feet: 'The sun is getting round to us. Time to go, perhaps? Your man struck me as someone who would always be better than his word. Who knows? He may have the engines working already. I can hardly tell you how I long to see the *Helena* with steam up. Is that the phrase, *kyria*?'

'Absolutely. You're simply amazing, Mr.–' She stopped, blushing.

'Please, call me Alex. Everyone does.'

'Thank you.' Doubtfully. Call him 'Alex' and go on calling Brett 'Mr. Renshaw'?

'If you do that, Miss Vannick,' Brett himself came to the rescue, 'I shall be sadly affronted if you don't start calling me "Brett". After all, compared with Alex here, I am an old, old friend.'

'You are indeed–Brett.'

She had forgotten to expect Aunt Cassandra's look of outrage when she heard this use of Christian names. 'But what else could I do, Aunt, when Alex doesn't seem to use his other one?'

'That young Greek!' Cassandra's tone was surprisingly sharp. 'Frankly, I'll be delighted to see the last of him. I wouldn't trust that one an inch, and don't you, Phyllida. I blame myself for letting you go ashore alone this morning. If I'd known Captain Barlow wasn't going too, I'd never have stayed behind.'

'Oh, Aunt.' Phyllida felt an odd little qualm of shame. She had known, and had taken very good care that her aunt did not find out.

'Picnics and wine drinking,' went on Cassandra. 'I tell you, Phyllida, I'll be glad when we see the last of him.'

'But he's Peter's friend.'

'And since when has that been a recommendation? Peter's a dear boy, but you know as well as I do that his choice of friends– Think of the ragtag and bobtail he used to go bowling with at Harvard.'

'But that was quite different. He was a boy at Harvard. Now he's grown up; everything's changed. Alex'–she coloured but ploughed firmly on—'Alex is a man. He's fighting for his country. He takes life seriously. Look how he had Peter teach him English.'

'And very useful it will be to him, too, in this war of theirs. Suppose Lord Byron had lived, Peter and this "Alex" might be his right-hand men by now, with a strong chance of getting into the first real Greek Government. I'd very much like to know what hopes of that beautiful young Greek's were snuffed out with Byron at Missolonghi.'

'Aunt, you're being horribly unfair.'

'Am I?' Something in Phyllida's tone had sounded a warning bell in her aunt's receptive ear. 'I'm sorry, child. I expect I am. Forgive me, I'm a little tired still, and crotchety to go with it. It's an old maid's privilege . . .'

Phyllida was glad to finish combing out her rebellious curls and return to the cheerful party on deck. She left her aunt with a good deal to think about. But, Miss Knight reassured herself, they would be parting from this too handsome young Greek at Nauplia. He was in the engine room now, watching Brown put the finishing touches to his repairs. No need to hurry after Phyllida, who had joined Brett up on deck. She sighed, rebuked herself for a shameless match-maker, and wished that Alexandros (wild horses would not have made her even think of him as Alex) had never rescued them.

They steamed into Nauplia just as dusk was falling, and Phyllida, standing eagerly at the forward rail, was delighted to have Alex and Brett, one on each side of her, to tell her about the temporary Greek capital.

'That's the Palamede,' Brett pointed up to the citadel, high above the town. 'It's as good as impregnable, they say.'

'Yes,' said Alex, 'but not, I'm afraid, a classical marvel for Phyllida.' It was the first time he had used her name, and she felt his quick glance ask her approval.

'Oh, is it modern then?' She smiled up at him.

'Comparatively. Like so many of our fortresses, it was built by the Venetians. You will see their arms over the great gate when I take you there.'

'But we must not trouble you with our sightseeing.' Brett was beginning to share Aunt Cassandra's feelings about the young Greek.

'No, please,' chimed in Phyllida. 'You are going to find out everything you can about Peter for me, are you not?'

'Of course I am. My own pleasure must come a long way second to that. Besides, what greater pleasure than to serve you?'

'Oh, thank you . . .' She had never much liked the compliment direct. 'What's that island?' She pointed.

'That's another stronghold. We call it the Burj. I'm glad Nauplia is to be your first Greek town, *kyria*. It's one of the few that have not been fought over. It's been in our hands ever since the first rising.'

'And the massacre of the Turks that went with it,' said Brett.

Phyllida felt Alexandros stiffen as he leaned on the rail at her side, but he spoke calmly enough: 'It's easy for the free to indulge in the humane virtues. Slaves must use what weapons they can. *You* must understand that.' He turned to Phyllida. 'You who have been in the hands of the Turk.'

'Yes.' She shuddered, remembering the massacre of the Janissaries, and her shoes caked with dried blood.

'Nonsense!' Aunt Cassandra intervened. 'Two wrongs don't make a right, young man. Never have and never will. I agree with Mr. Renshaw. You Greeks have done your cause untold damage by the innocent blood you have shed.'

'Innocent!' His eyes flashed. 'After four hundred years of tyranny, no Turk is innocent to us. Wait, Miss Knight, until you know what has happened to your nephew before you speak of "innocent Turks". And now, milord, ladies, I must leave you. Don't try to go ashore until I have spoken to my uncle about you. I am sure he will understand that since you have already been to Spetsai there is no need for you to suffer quarantine.'

'Your uncle?' asked Brett.

'The head of my family. Petro Bey, the Turks call him. He has some influence here in Nauplia. He will be glad to exert it in the interest of beauty in distress. Sister of my friend, I kiss your hand.' He did so, with emphasis, sending a curious little shiver through Phyllida and one of surprising irritation through Brett.

'And who is this Petro Bey?' Cassandra asked, after Alex had gone agilely down hand over hand into the *Helena*'s boat and been rowed away towards the shore.

'A very odd fish indeed,' Brett told her. 'The very name gives it to you. He co-operated with the Turks for all it was worth, so long as it was worth anything. Now he's the better part of the Greek Government, I believe. Such as it is!'

Phyllida turned from watching Alex leap lightly on shore. 'I do wish you'd try to speak more kindly of the Greeks, Mr. Renshaw.'

'I wish you'd try to call me Brett. If you can use that young pirate's first name–'

'How can you?' she interrupted him angrily. '"That young pirate", as you call him, has just saved us all–and your precious ship, too.'

'Yes, Miss Vannick, and have you thought at all about how he was able to do so? I admit I didn't understand all of what he was saying to the *Hera*'s captain, but I got a strong impression that it wasn't so much law and order he was preaching as might and right. If you're a small Greek captain, you don't lightly cross one of the Mavromikhalis.'

'And so much the luckier for us.'

'Oh yes, I agree with you there. I just wish I felt entirely happy about his motives.'

'His motives?' She flushed angrily. 'Friendship for my brother, of course. Didn't he tell us so?'

'Yes, so he did.'

Alex returned with depressing news. There was typhus in Nauplia. For their own sakes, they would be well advised not to go ashore. 'As for quarantine–' He spread his hands in a gesture that reminded Brett of the pirate captain. 'My uncle says that any friend of mine is free to do what he will . . . but the typhus is something else. And there is no coal in Nauplia. You will have to let me make you a larger sail, milord, and escort you to Zante so. There, you will certainly be able to get coal for your beautiful *Helena*.'

'Escort us?' Brett's reaction was predictable. 'What need have we of an escort?'

Alex smiled. 'Do you really think my friend and the *Hera* so far away? He was not at all pleased to have his beautiful prize snatched from his grasp. He will be waiting, trust me, somewhere down the coast between here and Matapan. And, down there, too, there are other hazards. We have been pirates of necessity for so many centuries, we poor Greeks, we cannot mend our ways all in a moment.'

'But Peter?' Phyllida asked. 'Have you any news of him?'

'A crumb.' He took her hand. 'A morsel of hope to feed a hungry sparrow. Don't make too much of it, *Kyria* Phyllida.'

'But what is it?' Cassandra moved between them so that he had to let go of Phyllida's hand.

'I have been out to the huts beyond the city wall, where the refugees from Missolonghi are living.' He turned on Brett, eyes aflash. 'If you saw that misery, you would not talk of massacres. Think of them, desperate, starving, planning their escape. And betrayed . . .'

'By one of themselves?'

'*No*! By a Bulgarian, a wretch, a turncoat . . . So when they had made their preparations, buried the type of the *Missolonghi Chronicle*, kissed each other the long good-bye . . . They broke out; the Turks were waiting, and death.'

'But my hope?' Phyllida intervened again. 'My crumb of comfort? What is it?'

'A very little crumb. I would not be your friend if I should bid you hope much. But one of the men I spoke to–a skeleton of a man, dying as he stands–I recognised him, just, as a friend of my Brother Petros. He told me that when the disaster struck, Petros was one of the band that cut their way out. He saw them, fighting gallantly, breasting the waves of Turks. And that is all he saw.'

'So we still don't know.' Cassandra summed it up.

'No, *kyria*, but we still have hope.'

It was hot in the landlocked Bay of Nauplia. The *Helena*'s deck was a scene of furious activity as the crew worked, under Alex's orders, to rig the new set of sails he had planned. Only in the evening could Phyllida and her aunt emerge from the saloon to enjoy the cooling air and watch the stir of life in the town across the bay. No one was allowed on shore. Brett had gone once, and had returned, very gloomy, to confirm Alex's warning about typhus and condemn Nauplia as a stinking hole. 'You're not missing much in staying on board,' he told Phyllida. 'It looks better from here than close to. And smells better. And there's no news that one can believe. And no mail from England. We shall have to wait until Zante for that.'

Here, Phyllida was sure, lay the reason for his gloom. Had he, perhaps, expected some word from Helena?

Even Alex was growing impatient with the dilatory behaviour of the Greek Government. 'It's over a month now since Missolonghi fell,' he told Phyllida, 'and what have they done? Put on mourning–and talked. And meanwhile the Turks have laid siege to Athens. It only remains for Ibrahim to attack Nauplia and we Greeks might as well jump off a cliff, as the women of Suli did when they were defeated.'

'You don't mean that?'

He flashed his smile at her. 'No, *kyria,* I don't. If I were the last Greek alive, I would still die fighting the Turk. If only we had more money–'

'Money–' Brett had joined them on the foredeck. 'What happened to the immense loan that was raised in England when the rebellion first broke out?'

'It's all been spent long since.' Phyllida did not think Alex much liked the question. 'Even a *pallikar*–a Greek soldier–must eat, milord.'

'And wear silver-mounted pistols?'

'It's true.' Alex flushed angrily. 'That first English loan was misspent. We Greeks are children still when it comes to government. It was madness to hand over the money without making any conditions about its use. If only Lord Byron had lived . . .'

'He'd have washed his hands of the whole affair long since. From all I've heard he was getting impatient enough already with the bungling and cadging at Missolonghi. Maybe it was a stroke of luck for your cause that he died when he did and provided you with a famous martyr.'

'Milord!' Suddenly Alexandros' hand was on his own silver-mounted pistol. 'You go too far.'

'Do I?' The quiet words fell heavily.

'Missolonghi!' Phyllida broke in. 'Alex! Tell me if you've had any more news from there. Please?' The plea was tacitly addressed to them both. But Alex's hand was still on his pistol. She touched it lightly, pleadingly. 'Say you've another crumb of comfort for me?'

'In fact, yes.' She could feel the tension drain out of him. 'There is news today that a group of soldiers from Missolonghi did manage to join Karaiskakis in the mountains. That at least was not mere rumour. As to the rest of it–I don't want to raise false hopes–'

'Please?'

'You could persuade a man to anything, *kyria*. Well, you shall have it then, your crumb. There is talk that one of them was a Frank–a Philhellene. Well, why not? Petros is young and strong. And he was not cumbered with womenfolk as were so many of the men who escaped. If they could have brought themselves to leave their wives behind, it might have been a different story.'

'Just the same, I'm glad they didn't,' said Aunt Cassandra. 'The women who stayed behind weren't spared, were they?'

'There was no hope for them,' he said. 'Knowing this, it was arranged that when the Turks were well into the town, the tower they were in should be blown up. They went to heaven, *kyria,* and sent a good number of Turks to hell at the same time.'

Phyllida shivered. 'It's barbarous.' But at least the moment of danger between him and Brett had passed.

Brett thanked Phyllida later. 'If you hadn't intervened, I really believe that mad young Greek and I would have come to blows this afternoon.'

'Not blows,' said Phyllida. 'Pistols for two.'

'Yes. The last thing we want. Quite apart from the debt

of gratitude I owe him, I don't at all wish to get in bad odour with the Greeks by killing him.'

'You're so sure you would?' She found his confidence irritating.

'My dear Miss Vannick, have you seen that silver-plated blunderbuss he uses for a pistol? It might just as well have come out of the ark. I doubt if he could hit a barn door at ten paces, still less a man. They're all the same, those Greeks. The only weapon of theirs that's any good is their musket–and it's so heavy they have to lean it on a rock to fire. That's why they're no use in hand-to-hand combat. Give me a regiment of English infantry, with the bayonet, and I guarantee to defeat any army the Greeks can field.'

'So long as you get near enough.'

He laughed. 'I hope I never do. But, Miss Vannick–'

'I thought you were to call me Phyllida.' His tone was more serious than she liked.

'Phyllida, then–' He moved closer, as if to take her hand; then, to her relief, turned suddenly on his heel. 'What am I thinking of? Forgive me; I must make sure that Barlow's set a good watch. I don't trust those Greeks for an instant. They'd steal the hair off your head and say it was in the cause of the revolution. I'll be glad when we've got the *Helena* safe to Zante.'

'So shall I,' said Phyllida.

# 8

On the surface, Brett and Alex were as good friends as ever, but just the same Phyllida was relieved that Alex would escort them to Zante on his own ship, the *Philip*. To see the two of them together, now, was to see tinderbox and gunpowder.

'I shall keep always within hailing distance.' Alex was saying good-bye. 'Even with your new sails, you've no chance of outdistancing the *Philip*. Set your own pace, and rely on me to keep close. You'll be in no danger rounding Cape Matapan with me behind you.'

'The piracy's so bad?' Brett had not much liked the implied criticism of the *Helena*.

'This is war, milord.'

'I've been thinking about that.' As so often, Phyllida felt it best to intervene. 'Ought you to be wasting your time escorting us?'

'Time is never wasted in the service of beauty. Besides.' On a more practical note. 'I am charged with messages from our government to Sir Frederick Adam, the British High Commissioner for the Ionian Islands.'

'Then we must delay you as little as possible.' Brett sounded equally businesslike.

'No indeed. Only–' Phyllida held out her hand to Alex: 'There's no more news?'

'Of Petros? None. I'm sorry. But my friends are still making enquiries. Don't despair, *kyria*. When I have seen you safe to Zante, and taken my despatches to Sir Frederick on Corfu, I propose to treat myself to a run up the gulf to Missolonghi. Who knows what information I may not be able to pick up there?'

'But is it safe? Now that the Turks hold the place?'

He raised her unresisting hand to kiss it. 'Your concern would make any danger worthwhile, but, frankly, there's none. What do the Turks hold? A few blackened ruins, full of the bones of gallant Greeks. They don't hold the countryside; they never do. That's why, in the end, they will lose this war. Have no fear for me. I shall find a way of getting in touch with friends on shore. Perhaps, at last, I shall have real news for you.'

'A very clever young man.' Miss Knight joined Phyllida at the rail, where she was watching Alex row himself vigorously back to the *Philip*.

'You don't like him?'

'I find him charming. But I don't quite trust him, Phyl.' She regretted it as soon as it was spoken and did her best to turn it off with a laugh. 'What was that phrase you and Peter used to use? "*Timeo Danaos* . . ." '

'"I fear the Greeks . . ."' She sighed, and her aunt wondered, anxiously, whether it was for her brother. 'But why in the world should we fear Alex, Aunt? Just think what he's done for us.'

'Yes indeed.' Wisely, Cassandra let it rest there.

With fine weather and a following wind they made good time down to Cape Matapan. Rounding it, they lost sight of the *Philip* for the first time but saw a pair of *mystics* ahead.

'They must have a lookout up there.' Brett pointed to a fortress on the headland.

'In that case he'll have seen the *Philip*,' said Phyllida. 'But not necessarily recognised her. Here they come.'

'They really are pirates?'

'It looks very much like it. I never thought I'd be so eager to see the *Philip*. Ah, there she is and signalling nineteen to the dozen. I wish I knew what it meant.'

'Yes.' Barlow joined them at the rail. 'I'd give a good deal to understand their code. But it seems to work. Look!' As he spoke, the two strange *mystics* had changed course and headed back towards the deep bay from which they had come.

'Interesting that they understand each other so well,' said Brett.

'What are you hinting at?' Phyllida's voice was angry.

'Oh, nothing, nothing at all.' He thought himself a coward as he spoke.

Sailing up the western shore of Messenia they got their first sight of the devastation wreaked by the Turks. Between Modon and Navarino smoke-blackened walls showed where villages had stood; the ravaged trunks of olive trees stood bitter as gallows against the deep blue sky. The fields were neglected, and they saw few signs of life until they drew almost level with Pyrgos. There, a black cloud of smoke hung above the land. 'Ibrahim Pasha must be back from Missolonghi,' said Brett.

Phyllida shuddered. 'Those poor Greeks. Do you think Alex will feel he must stop and try to help them?'

'I doubt it.' And then, sensing her reactions. 'He's the bearer of despatches, remember.'

It was an extraordinary relief to turn away from the

ravaged mainland, with its black pall of smoke, and see Zante's green and peaceful hills lying ahead. Since they entered the harbour there under sail alone, they did not cause the furore they had at Nauplia, but slid quietly to their anchorage to await the inevitable inspection and quarantine. Brett and Miss Knight both felt, and concealed, a deep relief that Alex had gone straight on to Corfu. Phyllida was equally careful not to show how much she missed him.

Quarantine over, there was plenty to distract her. Algernon Biddock was their first visitor, a long, lean Scotchman, with a prominent Adam's apple and an anxious expression. He had come to see Brett, and they were closeted together for a long time in the saloon while Phyllida and Cassandra sat under the awning on deck and tried to decide whether their first sightseeing visit should be to the Venetian fortress on the hill or the Church of St. Dionysus near the harbour. The idle talk concealed Phyllida's gnawing anxiety. When Mr. Biddock had finished his business with Brett, she must speak to him about her own affairs. He had been her father's agent in this part of the Mediterranean for years, but how was she to convince him that she was her father's daughter? It was galling, it was humiliating, it was intolerable to be penniless, dependent on Brett Renshaw for everything. Tomorrow they would be free to go ashore. She looked down at her Turkish costume, shabby by now, faded with sun and salt. She had always thought herself above caring about dress, and was irritated to realise how much she longed to go ashore and order herself a whole new wardrobe.

'Some new caps!' Cassandra must have been thinking along the same lines. 'Do you think they will have caps in Zante, Phyl?'

'If they do, you shall have six, Aunt.' Even if she had to humiliate herself and borrow the money from Brett Renshaw.

On the thought, he appeared, shepherding Mr. Biddock. 'Miss Vannick would also like a word with you, sir.' As he made the introductions, Phyllida was aware that he was holding himself on the tightest possible rein. Something was very wrong indeed. He was concealing it gallantly, but she knew him too well by now to be deceived. 'I've told Mr. Biddock the outlines of your story,' he said. 'I thought I could spare you that.'

'Thank you.' She accepted the man of business's condolences mechanically, trying to fathom the thoughts that lay behind them.

'More shocked than I can say,' he was ending. 'I knew that Mr. Vannick was sadly overdue, of course, but I'd heard nothing . . .'

'Nothing?' This was bad news.

'Just so. There's no use beating about the bush, Miss Vannick. You see, I call you that. I believe your story. Of course I do. But I'd not be worthy of the trust your father placed in me if I were to act on such verbal evidence alone. You've no documents whatever, Mr. Renshaw says?'

'None, I'm afraid. I'll remember to save them, next time I'm kidnapped!'

'Quite so. Precisely so. I can see you're your father's daughter, Miss Vannick. But how do we set about proving it? That brother of yours is off fighting in Greece somewhere, I understand.'

'I hope so.'

'Yes. Not much chance of getting hold of him. It really looks, I'm afraid, as if we will have to send to New York for someone to identify you.'

Phyllida's heart sank. 'But that will take months.'

'What about me?' asked Miss Knight.

The lawyer turned to her with heavy politeness. 'My dear madam, I hope you will not take it amiss, but you must see that if–which I do not for a moment believe–but *if* Miss Vannick here were an imposter–'

'I would be one too.'

'Exactly.'

'So that if, on the other hand, I am genuine–'

'Then so is she.'

'That's settled then,' said Cassandra.

'You can prove it?'

'You can,' she said composedly. 'I'm surprised at you, Algy Biddock. I never thought you'd have forgotten a lady you once asked to marry you.'

'I?'

Now she smiled. 'It was some time ago, I confess, and you were not very old. But don't you remember being brought South one Christmas and visiting a family at Steventon? And my cousin Jane reading aloud a book she'd just finished, called *Love and Freindship*, and how we all laughed ourselves into stitches, and you told her she couldn't spell, and went on to ask each of us to marry you in turn?'

'Good gracious,' he said. 'You're never Miss *Cassandra* Knight?'

'I am indeed. I can tell you a few other things you did on that visit, if you like.'

'No, no, I thank you, ma'am. I'm satisfied.'

'Good. In that case, allow me to present you to my niece, Miss Vannick.'

He took both Phyllida's hands in his own moist ones. 'I'm more happy than I can say, Miss Phyllida, that all our problems are so easily solved. You will let me be your banker, of course, until your father's will is proved. It will be a long enough business, I'm afraid. You'll be returning to New York, no doubt, to set about it?'

'No,' said Phyllida. 'We came, my father and I, to find Peter. I shan't go back until I know for certain what has happened to him.'

'Of course. We must set enquiries in train at once. We would need to anyway, since your brother is doubtless—if he is alive—your father's main heir, though I am sure that Mr. Vannick will have made ample provision for you.'

'Yes,' said Phyllida. 'As you say yourself, Mr. Biddock, there's not much sense in beating about the bush. Before we left New York my father signed a new will, making me his sole heir.'

'Good God! My dear Miss Vannick! I had no idea. But—there are millions—his steamboats alone—and the property—and the loans he made to Mr. Madison's government—if they are ever repaid . . . But even without them . . . Miss Vannick, you're quite sure?'

'Of course I'm sure. We quarrelled about it all the way across the Atlantic. My aunt knows . . . Oh, he meant to change it again, of course, once he'd persuaded Peter to come home with him. Poor father. I wish I hadn't quarrelled with him now. Even the night before he was killed . . .' She turned away suddenly, as if to look at blue sky over Mount Skopos.

'And the mills at Needham . . .' Mr. Biddock was still mentally taking stock of her estate.

'Yes,' said Cassandra, 'but for the moment we haven't a penny between us.'

'And we owe Mr. Renshaw a vast sum for bringing us here.' Her aunt's intervention had given Phyllida time to dry her eyes. 'I am going to be a great expense to you, Mr. Biddock.'

'It will be a pleasure. Yes, of course, your expenses . . . Most proper. We must work out a figure . . .'

'Nothing of the kind,' said Brett Renshaw. 'The two ladies were my guests.'

'But my dear Mr. Renshaw, under your special circumstances—'

'Damn my special circumstances.' And then. 'I beg your pardon, Miss Knight, Phyllida . . . Forgive me.'

'Of course. But, Mr. Biddock, Mr. Renshaw and I will discuss my indebtedness to him some other time. For the moment, you will think me horridly vulgar, I'm afraid, but we long, my aunt and I, for some spending money.' She smiled at him brilliantly. 'A great deal of spending money.'

'At once.' He was still getting used to the idea of her as an heiress. 'And the coal mine,' he muttered to himself. 'At Pittsfield, was it?'

'Pittsburgh.' She was longing for him to be gone. 'Father had great hopes of it.'

'But for your own plans, Miss Vannick. We will be most honoured, Mrs. Biddock and I, if you will stay with us while you are in Zante.'

'Oh?' This was a new idea. Suddenly the *Helena* seemed like home. 'It's very kind of you,' she temporised. Before she decided anything, she must find out what was the matter with Brett Renshaw. She looked down at the flowing Turkish trousers the lawyer had stolidly contrived not to see. 'You must see, Mr. Biddock, that before I can pay or receive visits, I must do some shopping.'

'Yes, yes, of course. Precisely so. I'll take my leave of

you now, Miss Vannick, and give myself the pleasure of calling again this afternoon with funds for you.'

'Thank you. I shall look forward to that.' She turned away, judging by the look in his eye that he had just remembered her father's English assets.

But he was saying good-bye to Brett Renshaw. 'Mr. Renshaw, I'm more sorry than I can say.'

'Then pray don't try.' In a moment, Phyllida knew, Brett's iron control was going to give way and he would say something they would all regret. She fluttered between them: 'And, Mr. Biddock, ask your wife to be so good as to send me the directions of the best mantua makers in town?'

'I will indeed.'

He was gone at last, though Phyllida thought she heard him muttering, as he went, 'And how many thousand in consols?'

'Aunt Cassandra,' she said, 'you look fagged out with all this talk. Shouldn't you rest awhile before luncheon?'

'Just what I was thinking.' Cassandra took the cue like an angel. 'I'm sure Mr. Biddock is an admirable man of business, or your father would never have employed him, but I remember finding him somewhat fatiguing even as a boy.'

Phyllida laughed. 'That reminds me to thank you, Aunt, for a most timely intervention. But why in the world didn't you tell me that you knew him?'

'Because I didn't know it myself. I remembered him, simply, as Algy. I wasn't even sure at first, but with that red hair, and those freckles–well, it was worth a try.'

'It was indeed.' An eloquent look urged her aunt to leave her alone with Brett, who had withdrawn to the rail and was leaning on it staring down into dark water.

'Brett?' She moved over to stand beside him. 'Please tell me what's the matter?'

He evaded the question. 'It seems I am to congratulate you, Miss Vannick. And apologise once again.' He was remembering their first encounter. 'I take it there really are diamonds in New York?'

'Who cares if there are? Do you think I wouldn't rather have my father, and no fortune? And must I be called "Miss Vannick" just because I happen to be the proud possessor of some coal mines and a cotton mill or two. As for Mr. Biddock! Did you see how his liking for me grew with each bit of property he remembered? I wonder what he's telling his wife about me? Brett, I don't have to go and stay with them, do I? He actually made me feel, by not looking at it, that this costume of mine was improper. Which is more than you ever did.' And that was not quite true, but never mind. At least it had raised the travesty of a smile.

'He'll warn Mrs. Biddock that you are a most unusual young lady–and so rich that it doesn't matter. But I think you should go and stay with them, Phyllida.'

'Why?' She noted his use of her first name with relief.

'Oh,' impatiently, 'for a thousand reasons. Surely I don't need to spell them out to you.'

'You're tired of slumming it in Mr. Barlow's cabin?' She intended to irritate him, and succeeded.

'Nonsense. And you know it as well as I do. It's not that at all. Sailing together, with your aunt on board, was well enough. Besides, we had no alternative. But now we're here, and safe, it's quite another thing. Your aunt will say the same.'

She sighed. 'Oh, you English. So many rules . . . You mean, just because we are safe, I must go and be bored to tears by Mrs. Biddock, who I am sure is a good little woman with five squalling children and nothing to talk about but the servants.'

He could not help smiling. 'I'm afraid so.'

'There,' triumphantly. 'I've made you smile twice. Brett, I do wish you'd tell me what's the matter. And don't pretend there's nothing. We know each other better than that.'

'Just the same, it's nothing I want to talk about. I'm only ashamed I've let it show. And don't think you can get it out of Mr. Biddock either.' He knew her well enough to anticipate her next move. 'Because he won't tell you, and will think the less of you for asking.'

'Yes. You English–' she said again. 'So what do I do? Say a gay good-bye, go ashore and leave you in worse case than I found you? I thought we were friends.'

'And so we are.'

'Well, then.' This was incredibly dangerous ground. 'As your friend, I don't propose to leave you alone like this.'

'What do you mean?'

'Do you really think I didn't know what you were doing, that first night at Constantinople? Oh, it took me a while to work it out. At first I thought you were just a boor, who didn't like women, but as I got to know you better I knew that wouldn't do. There had to be more to it. And then I remembered that glass of wine you spilt so conveniently when I wanted to give it to Aunt Cassandra. Yes–' She had seen the betraying flush along his cheekbones. 'No need to say more about it. But, knowing that, if you think I'm going to leave you alone on board, you're crazy.' She spoke more boldly than she felt, and watched anxiously as he took a furious turn across the deck.

Returning, he spoke with an irony more disconcerting than rage: 'Good of you to appoint yourself my keeper, Miss Vannick, but it won't do, you know. You must just leave me to go to the devil in my own way. It's been a pleasant interlude, and I'm grateful for it. Now, it's over. I'd be most obliged if you and your aunt would arrange to move ashore at your earliest convenience.'

'Oh, very well.' She was angry too, with herself as much as with him. Folly to have imagined that he was beginning, a little, to care for her. Now, with news no doubt of Helena, he was eager to be rid of her. 'I'll talk to Mr. Biddock this afternoon. With luck, you should be quit of us by tonight.' And she turned away, unaware of his quick, almost involuntary movement after her.

Arriving with the invitation he had forced out of his reluctant wife, Mr. Biddock was surprised to have it instantly accepted. He had brought a voluminous cloak for Phyllida. 'We thought you would not wish to be seen in town like that . . .'

'Did you so?' He did not know her well enough to recognise the anger in her tone. 'Good of you, but I have quite decided to set up as an eccentric. As to wearing a cloak in this heat: nonsense.' She turned to say good-bye to Brett and the crew of the *Helena,* who were all on deck to see them go. 'You'll be here for some time?' she asked Brett. This was not the moment, she knew, to raise the question of payment for their passage. She rather thought she would make Mr. Biddock do this for her, and also take care of the necessary vails to the members of the crew.

'I expect so.' His voice was toneless, and there was no inducement to prolong the farewells. Only, shaking Price firmly by the hand, Phyllida paused for a moment, struck by his reproachful look. But what else could she have done?

# 9

Something in Mr. Biddock's tone had prepared Phyllida for his wife. Hot weather had made Cissie Biddock sallow, discontent had marred a face that should have been plump and pretty. Visibly taken aback by her guest's unusual garb, she hurried her up to her bedroom. 'For fear the servants should see,' she explained with unlucky frankness. 'Or the children. My little innocents. I do beg, Miss Vannick, that you will refrain from discussing your—ahem—adventures in front of them. The bloom of youth is so precious, so fragile . . .' She trailed off into silence under Phyllida's basilisk stare.

'I will do my best, ma'am,' she said, 'to discuss nothing with your children. I take it they are the three boys I saw stoning a dog in the yard? If my brother had done such a thing, I would have whipped him soundly.'

'Yes,' said Cissie Biddock, 'and look what's become of him.'

It was hardly a propitious beginning, and relations were not improved when Phyllida found a shabby pink satin dress laid out on the bed in her room. 'I thought you would prefer to change for dinner,' explained her hostess, a trifle nervously.

'I intend to go shopping.'

'But it's a saint's day. Did Mr. Biddock not explain? There will be no shops open today. If they were,' she was pleased to point it out, 'you'd not get anything ready-made. And we expect company for dinner.'

'A pity your husband did not think to tell me.'

'My dear!' Mrs. Biddock lowered her voice to a conspiratorial whisper. 'He was frantic to get you off that yacht. Of all things: Brett Renshaw!' She gave it a kind of horrified gusto. 'How you endured his company all this time! Tell me, what was it like? If you can!' Her tone suggested things too bad for words.

Phyllida was staring at her in frank amazement. 'My dear madam, what in the world are you talking about?'

'You mean, you don't know? You've not heard? Well, of course, how should you have? Mind, Mr. Biddock tells me nothing; one might as well be married to an oyster; but I heard it from my sister at home. It was in all the gossip columns. Only think of his turning up for his own wedding drunk as a wheelbarrow! And his bride waiting half an hour in the church, all in her satin and lace . . . And when he did get there, he said one word'—she flushed unbecomingly—'*Not* a word I could mention to you—threw her letters at her feet, and walked out. Is it any wonder that his uncle has disinherited him? His mother's brother that's so rich!'

'What?'

'Well, of course.' It is always pleasant to describe the misfortunes of others. 'I imagine that is what Mr. Biddock, poor man, had to break to him today. A vast fortune, my dear, that he had counted on, and all left to the girl: "Who should have been my nephew's wife." Touching, is it not?'

'It's monstrous! Disinherited because of that scheming little piece! And in her favour. You mean, he has nothing?' Overtones of various conversations, unheeded at the time, echoed in her mind. Brett must have learned something of this at Constantinople, had been hoping, perhaps, to have better news from Mr. Biddock.

'Nothing but the *Helena*. And plenty of debt.' Cissie Biddock enjoyed the idea. 'He'll have to sell the yacht, of course. My husband's been making enquiries already. I know that,' she added a shade defiantly, 'because he spoke about it to the husband of a friend of mine.'

'Before Mr. Renshaw even got here?'

'Well, of course. Who do you think will be the prime creditor, but my poor Algy, who's been letting that young man draw on him all the way down the Mediterranean? And not for small sums either. I was tidying his study the other day and happened on some papers . . . And at Nauplia, too, when he must have had some idea . . . Right down dishonest, I call that, but it's all of a piece with the rest of his behaviour.'

'Where is your husband now, ma'am?' Phyllida had had enough.

'In his office, of course. Downstairs.'

'Good.' She moved towards the door.

'You're never going to tell Algy what I've told you?'

'Why not?' And then, taking pity on the woman's obvious fright, 'Well, I won't refer to you if I can help it. I suppose I owe you that for telling me. And doubtless I can get at it some other way.'

'But, Miss Vannick!' She fluttered anxiously between Phyllida and the door. 'Algy don't like to be disturbed while he's working.'

'Not even by several cotton mills and a coal mine? Don't worry, ma'am. I think he'll be happy to see me.'

She was right. Mr. Biddock had spent a delightful morning working out her total assets, and greeted her with enthusiasm. 'And what can I do for you, my dear Miss Vannick? You're never out of funds already?'

He meant it as a joke, and was taken aback by her answer. 'Precisely. Or rather, I am come to ask you to pay my debts for me.'

'In debt?' She amazed him more and more. 'But how in the world?'

'To Mr. Renshaw of course. Obviously my aunt and I owe him for our passage from Constantinople. He had to change his plans on our account. Otherwise he'd have coaled up at Smyrna and never gone near mainland Greece. I reckon I owe him not only for passage, but for the entire expense he was put to by those pirates. Repair of the engines; everything. He won't discuss it, so you and I will just have to work out a figure between us.'

'Generous indeed!' He cracked his knuckles enthusiastically. 'Leave all to me, Miss Vannick. Just give me the details insofar as you can. Unorthodox, of course, but, yes, most generous, and like your father's daughter.'

'Thank you.' She was amused to find how eagerly he cooperated in exaggerating the expenses she and her aunt had caused Brett. When they had arrived at a total that almost satisfied even her, he leaned back happily in his chair. 'Then it merely remains for you to authorise the expenditure, Miss Vannick.'

'Yes.' She had expected this, and found herself grateful to his tattling wife. Inevitably, his first thought would be to see that Brett's debt to himself was covered. 'And then for you to make me out a draft, payable to Mr. Renshaw. At once, if you would be so good. I mean to visit him directly.' And when had she decided that?

'To go back?' He was horrified.

'To pay my debts, Mr. Biddock. My father used to say that punctuality was the heart of business. And besides, I have a proposition to put to Mr. Renshaw. I don't know why I didn't think of it sooner. I hope, in a few days' time, to have news of my brother. Perhaps he'll be able to come here to me; perhaps not. Personally, I think it unlikely. So–I'll have to go to him. And how better than in the *Helena*? Do you think Mr. Renshaw might let me charter her? And, if he did, what should I pay him?'

'A charter? Now, that's an idea.' Had Mr. Biddock found it more difficult than he had expected to find a buyer for the *Helena*? His face, which had lengthened visibly when he saw he was not going to get his hands on the money Phyllida owed Brett, brightened again. 'It would be expensive, of course–a steam-yacht, fully equipped . . .'

'Of course.' Once again, they found it easy to agree on a figure.

'Right.' Phyllida rose to her feet. 'Then if you would be so good as to have one of your servants accompany me, Mr. Biddock?'

'I'll come myself.'

'No.' Not for the first time, she reminded him disconcertingly of her father. 'I'll go alone. This is a matter between Mr. Renshaw and me.'

'But you'll take your aunt?'

'I think not. For one thing, she's resting. For another, I shall do better without her. My father has left me with a man's responsibilities. I shall have to carry them like a man.' She dealt ruthlessly with his remaining objections, aware, all the time, of a swelling tide of anxiety about Brett. She should never have left him alone, would not have done so but for that misunderstanding about Helena. How could she have been so stupid?

It seemed an age before she was back at the harbour, being rowed out to the *Helena*. The heat had gone from the sun, and the brightness from the day. She would very likely be late for Mrs. Biddock's dinner party. As if that mattered. They were almost within hailing distance now and she could still see no sign of life on the *Helena*'s deck. Where was the lookout?

Ridiculous to be so anxious. She cupped her hands round her mouth: 'Ahoy there, *Helena*!' Would Brett remember, as vividly as she did, how she had called that, once before, back in the Golden Horn?

No answer. No sign of life above-decks, but suddenly something flew out of one of the saloon windows and fell with a splash into the still water of the harbour. She thought she could hear shouting, and was aware of the bright, enquiring glances of the Biddocks' servant and the oarsman, fixed first on her, then on the *Helena*.

'Row along the side,' she said. All was quiet again on board. She raised her voice and shouted as loud as she could: '*Helena*! Is anybody there?'

And now, with a sigh of relief, she saw a face pressed to a cabin window. 'Price!' But he had vanished, to reappear a moment later on deck.

'Miss Vannick.' He leaned over the rail. 'Thank God. I'll get help.'

'No need.' Lucky she had refused to change her Turkish dress. 'I've done it before.'

'Don't let them come on board,' Price said softly, for her alone, as he helped her onto the deck.

'No?' She turned to the servant, who was making as if to follow her. 'No need to come too. Take a message to Mrs. Biddock, will you? Give her my apologies and tell her I'll be late for dinner. Mr. Renshaw will send me back.' Would her reputation for rich eccentricity carry that for her? 'Hurry,' she said, and turned away. 'How is he, Price?'

Something splashed in the water close to the rowboat. Price watched for a moment as it began slowly to draw away. 'Mad drunk, miss, and dangerous. I oughtn't to be so glad to see you.'

'Oh yes you should. I ought not to have left. I know that now. I had no idea . . . But where is he? What's he doing?'

'Throwing Miss Helena's things out the cabin window. The captain and Mr. Brown are with him, but he's beyond minding them. He's been at it ever since you went ashore.' No mistaking the reproach in his tone. 'And eaten nothing.'

'Lamentable.' She moved briskly past him and down the companionway to surprise several members of the crew loitering in the yacht's long corridor, listening to the sounds of strife from the saloon. 'Good evening.' Her chilly glance sent them scurrying back to their own quarters, and she waited till they were out of sight before pushing open the door of the saloon.

Chaos. Brett, wildly untidy, in his shirt-sleeves, had his back to her as he delved in Helena's box. Barlow was beside him, vainly expostulating, Brown was trying to shut the saloon window. The room stank of brandy, and an empty bottle bore mute witness to how Brett had spent the afternoon. A chair lay broken at the head of the table, and another bottle had been hurled at the gold-framed looking-glass, which was cracked from side to side.

'Dear me,' said Phyllida.

'Oh, God!' Brett straightened up and turned to face her. His face was flushed, his hair wildly disordered. He was holding a tiny, silver-mounted pistol. 'You.' He pronounced each word individually, as if with a great effort. 'You should have stayed away. Or come sooner.' His hand was steady as he checked the little weapon. 'Loaded. Thought I'd never find it. Bought for Helena. Manton's. Tell her it came in useful in the end. Keep off, you—' Barlow had advanced a cautious step. 'And you, too.' Brown was immobile at the window. 'Can't you see I'm talking to a lady? To two ladies? A death-bed speech: "Here lies one whose name was writ in water." I should have known it was no good.' He was speaking directly to Phyllida now, the others forgotten. 'I should have learned. "Don't touch me," she said. Loathsome. Like a snake, a toad . . . Untouchable. Should have known.' Suddenly he smiled at Phyllida with immense charm. 'You knew. Just don't interrupt me this time–' His hand shook as he raised the pistol, and he had to steady it with the other one.

'Nonsense,' said Phyllida. Dared she try to take the pistol? No; movement would provide the final spur. 'So you'll let Helena win?' she said.

'She's won already. You don't know the full humour of it. Mr. Bidd . . . Bidd . . . Biddock told me today. My uncle's leaving her his estate. To make up for my cruelty. Mine! Drunk in church. Shame! And she waiting in her val . . . her valenciennes. "Don't touch me!" Rich Helena; lucky Helena! Give her my con . . . my congratulations.' Once again the pistol wavered upwards.

'You care so much for money, Mr. Renshaw?'

'Who doesn't?' But the contempt in her voice had got through to him. 'You shouldn't have come. No sight for a lady. Blood. Should be Helena. "Don't touch me." Blood on her little white slippers. Blood on her veil.'

Keep him talking. And, suddenly, inspiration: 'Have you made your will, Mr. Renshaw?'

Surprisingly, he laughed, a queer horrible croak of a laugh. 'That's the cream of it. Made it before my marriage. Everything to her; to Helena. All my debts . . . A present for Helena . . . A bride gift–a blood gift . . .'

'And the *Helena* too?'

'The–Oh!' This was something he had not thought of. She could see his drink-logged brain trying to grapple with the new idea 'The *Helena*?'

'For another honeymoon?' She had his attention now and pursued her advantage. 'Mr. Renshaw, what you do to yourself is your own affair, but first listen to me: I've come to see you on a matter of business. Surely you'll pay me the courtesy of a hearing?'

'Courtesy?' He was coming back to them as from a great distance. 'Business? At your service–Brown, a chair for the lady.' And then. 'But you were to call me Brett.' He dropped the pistol on the table and looked down at his crumpled shirt. 'No state for business. Ladies present . . . A thousand apologies.'

'I should just about think so, sir.' Price bustled forward. 'In your shirt-sleeves indeed! And the saloon looking as if a tornado had struck it! If you'd be so good as to step up on deck for a moment, ma'am, we'll have all shipshape for you in a jiffy.' One hand adjusted Brett's straying cravat while the other whipped the pistol out of sight. 'Give us five minutes, ma'am?'

It was longer than that before Barlow joined her on the deck. 'Thank God you came.'

She did not want to discuss it. 'How is he?'

'Asleep. He sent you a thousand apologies and fell asleep as he spoke. Don't blame him too much, Miss Vannick. And —another thing. He thinks you're staying. He insisted on being put in my cabin . . . the one he's been using. If he should wake and find you gone . . . Miss Vannick, would it be asking too much?'

'Of course I'll stay.' She was delighted to have the decision made for her. 'I'll write a note to my aunt at once. She can explain to Mrs. Biddock. Mr. Renshaw's ill—' She was working it out as she spoke. 'I can't put my proposition to him till the morning —till he's better. I feel in honour bound to stay and nurse him. It would never do to leave him to the tender mercies of a lot of men. Price is with him?' She broke off to ask it anxiously.

'Yes, and Brown is tidying the saloon. The less the crew know of this, the better. There's rumours enough going about the ship as it is. Miss Vannick—'

'Yes?'

'I've no right to ask it, but you said something about a proposition?'

'Yes.' Why not tell him? 'I want to charter the *Helena*, Captain Barlow.'

'Thank God.'

By the time Cassandra was rowed out to the *Helena*, the saloon was tidy again and Price was setting the table for dinner. 'I knew you'd come!' Phyllida kissed her warmly.

'Of course I've come. If Mr. Renshaw needs nursing,

I'm the one to do it. Poor man–' A bright, intelligent glance suggested that she knew exactly what was the matter with Brett. 'Frankly, Phyl, I was delighted to get your note. One afternoon of Cissie Biddock was enough for me. Where her poor husband can have found her is more than I can imagine. Underbred, a gossip . . .' She coloured angrily, remembering the questions Mrs. Biddock had asked about Phyllida. 'And as for her children–'

'Horrid little boys,' Phyllida agreed. 'Poor Mr. Biddock.'

'He was a horrid little boy too.'

'Yes . . .' Thoughtfully. 'Really, if it were not for the convenience of his handling Brett's affairs too, I'd be inclined to move my business to Mr. Barff, of whom everyone speaks so well.'

'But you can't until the will is proved. What are we going to do, Phyl?'

'Stay here until we hear from Alex. And then–I've a plan, Aunt.' She told her about her idea of chartering the *Helena*. 'Poor Brett! I've no doubt Mrs. Biddock told you how things are with him. You'll help me persuade him, Aunt Cass?'

'I'll try.' If Cassandra had noticed that the gold-framed looking-glass was missing from the wall, and one of the chairs from the table, she did not remark on it, and Phyllida was grateful to her. The yacht was too small for any discussion of Brett's state.

He did not appear in the morning, and Price reported him as still far from well. And that was likely enough, Phyllida thought, after the amount of brandy he had drunk. So long as it was only that. But suppose he felt he could not face her, after yesterday's scene? She half smiled to herself. Last time they had quarrelled, it had taken capture by pirates to restore them to speaking terms. Perhaps this time she would have to wait until Alex returned with news of Peter. She refused to believe that there would not be news. Alex had promised to find out: he would do so. His return would solve everything.

She was waked early next morning by a bustle in the harbour, and hurried eagerly up on deck. How like Alex to have made such good time. But it was a strange ship that was being moored inland from them. 'It's the British packet, miss,' the lookout told her. 'No quarantine for them, I reckon.'

And indeed Phyllida, swallowing disappointment, could see a lively going and coming to the new ship. She saw Biddock being rowed out to her and wondered if by any miracle the packet might bring news that Brett's uncle had changed his will once more. Summoned below by Price, she found her aunt already at the breakfast table. 'It's the British packet, Aunt Cass. Do you long to go home on her?'

'Not so long as you're staying.'

'Bless you. I knew you'd say that. Good gracious! Can we have company already?' A boat had scraped against the *Helena*'s side.

'It sounds like it.' Aunt Cassandra calmly finished her coffee. 'It might not be a bad thing either.'

'No.' Anything to get Brett out of that dismal cabin.

Captain Barlow appeared, looking flustered, at the saloon door. 'There you are, Price! Excuse me, Miss Knight, Miss Vannick. You must call Mr. Renshaw. At once. I've never been so surprised in my life. Perhaps you ladies– In the meantime– It seems an odd kind of welcome for the poor young thing. Really, I don't know what to do for the best.'

'Captain Barlow!' Phyllida could hardly help laughing. 'If you'd be so good as to explain. Price will need to know what to say to Mr. Renshaw.'

'Of course. Forgive me. It was having it come plump like that. I'm just a seaman, these are too deep waters for me.' And then, pulling himself together. 'It's Mr. Biddock. Up on deck. He's come from the packet. No, that's not right. He's come from his home, he says. He thought it best to take her straight to Mrs. Biddock, he told me.'

'Her? Good God, Mr. Barlow, not Helena?'

'Helena! Lord bless you, miss, not her. No, it's Miss Renshaw come out on the packet to join her brother, and what Mr. Biddock was thinking of to take her ashore I'm sure I don't know.' But he looked uncomfortable, as if he had a pretty good idea.

'Well! If that isn't the outside of enough.' For once, it was Cassandra who took command. 'Price, tell your master I will be delighted to accompany him on shore to fetch his sister. Unless he would prefer my niece to go with me? Tell him, would you, that the sooner his sister is out of Mrs. Biddock's house, the happier I shall be.'

'Thank you, ma'am.'

As he withdrew, Cassandra turned to Phyllida. 'Tell me, did you even know he had a sister?'

'No. But then, he talks so little of his life in England. Captain Barlow, you must know. How old is Miss Renshaw?'

'A mere child, miss. She lived with their aunt and uncle, you know. Ever since their parents died.'

'With . . . Not with the uncle?' No good pretending Barlow did not know everything about Brett's being disinherited.

'Precisely, miss.'

'Good God. And he's had *her* on his mind, too. No wonder–'

She paused at the sound of an altercation from Brett's cabin. 'Of course I'm going like this.' His voice was raised in a vigorous anger that she found most encouraging. 'This is not a morning call, you fool. I'm fetching Jenny. And why on earth that idiot took her there in the first place–'

Suddenly conscious that they were all listening, Phyllida and Cassandra both spoke at once. 'I'll just fetch my–' said Cassandra, and: 'I'd best go up on deck and speak to Mr. Biddock,' said Phyllida.

She opened the saloon door as Brett burst out of his cabin, with Price, still protesting, behind him. 'Be damned to Mrs. Biddock.' Brett was wearing his sailing costume of loose shirt and duck trousers. 'I'm in a hurry, man.' And then, suddenly aware of Phyllida: 'Forgive me.' Surprisingly, he laughed. 'There seems no end to the apologies I owe you. But no time for that now. I must get that fool of a girl back on board the packet before it's full up.'

'You're never thinking of sending her back?'

'What else can I do with her? I suppose she has quarrelled with my uncle on my behalf, bless her silly little heart. Well, she can't afford to. You'll have to help me make her see that, Phyllida. Or, better still'–he looked past her into the saloon: 'You, Miss Knight? I'd be most grateful if you'd come with me. It's good of you to offer.'

'Of course I'll come. But I think you should listen to what your sister has to say for herself, before you decide what to do with her.'

'Of course I'll listen.' Impatiently. And then, with a half laugh, 'You don't know Jenny. I'll have no option. But she'll have to go back just the same. You know as well as I do, Miss Knight, that this is no place for her.'

Phyllida threw back her head in a laugh her aunt suspected of being near hysterical. 'You sound for all the world like Mrs. Biddock. Another reputation dies!'

'Nonsense!' He turned on her furiously. 'You know I don't mean that. But she's a child, I tell you. There's her education to be considered; her future. What's to become of her, wandering about the world with a lost cause like me? I can't *do* anything for her, don't you see?' It had been eating into him. 'She's got to go back to my uncle, however much she dislikes it. And however much *I* do. But at least I hope I'm beyond considering myself.'

'Yes,' said Cassandra Knight. 'I see all that, Mr. Renshaw, but I still think you should wait to see what the child–Jenny –has to say. And as to education, I think I could make shift to help you there.'

'You're too good. But we must be going. God knows how many people will have booked passage on the packet already.'

# 10

They reached the deck to find it in a state of unusual bustle, with Mr. Biddock gazing pop-eyed over the side. Most of the crew seemed to be there too, and now Brown and another man leaned over the rail to steady the arrival on board of the prettiest girl Phyllida had ever seen. Everything about her was perfect, from her golden ringlets to her exquisitely fitted travelling dress, but her smile, when she saw Brett, was best of all.

'Brett!' She dropped the bandbox she had been carrying and hurled herself at him. 'Darling, horrible B., are you all right?'

'Of course I am, Jenny.' But Phyllida thought she heard a catch in his voice. Was he thinking, as she was, how nearly he had not been here to welcome his sister? 'But'—he held her back to look her up and down with almost comic dismay—'Jenny, you wicked little wren, what's happened to you?'

'I'm grown up, love. Didn't anyone tell you? Not that they would! Anyway, I've come to keep house for you, now we're alone in the world. And what *you* meant'—she turned on Biddock with a fierceness suddenly reminiscent of her brother—'by not telling me Brett was right here all the time is more than I can understand.' She coloured a little and turned to Phyllida, who thought that, in fact, she probably understood very well. 'You must be Miss Vannick. And Miss Knight?' She bobbed a charming schoolgirl's curtsy for Cassandra. 'Mrs. Biddock told me about you.' Her colour was higher than ever, but she ploughed gallantly on, addressing Phyllida now. 'Are you really going to charter the *Helena* to look for your brother? It's the most romantic thing I ever heard of. But, please, you'll let me come too? I'll be good as gold, I promise.'

Phyllida, looking quickly from one to the other, did not know whether Biddock or Brett was the more taken aback by this speech. Biddock, she thought, was swearing to himself. Like her, he must realise that his wife had eavesdropped on their conversation and reported it to Jenny. And Brett? What would he be thinking? She smiled warmly at Jenny. 'Of course you shall come,' she said. 'If we go. But first you must persuade your brother to let me charter his yacht. He's been ill, you see. He knows nothing about it.'

'Oh, lawks!' She looked round the circle of surprised, admiring faces. 'Have I put the cat among the pigeons again?' It did not seem to trouble her. 'I do do it. But, darling, idiot B., you *are* going to let Miss Vannick have your yacht, aren't you, so she can search for her brother? And we three'—the bright, friendly gaze embraced Phyllida and Cassandra—'will sit in a circle and chaperone each other, so that even Mrs. Biddock cannot cry "shame".' She flashed a wicked glance at Mrs. Biddock's husband, then back to her brother: 'Dear, dreadful B., say yes.'

'But, Jen, you don't understand. I'm penniless. I can do nothing for you . . .'

'Idiot! Why do you think I came? When uncle told me he'd stopped your allowance I went straight to Mr. Coutts and asked for mother's jewels. He gave them to me too, though he said it was "against his better judgment", bless his heart. You'd forgotten about them, hadn't you? We can live on them for ever. Those detestable ruby ear-rings paid my passage, and here are the rest–' She retrieved the bandbox and handed it to him. 'You can take care of them now. I'm sick of carrying them about with me.'

'Oh, Jen–'

He was near breaking down, Phyllida thought, and hurried to intervene: 'Shall we move down to the saloon? I think all your baggage is on board now, Jenny–you will let me call you that? Perhaps there is some message you would like Mr. Biddock to take to his wife for you?' Was that rash? Her warning glance met Jenny's sparkling one.

'Yes, of course.' Brett's sister was no fool. She turned at once to Mr. Biddock. 'You will say everything that's polite to your wife from me and explain that I prefer to stay with my brother? I'm afraid I came off in some haste. She may, just possibly, be wondering what has become of me.'

'And that got rid of him.' In the saloon, Jenny pulled off her expensively ravishing bonnet and threw it on the table. 'Thank you for the reminder, Miss Vannick. With such a tattletale for a wife, he's the last person we want listening to our family affairs.' And then, sensing an instinctive withdrawal in Phyllida. 'You are going to be a sister to me, I hope?'

'Who could help but be your friend?' Aware of Brett, darkling behind her, she felt as if walking on eggs. 'Lord knows what kind of gossip Mrs. Biddock has been regaling you with.' She turned to Brett. 'You've not met her. I warn you, she's an experience. But [to Jenny] the plain facts of the case are that your brother rescued my aunt and me from the Turks in Constantinople and has been so very kind as to bring us here to safety. And that is all. And that reminds me.' She turned back to Brett. 'Mr. Biddock and I worked out the extent of my aunt's and my indebtedness to you.' A deep breath. 'Here is a draft for the amount.' He would not take it. 'Since you have her jewels, perhaps I will give it to your sister. You'll take care of it for him?' She handed the folded paper to Jenny.

'Indeed I will. And, thank you. You see, B., we're not penniless after all. Now it merely remains to let Miss Vannick charter the *Helena,* and our troubles are over. Oh–and to tell Price where my luggage is to go. Dear Price–' He had appeared in the doorway of the saloon. 'I am so very pleased to see you.'

'And I you, Miss Jenny. As to your luggage: it's all safely stowed long since, and merely awaits your abigail's arrival to unpack it.'

'Then it will wait a long time. No, no. Don't look so scandalised. I started out with one, all right and tight. By Gibraltar, she was seasick half the time and grumbling the rest. At Malta, she got the offer of a passage home in company with "a very good sort of body".' Jenny's cockney was perfect. 'And I urged her to take it. Thank God she did. So–no abigail, Price.'

'Then I'll unpack for you, miss, with your permission.'

'I expect you'll unpack for me, permission or no. And very well you'll do it.'

'Thank you, Miss Jenny. But first–Mr. Renshaw–' Why was he looking so miserable? 'Mr. Brown has asked for a word with you, urgently. Before you discuss the question of a charter, he says.'

'Good God!' Predictably, Brett exploded. 'Has everyone on this boat been discussing this charter before it was so much as broached to me?'

'It's my fault,' said Phyllida. 'It seems I'm as bad as Mrs. Biddock. I'm afraid I told Captain Barlow. Forgive me, Brett? You must see we've all been at sixes and sevens while you've been ill.' She did not add that she had been quietly paying for the coal and supplies that had been coming on board.

'Ill!' He was furious with himself. 'Sulking in my tent, you mean, like Achilles, only with less excuse.'

'Oh well,' said Phyllida soothingly. 'Achilles gave a good account of himself, I seem to remember, when he emerged. And you are going to help me look for Peter, aren't you? Please?'

And then, on a wicked inspiration, 'I suppose I could charter the *Philip* from Alex, but I'd feel a good deal safer with you.'

'Good God! You can't do that. Of course you shall have the *Helena*. What I find hard to bear is that I must at least let you pay her expenses, since I cannot do so myself.' It hurt him horribly to admit it.

And, for the time being, it was concession enough. 'Thank you. I knew you would not fail me. But should we not hear what Mr. Brown has to say?'

It proved depressing. With coal at last on board, he had given the engines a trial run the day before, or tried to. 'It's the gudgeons,' he said. 'Those pirates!'

'Pirates?' exclaimed Jenny.

'But you've spares?' asked Brett.

Brown shook his head. 'We fitted them at Malta. No, sir. It means sending to England for them. With your permission, I'll write a note to go by the packet.'

'And in the meantime?'

'Sail only, I'm afraid. Of course, with that jury rig of Mr. Alex's we're not so bad as we used to be, but it's no good thinking we'd have a chance of getting away if we were to meet any more of those pirates.'

'And the packet takes six weeks or so each way,' said Jenny. 'Oh, poor Miss Vannick, what are we to do?'

'To begin with,' said her brother, 'we must wait till we hear what Alex has to say. But I'm afraid Brown's right, Phyllida. With steam, and a good lookout, I might consider venturing again into Greek waters with you three ladies, but you must see–' His look was appealing.

'I do indeed.' It was one thing for her to risk herself and her aunt, quite another to take Jenny into such danger. And it was she herself who had urged that he let Jenny stay.

'Miss Vannick, I am so sorry.' Jenny was no fool. 'You mustn't mind about me, Brett. I think an encounter with pirates would be the most romantic thing.'

'It's not, you know,' said Phyllida. 'And I thought you were to call me by my name.'

'Oh, thank you.' And then, heroically. 'If it's only I

who prevent you from going, you could leave me behind with Mrs. Biddock.'

'No.' Phyllida and Cassandra said it in the same breath. 'Let's not worry too much about it for now,' Phyllida went on. 'There's nothing to be done anyway until Alex gets here.' It frightened her that they had all been assuming he would bring news that Peter was alive.

'And who, pray, is Alex?' Jenny had been longing to ask the question.

The *Philip* swooped into harbour two days later and Phyllida's heart beat fast as she watched the dramatic landfall she had seen on Spetsai.

Ten minutes later, she greeted Alex with an eager question. 'Any news?'

'Do you think I would look so happy if I had none, *kyria*? I would have shipped a black sail, I think, rather than raise your hopes for nothing.'

'You mean?'

'He's alive. That's certain. I talked to a man who actually saw him in the hills.'

'Oh, thank God.' Tears trickled unchecked down her cheeks. 'And thank *you*, Alex. There was no danger?'

'There's always danger. Serving you, who cares?' He broke off to stare past her. 'But who is the nereid?'

'The—? Oh, you mean Mr. Renshaw's sister. She has just joined us from England.' Making the inevitable introductions, she watched, without pleasure, as Alex fixed his admiring glance on Jenny.

'I thought you a water-nymph,' he told her. 'The genius of the harbour.'

' "No spirit, sir," ' she quoted, and laughed, and coloured. 'So you're the hero who rescued them all? I must say—' Thoughtfully. 'You look just as a hero should.'

'Thank you, *kyria*.'

' "*Kyria*"? That's pretty. What does it mean?'

'It means "My lady".'

'Very pretty too. I must say,' she went on approvingly. 'You speak beautiful English.'

'My Brother Petros taught me. Each time I mispronounced a word, I had to pay a forfeit.'

'A forfeit. How do you mean?'

'Oh.' Carelessly. 'Bring him a Turk's head. Something like that.'

'Ugh. Horrid.' She turned a little away from him, and then, eagerly. 'But is there news?'

'Of Petros. Yes.' He repeated what he had told Phyllida.

'Oh, I am so glad. But what now?'

'I'm afraid, once again, there is nothing for it but to wait,' Alex said. 'I am only happy that you'–to Phyllida–'will be able to do so in such good company. The word is,' he explained, 'that Karaiskakis has gone across the mountains to join the defenders of Athens. Well, it's the logical thing for him to have done. I am on my way back to Nauplia now. I shall hope to get in touch with Petros and tell him you await him here.'

'But can't we come with you?' Phyllida explained quickly about her chartering of the *Helena*. 'It would have to be under sail, I'm afraid, since our engines aren't working.'

'Yes, so I'd heard.' He was well informed. 'And–I'm sorry, *kyria*, but this time I bear messages that brook no delay. I should not really have stopped here. I must give the *Philip* wings to make up for this happy visit. And your poor *Helena*–' A rueful glance drew their eyes upward to the mast he had had rigged. 'But I promise you, so soon as there is news, you shall have it, if all Greece suffers for my absence. Or, best of all, I will bring Petros here to you.'

He would not even stay to dine. 'The sooner I leave you, the sooner I shall return.' He kissed first Phyllida's hand, then Jenny's. Did he hold it a little longer than he had hers, Phyllida wondered, and disliked herself as she did so. But no wonder if he did . . . Jenny in sprigged muslin for dinner was more enchanting than ever.

'Isn't he beautiful?' Jenny gazed after Alex as he rowed away towards the *Philip*. 'The Corsair, and Lara and all the rest of them rolled into one. Much, much better than Lord Byron himself, poor man, from all one hears about him. Oh, Phyllida, I am so glad I came.'

'Yes.' Still watching Alex, Phyllida was ashamed not to be able to manage a greater show of enthusiasm. Characteristically, she turned the conversation into a practical channel. 'The question is,' she said, 'what's to do now. Three months till there's a hope of our getting spare—what were they called?—dudgeons?—from England, and God knows how long till Alex returns. I love the *Helena* dearly, but I think I shall hire a house on shore. You'll persuade your brother that you and he should come and stay with us? Even here, under British rule, I don't think my aunt and I would feel safe without a man in the house.'

'What a story!' Jenny laughed. 'I may only have known you three days, but you can't tell me you're afraid of anything. Of course I'll help persuade B., but I think you're much more likely to bring it off.' And, with a wicked smile, 'I shall enjoy watching you play the timid maiden.'

'A trifle ridiculous after my experiences?' Phyllida just failed to hit the light note she had intended, and turned, with relief, to greet her aunt. 'The very person. Jenny and I have decided to take a house in Zante. It only remains to persuade Brett that we can't do without him to protect us. How do we set about that?'

'You might try asking me.' Brett had followed Cassandra out on to the deck. 'I'm not completely unapproachable, I believe. Of course we'll be your guests, Jen and I, if you are so good as to invite us.'

'Oh, bliss,' said Jenny. 'A proper bedroom at last.' And, later, to Phyllida, 'You're a magician, that's all. To think I should see the day when Brett consents to be indebted to a woman! But he won't take my jewels.'

'I should think not indeed.' And then, to change the subject, 'I suppose I shall have to see Mr. Biddock about a house.'

'Let Brett do it for you. He'd like to, I'm sure. And it will spare you that dreadful woman.'

'And those little boys.' Phyllida's first instinct had been to say that, since she was to pay for the house, she would prefer to choose it herself, but she restrained herself, recognising the soundness of Jenny's advice. She was glad she had when Brett accepted the commission with pleasure. He spent several days on shore with Mr. Biddock, returning in the evening with comic tales of the hovels he had been shown.

'You see,' Jenny said to Phyllida, 'he's enjoying every minute of it. He looks much better. I was worried about him when I got here.'

'Yes.' Phyllida would never tell her how right she had been to worry. 'I'm grateful to you, Jenny.' Would Alex, too, prefer a woman who needed to be looked after, to have her decisions made for her? And, yes, she told herself ruefully, he certainly would. Cassandra, watching with quiet affection, saw her begin to practise a quite un-American submissiveness and felt at once pleased and sorry for her. Nor was she surprised to see her niece embark on a perfect orgy of shopping. When Alex returned, Jenny would not be the only one wearing sprigged muslin.

Thanks to Mrs. Biddock's unbridled tongue, Phyllida was already famous in Zante as a mad American millionairess, and she was surprised and delighted at the service she received. When Brett came on board, triumphant, one airless Friday night, he forgot his errand at sight of her. 'Good God, Phyllida!'

'You like it?' Her new dresses had been sent aboard that afternoon and she was wearing a cool, dark cotton, gold-edged with a characteristic Greek design. 'I'm finding it quite hard to get used to skirts, after all this time.' She let him help her down the companionway.

'Like it! You look like Astarte herself. But I am ashamed. Do you know I had entirely forgotten that you were still in mourning.'

'Oh, poor papa.' She looked down at her dark skirts. 'I'm afraid I sometimes forget myself. One can't, can one, go on being unhappy for ever?'

'No indeed. Even broken hearts mend—' But they were at the saloon door.

'What news?' Jenny jumped up to greet them. 'I know that look of yours, B., as if you'd swallowed the canary. You've got us a house?'

'I think so, if Phyllida approves. I was so amazed at her transformation that I quite forgot to tell her.'

'Isn't she lovely?' Jenny looked fondly at Phyllida. 'When Alex gets back he'll tell you you're Hera–just see if he doesn't.' And then, aware that this was, for some reason, not a lucky remark, 'But, quick, B., tell us about the house?'

'I hope you'll like it.' He turned to Phyllida. 'It belonged to an Italian family who have gone back to Venice. I doubt if you will do better. It's big–and expensive, I'm afraid–you might easily imagine yourself in a Florentine *palazzo*.'

'I mightn't,' said Phyllida cheerfully, 'not having ever seen one, but if you think it will do, Brett, let us by all means take it. As to expense, who cares! I've always wanted to live in a palace.'

'Well, you did, didn't you,' said Jenny. 'In Constantinople.'

'Goodness!' To her aunt's delight, Phyllida laughed. 'So I did. But it was not, somehow, quite the same thing. Shall we all go and see your palace tomorrow, Brett?'

'I have already arranged it with Mr. Biddock.'

The Palazzo Baroti stood high on Strani Hill. 'It's quite the best part of town.' Mr. Biddock had been knocked sideways by the sight of Phyllida in flowing skirts of midnight blue cambric and had not left her side during the hot climb up through the town. 'You'll have the poet Solomos for one of your neighbours. He's quite in the first society, here in Zante, even though he is a Greek. He actually writes his poetry in modern Greek.'

'And why not?' Phyllida suppressed a sharper retort. She must not alienate her man of business, however much his parrotting of his gossipy wife might annoy her.

They were all entranced by the house, with its arcaded central courtyard and high vine-covered terrace commanding a wide view of the mainland and the Gulf of Corinth.

'You can see Missolonghi on a clear day,' Biddock told Phyllida. 'You like it, Miss Vannick?'

'Oh, *yes.*' She turned impulsively to Brett. 'Thank you so much for finding it. When can we move in, Mr. Biddock?'

'As soon as I can find you servants. My wife is on the lookout already for a suitable housekeeper for you.'

'Oh, no!' Phyllida's reaction was instinctive. At no price would she have anyone recommended by Cissie Biddock. And then, quickly recovering herself. 'It's wonderfully kind of Mrs. Biddock–' She paused, searching vainly for a suitable excuse.

'But we won't need servants,' said Brett. 'With the crew of the *Helena* idle on our hands. It would be a real kindness if you'd employ such of them as you need, Miss Vannick.'

'Men?' Biddock was scandalised.

'Why not?' said Phyllida. 'If they can look after us on board, they can ashore. Of course we'll have them, Brett. And an interpreter, perhaps, for the shopping? I can't make head or tail of the dialect they speak here on Zante. It sounds more like Italian than Greek to me.'

'And no wonder,' said Brett, 'since the place was occupied by the Venetians for so long. But it's true; we shall need a dragoman if we're to be ashore for any length of time. I should have had one in the first place if I'd had any sense. Can you find us someone, Biddock?'

'And a cook,' said Phyllida. 'I really don't think your admirable man would be happy here, Brett. Besides, when in Greece . . .'

'Eat Greek food?' He laughed. 'I hope we don't all live to regret it.'

# 11

That was an extraordinary, idyllic interlude on Zante. The sun shone; grapes ripened on the vines; Marcos, their Greek interpreter, took them on moonlit autumn evenings to the wine festivals at neighbouring villages. Eating lamb roasted whole over fires flavoured with rosemary, drinking the light new wine and watching the endless, circular dancing of the *Romaika,* it was hard to realise what was happening in Greece.

But in the daytime, they could often see, from the vine-hung shade of their terrace, a pall of smoke over the mainland that meant Ibrahim and his Turks were at their work of devastation again. The new Commissioner for the Ionian Islands, Sir Frederick Adam, was more kindly disposed towards the Greeks than his eccentric predecessor had been, and pitiful families of refugees were often to be seen camped in the square by the harbour, waiting to be taken to the refuge that had been set apart for them on the island of Kalamos. Brett did his best to protect Phyllida from their tales of outrage. She spoke little of her anxiety for Peter–so little that he sometimes found himself wondering, gloomily, whether it was only for Peter that she was anxious. They had been on Zante nearly three months now. The harvest was all in, and the nights were getting colder. On the mainland, snow picked out the higher mountain peaks against the dark sky of morning or evening. And still there was no word from Alex.

'Perhaps he can't write,' suggested Jenny, only half in jest.

'Nonsense,' said Phyllida, rather more sharply than she intended. 'He went to a Lancasterian school, here on the Ionian Islands. He's as well educated as you or me.'

'Better than me, I expect,' said Jenny pacifically. 'Or than I used to be–' This with a special smile for Cassandra, who had taken her firmly in hand once they had got settled at the Palazzo Baroti. 'If we're really going to be here all winter, I might even be able to spell by spring.'

'I can't imagine what those governesses of yours were thinking of,' said Cassandra.

'Elegant accomplishments, of course, and the back-board. Now, if we only had a harp–'

'Thank God we haven't.' Brett had joined them in the Palazzo's high-ceilinged saloon. 'If your playing is anything like your singing–'

'Darling B., it's much worse. I can't tell you how I hated it. And Aunt Matilda listening with that frozen face of hers and wondering how she would ever help me to a husband. I do wish we had quarrelled with those two years ago. It's Aunt Matilda's doing now, you know. She never liked either of us above half, and she and Helena were thick as thieves. You should have heard them convincing each other that it would never do for me to be bridesmaid at that wedding of yours. I was far too volatile, they said. Of course I knew what they meant.'

'What did they mean?' Was Brett actually prepared to discuss that disastrous wedding day?

'Why . . .' Jenny jumped up and ran to the window to look at her own reflection against the darkening sky outside. 'That Helena and I are both blondes, and both beautiful. The difference is that I'm seventeen and she's thirty.'

'Thirty!'

'Ha!' Delighted. 'I thought that would surprise you. Well, it did me. It's the best-kept secret since the South Sea Bubble. But she's thirty all right. I met an old nurse of hers, once, and she told me. And not much else that was good of her either. That was a lucky escape of yours, B., and no mistake. Of course she was mad to let you go, but then she never did have much sense. I wonder if she caught the other fish . . .'

'The other what?'

'Poor darling B. You never knew, did you, any more than Uncle Paul. Well, of course, you two stayed in the country, most of the time. There was an old, old stick of an earl dangling after her in town, and she never could make up her mind, poor Helena, between being a countess for certain or a Duchess perhaps. Of course, when the real Duchess had that boy, there was no question what she'd do, but I'm not sure she did it right. Making you jilt her in church may have cooked your goose with Uncle Paul, but I rather fancy it cooked hers with the earl. Jilting's infectious, you know. She hadn't heard from him for several weeks when I came away, and was turning yellower by the minute.'

'Jenny!' Cassandra had been listening to this conversation with mounting disapproval. 'That's quite enough. Besides, it's time you practised your singing.'

'With that horrible piano!' Jenny pulled a face, then bent to give Cassandra a quick hug. 'Never mind, it's better than the harp. And, darling Aunt Cass, forgive me if I've shocked you, but don't you think, really, it's best to have things out in the open? Aunt Matilda and Helena were always whispering in corners—I hated it!'

'Just the same.' Cassandra turned to Brett as the sound of a one-finger accompaniment and unenthusiastic shakes began to falter out from the room next door. 'I'm worried about her, Brett. What's going to happen to her? She ought to be coming out this winter, establishing herself in life.'

'I know.' It was almost a groan. 'You can't be half as worried about her as I am. Sometimes I almost wish I had sent her back that day, on the packet . . .'

'Surely not after what she's told us tonight.'

'You're right, of course. I never saw much of my uncle's wife. As Jenny said, she preferred the town and spent most of her time there. I never liked town life much—nor my aunt either, I'm afraid. I'm ashamed now that it never occurred to me what it must have been like for Jen. I've not been much use to her, poor child, and, now, what's to become of her is more than I like to think of.'

Phyllida could not help laughing. 'You two! To listen to you, anyone would think *she* was thirty, instead of seventeen, with the world all before her. Time enough, surely, to start worrying when she's an old woman of twenty-seven like me. But, Brett, is it monstrously selfish of me to keep you here? Quite apart from Jenny, ought you not to be back in England, carving out a career for yourself?'

'What career?' he said bitterly. 'I'm educated for nothing.'

'Or anything,' said Cassandra. 'Had you thought of the diplomatic service at all?'

He looked at her with quick respect. 'Almost my first thought, Aunt Cass, when I found I needed a career. But, don't you see, that famous jilting cooked my goose, as my inelegant sister would say, for that too.'

'Then you'll have to do something about it, won't you?' said Cassandra placidly. 'I always thought it a crazy quixotic gesture of yours.'

'And what do you suggest I do?' Bitterly. 'Put an announcement in the *Times Newspaper*?'

'You could begin by explaining the true facts of the case to your uncle. With him on your side–'

'And have him think I was coming cap in hand to be reinstated as his heir? I hope I have more pride than that.'

She sighed. 'Sometimes I think pride's a deadly virtue–'

'I had an idea the other day,' Phyllida interposed diffidently. 'I don't know whether there might be anything in it. Only–why don't you write a book, Brett?'

'Write a book!'

'Yes. About Greece. Don't you see? Not just a travel and antiquarian kind of book, like Mr. Gell's, but a political one, about the people, and the war. You'd do it wonderfully well, I'm sure, and Peter will help you when we find him. Just think of the information he'll be able to give you. And Alex, too–' Infuriating to colour so when she mentioned him.

'If he ever reappears,' said Brett. 'But, do you know, it's not a bad idea. Mr. Murray was a friend of my father's.' He laughed. 'I told Barlow once I was going to write *Childe Renshaw's Pilgrimage.*'

'Byron's publisher?' Cassandra leaned forward in her chair.

'Yes.' The idea was growing on him. 'I'll write to him directly. Phyllida, you're my good angel! I must talk to the Resident here. Everyone knows I'm no Philhellene. Why should I not visit the mainland? Missolonghi? Murray would be bound to want a chapter on Byron. I could hire an Ionian *mystic*, as he did, for the crossing. Besides, when the *Helena* is repaired, what better cover for fetching Peter than the fact that we are collecting material for my book?'

'If only Alex would come,' said Phyllida, then wished she had not.

Brett plunged into the plans for his book with enthusiasm. 'I haven't enjoyed myself so much since Oxford,' he told Cassandra. 'I had hopes, then, that I might become a scholar–a fellow of my college, perhaps. I had plans for an edition of Homer. My father's death, and my elder brother's, changed all that. My uncle insisted that I leave the university at once–he would not even let me stay to take my degree. I must make the Grand Tour; must marry; must waste my time elegantly as befitted the heir to a title. I've wasted ten years, and now look at me. No title, no wife . . . Aunt Cass–' He and his sister had fallen naturally into the habit of calling her this. 'Do you think there's any hope for me?'

'I just don't know, Brett.' She understood him perfectly. 'But–go slowly, won't you?' How often, in the months that followed, was she to wonder whether it had been good advice.

Christmas was over. The marble floors of the palazzo struck chill against bare feet in the morning, and rain, lashing against the windows, kept Brett close to his work. 'It rained like this while poor Byron was dying,' he told Phyllida. 'A terrible, mismanaged business that, like everything else to do with the Greeks. The more I learn about this rebellion of theirs, the less I think it likely to succeed.' He watched hot colour rise in her cheeks and cursed himself for a fool. Luckily, Jenny bounced into the room to interrupt them.

'The packet's in,' she said. 'D'you think they'll have our gudgeons?'

Brett was on his feet, 'I'll send Marcos down at once. There should at least be mail. As to the gudgeons, we'll be lucky if they've come so soon.'

He was right. An apologetic letter from Galloway of Greenwich promised gudgeons by spring at the latest. The rest of the mail was equally discouraging. It was too early for an answer from Murray, but there was a long, angry letter from Uncle Paul, for whom Jenny's defection had been a last straw. They had chosen to defy him, had made him a laughing stock; they need expect no help from him.

'We thought you'd forgotten all about us,' Jenny greeted Alex when he appeared at last one bright January morning.

'*Kyria*, an impossibility!' He turned to Phyllida, who

had hung a little back among the general greetings. 'You have every cause to abuse me, but I hope the news I bring will earn my pardon.'

'You really have news?'

'Better than that.' He pulled out a leather wallet and carefully removed a stained and tattered piece of paper.

'A letter from Peter!' She took it with a trembling hand, read it quickly, and exclaimed: 'He's in Athens!'

'Yes, *kyria.* That's why it's taken so long. You heard that the French commander, Fabvier, fought his way in through the Turkish besiegers of the Acropolis just before Christmas? I was able to send a message in by him, and this is your answer. I confess I had hoped that Petros might contrive to escape through the Turkish lines. It would have made me so happy, *kyria,* to have brought him to you. But I have no doubt he tells you, as he did me, that he cannot abandon his friends at this time of danger.'

'Yes.' She was reading the letter for the second time. 'But, Alex, how dangerous is it? Can it be a real siege, if people get in and out?'

'Real enough. It would not be right to let you be too hopeful. But the Acropolis is as good as impregnable. If only our Greek leaders would stop quarrelling among themselves and take the Turks in the rear, there'd be an end of the siege in no time.'

'And what *are* your leaders doing?' asked Brett. 'We've heard nothing but gloomy reports all winter, of rival governments fighting each other instead of the Turks.'

'It's been bad,' Alex admitted. 'President Zaimis is a good enough sort of man, but he has no control over the *capitani.* My cousin, Petro Bey, does his best, but what can one man do? Don't look so downcast, *kyria,* it is but to wait until spring and everything will change.'

'For the better?' asked Brett.

'Yes. Lord Cochrane is on his way at last. And our good friend Sir Richard Church. When they arrive, with ships and funds, and their good counsel, you will soon see the Greek Government united and the Turks swept into the sea.'

'I wonder,' said Brett.

'Mr. Renshaw is writing a book about Greece.' As so

often, Phyllida must play peacemaker between the two men. 'We are relying on you for all the latest news, Alex.'

'*You* shall have it, *kyria.*' A slight but unmistakable accent on the first word. 'And there is good as well as bad. Karaiskakis has won a noble victory at Arachova, and Kolokotronis is harrying the Turks in the Morea.'

'You mean, when we see smoke hanging over the mainland, it is the Greeks who are lighting the fires?' asked Jenny.

'It's still Greek houses and olive groves that are burning,' said Brett. 'And what about that little matter of piracy on Hydra? Did Captain Hamilton really have to fire on your Greek ships in order to make them surrender their booty?'

'You are well informed, sir.' Alex did not like the question. 'But it was merely a misunderstanding.'

Phyllida laughed. 'The kind of misunderstanding you saved us from, Alex?'

'That was the happiest day of my life,' he said.

'I shall never forgive myself for having missed it,' chimed in Jenny. 'Only to think of being captured by real pirates! But, Alex, you haven't told us what you've been doing all winter.'

'My duty, I hope. Taking stores where they were most needed; keeping our lines of communication open; watching out for the Turks. I have longed to visit you sooner, *kyria*, with the good news of Petros, but my conscience to my country would not let me.'

'Of course not.' Phyllida's voice held warm approval.

'And now?' Brett asked.

'Once again I am the fortunate bearer of despatches to Sir Frederick Adam.'

'But you can stay with us overnight, Alex? And take an answer to my brother?'

'*Kyria*, I will dine with you gladly, but must sail with the evening breeze. As to your answer for Petros, I shall give myself the pleasure of calling for that on my way back. But you understand, of course, that it may be months before I am able to get it to him.'

Phyllida hurried away to stir up the cook into unwonted activity and then pause, irresolute, in her own room. It was almost a year, now, since her father's death. Surely the good news of Peter would justify her in celebrating with the white silk dress that hung temptingly in her closet?

She had had it made on severely classical lines, relieved only by the heavy gold embroidery she had found in the bazaar. 'Ravishing!' She turned from the glass at Jenny's voice. 'I'm sorry,' the girl went on. 'I didn't mean to startle you, but I can't do up my back buttons.'

Phyllida laughed. 'Better me than Price. Yes.' She was busy with the tiny silk buttons that ran all the way down Jenny's slim back. 'I thought this was an occasion that justified light colours.' There was the faintest hint of apology in her voice.

'Of course it is,' Jenny agreed warmly. 'I'm in my best too. Will he call us twin graces, do you think, or the spirits of the isle? What a man! What an air–thank you love!–and what a voice. When he calls me *kyria* as if I was the only lady in the world, it sends shivers right down my back. And then he does just the same for you, and I stop shivering.'

Cassandra, pausing in the doorway, heard the end of this speech and was delighted. She had been meditating some kind of carefully careless warning of her own to Phyllida, but thought Jenny had done it for her, and done it just right. They all went downstairs together and found Alex and Brett waiting for them in the saloon. Brett's evening dress was immaculate as usual, but no one had eyes for him. Alex had put on the white kilt, or fustanella, that was rapidly developing from the Albanian to the Greek national dress. They had seen it often enough, Isabella-coloured with much use and no washing, but this one was of brand-new, crisp white woollen and was worn with a dark velvet close-fitting jacket that made Alex every inch a figure from romance.

'Lord, aren't we all fine!' said Jenny irrepressibly.

'Fine!' Alex was kissing first Phyllida's hand and then hers: 'A pair of goddesses, no less.' And wondered why Jenny dissolved suddenly into delighted laughter.

It was a gay evening. Phyllida had felt a curious load lifted from her mind by Jenny's light-hearted comments on Alex. For the first time, she admitted to herself that she loved him. Madness, of course, but delicious madness. For tonight, she would simply let herself be happy in his company. It made it, somehow, easy to be unusually kind to Brett. Over dinner, she steered the talk to his book and was delighted to have Alex prove both enthusiastic and helpful. 'It's just what we need,' he said. 'Our story told for us by an Englishman who is known not be biased in our favour. Command me in everything, milord.'

'Splendid.' When the ladies left them alone together, Brett plied him with questions. But something had been puzzling him. 'You haven't suggested that we accompany you back to Aegina, where the government is?'

'Alas, no, since your *Helena* has still not got the use of her engines. You and the ladies must not risk yourselves near the Turks with only sail. Besides–I can hold out little hope that Athens will be relieved before spring. That will be time enough for you to sail round. By then, I hope, Cochrane and Church will have arrived; a very much happier scene will greet you.'

# 12

Phyllida read and reread Peter's short letter. 'Of course he cannot escape from Athens,' she told Brett. 'For one of the few remaining Philhellenes to behave in so cowardly a fashion–It's unthinkable.'

'I was afraid any brother of yours must feel that. Let us hope that the Greeks don't lose the Acropolis out of sheer incompetence, as they did Missolonghi. How Byron must have turned in his grave. Do you know, the more I find out about him, the better I like him–as an unlucky man, not at all the satanic figure I used to imitate.'

She was delighted with him. 'What in the world happened to that skull-shaped goblet you had?'

'I threw it overboard that night in Constantinople. Not out of good sense, I'm afraid, but bad temper.'

'Like all those bottles of sal volatile right here in the

harbour.' Hard to believe that episode had only been a few months ago. 'What a reformed character you are.'

'You know who's to thank for that–'

'Aunt Cassandra, of course.' She did not let him finish. 'She could reform a saint, if he happened to need it. But, Brett–I need your advice.' This was the best way she knew to get the conversation back to earth.

'Of course!'

'It's about Peter. He wants Mr. Biddock to sell up his share of our father's estate and devote the proceeds to the Greek cause.'

'He doesn't know he has no share?'

'No. And I don't mean to tell him. But I don't know what to do for the best. It's a great deal of money. Rightly used, it might make a real difference to the Greeks. But–how can I be sure that it will be rightly used?'

'You can't,' he said at once. 'Look what happened to the British loans at the beginning of this war. Squandered on silver-mounted pistols and yataghans–' He did not let himself add: 'Such as Alex wears.'

'I'll consult Alex, of course.' Had she read his thoughts, and was this her answer?

'You know what he'll say.'

'I suppose so: that I should give it to his government, the one at Aegina. But what do I know of Zaimis and Petro Bey? Father always said, "Never invest money in a ship you haven't seen." And this is Peter's money, not mine.'

'But it is yours.' He was not at all sure which side to take in this dialogue of hers with herself. In many ways, he would be delighted to see her give away the greater part of her fortune, since it would put them so much more on a level. But just the same . . .

'Of course it's not mine,' she said. 'Just because poor father left an angry will . . . I'd always meant to share half and half with Peter. If I do give his half to the Greeks, then, of course, we'll share what remains.'

'He may not agree to that.'

'Not if he knows about it. That's one of the many

reasons why I won't quarrel with Mr. Biddock, however impossibly his wife behaves.'

'You'll never get Biddock to connive at deceiving your brother.'

'You think not? I wonder . . . But in the meantime, what shall I say to Peter? I must have the letter ready for Alex when he comes.'

'I think you should tell him that you will keep the money until Cochrane and Church arrive. Alex himself said that he counts on them to unite the rival Greek governments. Your proposed gift might even help persuade them to quit quarrelling and work together for the relief of the Acropolis.'

'Of course! Brett, I do thank you. I knew you'd give me good advice. And by then, the *Helena* should surely be ready and we can go ourselves to make the offer.'

'If it's safe for you.'

'Dear Brett, no "ifs". You must see that I can only agree to delay the gift on that basis. I *must* be there to see that it is used, first and foremost, for the relief of the Acropolis. If I can't be sure of that, I'd best give the money to Alex right away.'

'No.' Every instinct cried out against this.

'Very well. Then promise me that whatever happens, you and I will sail round to Aegina–or wherever the legitimate government is by then–in time to greet Cochrane and Church. If you think it dangerous, of course we'll leave Jenny and Cassandra here, but I know you'll come with me.'

'Thank you. Very well, I promise. And, Phyllida–'

'Yes?'

'Will you tell Alex about this plan?'

'Of course. Why not?' Her tone warned him to say no more.

Phyllida and Jenny were out on the terrace a few days later, when the *Philip* made her characteristic daring swoop into the harbour.

'Beautiful!' Phyllida had watched, breathlessly, until the manoeuvre was successfully completed.

'And dangerous,' said Jenny. 'Like the man himself.'

'Dangerous?'

'Don't you think so? In some ways, he reminds me a little of Helena. They both have that glossy look of someone used to having their own way. It always makes me wonder what will happen if they don't. Helena used to throw things,' she added thoughtfully.

Phyllida nearly said, 'And so does your brother,' but restrained herself. She was to learn soon enough what Alex did when crossed. He arrived half an hour later, kissed both their hands with his usual ardour, and held Phyllida's for an extra moment. 'Tell me I am to have the privilege of taking my Brother Petros' gift to the Greek Government?'

'Peter's gift?' She should have expected this. 'He told you? But, Alex, I'm not sure–' It was surprisingly difficult to tell him her decision.

'So!' The furious tone drew her eyes up to meet the fire in his. 'Your brother's wishes–his orders even–are to be ignored! A woman's whim is to deprive Greece of the funds that would be lifeblood in her hour of need! I tell you, a Greek woman would know better than to behave so. But you will think again.' Something he saw in her face made him modify his tone. 'You have listened to the advice of cautious old men, *kyria,* when you should follow the dictates of your heart.'

'She has listened, in fact, to my advice.' Phyllida turned gratefully at the sound of Brett's cool voice.

'Just what I said. The voice of cold caution! I tell you, milord, the time of Greece's crisis is now! We have no money to pay our sailors; no money to send a relieving force to Athens! What will Phyllida think when she hears that the Turks have taken the Acropolis, and put its defenders to the sword. And knows that she herself has prevented her brother's own money from saving his life!'

'But how do we know that the money–if she should send it–will not be used in civil war against the rival government at Hermione?'

'You have my word for that–' Alex had never looked so handsome. 'And that of my uncle, Petro Bey.'

'Who served the Turks before 1821?'

'Milord!' His hand flashed to the pistol at his belt.

'You can't fight here,' said Jenny. 'Aunt Cassandra wouldn't like it.'

'What wouldn't I like?' To Phyllida's heartfelt relief, Cassandra herself appeared on the terrace.

'A fight,' said Brett cheerfully. 'But no need to look so disapproving, Aunt Cass. Alex won't waste powder on me. Not when I tell him I have promised to bring Phyllida round, funds and all, in the *Helena,* as soon as we hear that Cochrane and Church have arrived.'

'Madness to wait so long.' But the interruption had given Alex time to get hold of himself. 'And no need that I can see, since I, too, have a letter from Petros speaking of the gift as a thing of certainty. Since you will not do as he asks, *kyria,* I shall be compelled to speak to his man of business. This is men's work, after all. Had it not been you, of all women, I should never have considered consulting you.'

'I'm afraid you don't understand, Alex.' Phyllida looked appealingly at Brett. 'Mr. Biddock can do nothing. Will it be so very bad if you don't have the money till the spring?'

'Do nothing!' He ignored her last question. 'And why not, pray?'

'Because Miss Vannick is her father's sole heir,' said Brett. 'And I rather fancy that even if she should be so mad as to listen to your pleas, she would be unable to touch so much money yet. Biddock tells me that he has still not heard from New York about the settlement of the estate.'

'Oh–' This was a new idea to Phyllida. 'I hadn't thought of that. You mean I can't, even if I want to.'

'Exactly.'

'But surely she could borrow against her expectations.' Alex had had time to digest this new aspect of the affair and now bent his glowing gaze on Phyllida. 'Think, *kyria,* how Greece bleeds, how she suffers . . . You've seen the wretched refugees from the mainland, and heard their stories . . . How can you let such atrocities continue for a day, when there is something you can do to help?'

'The last family of refugees I talked to,' said Jenny, 'had

their house burned down by Kolokotronis and his Greek *pallikars.*'

'For treachery, no doubt.' He was red with anger again as he turned to Phyllida. 'So you will forget your brother, who lives on rats, and mice, and the dew he can gather on the marble of the Parthenon?'

'Is it really so bad?' She was weakening visibly. 'I thought Colonel Fabvier took in supplies.'

'No, *kyria,* he took nothing but gunpowder. Who knows? This is the second siege your brother has endured. Privation may destroy him before the Turk can. And then what comfort will you get from your riches? Will they help you to sleep sound at night, when you remember how your brother died, without a pillow for his head, or a glass of water for his thirst?'

'Alex, don't! Brett–' Once again she turned to him. 'Father never approved of borrowing, but surely in a case like this–'

'If you could be sure that the money would go to the relief of the Acropolis, I would agree with you,' he said. 'But, Phyllida, you must see that Alex can only speak for himself.'

'And for my uncle, who is a member of the government.'

'For the moment, yes. Of one of the governments. So long as they are at daggers drawn themselves, what hope is there of a relief of Athens? You must face it, Phyllida: if you send the money now, you have no guarantee that it won't be used in civil war. The blood of innocent Greeks will be on your head, and, when Church and Cochrane do get here, you will be unable to help them. Alex'–it was an appeal–'tell her I'm right. You must see what an agonising decision it is for her. As soon as we hear that Church or Cochrane have arrived, we will set out for eastern Greece. By then, Mr. Vannick's will should have been proved–the *Helena* will be ready for sea again–'

'You'll come in the *Helena*?' Alex asked.

'Under sail, if need be, but we'll come.'

'I believe, after all, you are right.' His capitulation surprised Phyllida almost as much as had his fury. 'Forgive me, *kyria,* if my anxiety for my Brother Petros made me say more than

I should have. It's true, I may have let it cloud my judgment. Milord Renshaw sees more clearly, since his emotions are not involved. How should I ever forgive myself if I were to take charge of my Brother Petros' fortune now, and return to Aegina to find that those rascally *capitani* from Hermione had taken over the government? If Kolokotronis and those brigands of his were to lay hands on the money, it would be good-bye to any hope of rescue for Petros. More than ever, I shall count the days till spring, since it will bring not only, I hope, Cochrane and Church, but you, *kyria*, like an angel of rescue for the heroes in Athens. In the meantime, I only beg you will forgive me.'

'Of course.' She could not resist that melting glance. 'And you'll try to get my letter to Peter? I've said nothing, by the way, about our father's will.'

'That's like you! In my anger, I misjudged you, *kyria*. I shall do penance for it until we meet again.'

'He changed his tune very suddenly.' Jenny caught Brett alone on the terrace after Alex had gone. 'I don't like him, Brett.'

'Oh, nonsense, kitten. He's a good enough sort of fellow in his flashy way. You've not seen him at his best. I can tell you, that day he saved us from the pirates, I thought him a perfect paladin.' He laughed, and pulled one of her golden curls. 'Confess, Jen, that what you really have against him is that he makes bigger eyes at Phyllida than he does at you.'

'Stupid!' But she said it in sympathy rather than anger.

# 13

That year, February was the longest month in the calendar. Nothing happened. Lord Cochrane was still somewhere in the western Mediterranean, making his dilatory way towards Greece. Biddock had not heard from New York and nor had the *Helena*'s gudgeons arrived. Phyllida's only comfort was a letter from Alex, delivered by the famous Greek Captain Kanaris on his way to throw supplies into the Greek fortress at Corinth.

'He managed to send my letter to Peter!' Her colour was high as she read. 'I knew he would. Peter sent me a message. Have they no paper, perhaps? He's well, thank God. And hopes to see us in the spring. So does Alex.' By the length of the letter, Alex had said a good deal more than that.

'It's spring already,' said Jenny. 'The sun's as hot as in full summer at home, and there are a million flowers I never saw in my life. Won't you put a chapter about them into your book, Brett? I'm sure you could find them all in Homer if you tried. You know, asphodel and all that?'

'I keep telling you, Jen, it's not that kind of book. I'm writing about Russia and Turkey just now. Do you know they've exchanged ambassadors?' This was rather to Phyllida than Jenny.

'No? Have they? That's bad, isn't it?' Phyllida had been copying one of his finished chapters, but put down her pen to look anxiously up at him.

'For the Greeks? I'm afraid so. I wish Cochrane and Church would get here.'

She smiled at him warmly. 'I believe writing about them's making you begin to care about the poor Greeks.'

'You can't help but be sorry for people who make such a muddle of their affairs. But there's one good thing: the Resident told me this morning. Great Britain and Russia have offered to mediate between the Greeks and the Turks. The Turks have refused. If the Greeks have the sense to accept, it may mean a real step forward for them.'

'Surely they will?'

'You never can tell with the Greeks. Besides, first they must produce a single government capable of accepting.'

'I know! Goodness, how right you were, Brett, not to let me send that money. God knows what would have become of it by now. But, poor Peter . . . This waiting is bad enough for us: what must it be like for him!'

'The packet's in!' Jenny had grown bored with the

political talk and drifted out into the sunshine on the terrace. Now she hurried back: 'Maybe this time it will have news for us.'

'I'll go down at once and see.' Brett had seen Phyllida's look of almost painful eagerness. The waiting had indeed been hard on her. Anxiety for her brother had been exacerbated, he knew, by doubt as to whether she had been right about the money. If the Acropolis fell, she would never forgive herself, or him.

But at last the packet brought good news. There were two sets of gudgeons, and an apologetic letter from Mr. Galloway; there was a great packet of American mail for Biddock and Phyllida; and, perhaps best of all, was the news that both Cochrane and Church were actually on their way to eastern Greece at last.

Arriving at the Palazzo Baroti later that afternoon, Biddock found a scene of frenzied activity. Cassandra was sorting linen; Jenny was packing Brett's winter-long accumulation of papers; Phyllida was checking over the consignment of medical supplies she had ordered from London. She greeted him with pleasure. 'Mr. Biddock! I was sure you would come at once.'

'Yes indeed. It's all in order, I'm glad to say. You could not ask for a tidier will. Not even Mr. Peter could break it.'

'As if he'd try! And you can let me have the funds I need?'

'You're an immensely rich woman, Miss Vannick.' Had he never quite believed in that will of her father's? 'But if you insist on making this lavish gift to the Greek Government, I must beg you to think hard about how you are going to get it to them safely.'

'Yes.' She had, somehow, assumed that when the time came to sail back round the pirate-infested coasts of the southern Morea, Alex would be there with the *Philip* to escort them. But he had explained that he was desperately busy taking supplies to the little army General Gordon had landed at Munychia in the hope of relieving Athens.

'What do you suggest?' she asked Biddock now.

'That you entrust the money and the stores you ordered to Captain Hamilton in the *Cambrian*. Best of all, I think you should arrange to travel in company with him. If you really feel you must go.'

'He's sailing soon?'

'He's at Corfu now. You'd best lose no time in your preparations. You'd like me to get a message to him?'

'Oh, yes, please.'

But Brett, returning from a visit to the Resident, with whom he had made firm friends in the course of the winter, told her that he had anticipated Biddock. 'It's the obvious answer,' he said. 'I'll feel very much safer rounding Cape Matapan in company with the *Cambrian*.'

'So we're all going?' Jenny jumped up from where she had been sitting on the floor, packing books.

'I see no alternative,' said her brother. 'Phyllida and I can hardly go jaunting off on our own, and I'm certainly not going to leave you here without Aunt Cass to look after you.'

She kissed him impulsively. 'Darling, dearest B. I was so afraid you'd decide, after all, to leave me behind with Cissie Biddock.'

'Heaven forfend,' he said. 'God knows what mischief you'd get up to. There's a letter from my uncle, by the way.'

'Full of reproaches?'

'Naturally. Helena's married.' Even now, he found it hard to say it.

'Not really!' Jenny did not share his difficulty. 'Has she caught her earl at last? I'd never have thought it.'

'My uncle does not name the lucky man.' His tone was repressive. Then, relenting. 'From what he says, it does not sound as if he thought it a good match. And that, of course, is all my fault, like everything else.'

'Oh, poor B.!' And, irrepressibly. 'Aren't you just glad you're safe out of it? But when do we start? How is Mr. Brown getting on with his blessed gudgeons? Will Captain Hamilton really let us go along with him? Tell me quick!'

'In one word, I suppose?' He could not help laughing at her. 'Well, to begin at your last question and work back: the Resident's written a moving plea to Captain Hamilton on our behalf. He seems sure he will help us. Hamilton's a good friend to the Greeks.' He might be answering Jenny, but he was speaking to Phyllida. 'And Brown says the gudgeons are perfect, much to his surprise, and he should be able to get steam up tomorrow. Then it's merely a question of waiting for the *Cambrian.* I think it will be best if we all move aboard at once. We'll be a tight squeeze, I'm afraid, since I intend to take Marcos along. My Greek's still not nearly as good as yours, Phyllida, for all my studies this winter, and I'm not sure how the Greek Government would feel about your acting as my official interpreter.'

'No,' said Phyllida thoughtfully. 'They do seem to treat their women as beasts of burden, don't they? I've noticed the refugee families; the father walks along with nothing to carry but his pistols and yataghan, and his poor wife follows bowed down with such of their possessions as they have managed to save. But, surely, with intelligent Greeks like the government it would be different?'

Brett was discouraging: 'I doubt it, and so does the Resident.' Had he succeeded, at last, in putting a doubt into her head about Alex? He hoped, but did not think so.

The *Helena*'s engines were as good as new. Sailing swiftly and safely in company with the *Cambrian,* they reached Aegina to find chaos compounded. Penniless and without authority, President Zaimis' government had made a feeble and unsuccessful attempt at relieving Athens, but was really more occupied by its feud with the opposing factions of Kolokotronis at Hermione and Kondouriotis on Hydra. The Navy had turned to piracy, and what remained of the Army to brigandage for lack of pay. The inhabitants of Argos had been reduced to closing their city gates and threatening to fire on anyone who approached. Worst of all, the Egyptian leader, Ibrahim Pasha, had taken astute advantage of the chaos in the Morea to persuade whole Greek villages to submit to him as a lesser evil than their own predatory soldiers.

'I don't know what to do.' It was their second night in harbour at Aegina, and the bad news had been coming in all day. 'I just don't know what to do,' Phyllida said again as she stood at the rail, gazing unseeingly southwards to the blue-shadowed mountains of the Morea.

'Wait.' It was the only advice Brett could give, and his heart bled for her. 'If Hamilton cannot persuade the rival governments to unite,' he went on, 'perhaps Cochrane will manage it when he gets here. In the meantime, I'm sure Hamilton is wise when he urges you to say nothing about your proposed gift. If news of it gets out, you'll be badgered as poor Byron was. I'm delighted to find that Alex has had the sense to say nothing about it.' He was also, privately, a good deal surprised, but that was not a thing to say to Phyllida.

'Anyway.' Jenny gave a great sigh of pure happiness. 'We're here. We're actually in Greece itself! I never really believed we'd get here. B., darling B., say we can go and look at the Temple of Aphaea tomorrow?'

'I'll see, kitten, but I'm not sure that this is really a time for sightseeing.' He had been on shore himself that day and did not much want Phyllida to see the crowded refugee camps on the island, or hear the stories of the fugitives who had escaped from the Acropolis when Fabvier fought his way in at Christmas.

Jenny jumped up to join Phyllida at the rail. 'It all looks so beautiful–and so peaceful–those delicious little white houses, and the men sitting about on the quays–it's hard to believe they're at war.'

'It *is* hard to believe it,' said Brett. 'The men idling on the quays there are soldiers who ought to be with Gordon and Karaiskakis outside Athens.' Too late, he saw where this was leading.

'Why aren't they?' asked Phyllida, and answered herself: 'For lack of pay, I suppose. Oh, Brett, shouldn't I–?'

'No,' he said. 'If you'd met the chiefs of this government, as I did today, you'd know it would be madness. Pay their soldiers and they'll send them to Hermione to intimidate Kolokotronis and his gang.'

He was actually relieved to see the *Philip* come swooping into the harbour a couple of days later, and even more so when Alex urged Phyllida as strongly as he had to do nothing for the time being. 'I know it's maddening for you, *kyria*, but we must wait, now, until Lord Cochrane gets here. Nothing's happening, over there at Athens. Gordon and Karaiskakis are sitting in their two camps, and the Turks are between them, at Saint Spiridion, laughing at them. But I've good news for you, just the same.'

'Another letter? Oh, thank you, Alex!' Once again it was an indescribably dirty and tattered old piece of paper, but the message it carried was reassuring. 'He says I'm not to believe all I hear,' she exclaimed. 'Things up there aren't so bad as Fabvier's been painting them. I wonder why?'

Alex laughed. 'Think, *kyria*! You can't blame General Fabvier if he's drawing it a bit strong; he wants to be relieved, doesn't he? I've heard it said he's not best pleased to be shut up there in the Acropolis while Sir Richard Church is made Commander-in-Chief outside. He didn't at all intend to stay there, in the first place. He meant merely to throw supplies into the Acropolis and fight his way out again. No wonder if he's getting impatient!'

'But, Alex, isn't there something we can do?'

'Not for the moment, *kyria.* That's just what I have come to talk to you about. I'm ashamed to have to confess it, but I don't think it's safe for you to remain here.'

'Safe?' She could not believe her ears. 'Here? At Aegina?'

'It's the *Helena*,' he explained apologetically. 'Your beautiful steamship, milord. You've heard, of course, of the excitement Captain Hastings' steamship, the *Karteria,* created when she arrived? And she was invaluable up at Athens until she was damaged. We miss her badly now she's being repaired. Well, you can see, the *Helena*, being so much smaller, might be even more useful for reconnaissance and inshore work. She's a daily temptation to Kondouriotis and his pirates on Hydra and Spetsai. Suppose they should get control of the government, what's to prevent them from seizing her, on some trumped-up charge, one day when there's no ship of the Great Powers in port?'

'Yes,' Brett said. 'I've been afraid of that. Captain Hastings himself warned me not to let any of the Greek captains on board, on any pretext whatever.'

'You're wise,' said Alex. 'Though I hate to admit it.'

Jenny laughed. 'But you're a Greek captain yourself, Alex. Shall we throw you into the harbour?'

'Why, so I am, *Kyria* Jenny, but also, I hope, your friend.'

'Of course. I was only teasing. But what do you want

us to do? Disguise the *Helena* as a caique, or hide her in one of those secret bays Greece is so rich in?'

'Precisely that. I should feel much safer if you were where only I could find you. Just until Cochrane gets here–' He turned to Phyllida and Brett. 'There's a bay under Cape Sounion that we use, my friends and I. If you'd let me guide you there–'

'On the mainland?' Brett was amazed. 'But the Turks?'

'Would never come there in a thousand years. It's as good as inaccessible by land, and invisible by sea. And it's known as a haunt of mine and my friends'. You'd be safe there. No Greek would dare molest you; no Turk would ever find you.'

'That may be true enough,' Brett agreed reluctantly. 'But still I'm not sure–'

Alex took his arm to lead him a little apart from the others. 'There's something else.' They were out of earshot now, their voices drowned by a fiddle being unmelodiously played on the crew's bit of deck. 'I was glad to hear you had not let the ladies go ashore. There's talk of the plague in that camp of huts outside the town. It may only be talk, but if you've been there, you know what the conditions are like. And if it should get a hold–in a place as overcrowded as Aegina–anything could happen. Quite aside from the infection, there's the question of panic. Suppose someone were to decide that the *Helena* would be a good way to escape?'

'But this secret cove of yours: you really think we'd be safe there?'

'My life for yours, milord.' He held out his hand. 'You know, I think, how I feel about the *Kyria* Phyllida. Do you think I would put her at risk?'

'No, I don't.' Brett took his hand. 'When shall we start?'

They encountered an unexpected obstacle in Phyllida herself. Their brief conference had given her time to think. When they returned to announce that they intended to sail that same night, she surprised them both with a decisive, 'No.' And then: 'I'm sorry, Brett . . . Alex . . . I know you mean it for the best, but I can't. Go and hide–out of touch–without news–while Peter is in danger every moment? Don't you see, Cochrane might arrive when you were away, Alex. We might not hear of it–the moment for my intervention might pass without my even knowing about it. Besides, I *cannot* believe the *Helena* won't be safe here at Aegina—safer, if you ask me, than hidden as you suggest. After all, the ships of the Allied Powers are in and out of the harbour here all the time. And I, personally, think better of your fellow countrymen than you seem to do.'

'But there's more—' Brett intervened to explain about the threat of plague.

'I'm sorry,' she said again when he had finished. 'Of course in that case we'll all stay on board the *Helena*. You and Marcos will have to go ashore, I suppose, Brett, but I know you'll take every precaution.'

'But, Phyllida, think of the danger. To you, to your aunt, to Jenny—'

'I am thinking of it, and I mind, horribly, that I must expose the rest of you to it. But—I'm sorry to have to remind you of this—I've chartered the *Helena*; I have the right to decide where she goes. And, please understand this, Brett, I have decided.'

'Oh.' His face tightened. 'Of course, if you put it like that, there's no more to be said.'

# 14

'Forgive me, *kyria.*' Alex contrived to snatch a moment alone with Phyllida in the lee of one of the paddle wheels. 'I understand now that I should never have suggested your hiding. There's no end to the surprises you have for me. An Amazon! An Athene! But you will let me leave one of my own men on board with you, as a protection?'

'Oh, thank you, Alex! You think of everything. I *should* be grateful! I'd never forgive myself if anything were to happen to Jenny and my aunt.'

'And I, *kyria,* would never forgive myself if anything

were to happen to *you*. I'll speak to Milord Renshaw about the man, with your permission?'

'Oh, yes, please do. He's angry with me, I'm afraid. It will come much better from you. And stay to dinner, Alex? It will make things easier . . .'

Was this a mistake? She wished, afterwards, that she knew just what Alex had said to Brett. It was certainly very far from having the effect she had intended. He treated her throughout the evening with a tight, controlled courtesy that she found hard to bear. But Alex was at his most charming and kept them absorbed with his stories of alarms and adventures at sea. Many of these involved Peter, and Phyllida could have listened to him for ever. 'Oh, yes,' Alex said. 'He's one who can take care of himself, my Brother Petros, but how should he not be, brought up by such a sister! You have never asked me, *kyria*, what Petros told me about you.'

'Why, nor I have.' She laughed. 'That I was a domestic tyrant, I expect. I've always felt I must have failed him somehow, or why did he run away as he did?'

'For love of a cause, *kyria*, an ideal. For freedom, and for us poor Greeks. He's a man in a million, your Brother Petros.' And, seeing how she enjoyed it, he embroidered on this theme for the rest of the evening.

Their self-imposed quarantine in the bay of Aegina was no pleasure. Each day, now, was hotter than the last, and as they sat under the awning on the burning deck, the sight of wooded hills and blue distances was merely maddening. Worst of all, for Phyllida, was the knowledge that she was responsible for this discomfort. And Brett continued equally polite and withdrawn. It would have made her furious, if it had not made her so unhappy.

It was no comfort to wonder if he might not have been right in urging her to take Alex's advice and quit the hot and crowded harbour at Aegina. He never raised the subject again, or commented on the discomforts of their enforced confinement. He did not need to. She saw that Jenny was losing weight, and knew that her aunt was not sleeping. She herself was, simply, miserable. To watch Brett laughing and joking with Jenny, and then suffer his invariable cool courtesy to herself was curiously hard to bear. And yet, she told herself, she ought to be grateful. If she had been afraid, once or twice, on Zante, that he was beginning to forget Helena for her sake, she had certainly managed a most effective cure. It made things, she kept telling herself, much easier. But it still made her miserable.

So she was immensely relieved when Lord Cochrane finally sailed into Aegina harbour one fine March morning. The handsome eighteen-gun brig bought for him by the Greek Committee of France had hardly downed anchor before emissaries began to swarm on board, both from the shore and from Hamilton's *Cambrian*.

'He's getting a tremendous welcome.' Phyllida had watched the whole scene from the deck of the *Helena*.

'Yes.' Brett joined her at the rail. 'They seem to think that his coming will solve all their problems. I only hope they are right.'

'You don't think so? Do you know Cochrane, Brett?'

'No. He's been a semi-exile since that disgraceful business in 1814. You must have heard about it.'

'No.' She was delighted to have him talking to her again. 'What happened?'

'It was a tremendous scandal at the time. Of course.' He remembered. 'Britain and the United States were at war then. You would not have heard. Cochrane engineered, or was supposed to have engineered, a false rumour of peace with France, and made a fortune on the stock exchange in the resulting confusion. It was an extraordinary business altogether, and I don't think anyone really knows the rights of it. There was immense popular sympathy with him at the time. He was gaoled . . . escaped . . . stood again for his seat in Parliament and was actually re-elected. He may have been innocent for all I know, but it finished his career in the Navy. He's seen a good deal of service in South America since then. He's —well, I suppose you'd call him an adventurer.'

'Then he should just suit the Greeks.'

'I'm not so sure. What they need is someone who'll restrain their tendencies that way, not pander to them. I'd rather see Frank Hastings in command of their Navy any day, but I don't think there's any question but that Cochrane will carry all before him now he's here. I just hope it works out for the best.'

'And quickly, so they can set about the relief of Athens. I wish Alex would get back with news.'

'We don't need Alex to tell us that everyone admits the supreme importance of relieving Athens. Hastings says there's a rumour going about that the Great Powers intend any liberation of Greece to apply only to such territory as the Greeks hold when the truce finally goes into effect. So they are bound to make every effort to hold the Acropolis, in order to be able to claim possession of at least part of northern Greece.'

'I see.' She found it cold comfort. 'And, on the same grounds, the Turks will be equally determined to take it at all costs.'

She met Cochrane at dinner on the *Cambrian* a couple of days later, and did not like him. 'Though I can't think why not,' she admitted to Jenny afterwards. 'He has charm enough for ten; I thought he didn't much like us Americans, but he was certainly courtesy itself to me. And wonderfully confident and reassuring about the Acropolis.'

'Too confident,' said Jenny. 'And did you notice how carefully he apportioned his favours?' She laughed. 'Will you think me a jealous cat, love? It did occur to me someone might have told him you were thinking of giving money to the Greeks.'

'Wretch! If Aunt Cass wasn't watching, I'd pull your hair for that! And I so proud of my moment of triumph! No, seriously, it bothered me a little. Who could have told him?'

'Not Brett, that's certain.' Wisely, Jenny left it at that. 'I'll tell you something else I didn't like about Cochrane. Did you see him not seeing Aunt Cass?'

'Yes, indeed,' said Phyllida. 'And how your brother came to her rescue when Cochrane left her stranded. I *was* grateful.'

'Oh, you can always count on Brett.'

Likable or not, Cochrane succeeded where everyone else had failed. The rival Greek governments managed to compound their differences after a series of noisy meetings, and sent for Count Capodistrias to take office as the first President of the Republic of Greece. Cochrane was made Commander-in-Chief at sea, and Church on land, and a committee of three was elected to govern until Capodistrias arrived.

Oddly enough, it was Alex, now, who urged that Phyllida delay handing over her gift of money to the new government. 'Pay it in instalments, *kyria,*' he said. 'That way, you will have some control of what is done with it. Besides, who knows, now Lord Cochrane is in command, Athens may be relieved any day. We may have my Brother Petros back with us, able to decide, himself, what's best to do with it.'

'What do you think, Brett?'

'I think it very good advice. There are rumours, you know, that Lord Cochrane is living pretty lavishly at the expense of the Greek Government. You don't want to find yourself contributing to the upkeep of his establishment.'

'No indeed!' The frugal American housewife in her was revolted by the idea. 'Very well, by instalments it shall be. I'm glad your cousin George is one of the council of three who are to govern until Count Capodistrias gets here, Alex. But I do wish they would hurry up with the relief of Athens.'

'Take comfort, *kyria.* Lord Cochrane is quite as impatient as you.'

'Yes,' said Brett. 'I believe he's told the Greeks that if they don't mount an attack soon, he'll throw up his command and find himself a new adventure.'

'Would he really do that?'

'I wouldn't be surprised. He likes results, does Lord Cochrane.'

They heard, next day, that the new government intended to move its headquarters to Poros. Alex advised that they go there too. 'It's a magnificent, landlocked bay. You should be able to find a private anchorage. But first, I hope you will let me take you to see the Temple of Aphaea here on Aegina. I know Miss Jenny has her heart set on that.'

'Oh, yes, please!' Jenny had been gazing at the blue distances of the Morea and only half listening to the talk, but now joined in eagerly. 'It's so mortifying to have been in Greece all this time, and never seen so much as a bit of a classical ruin. Do let's go. You'd like it, wouldn't you, Phyllida?'

'Yes, immensely–if you think it's safe?' She addressed the question equally to Brett and Alex.

'Perfectly,' said Alex emphatically. 'We'll sail round to the bay under the temple–no threat of plague there.'

'No,' said Brett. 'And, in fact, I've not heard any more talk of it here at Aegina.'

'Very likely it was a false alarm,' Alex agreed. 'But–what is it my Brother Petros says? "Better safe than sorry."'

'You do speak English beautifully, Alex! You must have worked at it like a Trojan.'

'Or like a Greek? How glad I am, now, that I did.'

Next day dawned fine and windless, so Alex made the short trip round the island on the *Helena* with them. On his advice, Phyllida and Jenny had both put on full-trousered Turkish costume. 'We shall need to go ashore and walk a little to get the best view of the temple,' he explained.

One glance at the pine-covered hillside was enough for Aunt Cassandra. 'I shall stay on board. You won't go far, Phyllida?' It was a plea.

'No, Aunt.' Phyllida had hoped that they might be able actually to climb up to the temple that stood high above them, brilliant white against the sapphire midday sky. But if she even breathed the idea of so extended an expedition, her aunt would feel in honour bound to come too. She would never get used to these English ideas of chaperonage, and might, perhaps, have resisted on her own account, but there was Jenny to be considered. So she sighed and resigned herself to the compromise Alex proposed. A short walk through the pine woods, he explained, would take them to a clearing from which they could get the best view of the temple, short of actually climbing up to it.

'Better so,' he consoled Phyllida as he helped her ashore. 'Even here, you know, the modern Vandals have been at work. The carvings from the temple have been carried off to Bavaria, and the workmen who took them for Prince Louis were no respecters of antiquities. From down here, you will be able to imagine the building perfect as when it was first dedicated.' Leading her along the shady path through the woods, he proved surprisingly knowledgeable about the temple. Absorbed in his account of the various theories about its dedication either to Aphaea, Pallas Athene or even Jupiter Panhellenius, Phyllida did not notice for some time that they had left Jenny and Brett far behind. But that was not surprising. As they pushed their way through thickets of flowering almond or purple Judas trees, each sunlit glade they reached had its own splendour of spring flowers, white drifts of narcissi and daisies, scarlet ones of anemones and everywhere the purple and crimson of poppies. Jenny could never resist a flower she did not know, and any walk with her was punctuated by her exclamations of delight as she darted this way and that to investigate here an unusual iris or there something yellow she had never seen before. And after all she was safe with her brother. But just the same . . . Phyllida thought of Aunt Cassandra and slowed her pace: 'We'd better wait for the others, Alex.'

'But we're just there. One more turning and you shall have your view of the temple and think of Aphaea while you wait.'

'Oh, in that case . . .' She moved forward again at his side. 'But will they be able to find their way?' Distracted equally by his talk and by the spring glories all round them, she had still noticed that the path was little more than one among many sheep tracks.

'They can hardly fail to. It's just to keep going upwards as we have done. Miss Jenny is doubtless after her wild flowers again.'

'I expect so.' She continued by his side, but a little slower now, listening for the sound of Jenny's voice and gay laughter.

'Phyllida—' He took her arm to guide her round a projecting piece of rock. 'Forget about Jenny for once. She's with her brother. They'll catch us all too soon. Think of me. Think how I've schemed, planned, hoped for this moment.'

'Planned?' A little breathlessly, playing for time.

He laughed. 'Why do you think I wanted, so badly, to get you to Sounion? How could we speak our hearts to each other, on the *Helena*, surrounded by a thousand eyes? I began almost to believe in our old fable of Argus; I would have despaired, I think, if your beautiful eyes had not sometimes told me to hope. *Kyria,* tell me I was not wrong! Oh–I've no right to ask you this! What have I to offer but a heart that beats only for you, and a castle on the bare rock, down in the Mani? Not even that, if the Turks should conquer us. But that I'll never believe. And you, you're rich, beyond imagination. Sometimes, I'm ashamed to have let myself dream of you. But, Phyllida, we shall not be beaten! We Greeks are a nation at last; a nation with pride, with a future. When the fighting is over; when the Turk has been driven from our shores and we establish our kingdom, once more, at Constantinople, who will govern the new Greece but men like me, men who fought and suffered for her? In the present, *kyria,* I offer you my poverty, but in the future I build you a palace of dreams.'

'Constantinople?' Even now, the word sent a little shudder down her spine.

'Of course.' Impatiently. 'A new empire of Byzantium, and you and I among its princes.'

'Princes? A kingdom? But, Alex . . .'

He laughed, but the colour was high on his cheekbones. 'I'm speaking figuratively, though indeed Petros and I have often agreed that we Greeks might need, at first, one strong man, one Pericles to set us on our way to liberty. And that brings me to something I should have said before. *Kyria*!' Formal now. 'I have your brother's permission to pay you my addresses.'

'Peter's!' Do what she would, she could not help laughing. 'Oh, Alex, you never asked him?'

He did not like it. 'Why do you think I have waited so long, but for his answer. And this opportunity. In Greece, we do it like this, by consultation with heads of families.'

'I'd rather you'd asked Aunt Cass!' It came out almost despite her, and she anticipated his answer.

'A woman!' With undisguised scorn. And then, quickly, taking both her hands. 'Phyllida, you must know that you are the only woman in the world whose judgment I respect. The only woman in the world for me.' He pulled her towards him. 'Don't think of anything but that. What do they matter, my poverty, your riches; the past, the future, when you and I can come together, like this?'

He was right. Nothing mattered. She was dizzy, drowning in his kiss. His body was hard against hers; his weapons hurt her through the thin stuff of her tunic; time whirled past as if they two were its centre.

When his lips left hers at last, she was glad of his arm, still supporting her. 'I didn't know it could be like that.' She looked up at him, shakily, the whole world changed about her.

'Nor I. Believe that.' He met her, look for look. 'I'm yours. You're mine. For ever. Only, for the moment, love, shall it be our secret?'

'Why, yes, if you say so. But why?' She was both puzzled, and, oddly, relieved.

'For all kinds of reasons, but mainly for your safety. I have enemies, Greeks, alas, as well as Turks, who might be glad to strike at me through the one I loved. And besides'–his smile warmed her–'I must confess that I don't much like the idea of being thought a fortune hunter. When I take my rightful place in a free Greece I shall have position to offer you, if not fortune. And you will be my good genius, mine and my country's, helping us with your wisdom to plan a government fit for free men.'

It was a dazzling prospect. 'But, Alex, you won't mind if I tell my aunt?'

'My little love, I should mind beyond bearing, beyond reason. She doesn't like me, your good aunt. She'll do her best to poison your mind against me. And I–I must leave you, tomorrow, on a mission not without danger. Don't let me be plagued with doubts of what she will be saying to you. Besides, my life, there's something else, something we should face. Suppose I should not return? You're brave enough, I know, to admit that chance, but it will be easier–and safer–for you if nothing is known of this.' She was still silent, doubtful. 'My love, grant me this, the first thing I've asked you?'

'Of course.' Impossible to resist that plea. 'But, what's that?' She turned away from him, listening.

He was laughing. 'Milord Renshaw, I have no doubt,

shouting for guidance. Perhaps my directions were not quite so clear as they should have been.' And then, quick to see the change in her expression, 'We Greeks have a saying, my life. "Love and war make all things even." So, one kiss more before we go to find them?'

# 15

Over and over again, Phyllida was to regret that rash promise of secrecy. It was bad enough when Brett and Jenny caught up with them and she was aware at once of her own confusion and of Jenny's bright enquiring eye upon it, but it was much worse to return to the *Helena* and find herself, for the first time, keeping an important secret from her aunt. It tarnished, ever so slightly, the golden glow of her happiness, but she had given her word, and there was nothing she could do about it until Alex returned to release her.

Her comfort was that things seemed at last to be moving quickly towards the liberation of Greece. Soon Alex would take his rightful place and there would be no more need for secrecy. Preparations for the relief of the Acropolis were going on apace, and she had the happiness of knowing that some of the soldiers assembling for the attack had been paid for by her money, or rather by Peter's. But now, anxiety for Peter was compounded by that for Alex. If only she knew where he was . . . He had said no more about his dangerous mission when they had parted, so publicly, on the crowded deck of the *Helena.*

She was delighted when Brett raised the subject a few days later. He and Marcos the interpreter had been ashore from their new anchorage at Poros and he returned with the news that he had met his friend Frank Hastings. 'It's not much of a secret, I'm afraid, that he's preparing for a raid on the Turks' supply lines up in Euboea. Frank thinks, and I agree with him, that the Greeks would do much better to concentrate on cutting those, rather than mounting the frontal attack on the Turks that Cochrane wants. From something Frank said, I rather suspect that Alex has been up in the Gulf of Euboea spying out the land for him.'

'Oh!' Blushing over the inadequate monosyllable, Phyllida felt enquiry in Brett's gaze, and was grateful when he went calmly on: 'Do you know that the greater part of the Turks' supplies come from Greece itself?'

'No!'

'I'm afraid so. And in Greek ships, which should at least make Alex's task that much safer. But it does make one wonder about the chances of a free and united Greece.'

It was her chance to ask a question that had been on her mind. 'Brett, do you think there's any hope that the Greeks will ever regain Constantinople?'

'Constantinople! Good God, what put that idea into your head?' And, answering himself: 'Alex, of course. The *megali idea,* the great idea. It's been a Greek dream, I believe, ever since they've been aware enough for dreams. To throw the Turks back out of Europe and revive the Empire of Byzantium! Frankly, I think it nothing *but* a dream. They'll be lucky if they get them out of Athens.' And then, remembering, 'But whatever happens, your brother should be safe enough, I hope. The Turks must know, by now, how European opinion is building up against them. It's an odd thing, but the fall of Missolonghi seems to have helped the Greeks, who lost, more than the Turks, who won. I wonder if Missolonghi won't go down to history, like Thermopylae, as a great victory that weighed the balance of war against the victors.'

'Do you really think so?'

'I wouldn't be surprised. It's meant more even than Byron's death in terms of support and sympathy from abroad. And for that very reason I think the Turks will be careful, now, how they behave to the Philhellenes.'

'Yes, I see. But, Brett, you talk as if you thought there was a chance of the Acropolis falling.'

'In war, anything is possible. I know the Greeks have got Ibrahim Pasha on the defensive now–he's almost as much beleaguered himself as he is besieging the Acropolis, but he has the advantage of a unified command—and the courage, I should think, of near despair. So long as he holds his chain of communications with the sea, and the monastery of Saint Spiridion between the two Greek camps, I think he's in too strong a position for any army the Greeks can field. They're splendid fighters as individuals, but I just can't imagine them mounting a major attack. Well, look at those guns of theirs—so heavy that they have to be balanced on a stone to fire. And no bayonets, no training, no discipline. Give me one regiment of English infantry, and I'll guarantee to relieve the Acropolis tomorrow, but that's just what we haven't got.'

Alex, returning from Hastings' successful raids in the Gulf of Euboea surprised Phyllida by taking much the same line. 'Why risk a frontal attack when we could starve them out in six months? Give me money to pay the sailors of Hydra and Spetsai, and Ibrahim would be asking for terms before the currants are ripe.'

'Asking for terms?' asked Brett. 'Do you really think he would?'

'Why not?' But Phyllida thought Alex was on the defensive.

'Because of the chance of a massacre. Oh, I know there have been wrongs on both sides in this war, but that's just what makes the situation of anyone who surrenders so precarious.'

'Not now,' said Alex. 'Those barbarous days are past.'

'I hope you're right.'

'I'm sure I am.' His glowing gaze was for Phyllida. 'We Greeks are a free people now. When we were slaves, we behaved like slaves; now everything is different. You agree with me, don't you, *Kyria* Phyllida?'

'Of course I do.' If only she could catch a minute with him alone and urge that the time had come to announce their engagement. But what hope was there in the crowded *Helena*? Perhaps he would suggest another shore excursion?

His next words put an end to this hope. 'I must leave you, alas. Shall I blow a kiss to the Acropolis for you, *kyria*?'

'You're going back?' It was hard to believe, seeing him so handsome and so casual, that he was returning to the fighting.

'Yes, to Saint Spiridion. The Turks' garrison there

can't possibly last much longer. And then, *kyria,* then the way will be open to the Acropolis.' Kissing her hand, in farewell, he held it a second longer than he had Jenny's.

'Alex?'

'Yes?' His bright gaze held a warning.

'You'll be careful?' What else could she say?

'I'm always careful.' He smiled at her. 'We Greeks have so much, now, to live for.'

Phyllida was actually grateful that, with the *Helena* so crowded, private conversation with anyone was a near impossibility. She was aware, from time to time, of her aunt's anxious, speculative gaze on her. Given the opportunity, she thought, Cassandra would, however delicately, begin to ask questions that could only be answered by lies. She should never have made that promise to Alex. At all costs, she must see him alone next time he arrived.

Life was pleasanter at Poros, with hope for company. The four of them were sitting on deck in the cool of evening a few days later watching the slow melting of sunset over the mountains of the mainland.

'Something's happening!' Brett turned to gaze towards the crowded shipping at the other entrance of the harbour. 'Look!'

'It's the *Philip*!' Phyllida was on her feet. 'No one else comes in like that. Brett, do go and find out what the news is. Maybe Alex would come to supper and tell us what's happening? Just think, Saint Spiridion may have fallen. The way may be open to the Acropolis!'

'Yes. I'll go directly.' Something chilly about the courteous reply made her wish her impulsive request unspoken. But it was all imagination, merely her strained nerves that made her feel her secret about Alex as a kind of invisible barrier between her and her companions.

'It's getting cold.' What had Jenny noticed? 'How fast the sun sets here! I'll tell Price there may be one extra for supper, shall I?'

'Yes, do.' Brett turned away to give his orders for a boat, and Cassandra went below with Jenny. Only Phyllida sat on, gazing at the mountains as they turned from palest lavender to silver-grey, and promising herself that this time she would have it out with Alex.

She forgot all about it when he and Brett returned together. 'Alex! What's the matter? You're hurt!'

'It's nothing. A couple of scratches.' Dried blood caked the side of his haggard face, and his left arm was in a rough sling. 'If that were all!'

'Why? What's the matter? It's not—Not the Acropolis? Tell me!' She looked from one gloomy face to the other. 'Tell me!'

'No, no.' Brett hurried to reassure her. 'Not the Acropolis. But it's bad news, just the same. Terrible news. Saint Spiridion has surrendered.'

'But that's not bad news?' Puzzled. 'I don't understand. You said, Alex, that when Saint Spiridion fell, the way would be open to the Acropolis.'

'Yes. A way of blood. I wish I'd died before I saw this day.'

'Alex! You can't mean that!'

'No.' For a moment, the old smile flashed for her, softening the grim set of his face. 'But I'm almost ashamed not to. Ashamed to be a Greek, God help me. God help us all.'

'But what is it? Brett! Explain.'

'I'm afraid it's the garrison of Saint Spiridion. All massacred.'

'No!' It was too bad to be true.

'Yes.' No wonder Alex looked so ghastly. 'When I realised what was going to happen, I went ashore. I did what I could, *kyria*; so did Karaiskakis and a few others. But what could we do, against so many madmen? I got these wounds from Greeks.'

'Horrible!' She shuddered. 'Unbelievable.'

'But true,' said Alex. 'Church should have supervised the surrender himself. Madness to leave it to the Greek *pallikars.*' And then, aware, perhaps, of a change in Brett's expression. 'Oh, you're right. I'm making excuses, but can you blame me? God knows what harm this day's work has done to our cause.'

'Not to mention to those poor Turks,' said Brett dryly.

'Oh, as to them—' Alex showed his teeth in a smile that

struck Phyllida disconcertingly as savage, almost wolfish. 'I've no doubt they deserved their fate. Think of Chios! Think of Missolonghi!'

'Alex, you don't mean that. You're ill.' Shocked, Phyllida saw that he was shivering convulsively. He was feverish, near delirium, or he would never talk so wildly. 'Oh, thank God! Price!' He had appeared with her box of salves and dressings.

'I saw Mr. Mavromikhalis come aboard, miss, and was sure you'd want these.'

'Bless you, Price. Alex, you must let me dress that wound.'

'Never!' He recoiled at the thought. 'Not you, *kyria*, not your hands. How could I?'

'Let Price do it,' said Brett. 'He's as good as a surgeon any day. Take him to my cabin, Price, and let him rest there till supper.'

'Thank you.' Alex put his good hand to his head. 'Forgive me, *kyria,* if I've said anything amiss. I'm not myself.'

'Of course not.' Warmly. 'You'll be well enough to join us at supper?'

'Death wouldn't stop me!' But he was obviously glad to let Price lead him away below.

'It's bad.' Phyllida had been realising all the implications of the massacre.

'As bad as can be.' Brett could be relied on for a straight answer. 'Both as a threat to the safety of the garrison in the Acropolis, and as one to the unity of the Greeks. There's a rumour already that Church is talking of throwing up his command because of this day's work. Mind you, in some ways, that might not be a bad thing. If only they could get my friend Charles Napier to take his place—but I think it's too late for that now. Any change of command must do untold damage at this point.' He took her cold hand. 'Don't look so anxious, Phyllida. I still think your brother should be safe enough. Frankly, I think Reshid Pasha has more sense, and more control of his troops, than the Greeks. Even if it should come to a surrender of the Acropolis, I should expect him to keep his men in hand.'

'Even after this?'

'Yes, even after this. But, you're shivering. It's almost dark, and the wind's getting up. Come below, Phyllida. Things will seem better in the morning, I promise you.'

'They could hardly seem worse.'

Alex emerged from Price's ministrations looking very much more himself, and protesting all over again that his wounds were mere trifles. He set out to behave as if nothing was the matter, but there was a strange, hard glitter about him all evening that Phyllida found almost frightening. That night she dreamed that he and she were climbing the path to the Temple of Aphaea. It grew narrower and incredibly steep. Drifts of scarlet anemones and purple poppies on either side encroached more and more closely: in a moment they would be wading through them. And they were not flowers, they were rivers of blood.

'Phyllida! Phyllida, child, what's the matter?' Cassandra was beside her, holding her hand.

'Nothing, Aunt. A nightmare. I'm sorry if I waked you.'

'No matter for that.' Her aunt's cool hand lay for a moment on her forehead. 'I'm anxious about you, child. There's something on your mind, isn't there?'

'Oh, Aunt Cass!' Suddenly, helplessly, she was crying. 'I can't tell you. Don't ask me. I gave my word.'

'But should you have? This isn't the first time I've heard you talking in your sleep.' Cassandra felt her way over to the lamp and lit it. 'I've wanted to talk to you, but it's impossible in the daytime. There's no privacy, not even in here, with the saloon so close. But I can't bear to see you looking so burdened, so withdrawn . . . Tell me about it?'

'I can't,' she said again. 'I promised . . .'

'Not a promise you should have given, nor one that anyone should have asked of you.'

'Maybe not.' The hot horror of the dream was fading now, and she could think clearly again. Oddly, her first thought was that only yesterday, under such loving pressure, she would have broken her promise and told her aunt of her engagement. Why had

Alex's behaviour last night made this impossible? She temporised. 'Father always said one's word must be one's bond.'

'Sometimes,' said Aunt Cassandra oddly, 'I wish your father had not been a sea captain.' But to Phyllida's grateful relief, she asked no more questions, merely smoothing her rumpled sheets and pouring her a glass of lukewarm water. Only, the lamp blown out, she said, 'You shouted, "blood", Phyllida. It frightened me.'

'I must have been dreaming about that night we escaped from Constantinople.' Phyllida was ashamed of the suggested lie the moment it was spoken. Angry with herself, she was angry, too, with Alex for getting her into this position. Tomorrow, she would speak to him.

But tomorrow the *Philip* had sailed.

# 16

Easter passed gloomily. It was hard to put one's heart into the traditional 'Christ is risen' with memory of Saint Spiridion still fresh as a wound. And though its fall should at least have left the way open for the relief of the Acropolis, nothing was done. The Greeks seemed paralysed, absorbed in mutual recriminations, while the Turks, inevitably, prepared to fight to the death. It was not only Phyllida who woke each morning to a deep, unreasoning burden of misery.

'But at least Church hasn't resigned.' Brett was doing his best to be cheerful. 'Those three ciphers who pass for the Greek Government have arrested John Notaras, who had nothing to do with the massacre, and propose to make him the scapegoat. What worries me more is that Church and Cochrane seem to have learned nothing from the disaster.'

'What should they have learned, B.?' Phyllida was increasingly silent and withdrawn these days, and it was Jenny who asked the question.

'Why: the obvious. That they cannot hope to control the

Greek troops. How on earth do they expect to carry an attack across the plain to Athens, in the teeth of the Turkish cavalry, when they can't even control their men in a minor victory?'

Jenny flashed him a warning glance. 'You're just an old raven, B.! Surely now Spiridion has fallen, they've got the Turks in a trap. They can't lose. And anyway you said yourself that what happened there makes a negotiated surrender almost impossible.'

'I did indeed.' Grimly. 'Would you surrender, if you were Reshid? To a pack of bloodthirsty barbarians?'

'Oh, really, B.' Once again her look was a warning. 'You're so prejudiced against the Greeks you won't see reason. I'm sure this will have been a warning to them. They'll do better from now on.'

'I hope you're right.'

'Of course I'm right. You may be a great author, but I've got female intuition. And that reminds me, I've another chapter copied out for you. Come down to the saloon a moment and I'll give it you.' And then, as he followed her down the steep companionway, 'Brett, I'm worried about Phyllida. She doesn't look a bit well.'

'I know. I wish to God I'd never agreed to let her charter the *Helena*. She'd be infinitely better back on Zante, away from all this.'

'You're talking about Phyllida?' In the saloon, Cassandra had heard his last sentence. 'I'm anxious about her, Brett.'

'That's just what Jenny was saying. But what can we do? She'd never consent to go back to Zante now.'

'No, of course not. But I think we must do something, just the same. She's having nightmares, night after night. She wakes up screaming. It's the same dream, I'm sure, over and over again. Anxiety, of course. I think it's too hard on her to be here, right in the thick of things like this. Besides, let's face it, the *Helena* wasn't designed to accommodate so many people. I think it does us the greatest credit that we're not quarrelling like cats.'

'Yes.' He smiled at her with affection. 'But what can we do, Aunt Cass?'

'I've been thinking about that. In the night, listening to poor Phyllida, I've had a lot of time for that. I think I've hit on it. In fact, I can't think why it didn't occur to us sooner. When the attack on Athens comes, you'll want to take the *Helena* up as near as possible, won't you?'

'Not with you women on board.'

'Precisely. So we must go ashore. There must be somewhere safe on the mainland, Brett? Where Phyllida can hire another house?'

'Nauplia, of course. It's as good as impregnable. And not a chance in the world of the Turks attacking it now, when they are so closely threatened at Athens. It's not much of a place, I'm afraid, but it should be safe enough.'

'What should be safe?' Although she longed to be alone, Phyllida became restless when she was, and had come down to join the others in the saloon.

'A house in Nauplia,' said her aunt. 'We've been holding a council of war, love–a fine thing to do without you there, who will have to pay the shot!'

'A house in Nauplia! But why in the world?'

'Because we've none of us been thinking,' said Brett cheerfully. 'The attack on Athens is due to start any day now and if you think I am going to stay down here when that happens, you're crazy. Crazier still–' He anticipated her reply. 'If you think I'm going to take you with me. So, this afternoon, we are going to sail round to Nauplia and establish you three in a house there. You must see, Phyllida, that even if I would let you, I can't take Jenny into the war zone.'

'No, of course not. I've been a fool not to think of it myself. But, Brett, do let's lose no time! You'll really go up to the Piraeus when they attack?'

'What else? And bring Peter straight back to you. It's another argument for a house. He's bound to be exhausted after all these weeks of siege. He'll need all the comfort he can get.'

'Yes, indeed.' It did her good to have him talk as if Peter's rescue were a matter of course. 'But, Brett, it's not just Peter–' She hesitated, horribly aware of her betraying blush.

'You're thinking of Alex?' For once, his cool, matter-of-fact tone was balm to her. 'Of course I'll bring him, too, if I can get him to come. Price says he should hardly be noticing those wounds of his by now, but once the Acropolis has been relieved, he, too, may feel glad of a rest.'

'You really think it's going to be relieved?'

'Church and Cochrane seem sure enough about it.'

It was not quite an answer, and Jenny darted him one of her quick, bright glances, but it satisfied Phyllida. 'Let's start at once,' she said.

Since the Greek Government was now on Poros, Nauplia was considerably less crowded than when they had been there before, and Brett was able to find them a house set close between the shore and the towering cliff. 'I've accepted it on your behalf,' he told Phyllida next day. 'I hope you'll forgive me, but I thought you ladies would like it better if I had it thoroughly cleaned before you even saw it. Price is taking a detachment of the crew ashore first thing tomorrow to do so.'

'Oh, thank you, Brett, you think of everything.'

But the house in Nauplia was a sad come-down after the Palazzo Baroti. Brett had explained, ruefully, that the Greeks, in their extravagant fury, had destroyed most of the Turks' houses when they captured the town at the outbreak of the rebellion. The best of those that remained had been taken over by Prince Mavrocordatos, and Brett had been lucky to rent a smaller one belonging to a member of the government, now at Poros.

'Well, at least, under the cliff like this, it should be shady enough.' Phyllida mustered the best enthusiasm she could. 'And what a wonderful job you've done, Price, in making it habitable.'

'Thank you, miss. It looks a bit odd, the *Helena*'s furniture in these outlandish rooms, but never mind. We'll be settled in no time, you see if we aren't.'

'And just think of all this space,' said Jenny. 'A study for you, darling B., and rooms to ourselves all round. You should get on like a house afire with your book now. But when can we go sightseeing? I'm dying to look at those romantic castles!'

'I don't know about that,' Brett said doubtfully. 'I've been talking to Marcos. I'm afraid you ladies are going to have to resign yourselves to a fairly cloistered life while I am away with the *Helena*. Greek ladies don't go out much, you know. Of course Marcos will stay with you, but I can see he's a little anxious about your safety. It's a great responsibility for him, and I rely on you to make it as easy for him as possible.'

'Oh B.!' It was almost a wail. 'You mean we've exchanged the deck of the *Helena*, and all those wonderful views, for this tiny airless courtyard.'

'Well, not entirely. Marcos seems to think that it will be "suitable" if you join the evening promenade in the main square –I'll take you there tonight. It's not much of a place, I'm afraid, but better than nothing.'

So, that evening, he led the way through the narrow, noisome lanes of Nauplia to the small square, with its huge rustling plane tree, where the Greeks took their evening walk. 'There aren't many women, are there?' Jenny had been watching everything with her usual lively interest. 'And look at them! Wrapped up in shawls and veils like so many mummies! Only a good deal more shapeless. Something tells me we're not going to have much social life here. Really, B., I don't see what good it's done the Greeks to free themselves from the Turks if they go right on behaving like them. I'd as soon be a Turkish woman as a Greek one any day. At least the Turks have a chance of ending up in Constantinople and the Sultan's harem! What do you think, Phyllida?'

'I think you talk a great deal of nonsense!' It came out more sharply than Phyllida had intended, and, to make amends, she went on. 'But tell me about the fortresses, Brett. Which is the Palamede and which the Itchkali? And are we going to be able to take Jenny to see them before you go?'

'I'm afraid not. I made some enquiries about it today and it's perfectly clear that visitors–and most particularly female ones–are far from welcome. Well, it's understandable enough in time of war, but also I hear there's a good deal of ill feeling, just now, between Grivas, who commands the Palamede, and Fotomarra at Itchkali. There's been one outbreak of actual fighting between them already. I'm afraid it's hardly the time for sightseeing trips to their strongholds.'

Jenny sighed. 'And I know you're going to tell me it's quite impossible to ride over to Argos–we've got to be content with the distant view of the ruins there . . . and with imagining the Lernean swamp, and Tyrins–Not to mention Mycenae . . .'

'I'm afraid so, for the time being. Even for men, sight-seeing would be a chancy business these days. For you, I'm afraid it's, simply, impossible.'

'Heigh ho,' sighed Jenny. 'Do you know, sometimes I quite find myself looking forward to getting back to England.'

'Oh, Jenny!' Something about her tone roused Phyllida from her abstraction. 'I'm sorry!'

'Nonsense!' Jenny gave her a quick kiss. 'It's I who should be sorry. I'm a brute to grumble, when you've been so angelic to me. It's only—at Zante there were the flowers, and the walks . . . Even on the *Helena* there was always something going on in the harbour that one could watch. But what are we going to *do* here?'

'Let's hope we won't be here for long,' said Brett.

'You think the attack will come soon?' Phyllida asked.

'Very soon. If you feel you can manage without me, I propose to go back to the *Helena* tomorrow. I want to be ready, with steam up, when Cochrane gives the order for the attack.'

'Brett, you'll be careful! I'd never forgive myself if you were hurt—or the *Helena*—on my account.'

'Nonsense.' He had been ready for this. 'You mustn't look at it like that. Don't you see how selfish I am to dump you in this airless hole, so that I can go off and watch the fighting? It's going to be the making of my book! When Murray wrote and approved my plan for it, he made a special point of that. He says a good set piece of a battle scene should be worth a fortune to me in sales. I know that must sound heartless to you [he intended it to] but remember I've got my way to make in the world, and Jenny's too. This book *must* be a success.'

'So you'd want to go anyway, even if it wasn't for Peter?' This was a new idea to her.

'Of course I would. So, if by any chance I should get hurt, you are not to imagine it has anything to do with you. I'm just immensely grateful to you for making it possible.'

'I see.' She thought him disconcertingly mercenary, but Cassandra, understanding it all, gave him a warm, approving smile.

Alone in her tiny room in what had been the Turk's harem, Phyllida sat for a long time savouring her solitude. She had much to think about. The day had been one long succession of unpleasant discoveries. Living in the comparative luxury of the Palazzo Baroti, on peaceful Zante, she had thought she was learning about life in Greece. Now she began to understand that she knew nothing about it whatever. It brought her back, as everything did these days, to Alex. Watching the veiled Greek women, huddled up in their shapeless garments, spinning as they walked meekly behind their husbands, hearing Brett's description of the cloistered lives they led, she could not help wondering if Alex expected her to live like this. What would it be like down there in the primitive castle he spoke of in the Mani?

She shook herself and began to prepare for bed. Nonsensical to think like this. They would not be living in the Mani. Even if the Greeks did not recapture Constantinople (a dream, Brett had called that) surely they would soon retake Athens. That would be their capital. She and Alex would live there, working together for a new and happier Greece. She remembered how he had spoken of her help in civilising his country, and thought she began to understand how much there was to do. She went to bed, contented, or nearly so, planning the schools she would run–for mothers as well as their children? . . . And waked, a long time later, in the chill of the dawn, sweating, from her nightmare of flowers and blood.

Brett sailed back to Poros next day taking the smallest possible crew for the *Helena.* 'But how in the world will you manage without Price?' Jenny had asked; and Brett had laughed and said, 'Deplorably, I'm sure, but I'll feel much safer to think he's here with you.'

Jenny laughed. 'Don't worry, Brett, we'll look after each other, and Price will look after us all. If you ask me, our worst enemy is going to be bordeom.'

But in fact they soon found a small society of Philhellenes in Nauplia, and notably a young American doctor called Samuel Gridley Howe, who had acted as surgeon on Hastings' *Karteria* but was now convalescing from a fever caught when he had been compelled by Greek inhospitality to spend a stormy night in the open on an islet near Hydra. He and his friends became constant visitors at the house under the cliff, and in return for Phyllida's lavish hospitality brought the most precious of all commodities, news.

'Won't Brett be surprised to come back and find us running a salon,' said Jenny one bright May morning when even their dark little courtyard was full of sunshine.

'I wish he'd come,' said Phyllida. 'Do you think they may call off the attempt to relieve the Acropolis now Karaiskakis has been killed?' Yesterday's piece of bad news had given her a sleepless night. 'Dr. Howe and his friends are so young,' she said now. 'I do wish Brett was here to tell us what's really happening.'

'But you know he won't come so long as he thinks there's a chance of an attack on the Turks.' Jenny was determinedly hopeful. 'So really his not coming is the same as good news.'

Dr. Howe and his friend Townshend Washington called on them next evening bringing a bottle of raki to drink with the curious brew Price called coffee. Dr. Howe had just returned from a trip down the coast, and appalled them with his tales of conditions there. 'The fighting's gone on too long. The peasants have no seed to sow; if they don't get help soon, there will be mass starvation this summer. And all the government thinks about is the Acropolis.' He remembered. 'I'm sorry, Miss Vannick.'

'No need. I'm ashamed not to have thought of this sooner. They lack seed, you say?'

'They lack everything! I've written to the Greek Committee in Boston urging that they send what they can—at once. But think of the time lag.'

'Surely one could buy supplies nearer?'

'With money, of course. But, look at us! We were almost ashamed to come here tonight. And to see you ladies, so beautiful, so elegantly dressed.'

'It's we who should be ashamed,' said Phyllida. And then, 'What's that?'

A commotion in the outer rooms of the house. Price's

voice raised in remonstrance. Then the door of the room burst open and Alex appeared. 'A party!' His scornful glance swept the little circle, then settled on Phyllida. 'Greece bleeds from her death-wound, and you gather your jackals round you to make merry.'

'That's no way to speak to a lady.' Howe was on his feet, looking absurdly young in contrast to the swarthy Greek.

'Never mind.' Phyllida took control. 'Sit down, Dr. Howe, and you, too, Alex. Price, fetch some coffee for Mr. Mavromikhalis. And a glass.'

'Coffee!' But Alex dropped into the chair Price set for him. 'A Judas feast. What do you think your brother is eating to-night, *kyria*? Dust and tears?'

'Alex, what is it? Tell us!' At first, she had thought him drunk; now she began to fear it was worse.

'What do you care? Sitting there, entertaining your fine friends in your fine rooms. "Coffee for Mr. Mavromikhalis!" ' His voice was a cruel parody of hers. 'And wine! A libation! A sacrifice, like those brave men in the Acropolis? Oh, yes.' He emptied the glass Price had given him. 'Their race is run. No doubt of that.'

'What do you mean? What is it?' Her voice shook.

'Disaster. Defeat. Crushing; absolute; final. There is no Greek Army any more.' He drank again. 'If Karaiskakis had lived, they might have listened to him. If Cochrane and Church had troubled to go ashore, they might have been obeyed. But–to order a mass attack, and then watch it from their ships through field glasses! Well, they saw.'

'What happened? Try and tell us, Alex.' Cassandra's calm voice was meant to steady him.

'Cochrane insisted on a direct attack on the Turkish positions. He'd been urging it all along. He said he wanted to eat his dinner in the Acropolis. Tonight!' Savage irony in his tone. 'He gibed and goaded at the *capitani* until they agreed to lead their men down from the heights and across the plain. He didn't understand.' He was trying to explain the disaster as much to himself as to them. 'It's not the way we Greeks fight. I think he must have deluded himself that he had an English army. "Fix bayonets! Charge!" ' The parody of a clipped British accent was cruelly accurate. 'Of course, when our *pallikars* got down into the open plain, they wanted to stop, to build their *tambourias*. You know.' He picked Howe as the most intelligent listener. 'The little earthworks they rest their guns on to fire. The *capitani* urged them on. They swore, they shouted. Some obeyed, some went on digging. And then, the Turks charged, with cavalry, with the bayonet. It was a massacre, I tell you. We've lost the flower of our soldiers today. It's the end of organised resistance, the end of everything.'

'I don't believe it,' said Phyllida.

'You're calling me a liar?' His eyes flashed fire.

'Nonsense,' said Cassandra. 'You're exhausted, Alex. It's terrible news, but it can't be so bad as you think.'

'No? I tell you, *kyria,* it's the end. The Acropolis will surrender; God knows how long you ladies will be safe here, giving your parties in Nauplia.'

'Alex!' Jenny leaned forward to intervene. 'What of the *Helena*?'

'She was still taking off the wounded when I left.' And then, aware of a sudden chill in the room. 'The *Philip* had all she could hold. As to the *Helena*, she'd been under fire, of course, but should be safe enough, with British colours. And so will Church and Cochrane, God damn their souls! All very well for them to play at war with other men's lives, and stay safe on board to watch them die.'

'Mr. Mavromikhalis.' Cassandra was on her feet, speaking very quietly. 'I think you forget where you are. It's terrible news.' Her voice was not unsympathetic. 'It will be better discussed in the morning. If you will forgive us, gentlemen, we will say good night. Price, you will look after our guests?'

But they had all risen. In the subdued murmur of farewells and thanks, Alex cornered Phyllida. 'Forgive me! I'm not myself. In the morning . . .'

'Yes, Alex.' Very gently. 'In the morning.'

# 17

'I wish Brett would come.' Jenny pushed back her chair from the breakfast none of them had eaten. And then, aware of Phyllida's drawn face: 'But I'm sure it can't be so bad as Alex said. He was exhausted, beside himself, poor man.'

'Yes.' Phyllida had lain awake for hours; had made up her mind at last what she must say to Alex, and, surprisingly, had then slept dreamlessly till morning. 'When did Mr. Mavromikhalis say he would come, Price?'

'As soon as he could, miss. I think he was worried about what might happen to the *Philip* if he wasn't there. Marcos says there's a proper panic in town this morning, and no mistake. He wants us to start packing up, but I said we'd wait for orders from Mr. Renshaw. I hope that was right, miss?'

'It certainly was, Price.' And then, echoing Jenny. 'I wish he'd come!'

'I don't expect he much likes to leave the *Helena*,' said Jenny. 'If Alex doesn't even trust his own crew.'

'He'll come as soon as he can.' It was comforting to be so sure of that. 'But if things are really so bad for the men in the Acropolis–' Her voice shook as she faced it. 'I know he'll stay, just in case . . .'

'Of course he will,' said Jenny. 'And when Brett really puts his mind to something, I wouldn't want to be in his way.'

'Oh, Jenny.' Somewhere between laughter and tears. 'You sound as if he would relieve the Acropolis single-handed.' And then, the tears choking her. 'Poor Peter! Just think. They must have been able to watch it all from up there. To see the attack that was to save them. And what happened to it.'

'Don't, love.' Jenny handed her a clean handkerchief. 'It will all come right, you see if it doesn't. Yes, Price?'

'Mr. Mavromikhalis is here.' Price's voice was disapproving. 'He asks to see you, Miss Vannick. Alone.'

'No!' said Cassandra.

'Yes,' said Phyllida, drying her eyes. 'I must, Aunt. I owe it him.'

'I see.' Phyllida thought she probably did. 'Well, if you think so, Phyl; but I shall be in the next room. And, Price?'

'Yes, ma'am?'

'You won't be going out for a while?'

'No indeed, ma'am.'

'Very well.'

It was a little like a military plan of action, Phyllida thought ruefully. And all her fault. 'I'll see Mr. Mavromikhalis in the little saloon, Price.'

'I shall be in the courtyard,' said Jenny cheerfully. 'Watering the plants. If you want me to burst in on you, by accident, love, just raise your voice.'

'Bless you.' Tears threatened again. 'I've been a terrible fool.'

'Never mind that,' said Cassandra bracingly. 'So long as you've realised it.'

Alex was a different man this morning, chastened, subdued, deferent. 'Phyllida.' He took both her hands in his. 'It's like you to see me, to forgive me, to understand . . . I was a little mad last night, I think, with despair. I don't even rightly remember what I said, but I know, being you, that you will have understood.'

'Of course I did. I've forgotten, too. Only, is it really so bad?' She must ask this before anything else.

'As bad as can be. It's the worst disaster of the war—worse even than Peta. It's a miracle Reshid didn't go on and recapture Phalerum and Saint Spiridion—but he was too busy taking vengeance on his prisoners. Yes, *kyria,* he lined them up, hundreds of them, the flower of our *pallikars,* and had them beheaded.'

'Horrible! But where are Cochrane and Church?'

'Cochrane's gone off to Hydra. Church is holding out in Phalerum, but God knows how long he'll be able to. A friend of mine was there before Saint Spiridion fell. It's terrible, he says;

brackish water to drink, and sometimes no bread for days. They'll never hold out long; not after a disaster like this one.'

'Then what about the Acropolis?' She hardly dared ask.

'That's just it. That's why I was in such despair last night. There's no more hope for the Acropolis; we have to face that. It's merely a matter of time. If they try to fight their way out, they're dead men.'

'And if they surrender?'

'Think of those Greek prisoners yesterday. There's your answer. Petros might just possibly be spared, as a Philhellene, but I doubt it. There were twenty or so Franks killed on the field yesterday. No: it's every man for himself from now on. We must make Petros see that. He must escape, by himself, as soon as possible.'

'But will he agree to? And even if he should, is it possible?'

'If we put it to him right, I think he'll agree. And, yes, I think it's possible. It will cost money of course.'

'As if I cared about that. But how shall we persuade him?'

'You're his sister, *kyria,* surely you can think of some way. Tell him you're ill, in danger, that you need him . . . That will bring him.'

'But I'm not.'

'Does that matter? It's his life we're talking of.'

'Yes.' Doubtfully. 'You're sure, if I manage to persuade him, that you can arrange it?'

'If he's my brother. Yes.'

'What do you mean? I don't understand.' She was afraid that she did.

'Phyllida.' He took her hands. 'You must try and understand how things are today. The Greek *pallikars*–those who survive–feel betrayed. They feel, and I don't blame them, that Cochrane and Church sent them and their friends to their deaths yesterday, and stayed safe themselves. You won't find many Greeks, this morning, ready to risk their lives for a Frank. But if he's my brother, it will be another matter. I know twenty men who would take your message to the Acropolis tomorrow–for a price–and bring Petros back with them. Albanians, of course. Who's to know whether they serve the Turk or the Greeks? Frankly, many of them do serve both. It's merely a question of who pays most.'

'I see.' She liked no part of it. But that was not the point. The point was Peter, Peter's safety . . .

'I knew you would. It's not what I had intended for you, for us, but we must be married today, Phyllida, for Peter's sake. Then, and only then, can I save him.'

'Alex, I can't.' It came out instinctively, from the very depths of her.

'Can't? What madness is this? Have you forgotten Aegina, my little love, and the promise you made me there, under the Temple of Aphaea?'

'Not forgotten.' This was far worse than she could have imagined it. 'But regretted it many times. Forgive me. I've realised, too late, I know, that it's not possible. You say you were a little mad last night. I think I was that day on Aegina. I'm ashamed–disgusted with myself. But, thank God, you made me promise to tell no one. It's not so bad as it might be. Nobody need ever know . . . Because it won't do, Alex. We come from different worlds, you and I. I'm no wife for you. You must see that. I can't understand how you should think of it. And as for me, I was a fool that day: I didn't understand anything. Forgive me?' She said it again, pitifully.

He had dropped her hands as if they burnt him. 'So! It was one thing to engage yourself to me when we Greeks were winning. You would reign with me at Constantinople. But when it comes to being my comfort in exile, down in the Mani, you think again. Phyllida, I would not have believed it of you!'

'It's not that!' But how horribly convincing it sounded. 'Alex, try to understand. I didn't know, back at Aegina, what it was like to be a woman, here in Greece. I can't do it. Even if I loved you–'

' "If"?' He pounced on it. 'They were all lies, then, those kisses back at Aegina?'

'Not lies, Alex. A mistake.'

'An unlucky one for me, *kyria*. And for your brother.' It sounded, incredibly, almost like a threat. 'But you'll think again of this. You're distraught today, and I don't blame you. And angry, too, because of last night. Take your woman's revenge then;

make me suffer. I deserve it. But not for too long, *kyria,* if you don't wish to know yourself your brother's murderer.' He watched it hit her. 'I must go now and tell the priest we don't need him—yet. I'll come again tonight and hope you've returned to your senses. We're all a little mad today, Phyllida. Don't, in your madness, make a mistake that will ruin our lives, yours and mine, and end your brother's.'

'But, Alex—'

'Not now, little one. I will come to you again tonight. There's a hairsbreadth of time, still, for the Acropolis, and for Petros. Use it well, my love, for all our sakes.' To her infinite, unreasoning relief, he merely bent, kissed both her hands, and left her.

'Oh, God.' She was actually wringing her hands. 'What shall I do?' But at least, since he wanted her to marry him today, Alex could be assumed to have absolved her from her promise of secrecy. She found her aunt peacefully darning sheets and poured out the whole story. 'I'm so ashamed. I've been such a fool. But what shall I do? If I don't marry him, Alex will do nothing for Peter.'

'It hardly makes him seem a good bargain as a husband.'

'Oh, I know. I was crazy, moonstruck, sunstruck; I don't know what, back there on Aegina. But that's not the point. If Alex doesn't get Peter out . . . If they're all murdered . . . It doesn't bear thinking of.'

'No,' said Cassandra. 'But we have to.' And then, 'I wish Brett was here.'

'Oh, God, so do I. But there's not even time to send for him. Alex is coming back this evening. I suspect he'll bring a priest. I suppose it would be legal?'

'I very much doubt it. But that's neither here nor there. You can't do it, Phyllida, and you know it. This is what those nightmares have been about, isn't it, not what happened at Constantinople at all?'

'Yes. Aunt Cassandra, I'm sorry—'

'No need to be. You'd given your word. Foolishly, but never mind. The question is what to do now. First of all, you're not going to see Mr. Mavromikhalis alone. I'm not sure we oughtn't to send for Dr. Howe.'

'Oh, no. It would make Alex too angry! Think what he was like last night!'

'Yes, scratch the charming surface, and you find the barbarian. But you're right, just the same, we can't afford to alienate him, for your brother's sake. I think you and I will have to see him together, and try a little genteel bribery. The only question is, how high will we have to go? I wish you had your diamonds here.'

'You think it might work?' Here was a new horror.

'If we go high enough, I should hope so. After all, this thing works both ways. Mr. Mavromikhalis is no fool. He must see that you would make a very different kind of wife from the usual Greek beast of burden. He might be quite glad to take the fortune without the bride.'

Phyllida actually smiled. 'You're not very flattering!'

'That's better.' Her aunt smiled back lovingly. 'These last few weeks I was beginning to think you'd never smile again, poor lamb.'

'I've been a proper fool, haven't I?'

'Yes, dear, and the best thing you can do now is to forgive yourself and tidy up as best you may. How much actual cash do you think you can raise in the course of the day? Failing diamonds, I think the clink of sovereigns might be a powerful argument with Mr. Mavromikhalis.'

'I can't believe it.' Suddenly, she found she almost wanted Alex to refuse the offered bribe. And yet, where would that leave her? Either way, it was sordid, horrible . . .

But she sent off an urgent message to Mr. Biddock's representative in Nauplia and was anxiously awaiting his arrival when Jenny bounced into the room. 'Marcos is back from the market! He says the *Helena*'s in.'

'Oh, thank God!' And then, appealingly, 'Aunt, will you explain to him?' No need to say she meant Brett.

'I think it would be better if you did, my dear.'

'Explain?' Jenny looked from one to the other, puzzled.

'It's Alex–' Telling Jenny was bad enough; how in the world would she tell Brett? But her aunt was right; she must do it.

When Brett arrived, she forgot everything in shock at his appearance. He was immaculately neat as always, but the efforts he had made to look as usual merely accentuated his ghastly pallor, the nervous twitch under one eye, and, worst of all, the path of dried blood across the top of his head that he had tried so hard to hide by a rearrangement of his Byronic curls.

'Brett! You're hurt!' Jenny had flung her arms round him and was sobbing on his shoulder.

'It's nothing; a ricochet; I was lucky.' He patted her soothingly, his eyes on Phyllida.

'You certainly were.' This was Cassandra. 'An inch lower . . .'

'Just so.' He did not want to discuss it. 'You've heard the bad news, I take it.'

'Yes.' Phyllida took the plunge. 'Alex came last night. He told us. Is it as bad as he said?'

'It could hardly be worse. It was a shambles . . . a disaster . . . When I think that I wanted to see a battle, for my own selfish reasons, I can hardly bear myself. We saw it all, from the *Helena*. The Greek prisoners lined up–' He stopped. 'Why should I inflict it on you? Besides, I mustn't waste time; I must be back at the Piraeus by morning. Thank God the *Helena*'s engines weren't damaged.'

'And the crew?'

'Nothing serious–a few scratches–spent balls mainly. We were wonderfully lucky. The tricky bit was getting the wounded off the beach–I got this on the last trip–' A shaking hand made another attempt to hide the wound.

'You'd much better leave it uncovered,' said Cassandra. 'And I never heard such nonsense as to suggest that you're going back on board tonight.'

'Oh, I must.' He said it with a sort of absent-minded firmness that was more final than any amount of argument. 'I only came to tell you not to worry–too much. You should be safe enough here. At least for the time being. It's Peter we have to think about. This is the end for the Acropolis, I'm afraid.' His steady eyes met Phyllida's.

'That's what Alex said. He says Peter must escape. There were twenty Philhellenes killed yesterday, he told me.'

'He thinks it still possible? An escape?'

'Yes.' She must tell him. But how could she?

'Jenny, my dear,' Cassandra picked up her sewing. 'I think we had best leave your brother and Phyllida to talk it over.'

'Yes, Aunt Cass,' said Jenny meekly. She flung her arms round Phyllida. 'Don't look so frightened, love. He won't eat you. He's a kind old monster, aren't you, B.?'

'Naturally.' Brett closed the door behind her. 'What is it, Phyllida? Something's very wrong. I knew the moment I saw you.'

'Brett, I'm so ashamed.' How many times must she make this confession? 'But, sit down, do. You look exhausted.' She sat, herself, on one of the set of chairs from the *Helena*'s saloon, remembered, as she did so, the one he had broken that night at Zante, and was frightened, for a moment. But that was absurd. 'I've been such a fool.' He was facing her across the table, but she could not look at him. 'And now I don't know what to do.'

'Tell me.'

'You remember that day at Aegina? When we went to the temple?'

'Of course I do. What of it?'

His tone frightened her again. Get it over with. She bolted into it. 'Alex asked me to marry him.'

'Yes?' Very quietly.

'I don't know what possessed me. I said yes.'

'What?'

'Yes. Don't look at me like that, Brett. He said it must be a secret, for the time being, because he'd be ashamed–he didn't want to be thought a fortune hunter. And, like a fool, I promised–And then you and Jenny came, and I never had a chance to ask him to . . . to . . .'

'To release you from the engagement?' He pounced on it. 'You realised at once, then–'

'No. If only I had. To release me from my promise, I meant. I knew I should never have given it. I've felt so dreadful, all this time, acting a lie to you three who . . . who . . .

who've been so good to me. But what could I do? I never had a chance to speak to him alone. You know what it was like on the *Helena.*'

'Yes?' He was not going to help her.

She gazed down at her hands. 'And now . . . Brett, I don't see how I can. Marry him, I mean. And yet, I have to!'

'What in the world do you mean?'

Open rage would be easier to bear than these cool questions. 'Brett, he says he can only help Peter escape if he's his brother. He wants to marry me today. He says the Greeks are angry with Cochrane and Church; they won't help a Frank. But if we're married, if he's his brother-in-law, he says, he could do it.'

'And you want me to give away the bride?'

'No!' She bit back first anger, then tears. 'Brett, don't make it harder for me than it is already. Don't you see; I've realised, been realising . . . Do you remember the way he talked about the massacre of Saint Spiridion? It began then. And, now, I don't even think I *like* him.'

'A pity you didn't realise it sooner. To let yourself be charmed by an adventurer–a flashing smile and a pirate's swagger!' He paused, took hold of himself. 'And now he's trying to blackmail you into keeping your word?'

'That's not a very nice way of putting it.' Once again she felt bound to defend Alex.

'It's not a very "nice" situation.' Savagely. 'Well, you asked for my advice, Phyllida. Here it is. I'll see Alex for you and give him your refusal. It's impossible, and you know it. Imagine how your brother would feel, if Alex did, in fact, manage to save him.'

'Peter? But he's given his consent. Alex wrote and asked him.'

'He did, did he? You've seen the letter?'

'No, of course not. Alex told me . . .'

'And you believed him! God give me patience! Have you no sense, Phyllida? Don't you see that if Alex has been in such close touch with Peter, he could have got him out long ago if he'd really wanted to.'

'But Peter wouldn't come. You know that. He wrote me . . .'

'And how do you intend to persuade him to come now?'

'Alex said I must make something up—tell him I needed him—'

'Lie to him, in fact. And you're prepared to?'

'If it's the only way. Aunt Cassandra says she thinks if we offer Alex enough emoney, he will get Peter out without—' She boggled at it.

'Without your marrying him? Maybe he would—for enough money. But have you thought what this tells you about Alex? Pay him, if you like, but how do you know someone else won't pay him more?'

'The Turks? It's not possible.'

'Anything is possible. If he'll stoop to blackmail . . . To have persuaded you, in the first place, to keep the "engagement" secret was bad enough, though, mind you, I thank God for it. But, now, I think we must believe him capable of anything. You must realise, Phyllida, that this is the end for the Greeks. No wonder if Alex wants to ensure himself a snug life in America.'

'You think that?'

'Well, what do you think? You've not, surely, persuaded yourself that Alex wants you for your intellect?'

'Brett!' She was crying helplessly now. 'Don't.' And then, pleading, 'He said I'd be a help to him, in creating the new Greek state . . .'

'At Constantinople, I suppose! I remember your speaking of that. I should have guessed. And you believed him! I tell you, Phyllida, Jenny would have had more sense.'

'And you were so wise about Helena?'

'We will leave Helena out of this.'

'Brett, I'm sorry. I didn't mean—'

'No? But we've no time for apologies. They are a peacetime luxury. I must be back at the Piraeus by morning. I've an appointment to see Admiral de Rigny. I hope he'll arrange a flag of truce for me to visit Reshid Pasha. Ostensibly for my book; in fact, to speak to him about Peter. To try and get it across to the

Turks that your brother is powerfully connected—that it would do them infinite harm with the Great Powers if anything should happen to him. I really think you will find this a more practical way of helping Peter than any wild scheme of Alex's.'

'Oh, thank you, Brett.' She was too grateful even to mind his tone.

'So you had best sit down and write a note to Mavromikhalis,' he went on, almost as if she had not spoken. 'I'll take it to the *Philip* on my way back to the *Helena.* It will spare you having to see him. Frankly, I'd very much prefer that Jenny should be spared the kind of scene he's quite capable of making.'

Jenny! But she had deserved it all. 'Thank you, Brett,' she said again, meekly.

# 18

The letter to Alex was indescribably difficult to write, and knowing that Brett was waiting for it in the next room was no help. But it was done at last, full of almost incoherent apologies, scratched and blotted here and there, a letter she would normally have been ashamed to send. But what was normal about today?

'Brett?' She gave it to him with a hand that would shake. 'You won't let him quarrel with you?' This fear had been uppermost in her mind as she poured out those pitiful apologies.

'Quarrel?' His tone was scornful. 'With—' He stopped. 'I'm not a quarrelling man. Besides, I've your brother to think of.'

'Not a quarrelling man!' Jenny interrupted him. 'I like that! Please, B., you will be careful, won't you? He's rather frightening, that Alex, when he loses his temper.'

'Nonsense, Jen.' He pulled one of her curls. 'I shall be the complete English gentleman, cool as a cucumber. You know how impossible it is to quarrel with one of them!' His tone of affectionate teasing was in such marked contrast with the one he had used to Phyllida that she found herself angrily swallowing tears.

It made it impossibly difficult to thank him properly. 'I wish you'd take Price back on the *Helena* with you,' she concluded, pleadingly.

'As a protection? I believe I can take care of myself, thank you.'

'No!' Now she had made him angrier than ever. 'But to look after you, to dress your wound . . .'

'And leave you three with only Marcos? I think not. I hope, of course, that Alex will take this'—he still had the letter in his hand—'like a gentleman, but God knows it seems unlikely enough. I think you should prepare yourselves for a visit from him. I'd rather know you had Price for that. I only wish I could stay, but there it is. I rely on *you,* Aunt Cass.'

'Thank you, Brett.' Cassandra was horribly sorry for Phyllida, but could not help feeling that she was learning a well-deserved lesson. 'And you'll let us know what Reshid Pasha says?' She asked the question Phyllida had longed to.

'As soon as I can. But don't worry if it's not for a little while. God knows how long it will all take to arrange. So—good-bye, and take care of yourselves.' A quick hug for Jenny, a warm shake of the hand for Cassandra, a bow for Phyllida, and he was gone.

'He's furious with me.' Phyllida could not help it.

'Well, love,' said Jenny cheerfully, 'you can hardly blame him, can you? So now, here we sit, we three, and wait to see if your Alex is going to come and blow our house down.'

'Not my Alex!'

'No, thank God.' She laughed. 'You and Brett are a proper pair, I must say. Talk about moon-mad. His Helena and your Alex—' And then, quickly, 'I'm sorry, love, it's too bad for teasing, isn't it?'

'Yes,' said Cassandra. 'We'll say no more about it.'

The evening dragged out interminably. Phyllida had secretly been almost certain that Alex would come storming ashore, priest and all, to claim her hand, but nine o'clock came, and ten, and still there was no sign of him.

Cassandra sighed comfortably and put down her sewing. 'I really think,' she said, 'that we might go to bed.'

'Do let's.' Jenny yawned unashamedly. 'I'm worn out with all this excitement. And it really does look, doesn't it, as if the gallant isn't coming, late or otherwise. Thank goodness.'

'Yes.' Phyllida had been experiencing a curious sense of let-down. Naturally she had hoped that Alex would not come and make a scene, but surely he should have written, sent a message, done something?

The feeling was more pronounced than ever next morning, when Marcos returned from market with the news that the *Philip* had sailed the night before.

'So we can breathe again,' said Jenny.

'Yes.' Phyllida had never disliked herself so much. She looked so wretched that her aunt was sorrier for her than ever, and glad that they could all pretend it was only anxiety for Peter that was upsetting her so. A long week dragged by with no news of any kind except the further details of the disaster at Phalerum, which she and Jenny did their best to spare Phyllida.

But their house was too natural a centre for Dr. Howe and his friends for there to be much hope of succeeding in this. Inevitably, they talked of nothing else. Most of them had lost friends in the battle; each had his own explanation of the disaster, none of them either flattering to Church and Cochrane or hopeful for the future.

'It will need a miracle,' said Howe, one hot morning when they were all drinking the curious coffee Price still managed to provide.

'Perhaps Capodistrias is busy arranging one,' said Townshend Washington.

'More likely he's arranging to hand Greece over to Russia. After all, he's as much a Russian as a Greek by now. Do you know what Hamilton told old Kolokotronis when he heard of Capodistrias' election?'

'No?'

'He said, "Take Capodistrias or any other devil you like, for you are quite lost." Or that's what Kolokotronis says. Hamilton may not have put it quite like that.'

'And do you know what your friend Kolokotronis is doing now? He's harrying those poor Moreot Greeks who've been so foolish as to submit to Ibrahim Pasha. "Fire and the sword to those who have submitted," is his cry.'

'While the defenders of the Acropolis count the days they have to live.' And then they remembered Phyllida and all began busily to talk about something else.

Phyllida was having nightmares again, different ones this time. Now they really were set in Constantinople, that night she and Cassandra had escaped. Over and over again she heard the screams, the sounds of pursuit, felt the blood slippery under her feet . . . But the figure she saw chased, caught and beheaded by the Turks was sometimes Peter, sometimes Brett.

'Suppose Reshid Pasha knows that Brett helped us escape from the Sultan. Just think what he might do to him!' She had said it to her aunt countless times, but kept coming back to it, hoping for impossible reassurance.

'But why should he, child?' Cassandra still managed to speak patiently. 'You mustn't frighten yourself unnecessarily.'

'I shouldn't have let him go to Reshid. It's too dangerous . . . If anything happens to him, I'll never forgive myself.'

'Yes, love.' Jenny had come in from the courtyard in time to hear the end of the familiar conversation. 'But, think a little. You know Brett, or you ought to by now. How could you have stopped him?'

'Besides.' Cassandra thought of a new source of comfort. 'You must remember that Brett is not exactly nobody. If he goes to Reshid Pasha with an introduction from De Rigny, the Pasha will be bound to know that he is cousin to an English Duke. Even if, by any fantastic chance, Reshid should have heard about our adventures in Constantinople, I'm sure he'd think twice about harming a member of the English aristocracy.'

'Goodness!' Phyllida did not know whether to be relieved or irritated. 'You make it sound as if Brett were practically first cousin to God.'

'Phyllida!'

'I'm sorry. But really I find this business of "English milords" immensely tedious. Sightseeing round the world as if it belonged to them; taking it for granted they'll be given the best of everything wherever they are. And getting it.'

'And paying for it!' Jenny bristled up at the implied slight to her brother. 'And wasn't it lucky for you that Brett was "sightseeing round the world" as you put it?'

'Of course it was! Oh, Jenny, I'm sorry! I can't bear myself these days. Forgive me?'

Jenny laughed. 'I ought to be saying the same thing to you. After all, love, let's face it, if it weren't for you, Brett and I would very likely be starving by now. I'm a fine one to talk about paying for things.'

'Nonsense,' said Cassandra. 'You know perfectly well, child, that Mr. Murray sent your brother a simply immense advance payment for his book.'

'Yes,' said Jenny. 'Wasn't it splendid? I don't believe I've ever seen Brett so pleased. So stop worrying, Phyl, and remember what a triumph an interview with Reshid Pasha will be for the book. Really, when you think about it, so long as he just manages to keep his head–literally, as well as metaphorically–B. can't lose.' She laughed wickedly. 'Just think if the book's really a success! Won't poor Helena be cross! I do wish we'd ever heard who she married in the end. That's the worst of being in disgrace; nobody writes to me. I don't suppose Aunt Matilda has even told my friends where I am. I find I rather wish I knew what kind of lies she was spreading about me.'

'Never mind.' Cassandra had noticed that Jenny seemed increasingly eager for mail from home. 'Perhaps in a week or so Peter will be safe and we can think of setting sail for England.'

'Getting steam up, you mean!' But Jenny sighed. 'Wouldn't it be wonderful! It's ungrateful of me, I know, but I'm tired to death of Nauplia.'

'So am I,' said Phyllida. 'And Marcos gets gloomier and gloomier about the state of affairs between the two forts. He seems to think they may come to blows any moment.'

'And here we sit between the two!'

'Yes. I do wish we'd hear from Brett.'

Jenny laughed. 'When I write my *Don Juan* about this adventure, I shall use that for the chorus. Let's think: how would it go? All kinds of permutations and combinations: "And every time they found the weather wet, They only said, 'I wish we'd hear from Brett.'" And so forth.'

'You talk a great deal of nonsense, child,' said Cassandra indulgently. She had grown very fond of Jenny, whom she found a good deal easier to understand than her niece. She had done her best to make light of Phyllida's secret engagement, because there seemed nothing else to be done, but it had shocked her deeply. Judging Brett's reaction by her own, she had quite given up that secret hope of hers that he and Phyllida might end by making a match of it. He would see them through their troubles, like the gentleman he was, and then wash his hands of them, and the worst of it was that she entirely sympathised with him. And when Phyllida compounded her offence by acid comments on the English aristocracy she sometimes found it quite hard not to lose her temper.

Jenny saw this. 'You mustn't be cross with Phyllida, Aunt Cass.' They had been working together at Jenny's indifferent French in the little room set aside as a study, and Jenny said this, haltingly, in French. 'She's so unhappy, sometimes I don't think she quite knows what she's saying.'

'I know. But, Jenny, how could she do such a thing?' It was a relief to have said it.

'I expect they'd think nothing of it in America,' said Jenny cheerfully. 'But it's a pity about Brett.'

'Hopeless, I'm afraid.' They understood each other perfectly.

Inevitably, Phyllida was aware of this understanding between them, and it put the final touch to her general misery. Everything had gone wrong, and most of it was her fault. She who had been used to being so self-reliant found herself wretchedly anxious for any kind of approval and reassurance. She threw herself into helping Dr. Howe with his relief projects, but could not help, like Jenny, longing to be away from Nauplia, with its constant reminders of Greek misery. And yet, if by any miracle Brett did manage to secure Peter's escape, and they were able to leave, it would mean a parting of their ways. As realist as her aunt, she knew that the end of their adventures would mean the break-up of their strange ménage. And she found it extraordinarily hard to bear the thought of parting from Brett in anger. But perhaps the question would not arise? May dragged into June and there was still no word from him.

At last a member of the *Cambrian*'s crew brought them a reassuring note from Brett. It was addressed to Miss Knight, and Phyllida felt a familiar pang as she watched her aunt open it. In happier days, surely, he would have written to her?

'Good news!' Cassandra had read it rapidly, aware of the two girls' anxious attention. 'He's seen Reshid Pasha—a great success, he says—"tell Jenny several chapters for the book". And, best of all, Reshid gave him his word that the garrison of the Acropolis will be spared if they surrender. He seems to think it will happen any day now. Church has written Fabvier advising that he give up, and Admiral de Rigny has undertaken to supervise the evacuation. I think it's as good as one could hope for.'

'Yes.' Phyllida was longing for a personal message like the one to Jenny. 'What else does he say, Aunt?'

'Not very much. Read it if you like. It sounds as if it were written in haste . . .' There was no mention of Phyllida.

Howe and his friends were not much comfort. They were appalled at the idea that the defenders of the Acropolis might really mean to surrender. 'It can't be necessary,' said Townshend Washington. 'That position should be impregnable, and we all know they're getting a certain quantity of supplies through the lines. If you ask me, the truth of the matter is that Fabvier doesn't much like being shut up there. That's why he's writing such desperate letters.'

'Yes,' said Howe. 'What he doesn't realise is that to hold out there is the most important thing he can do for Greece. It's like Missolonghi; it catches the attention of the world.'

'But that works both ways,' said Phyllida. 'Mr. Renshaw once told me he thought Missolonghi might be like Thermopylae—a victory that turned things against the victors. It struck me very much at the time. Don't you think the fall of the Acropolis might be the same?'

'Not if the Turks behave well,' said Howe, and, as so often, a cold little silence fell.

Next day, Nauplia was seething with rumours. The Turks had stormed the Acropolis by a trick; the garrison had marched out with flags flying and been cut down to a man; Church had launched a counter-attack and cut Reshid Pasha's lines of communication.

'That I don't believe,' said Jenny. 'Nor the gloomy stories either. If you ask me, they're merely rumours put about by Grivas or Fotomarra to mask their own quarrel. Marcos gets gloomier about things here in Nauplia every day. There's something going on to do with old Kolokotronis and his son John. Nobody quite knows what, but they're both in town, with more of those ragged desperados of theirs than anyone much likes to see.'

'I know,' said Phyllida. 'Sam Howe's had to put a guard on the American relief ship that came in the other day. Even when he gets the food distributed, he says he's afraid the soldiers will just take it away from the poor peasants.' She had been working steadily with Howe and his friends since the long-awaited ship had sailed into harbour.

'Not really a very nice lot, the Greeks,' said Jenny.

'But, poor things–' Phyllida could still be relied on to spring to their defence. She broke off. 'Yes, Price?'

'The *Helena*'s in, miss.'

'At last!' They were all on their feet. Phyllida turned pleadingly to her aunt. 'Surely we could go down and meet them?' Meet whom? She hardly dared ask herself the question.

'If you'll excuse me, miss.' Price had hovered in the doorway. 'Things are on the boil in town today, Marcos says. He told me particularly not to let any of the English servants out of the house.'

'Anyway,' said practical Jenny, 'there are so many ways to the harbour, we'd be bound to miss them.' She, too, carefully did not specify to whom her 'they' referred.

'And in the meantime,' said Cassandra, 'we'd better make up some beds.' She kept Phyllida and Jenny busy tidying and retidying Brett's room, and the one intended for Peter, until a commotion in the street sent Jenny rushing to the window.

'They're here,' she said. 'Oh, Phyllida!'

Hard to recognise Peter in the gaunt, heavily bearded figure who walked unsteadily beside Brett. 'Both of them!' It was a prayer of thanks. 'Quick, let's go down.'

Peter was exhausted, at the end of his tether, and furious. 'We should never have yielded! Two thousand pounds of powder, and grain for several months, and Fabvier surrenders the heart of Greece!' He still had his arms round Phyllida, and she recognised, with an odd little shock, that he was wearing a suit of Brett's clothes. 'Not that I'm not glad to see you, Phyl,' he went on, 'or to be here, come to that–but it's a black day for Greece. If I'd been Fabvier, I'd have held out to the last man.' He turned, with the smile she remembered, to Brett: 'In a way, sir, you've done Greece a disservice.'

'Oh?' Brett looked almost as tired as Peter.

'A massacre would have been better than this ignominious surrender! Now what will the world say? That the Turks are civilised, the Greeks barbarians. That the garrison of the Acropolis marched out with the honours of the war– And what happened at Saint Spiridion?'

'Perhaps the world will be right,' said Brett.

And, 'Peter,' intervened Phyllida. 'You mean you'd not have escaped, if Alex had arranged it for you?'

'Escaped? From the Acropolis? Have you gone crazy, Phyl?'

'Oh.' She was aware of Brett's disconcertingly sympathetic glance. 'I've been stupid,' she said.

'I expect so!' Peter's tone told her that everything had changed between them except affection. He was a man now. Odd to think that the last time she had seen him, she had been insisting that he take warm underwear to Harvard. 'But what's the news of Alex?' he asked. 'I rather expected to find him here.' It was all kinds of questions rolled into one.

Phyllida turned an anguished, questioning glance on Brett. 'Alex?' she temporised. 'We've not seen him for some time.'

'Your brother's been asleep all the way from Phalerum,' put in Brett. 'Some food, and I think the best place for him is bed again. There'll be plenty of time for talk later.'

'Yes.' Peter's laugh came oddly from that gaunt face. 'This tyrannical friend of yours, Phyl, has kept me on iron rations, and in bed, ever since we met. And don't think I'm not grateful,' he finished.

'And more iron rations, and bed, are what you're going to have now,' said Aunt Cassandra. 'How much, Brett?'

'I told Price. It should be ready directly. That sour milk the Greeks eat so much of is the best thing for the moment. Never mind–' Peter had made a face that reminded Phyllida almost unbearably of the boy he had been. 'We'll soon be dressing the fatted calf for you.'

'It's too good to be true,' said Phyllida. 'Oh, Brett, I do thank you.'

'It's been a pleasure.' Something extraordinarily daunting about the social phrase. If she had hoped that in the excitement of the reunion he had forgotten to be angry with her, this brought her back to reality with a start. And, worst of all, she was aware of Peter's speculative eye taking it all in.

'Food and bed,' he said. 'It sounds like heaven. It's what we dreamed of, up there on the Acropolis, with the vultures waiting overhead.'

'What a vulgar idea of heaven.' Jenny broke the moment of tension.

'Ah, but you see, Miss Renshaw, I'm an American.'

He ate his curdled milk with gusto, drank the one glass of watered wine that was all Brett would allow him, and agreed again that bed would be very pleasant. 'And if I were you,' Brett said to Phyllida afterwards, 'I would send for that American doctor friend of yours. Your brother's made a great effort today, but I'm not at all happy about him.'

'No.' Phyllida had seen the suddenly admitted exhaustion with which Peter collapsed on to the bed they had made ready for him. 'Brett–'

'Yes?' The monosyllable was forbidding.

'Just: thank you.' What else dared she say?

# 19

Dr. Howe took a comparatively cheerful view of Peter's condition, prescribing merely rest and cautious diet. 'It will take a bit of time, of course. I certainly wouldn't recommend moving him until he's a good deal stronger. Unless things get so bad here in Nauplia that there's no alternative.'

'You expect them to?' Brett asked.

'I wouldn't be surprised at anything. Something very queer seems to have happened up at the Palamede last night. As far as I can make out, old Kolokotronis tried to bribe Grivas' men to surrender the fortress to him, but was betrayed in his turn. He and his son have retreated ignominiously to Argos and are the laughing-stock of the town today. Personally, I think the Greek Government crazy to move back here to Nauplia, with things in such a state of confusion. Kolokotronis may be out of it, but I wouldn't be surprised if fighting broke out between Grivas and Fotomarra any moment.'

'As bad as that?' Brett drank coffee thoughtfully. 'I think I shall call my book *When Greek Meets Greek*. So far as I can see, it only takes two of them to make a civil war. But you really don't think we ought to move Peter Vannick?'

'It would be risky. All very fine if the weather holds, but you know how quickly a storm can blow up in these waters, and, frankly, I'd not much like to be on board that pretty little *Helena* of yours in one of the real Aegean tearers.'

'That's what my captain says. We've been incredibly lucky so far; we'd best not chance it. Besides, I'd much rather keep Peter under your eye so long as possible.'

Peter himself had made a gallant attempt, the first day, at getting up and behaving normally, but half an hour of it had been enough and he had given in gratefully when Cassandra bullied him back to bed. After that, he lay there peacefully while the three women took it in turns to read aloud to him out of their exiguous store of books. Brett had shut himself up in his study to write his chapters about Reshid Pasha and the disaster of Phalerum and only appeared at meals. Invariably courteous to Phyllida, he contrived never to be alone with her. Sometimes she thought she would have minded less if he had lost his temper.

Peter did not improve matters by asking fretfully over and over again when Alex was coming to see him. 'Not till you're a great deal stronger than this.' Jenny had arrived to take over from Phyllida by his bedside. 'Look at you! Working up a fever over that Alex, who is doubtless busy committing piracy for the greater glory of Greece. I don't suppose he even knows you're here.'

'No, very likely not.' He lay back obediently among the pillows she had plumped up for him. 'Read me some *Rob Roy* Jenny, you do the Scottish much better than Phyllida.'

And Phyllida, retiring to her own room, recognised as yet one more last straw the fact that he preferred Jenny's ministrations to her own. She sat for a while, wondering what he would say when she told him she had refused Alex, then shook herself and sent for Marcos to escort her down to the ramshackle dockside warehouse where Howe and his friends were still busy sorting American relief supplies.

Returning, much later, with hands blistered and filthy, she was at once aware of tension in the house. Price materialised between her and the door of the main saloon. 'Mr. Mavromikhalis is here, miss. He wants to see Mr. Peter. Mr. Brett thinks we ought to send for the doctor first, and get his permission. They're discussing it.'

'They certainly are!' Alex's voice rose in anger in the next room. She looked down at her dirty hands. 'Price, Dr. Howe is down at the warehouse. Send Marcos right away?' She pushed open the saloon door and found Alex pacing furiously up and down the room, shouting at Brett. 'There you are!' He turned on her. 'What's this I hear about you running round the town with a pack of young Americans who haven't even the guts to fight for us? And–look at you! A Greek lady would be ashamed to appear in such a state.'

'A Greek lady would probably not be allowed to appear at all,' said Phyllida. 'Besides, I fail to see what business it is of yours. Price said you wanted to see Peter, and I think I'm the one to explain to you just how quiet the doctor wants him kept. He's not to be worried about anything–yet.'

'And what do you mean by that?' His tone was dangerous, and Brett, who had risen and held a chair for Phyllida, gave her a quick glance, then left her to deal with it in her own way.

'That I have said nothing to him about you–about us.' She made herself clarify it. 'He's been asking for you a great deal. I think it possible he imagines that we are engaged to be married. If you are to be allowed to see him, I would want your promise not to discuss me.'

'If!' He was angrier than ever. 'Promises! To a woman! I don't much like your tone, *kyria*.' And then, getting hold of himself with an effort. 'I'm forgetting myself. Forgive me, Phyllida. It's all been too much. And now, to be kept from my brother's bedside, after all he has been through, by this–'

'Gentleman,' Phyllida interposed, before he could use a more contentious word. 'Who saved Peter's life. I think he has every right to protect my brother from the kind of scene you seem set on making.' She folded her dirty hands in her lap and noticed, for the first time, the fringe of dust edging her muslin skirts. 'Sit down, Alex. I've sent for Dr. Howe. He will decide whether Peter is well enough to see you. In the meantime, tell us what has been happening to you.'

'What's been happening!' He threw himself into a chair. 'Disaster! You've not heard?'

'Another disaster?' Brett's voice was a shade too cool.

'Yes. There's no Greek fleet any more. I'm ashamed to have lived through the day it happened, but what could I do? One man, among so many?'

'What did happen?'

'Lord Cochrane assembled the fleet at Poros, to replan his strategy in the light of the Army's defeat at Phalerum. And the Hydriot and Spetsiot captains demanded a month's pay in advance. Well, you can't blame them. What other security have they? Lord

Cochrane understands nothing. He would only offer a fortnight's money. There he was, flying his flag as Lord High Admiral of Greece. The sun was setting behind the mountains of Argolis; the shadow of the rock of Methana growing darker every moment. Darker than the water under the ships as they left him, one by one. Now he's alone. There is no Greek Navy.'

'What did you do?' asked Brett.

'I came here. To see my Brother Petros, to ensure his safety and that of this lady who has dealt so hardly by me. There is nothing more to be done for Greece; it is time to be thinking of one's friends. And you Franks would be much safer back at Zante. I am come to offer you the *Philip*'s escort there, as once before in happier times. That duty done, I shall retire to my castle in the Mani and hope that Ibrahim Pasha is fool enough to seek me out there.'

'Oh, Alex–' Phyllida was both touched and relieved. 'How good you are! It's true, we all long to be back at Zante, but the doctor says Peter's not strong enough to be moved.'

'No,' said Brett, 'and I, personally, don't take quite so dark a view of Greek affairs as you do, sir. I know the military situation looks black enough, but from all one hears it's only a question of time now until the Great Powers intervene with some kind of plan for a pacification.'

'Yes.' Savagely. 'Easy enough to make peace when every Greek worth the name has died either on the field of battle or from starvation.'

'Or fighting each other. As to the starvation, that's what Miss Vannick and her American friends have been working so gallantly to fend off. And here, unless I'm very much mistaken, comes Dr. Howe.'

Howe, too, was dusty from his morning's work, and apologised for it briefly. He saw no reason why Alex should not see Peter. 'You won't, of course, touch on any topic that might agitate him.'

'You ask a good deal,' said Alex gloomily. 'But I'll do my best.'

And Jenny, running downstairs from the sickroom,

settled the question by reporting that Peter had heard the bustle in the house, deduced Alex's arrival, and insisted on seeing him. 'He's getting rather excited.'

'In that case,' said Howe, 'I think you'd best visit him at once, Mr. Mavromikhalis, and do your best to calm him down.'

Alex succeeded to a marvel. Cassandra was sitting with Peter, and refused to leave, though as she said afterwards, she was not much the wiser, since what the two men said was, literally, Greek to her. 'But Alex really did cheer him up immensely,' she concluded. 'I don't know what he told him, but it did him a power of good.'

In fact, Peter's recovery seemed to date from that meeting, and Phyllida could not help blessing Alex for the good effect he had had, any more than she could help wondering what, in fact, he had said. But he had left at once, explaining that, since they did not need his escort yet, he felt in honour bound to take supplies to the gallant little garrison that was still holding out in the Acro-Corinth. 'But trust me.' He held Phyllida's hand for a long moment. 'Any new threat to Nauplia, and I will return on the instant. If it was dangerous last year for a Frankish ship—and so desirable a one as the *Helena*—to round Cape Matapan alone, this year it would be mere madness. I suppose you know that our miserable governors are issuing letters of marque to anyone who asks for them.'

'For a price,' said Brett. 'Yes, I had heard of it. Licences for piracy. But isn't one of those "ciphers" your cousin?'

'Yes, to my shame. I had thought better of him. He and his two companions are busy selling the good name of Greece for what they can get.'

'And, oddly enough, it may be the best thing they can do for the Greek cause,' said Brett. And then, in response to Phyllida's little gasp of astonishment, 'Don't you see? The Great Powers simply cannot afford to have this end of the Mediterranean degenerate into a nest of pirates. They're bound to do something. And, granted the immense public sympathy for the cause of Greek independence, I don't think they can possibly just restore the Turkish yoke. I've no doubt that they are busy, right now, trying to work out some kind of a compromise. But, in the meantime'—

to Alex—'if trouble really does break out here in Nauplia, we'll be most grateful for your escort round Cape Matapan.'

'You may rely on me.'

'So father cut me off without even a shilling?' Peter greeted Phyllida without a smile.

Alex must have told him. 'He didn't mean it to stand, of course. I told Mr. Biddock that as soon as you were safe, we'd arrange to share alike.'

'I knew I could count on you.'

'Yes.' Was it unreasonable to feel that a word or so of thanks would not have come amiss?

His next remark was still more disconcerting. 'And these vast sums you've been pouring out for the relief of Greek beggary,' he said. 'Are naturally your own affair.'

'But, Peter—You wrote and told me to send you your entire share—'

'That was to fight with. Not to cosset a lot of wretched babies who would probably be very much better dead. No, no, Phyl. Spend your own money on what mad philanthropy you please, but keep your hands off mine.'

His? But he was ill. She bit back the retort that had sprung to her lips, and he went straight on. 'I may need all my wealth if I'm to get Jenny. I don't suppose that stiff-necked brother of hers will let her go without a deuced amount of settlements and pin-money and so forth, and, if I don't miss my guess, a little something for Brother Brett as well.'

'Peter!' Now he had really shocked her. 'What in the world do you mean?'

'You hadn't even noticed! How like you, Phyl. You never did see the things that really concerned me. You haven't seen that I'm head over heels in love with that pretty little puss of an English girl! And what a wife she'll make! Absolutely of the top rank—my cousin the Duke, you know. Well, obviously you have to pay for that kind of thing, and you can tell Mister Brett that I'm quite prepared to do so.'

She was so horrified that it was hard to know where to begin. 'Mr. Renshaw and I are hardly on such terms–'

'Played your cards badly all round, haven't you? But never mind, Alex still carries the torch for you. God knows why. I told him he'd be hag-ridden as I used to be, but he just said, "nonsense". Well, it's his own business, and, of course, with things as they are now, he'll find the money handy. How much is there, by the way? Isn't it about time we sent to old Biddock for an accounting?'

'No need.' He had shocked her so much that the only thing to do seemed to be to treat the whole subject as the most ordinary one in the world. 'I have all the figures here. But we'll have to wait till we get to Zante to have the papers drawn up handing over your share. Biddock will have to do that.'

'And till then I'm to be dependent on you for every penny I spend! Just like the bad old days. You never knew, did you, how it irked me to have you dole out my pocket-money as if you were my mother.' He moved restlessly in bed. 'I wish that damned doctor of yours would let me get up and start getting my strength back. But in the meanwhile, what's this about you and Alex?'

'Just that I've refused him.' She must try not to let him excite himself further.

'But that's not the whole story, and you might as well admit it. You didn't refuse him the first time, did you? Got cold feet, I suppose, now the Greeks are losing.' It was what Alex had said, which did not make it any pleasanter hearing. 'Did he tell you I'd given my permission?'

'Yes.' Odd to remember that she had actually found this comic.

'I suppose that goes for nothing with you? I'm just the little brother you used to bully–oh, quite for his own good, of course. Harvard, and the law, when you knew perfectly well all I wanted was a chance to try my luck against those damned turncoat Canadians. Well, times have changed now, Phyl, and the sooner you realise it, the better. I'm the head of the family, and what I say, goes. That crazy will of the old man's would never stand for a moment if I were to fight it. Undue influence . . . Obviously his mind was going or he'd never have dreamed of bringing a couple of women here in times like these. Frankly, I thought him a little touched in the head the last time he was home, and I've friends who'd say so too. But no need to look so qualmish. I'm a fair-minded man. Fifty-fifty should do us both well enough . . . Of course, I ought to have the larger share, but there's Alex to be considered. The best friend a man could have.'

'But I've told you, Peter.' Here at least was a bit of solid ground. 'I've refused Alex.'

'Want to be an old maid, do you? Like dear Aunt Cass?'

She shivered a little at the spite in his tone. 'I can imagine worse fates.'

'Such as marriage to a real man like Alex, who'll expect a real wife? Scared of it, aren't you? Scared of anything real? A proper New England miss you turned out to be. Frankly, I can't think why Alex wants you, but he does, and, I tell you, Phyl, if you don't take him, I'll break that will, and you can starve, or turn governess for all I care. You'd make a good governess,' he concluded brutally.

'Who'd make a good governess?' Jenny pushed open the door, her arms full of flowers. 'Look what Marcos brought me! I thought they'd cheer up the sickroom a bit.'

'*You* cheer up the sickroom, Jenny.' His tone changed completely at sight of her. 'I was beginning to think you'd never come. And so, I'm sure, was Phyllida, who longs to be off counting okas of flour with those American friends of hers.'

'And a very good work, too,' said Jenny. 'I think you must be better. I've always found that bad temper is a great sign of convalescence. And just look at the state you've got your pillows into. Anyone would think you and Phyl had been having a fight!'

And so we have, thought Phyllida, retreating wearily to her own room. She could not even bring herself to go down to the warehouse, though she knew she would be missed, but sat, all afternoon, wondering wretchedly where she had gone wrong with Peter. And what should she do about it now? She longed to ask advice, but whose?

The roar of an explosion brought her out of her reverie with a start. She hurried downstairs and found the rest of the family already gathering. 'What is it?' 'Did you hear it?'

'Gunfire,' Brett had emerged from his study. 'It sounds to me as if the Palamede has opened up on the Itchkali.'

'And what happens to us?' asked Jenny.

'We leave, I think. Stay here, all of you; keep calm. There's no reason why a ball should fall here. Marcos and I will find out what's happening and make arrangements to board the *Helena*, if necessary. I just hope Peter's well enough.'

'Of course I'm well enough.' Peter himself appeared at the head of the stairs. 'So we're to run away are we?'

'Well,' said Brett reasonably, 'what would you suggest?'

'You'll be careful, B.?' Jenny said what Phyllida had longed to.

'I'm always careful, kitten. You should know that by now.'

'Yes, indeed.'

Something in Peter's tone made Jenny turn on him. 'He's been pretty careful of you, when you come to think of it, Mr. Vannick.'

'Yes. Forgive me, Jenny. I'm not myself.' A convincing stagger brought her hurrying to his side to help him back to bed.

'I hope we don't have to move him.' She rejoined Phyllida downstairs. 'He's not a bit well really. I'm sure that's what makes him so short-tempered, poor thing. I expect it was just one gun, don't you? An accident or something?' But her hopeful words were drowned by a new burst of gunfire. 'That's from the other direction!'

'Yes,' said Phyllida. 'From the Itchkali.'

Brett returned with more bad news. 'The town's in a panic, and the gates are shut. For the moment, no one's allowed out or in. Oh, I expect we could bribe our way through if the worst came to the worst, but the streets are in such a state I really think that for the moment we'd do better to stay here and take our chance of a stray ball. Under the cliff as we are, I think we should be safe enough.'

'And to think I used to complain of the overhang!' said Jenny. 'You don't think a ball might bring it down on us, Brett?'

'I hope not. They're wild shots, God knows, but not, I hope, so bad as that. It's what we thought. Trouble between Fotomarra and Grivas.'

'What are the government doing?' asked Phyllida.

'They're mixed up in it. It all started with trouble among the three regents. I wish to God Capodistrias would get here.'

'I'm not sure I wouldn't rather see Captain Hamilton and the *Cambrian*,' said Phyllida.

'You may well be right. Or Codrington himself, the admiral. I've never met him, but from what I've heard, he's not one to stand much nonsense. Oh—that reminds me of one good thing: Dr. Howe must have had early information of the trouble. The American relief ship that arrived yesterday, the *Six Brothers*, slipped anchor and sailed in the night. I imagine Howe didn't intend the government to take their tithe of her supplies, as they did with the *Tontine*.'

'Yes,' said Phyllida. 'It made him furious, and no wonder. I hope he's all right today. Did you see him, Brett? Should we ask him to stay here? It's much safer than those lodgings of his in the centre of the town.'

'That's what I was coming to,' said Brett. 'He sailed with the *Six Brothers*.'

'Oh! So—no doctor?'

'What a good thing Peter's so much better,' said Jenny cheerfully.

# 20

The intermittent gunfire between the two forts continued, the town gates remained shut, and food prices soared. Several houses were destroyed, and a ball from the Palamede hit the converted mosque where the government met, and wounded three senators. This had much more effect than a hundred civilian deaths and they promptly packed up and moved to the Burj, a fortified island in the bay out of range of the firing.

In the house under the cliff, things went on with an odd appearance of calm. Price, characteristically, turned out to have been building up a reserve of supplies, so that though their diet was dull it was perfectly adequate.

'I still think we're safer here.' Brett and Marcos, the only two who now left the house, had just returned from a walk to the central square. 'I don't a bit like the look of the soldiers at the town gate.' Nor did he much relish the idea of escorting the three women through the crowded and panicky streets, where looting and disorder of every kind were already rife.

'Besides,' said Jenny, 'Alex said he'd come for us if he heard of trouble in Nauplia. We really need his escort round Matapan, don't we, Brett?'

'Yes, I think we do. Unless of course the *Cambrian* or one of the other Allied ships is going that way.'

'Which seems extremely unlikely.' Peter joined them fully dressed. 'It would be madness not to wait for Alex. We can count on him.'

'In so far as we can count on anything,' said Brett. 'But at least, thank God, the *Helena*'s still there in the harbour, safe and sound.'

'Does that surprise you?' Peter's tone was belligerent. 'You don't seriously think she's likely to be attacked right here in the Bay of Nauplia, under the nose of the government?'

'Frankly, nothing would surprise me by now.'

'You don't understand the Greeks.'

'I'm not sure I want to.'

'I don't like to think what that book of yours is going to be like!'

'It's going to be a tearing success!' Jenny intervened, as so often when things began to go wrong between the two men. 'I hope you're making the most of this episode, B. What's the title to be now? *Between Two Fires*?'

'It's not a bad one,' said Brett. 'I suppose all we need now is an attack by Ibrahim Pasha to make it three.'

'Yes indeed!' Peter actually seemed to welcome the idea. 'If Ibrahim would only attack, the Greeks would unite at once.'

'Rather a drastic way of achieving it, surely?'

As so often, Peter took no notice of Phyllida's comment. Later, alone with Jenny, she made herself raise what she felt to be a difficult subject. 'I *am* grateful to you for smoothing things down between your brother and mine. Sometimes I almost wish poor Peter was still confined to his room.'

'Prickly, isn't he?' said Jenny cheerfully. 'I expect being defeated, and surrendering, and all that, was a perfectly horrid experience. He'll get over it.'

'I hope so.' It was on the tip of her tongue to warn Jenny of his intentions towards her, but what right had she to do so?

'Just the same,' Jenny went on, 'I can't say I'll be sorry to get away from here. Though mind you it's going to be no picnic on the *Helena.* Have you thought what a crowd we're going to be?'

'I have indeed! I'd even wondered whether Peter mightn't consider sailing on the *Philip*–if Alex really comes.' Odd to find herself actually wishing he would. 'Lord! That was a near one!' Most of the time they pretended not to notice the sporadic outbursts of gunfire, but this shot had been very much too close for comfort.

'Yes! Look at the dust. Poor Price, he'll be quite in despair. I do hope they mend their aim before they fire again. Do you think we ought to go and see if anyone's been hurt next door?'

But Brett refused to allow this. He and Marcos went and returned to report that the ball had merely set fire to an empty house.

'Merely!' said Jenny.

'Well, kitten, you know what I mean.'

'I do indeed. It's remarkable, isn't it, how one can get used to anything. Was it like this in the Acropolis, Peter? Did you get so you hardly noticed?'

'Good God! You don't delude yourself that this is anything like what we endured on the Acropolis! Compared to what we went through, this is merely playing at war.'

'It's playing quite hard enough for me. I can see I'm

not the stuff heroines are made of. Right now, I'd give my eye-teeth for a quiet country walk and a picnic of fruit at the end of it.'

'Just to get out!' said Phyllida. 'Are you sure we couldn't be out helping with the wounded, Brett?'

'Quite sure.'

'Idiotic!' said Peter. 'If you didn't faint at the blood, you would at the remedies the Greeks use.'

'I might,' said Jenny. 'But Phyllida wouldn't. She's game for anything.'

'Most unsuitable,' said Peter.

Jenny rounded on him. 'Really, there's no satisfying you today! I shall go and help Aunt Cass with the mending!' She flounced out of the room, closely followed by Brett.

'Promising!' Peter moved closer to Phyllida, who had been busy all this time with some copying for Brett's book. 'It's always a good sign when they begin to lose their temper with one. I wish I could decide whether to declare myself before or after you make over my estate to me. She's such a romantic little idiot, she might prefer to accept me for my *beaux yeux* alone, don't you think? Specially as, from what I can gather, she's got nothing herself except some shabby old family jewellery. Lucky I'll have enough for two! But what do you think, Phyl? Shall I throw myself at her feet in all my interesting convalescence, or wait till Zante?'

She looked up at him, troubled. 'Do you care about her at all, Peter?'

'Care? Of course I care! It's a chance in a thousand! You don't understand anything, do you? It's connection that counts in the world, and that's what she's got. Look at the way that brother of hers sails about the Mediterranean as if it belonged to him. I count on you to turn him up sweet about this, by the way. I wouldn't be surprised if he took against the idea at first, but you and my Jenny will bring him about between you.'

His Jenny? 'Aren't you taking things a bit for granted?'

'I might have known you'd take that line! Trust you to put a spoke in my wheel if you can! I warn you, Phyl, if you try and turn Jenny against me, you'll regret it to your dying day.'

'But, Peter!' No use. He had slammed out of the room. She sighed, picked up her pen and went on with her copying.

At least Brett still let her do this for him. Jenny and Cassandra might help with his first drafts, but the final version of the book would all be in her beautiful copperplate hand. Writing away, she could not shake off her anxiety about Peter. What ought she to do? Speak to Jenny? Speak to Brett? But how could she speak to Brett, when he contrived never to be alone with her? Besides, everything she did went wrong. Best let things alone? And blame herself for ever if Jenny should accept Peter, and be wretched? She was so young . . .

A tear fell, blotting the page. As if they were not short enough of paper already. She jumped furiously to her feet, and was aware, as she did so, of angry voices in the courtyard. Brett and Peter. Now what?

It must have blown up very suddenly. 'I'm going, I tell you!' Peter was still incredibly gaunt, and weak to match, and they had so far managed to persuade him not to leave the house. 'I'll be able to get more sense out of them in five minutes than you and Marcos can in days of pleading. I've fought for them, remember. I'm one of them.'

'Yes,' said Brett reasonably. 'Just so long as you don't happen to be on the wrong side. Have you considered that? There's a good deal of feeling in town about the surrender of the Acropolis. No, don't flare up at me! I know as well as you do that it was no decision of yours, but what's reason to an angry Greek? Besides, if you could persuade them to let us out, as, perhaps, you could, we'd merely have to wait on board the *Helena* till Alex arrives. If we're crowded and cross here, what will it be like there, do you think?'

His reasonable tone was wasted on Peter. 'You think I'm suffering with my "nerves", do you? Don't you realise how near that last ball came? Death's nothing to me. I've faced it a thousand times. I'm thinking of your sister. How will you feel when you see her lying dead—or, worse still, raped at your feet?'

'Surprised,' said Brett equably. 'Look, Mr. Vannick, I'm not a fool. I've thought, over and over again, of the risks to which my sister—and yours, too, and her aunt are exposed. I'm responsible for them, and I shall do my best to see them safe out of this danger, into which, by the way, they would never have run but for you. You've been a soldier; you must have seen the dangers of a divided command. I'm in command here, and I intend to remain so. And I've made up my mind. We will all remain here, together, to await Alex's arrival.'

Phyllida, listening unashamedly from the concealing darkness of the saloon, had a moment of terror, afraid it would come to blows. But—had Peter remembered that this was Jenny's brother?—his answer, when it came at last, was surprisingly meek. 'I'm sorry. It's this inaction. It's my anxiety for her, for your sister, for Jenny!'

'Believe me,' said Brett, 'I am anxious for her too. And for Phyllida and her aunt,' he added and brought uncontrollable tears to Phyllida's eyes.

'What's the matter, love?' Jenny joined her. 'Been listening, too? That was a turn-up for the books, wasn't it? Or for the book!' Wickedly. 'I wonder if we could persuade Brett to write it in. He put that suitor of mine nicely in his place, didn't he?'

'Suitor?'

'I'm not quite a fool. What I don't rightly understand is why he wants me. Not for love, I'm sure, nor yet for my riches, since I've none.'

'He says connection is the most important thing in the world.' There, it was out, and she was glad.

'So that's it. I did wonder. Thank you, Phyl; that will help. And now, dry your eyes for goodness' sake. They're coming in, and, remember, we've not heard a word of it. One good thing: there's less chance of the two of them coming actually to blows if Peter's after me. He's a cold-blooded one, that brother of yours.'

It was cool comfort to Phyllida. She wished now that she had thought up some pretext to make Peter defer his offer for Jenny till they reached Zante. What would happen if he should propose now, and be refused? She did not much like to think of it, and nor, apparently, did Jenny. The two of them found themselves in tacit conspiracy to avoid any dangerous tête-à-tête. It was easy enough, in that crowded house, but Phyllida had an uncomfortable feeling that Peter was beginning to recognise and resent their tactics.

She would not have imagined it possible to be so pleased when Alex walked into the house a few days later: 'Alex! At last.' And then afraid that he might interpret this in a more personal sense than it was meant: 'We've been waiting for you. Have you really come to escort us round to Zante?'

'Did I not promise I would? I'm only sorry I could not get here sooner, but there are so few of us, now the Hydriots and Spetsiots have deserted the cause. What remains of it.' Bitterly.

'Are things very bad?' Brett asked it when the first flurry of greetings was over. 'It's been impossible to get news of any kind, shut up here in Nauplia.'

'But you're none the worse I'm glad to see.' Alex had made a rapid circle of the room. 'As for the news, it's good and bad mixed, as usual. On the surface, things could hardly be blacker. Reshid Pasha carries all before him in Attica, and Ibrahim is burning and harrying here in the Morea. And as for Capodistrias, our fine new President, so far as I know he's got no further than Paris. But there is some good news, just the same. The Great Powers have come to our help at last. Great Britain, France and Russia have signed a treaty at London, calling for an immediate truce between Turkey and Greece and instructing their navies to see that it is observed. I understand that a messenger was sent at once to Egypt to prevent the new fleet we're threatened with from sailing from there.'

'Did he get there in time?' asked Brett.

'I don't know. But you can see what a difference this makes to everything. Our good friends like Hamilton will be able to help us now, instead of standing by to watch us bleed. It's the beginning of the end for Turkey.'

'And you want us to turn tail and go off to Zante!' Peter thrust his way into the conversation. 'I thank you, no!'

'I'm afraid we must, Peter.' Brett's tone was patient. 'Now that Alex is here to escort us. I know exactly how you feel, but you must see that we wouldn't be justified in exposing the ladies to the danger here a moment longer than we must.' The whine of a cannon ball, passing high overhead, added point to his words.

'He's right, *koumbaros,*' said Alex. 'Not even the news of the Treaty of London has brought these madmen here to their senses. Codrington has tried; Fabvier has tried; they'll listen to no one. Only God knows how long the fighting here will continue. And the town's in a bad state. It's not only stray cannon balls that the ladies have to fear. If you'll be advised by me, you'll make your preparations today and leave at first light tomorrow. Sooner, if possible.'

'Tonight?' said Phyllida eagerly. 'We've had everything ready since the trouble started, and I'm afraid I'm coward enough not to want to waste a minute. How stupid it would be to be killed now, when you're here to save us, Alex.'

'I'm glad to know you were so confident of me, *kyria.*'

'Well, I shan't come,' said Peter.

'That's entirely your own affair.' Brett rang the hand-bell for Price. 'If you can really take us, Alex, we'll sail tonight. Barlow has standing orders to get steam up the minute he sees the *Philip.* Thank God we've coal enough for the trip. We won't hold you back as we did last time.'

'Ah, but what a pleasure it was!'

Alex's glowing look for Phyllida warned her that he had indeed taken everything she had said in the wrong spirit. It would be all to do over again. Oh, why had she been such a fool in the first place? She sighed, and turned to Peter: 'You can't mean to abandon us now?'

'You surely don't imagine I'll abandon Greece?'

'But, *Petros mou,*' Alex intervened. 'Think a little. It's only to go so far as Zante. And, to tell truth, I'm short-handed on the *Philip.* I'd counted on you to sail with me and lend a hand as you have so often done before. Besides–' He took Peter's arm and led him away from the others out into the courtyard, throwing a reassuring glance back to Phyllida as they went.

Brett was busy giving his orders to Price, who received them with his usual calm. 'Packed and ready by this evening? Very good, sir, and glad to be going. But what about rations for the trip? We're pretty short by now, and I don't reckon they'll be much better off on the *Helena.*'

'I've been thinking about that.' Brett turned to Phyllida. 'Your friend Dr. Howe's back in town. Do you think he could be prevailed upon to let us have sufficient for the trip? For a good price, of course. He must still have some provisions left from that last American relief ship. I dislike to have to ask it, but you, at least, have certainly earned his help by all the work you've done for him, here in Nauplia.'

'I don't know–' Phyllida, too, hated the idea of putting such a request to Dr. Howe. His stories of the peasants of the Morea, living on herbs, and snails and more unmentionable food in frail wigwams made of poles and leaves had impressed her deeply. How could they take even a little food out of those starving mouths?

She was relieved when Alex, returning with Peter, picked up the subject and disposed of it in his usual definite way. 'Food? You've enough for a few days? Then we'll round Cape Matapan and stop at Kitries for what we need. I promise you, my people will never let friends of mine go hungry.'

It was nearly a month since the three women had left the house, and they were appalled at the change in the town. Most houses showed traces of gunfire, or looting, or both. Many of them were entirely destroyed, their wretched inhabitants camping among the ruins in huts made of poles and blankets. And over all hung a vague, indefinable odour–the smell of death.

'Dear God,' said Phyllida. 'I had no idea.' The three women were hurrying along, surrounded by the men of the party.

'No,' said Jenny. 'I'm just as glad I didn't. Lucky for us our house was under the cliff. But these poor Greeks; to think they've done this to themselves.'

'Yes. One of the few towns that didn't get destroyed in the fight against the Turks. It's heartbreaking. Oh, look! There's Dr. Howe!'

The young American was surrounded by a clamorous crowd of half-starved, ragged Greeks, but detached himself for a moment to join their little party. 'You're getting out? I'm glad. I'd been meaning to come and see you–but you can see how it is. Things are worse here than anywhere, I think.' He walked along with them, explaining that he had been delivering relief supplies to the islands and down along the coast of the Morea. 'But it's bad everywhere. How are you off for food?'

When he learned that they only had supplies for three days, he insisted on adding to them. 'Suppose you're becalmed? It's not safe to start with so little. At least the poor wretches on land can eke out their rations with snails and shellfish, prickly pear and what herbs they can still find.' He scribbled an order for flour. 'It's all I've left, I'm afraid.' And parted from them at the town gate. The soldiers on duty began by demanding immense sums to let them through, but Alex dealt with them rapidly. 'The name Mavromikhalis still has its magic,' said Brett.

'Even here,' agreed Alex. 'But just wait till you get to Kitries.'

'Shall we need to stop there now?'

'It depends on the wind. You may be independent of it, in your splendid *Helena*, but this time I'm afraid you will have to set your pace by mine. I don't intend to part from you till I have seen you safe in the harbour at Zante. And I don't know about your sailors, but I know mine won't work without their food–and their wine. I think we'd best resign ourselves to a stop at Kitries.'

# 21

'It's the most beautiful country I've ever seen.' Phyllida leaned her arms on the *Helena*'s rail and gazed back at the turrets of the Palamede outlined against the violent evening sky, with one cypress tree rising above them like a banner.

'And how glad I am to be leaving it.' Jenny laughed. 'I never thought I'd live to be so grateful to Alex. And don't you just hope he's making Peter do some work for a change?'

'Yes.' Phyllida, too, had been shocked at the way Peter had left all the work of the embarkation to Brett. Surely, by now, he was well enough at least to try and help? 'It will do him good to be with Alex,' she said hopefully.

'It might at that. He certainly seems to pay attention to him. Did you wonder how Alex persuaded him to come along with us? I know I did.'

'A little. But, surely, for your sake?'

'You think I'm still to expect a proposal in form? Oh well, not till Zante now, thank goodness.'

She was wrong. They had arranged to lie to at night for fear of losing each other, and as soon as the two ships were lying quietly as close together as was safe, Peter had himself rowed across to the *Helena* with an invitation. Alex wanted them all to dine with him on the *Philip* next night.

Brett was doubtful. Phyllida and Jenny exchanged speaking glances. Peter, predictably, blew up. 'You do understand, I suppose, what a sacrifice Alex is making for you? He'll never tell you himself, he's too proud; but it was almost at the expense of honour that he withdrew, at this crisis, from the depleted Greek Navy.'

'Yes. I'd thought of that. I suppose it would seem ungracious.' Brett still sounded doubtful.

'Ungracious! It would be barbarous! Besides, there's something else. Might I ask for a word with you alone, sir?'

'Alone?' Brett raised an eyebrow. 'It will have to be on deck then.' He turned to lead the way.

Jenny's eyes met Phyllida's. 'Oh dear,' she said.

Brett returned by himself ten minutes later. 'I've told him we'll go tomorrow night. If it's calm. I think it's the least we can do, in the circumstances. Besides—' He met one enquiring glance after another. 'No use beating about the bush, I suppose. I didn't know you'd made a conquest of him, Jenny. He has asked my permission to make you an offer.'

'Oh dear,' said Jenny again.

'Thank goodness!' Brett did not try to hide his relief. 'Just the same, I think you must give him his answer, kitten, and the sooner it's over with, the better. So—I said we'd go. No doubt he and Alex will arrange an opportunity between them. No use letting him hope a moment longer than necessary. Well'—he was glad to have it over—'that's settled then. We three will go.' Aunt Cassandra's refusal had been a foregone conclusion. 'And now, if you'll excuse me, I think I'll say good night. I promised Barlow I'd take the first watch on deck. He's had a hard day of it, and Brown too, and we're a bit nearer Nauplia still than I altogether like.'

'Brett!' Phyllida flung her scruples to the winds and followed him up the companionway. 'I don't like it.'

The moon had risen, turning the still water round the ship to liquid lead, and casting strange shadows of paddle wheel and mast across the deck. In its light, the lantern, up forward where Barlow was on watch, looked pitiful, a flickering pretence at illumination.

'Don't like what?' Brett turned, impatiently, to face her in the shadow of the hatchway. Incredible how long it was since they had been alone together.

'This dinner . . . this proposal of Peter's . . . Any of it. Can't we make an excuse, beg off, wait till Zante?'

'Why?' He wanted this over as fast as possible.

'I don't know. I'm–frightened. It's absurd, I know. But I am, just the same.'

'It *is* absurd. You ought to know Jenny well enough by now to be sure that that brother of yours is never going to talk her round. She's got a lot of sense, my Jenny.'

'Of course she has.' Angrily. Must he remind her how she had let Alex 'talk her round'? 'That's not what I meant at all. It's–' She hated to say it. 'It's Peter I'm afraid of. What he'll do if she refuses him.'

'*When* she refuses him,' he corrected her. 'He's been taking things for granted a bit, hasn't he? I can't say I altogether liked his tone when he asked my permission. A sharp set-down is what he needs, and that's what he's going to get from Jenny. About time too. Frankly, I was never more glad of anything than when Alex invited him on board the *Philip*.'

'I'm sorry we've been such a burden on you.'

'Nothing of the kind. I'm delighted to have you and your aunt, and you know it. It's made all the difference to poor Jenny. God knows what I shall do about her when we part at Zante.'

'I'm sure you'll manage admirably.' She spoke more sharply than she meant in an effort to conceal her dismay at the idea of that parting. 'You Renshaws always fall on your feet.'

'Always? I wonder. But, thank God, Jenny at least seems

to know her own mind. And now, if you'll excuse me. I ought not to keep poor Barlow from his bed any longer.'

'But, Brett–' How could she put it? 'I really am frightened. Of what Peter might do.' As he turned to move away, she came after him, out from the shadow of the hatchway into full moonlight, the pale oval of her face turned up towards him, pleadingly.

He was quite mad. More than anything in the world he wanted to take her in his arms, to comfort her, to promise–All kinds of absurdities. Only the other day she had engaged herself to Alex. Women were all the same. Helena . . . Phyllida . . . Not Jenny, thank God. 'Nonsense!' The word, the angry tone were as much for himself as for her, but she drew back as if he had struck her. 'It's not like you to let your nerves run away with you,' he went on more gently. 'But we're all tired out. Sleep on it. You'll see, in the morning, that you've been making much ado about nothing. Jenny will give your brother his dismissal, and the air will be the clearer for it. After that, we'll keep as much to ourselves as you like. I know it's awkward for you to meet Alex–'

'It's not that.' Furiously. And then, giving up, and turning away into the shadows, 'I'm sorry. I won't keep you any longer. Good night.' She got away from him before the tears submerged her, and waited, trying to swallow them, on the companionway.

Returning at last to the saloon, she found Jenny alone. 'Aunt Cass has gone to bed. What's the matter, love? Been quarrelling with poor old B.?'

'Not precisely. He doesn't think I'm worth quarrelling with. I was trying to persuade him we ought not to go tomorrow. He won't listen. He thinks I'm "letting my nerves run away with me".' She quoted it angrily. 'But, Jenny, I'm worried. If we must go; if Peter does propose to you–and I suppose he's bound to–don't you think you could hold out some kind of hope . . . just till Zante . . . say you need more time . . .' She dwindled into silence.

'No, love, I can't.' Jenny had never sounded more like her brother. 'And it's not like you to suggest it. After all, Peter can't eat me. If you ask me, he's been riding for a fall, and, frankly, I find I quite look forward to giving it him.'

'Oh, Jenny–' This was worse and worse.

'You really are overwrought, Phyl.' Jenny might have been ten years the senior. 'Wait a moment, while I find you my sal volatile.'

'I don't want sal volatile! Jenny, listen to me!'

'In the morning, love. It's late, and we're all exhausted. We'll be keeping poor Aunt Cass awake. Sleep on it.' She echoed her brother. 'I promise you, it will all seem mere moonshine in the morning.'

Phyllida sighed, and yielded, and let herself be fussed over and dosed with detestable sal volatile and finally sent to bed like an hysterical child. They were so confident, those Renshaws. Once they had an idea in their heads, there was no shaking them.

Jenny might send her to bed, but she could not make her sleep. She lay for what seemed hours, watching a narrow streak of moonlight creep across the wall of the cabin, listening to Cassandra's steady breathing and wondering how in the world she could prevent tomorrow's party.

She could not. Next day was August at its best, a golden calm over sea and land, sunshine turning the sea to saffron and the mountains of the mainland to a celestial vision from the illustrated *Pilgrim's Progress* she had read to Peter as a child. Sitting on deck, hands listlessly in her lap, she let the golden prospect soothe her. Of course Brett and Jenny were right. Peter was her brother. She had known and loved him all her life. It was absurd, it was wicked nonsense to be afraid of what he might do when Jenny refused him.

In the dead calm, the *Philip*'s sails hung lifeless from her masts, and they made no headway at all until a light breeze sprang up towards evening. Phyllida's hopes rose with the wind. They could not possibly make the difficult transit to the *Philip* if it held. But it was no use, as the sun set it fell again and the sea lay still as molten glass. 'As silent as a painted ship Upon a painted ocean–' she remembered the lines from that strange poem by Mr. Coleridge and felt a little, superstitious shiver run through her as she remembered the fate of that ship's crew.

'Time to go down and tidy ourselves.' Jenny's cheerful voice roused her from her abstraction. 'I rather like the idea of going out to dinner in trousers.' She looked with amusement at the Turkish tunics and trousers they were both wearing.

'Jenny?'

'Yes?'

'You'll be gentle with him?'

'If he is with me.'

The *Philip*'s main cabin might be cramped, but there was, apparently, no shortage of food on board. Caviare and champagne were followed by chicken and the mildly retsinated wine they had all got used to drinking, and then by fresh fruit, something that had been unobtainable in Nauplia. Best of all, Alex was simply the charming host—and how well he could do it. Sitting between them he divided his attentions equally between Phyllida and Jenny, and Phyllida thought with relief that he really had forgiven, or better still, forgotten the way she had treated him. By the time they were drinking delicious coffee, she was beginning to feel that, so long as nothing went too wrong between Jenny and Peter, she would be glad they had come. It was good, and more than she deserved, to be back on the old easy terms with Alex. And Peter looked wonderfully better for his day at sea, and was cheerfully letting Alex tease him about having degenerated into a lazy, good-for-nothing landsman.

'But we'll turn you back into a sailor yet.' Alex turned to Phyllida. 'I've even got him obeying the captain's orders. No mutiny on my ship. I'll show you. *Petros mou,* don't you think the wind's come round a point?'

Peter was on his feet at once. 'I'll make sure,' he said. 'If it's getting up, I'm afraid we must speed you back to the *Helena*, however regretfully.' He looked down at Jenny. 'Would you fancy a breath of air, Miss Renshaw?'

Jenny coloured, drank coffee, caught first Phyllida's anxious eye and then Brett's, and rose to her feet. 'Why, yes, I believe I would, Mr. Vannick.'

'Delicious coffee, Alex." 'Phyllida spoke into the little silence left by their going.

'A delicious dinner altogether.' Something faintly puzzling in Brett's tone. But then, she was all on edge tonight, and doubtless imagining things.

'Thank you,' said Alex. 'I will say for the islanders, they see to it that we ship's captains lack for nothing.'

On deck, Peter led Jenny to the farthest point from the lookout. 'Not that he understands a word of English. Jenny!'

'Yes?' She felt extraordinarily alone with him, up here where moonlight silvered the sea and played strange tricks with the mountains beyond. Surely she was not frightened? She, Jenny Renshaw?

'It's good of you to see me.' He began reassuringly enough. 'I gave up in despair, back there in Nauplia. Talk about a houseful of women! Cassandra bobbing about with that everlasting mending of hers, and Phyllida scribble, scribble, scribble in the saloon all day. I thought I'd go mad.'

'Was that why you were so short-tempered?' She found she was not frightened after all.

'Did I seem so? Forgive me. I'm not a patient man, I suppose. But then, no more is your brother. You must be used to it; know how to manage. Well, I've watched you; seen you soothe us down, the two of us. Mind you, if you'd not been his sister, I'd have killed him, long since, for some of the things he's said about the Greeks.'

'Oh? Should I thank you for that?' And then, incorrigibly, 'It had not occurred to you, Mr. Vannick, that he might have killed you?'

'Jenny!' He took both her hands. Here it came. 'Don't trifle with me. We've so little time. Your brother's told you what I want. As if he needed to! Your own intuition must have told you long since that I adore you, worship you, want nothing in the world but you.' He pulled her towards him. 'Say, "yes", Jenny, and make me the happiest of men.'

'No.' The bleak monosyllable surprised him so much that he let her go. 'I'm sorry, Peter.' Be gentle with him, Phyllida had begged. 'I truly am; but I can't marry you.'

'Why not?' He was making himself speak reasonably, but she could feel the effort it took. 'Jenny, have I gone too fast for you? I know there's not been much scope for a wooing, but surely you must have seen how I've borne with your brother for your sake. Or is it my prospects that worry you? I suppose I should have spoken to your brother about them, but you must know that when we reach Zante I'll come into my own. What do you want, Jen? A castle in

England? Or in Spain if you'd rather! I rather fancy England myself. I thought, once we're married, I'd approach my government for a diplomatic posting. My experience here will be invaluable of course, but I think the Greek cause itself's a dead duck.' He laughed. 'Don't tell Alex I said so! Let's be married in Zante, Jen, and then the world's our oyster.'

'Don't call me Jen!'

'Your brother does.'

'He's my brother!'

'And mine, too, I hope, when we get to Zante. Be a little realistic, Jenny.' His use of her full name was a concession. 'Your goods aren't for every market. Penniless, cast off by your family, drifting around the Mediterranean with a brother everyone knows is no better than he should be.'

'And what, pray, do you mean by that?'

'What do I mean? My dear girl, you must know! Of course, we've all put as good a face upon it as possible, but he's not at all the thing, that brother of yours. Jilting his fiancée in church, and then indulging in drunken orgies all over the Mediterranean! You hadn't heard, I suppose, about the scene he made at Zante before you arrived? Oh, shameful . . . But I'll spare you the details. Don't you see, that's why we must be married as soon as we get there. Then you, as a married woman, will be able to cast some slight veil of respectability over poor Phyl. Perhaps, by the time we get her back to England the worst of the gossip will have died down.'

Now she was too angry for thought. 'You're speaking of Phyllida, on whose charity you mean to live for the rest of your days.'

'Oh!' This was a new light to him. 'That's your trouble, is it? You want to be sure of the cash before you give your word. I always knew you British were a hard-headed people. Never mind, I respect you for it. It's all right, Jen, I have her promise. The half of the estate, absolutely, as soon as we reach Zante. But, don't you see, so much prettier to announce the engagement now, when I'm still penniless?'

'There's nothing pretty about this conversation. Mr. Vannick, do I have to spell it out for you? I wouldn't marry you, sir, if you were the last man on earth.'

'Strong words!' She had expected him to be angry, and was relieved that he took it so calmly. 'I've annoyed you, of course, by what I've said about your brother. I'm sorry. But you've had your revenge now. Next time I speak to you, I'm sure we'll come to a better understanding.'

'But there's not going to be a next time, Mr. Vannick.'

'I wish you'd call me Peter. Am I really in such disgrace?'

'Of course not.' She was at once surprised, and grateful to him for taking it so well. 'We're to continue friends, Peter, are we not?'

'More than that, I hope.'

'Oh, please!' She had promised Phyllida to try not to make him angry. 'Don't you see? I can't . . . There's someone else.'

'Someone else?' Now she really had surprised him.

'Yes. In England. Nobody knows but you.'

'And he, no doubt?'

'No!' It was almost a sob. 'That's just it, don't you understand? I'm paying you an immense compliment, Peter, in telling you this. It's hopeless. It's all over. Or rather, it never began.'

'In that case, you can hardly blame me if I refuse to give up hope.'

'Oh,' she flared up. 'You're impossible!' And hurried down to join the others. To her relief, Peter did not follow her, and Brett took her appearance as the signal to leave.

When they got up on deck, Peter was nowhere to be seen, and as Alex apologised for his absence, Phyllida had a curious feeling that he was pleased about what had so obviously happened. But why in the world?

'Well, that's over,' said Jenny, when they were well out of earshot of the *Philip*. 'I think!'

'And well over, I hope,' said Phyllida. 'You didn't make him angry, Jenny?'

'He made *me* angry, I'm afraid.' She would not tell Phyllida how deplorably he seemed to take her generosity for granted. 'He's one who won't take no for an answer. But he'll get over it, never fear. He doesn't care a straw for me, and you know it.'

'I don't think he cares for anyone but himself,' said

Phyllida sadly. It was painful to remember how, after her father's death, she had longed for the comfort of Peter's company. And now she was actually glad that he was on the *Philip* rather than the *Helena*.

# 22

They rounded Cape Matapan without incident this time, the *Philip* in the lead and the *Helena*, engines damped well down, keeping close behind her. Jenny claimed to be disappointed. 'Not even a sniff of a pirate. You have all the luck, Phyllida. I was so hoping for a romantic rescue by Alex and Peter. But I suppose they are all Alex's cousins round here. No wonder he keeps them at bay so easily.'

Once round the cape, the wind was against them, and it was maddening to have to keep the *Helena*'s engines slowed down to mark time with the *Philip*'s snail's pace as they beat their slow way up the desolate coast of the Mani, keeping as close together as they could safely manage. 'Every village is a pirate stronghold,' Brett told Jenny. 'And when they have no strangers to plunder, they fight each other. You see those square towers?'

'Yes?' Jenny could see the village clearly, its huddle of houses clustered round three high, square towers.

'They're not only for defence against the Turk. This is a terrible district for blood feuds. They arise out of anything, a trifle, a nonsense like who goes first in the *Romaika*. And once started, there's no ending them. The men of one family are in honour bound to wipe out those of the other.'

'And the women?'

'Aren't involved. In fact, their company can actually give protection.'

'Yes.' Phyllida looked up from her writing. 'So the poor women get left with the task of wresting some kind of a miserable livelihood out of that bleak mountainside, while the men build their towers higher and higher, or spend days ambushing each other. Will it be like that at Kitries, do you think?' It had long since become obvious that they would have to stop there for provisions.

'Alex says not, but I know one thing. You're none of you going ashore.'

Jenny laughed and protested: 'But darling, ridiculous B., by what you've just said, we're the only ones who would be safe. How do you know, if you go, that you won't get mixed up in some feud of Alex's?'

'Yes. I must confess I'm not sure I ought to go. It's not just the feuding. Kitries is at the very north of the Mani, quite close to Kalamata. Well, the Turks have been down as far as that already. I can't afford to get involved in any trouble while I'm responsible for you three.'

'Oh, poor B. Do you long to go?'

'I do rather,' he admitted. 'To see Alex at home, in his castle, living the life of a feudal chieftain. It would be the very thing for my book. Oh well, there's time still to think it over. At this rate goodness knows when we'll get there.'

It was golden evening when they finally sailed into the dark water of the steep, mountain-ringed harbour at Kitries. 'There's deep water right up to the cliff,' said Brett. 'You can see, Alex is going right in to tie up, but I think we'll lie to out here. Safer so.'

Alex had himself rowed over to them as soon as the *Philip* was moored. 'Welcome to Kitries.' He was in the gayest possible mood. 'Peter and I are going ashore at once to begin organising supplies. It will take us a couple of days or so at least, I'm afraid. Can we persuade you to come with us, milord? I won't, alas, invite the ladies. I've been away too long to be sure that my castle is fit for their reception.'

'Which is your castle, Alex?' Jenny pointed to the turreted medieval fortress at the top of the little town that climbed from ledge to ledge above the harbour. 'That one?'

'No. That belongs to my uncle, Petro Bey. Mine is a little further inland; you can't see it from here. But it's only a couple of hours away.' Like all Greeks, he measured distance by the time it took.

'Six miles or so?' Brett looked tempted, but then: 'Thank you, Alex. I should dearly like to come, but I think I should not leave the ladies alone on board.'

'I was afraid you would say that.' As on a previous occasion, Phyllida was puzzled to feel that Alex was pleased at this rebuff. 'And I'm afraid I can't offer Peter as a guard for the ladies, since I will need his help on shore. Oh well, another time, let us hope . . . I'll try and send off fresh meat and fruit for your dinner tonight, ladies.'

Price took advantage of next day's inactivity to give the saloon a badly needed spring-clean, so the three women settled themselves under the awning on the deck to watch the apparently peaceful life of the village. Black-garbed women were at work, here and there, in tiny plots terraced out of the cliff; a boy blew on a reed pipe as he watched a few scrawny goats.

'Not a man in sight,' said Jenny. 'Do you think they really are off stalking each other through the underbrush–what there is of it?'

'I suppose so.' Phyllida felt amazingly cheerful this morning. 'Rather them than me. From the look of it it's all thorn, and prickly pear and cactus . . . Those poor women, trying to grow anything! Where on earth do you think Alex got the fruit and salad he sent yesterday?'

'Honestly, love, I think I'd rather not know.' Jenny leaned forward. 'There comes a man now; riding hard. Bother this sun; it's shining directly in my eyes. Is it Alex, do you think?'

'I'm not sure. Oh!' Horse and rider had disappeared among the houses. 'He was riding hell for leather,' she went on. 'At the risk of his life–and his horse's. Jenny, tell Brett? Quickly!'

Brett returned with Jenny in time to see the rider emerge on the quayside, now unmistakably Alex. A crowd of children had appeared from nowhere to surround him, he threw his reins to a boy, and shouted an order to the man on watch on the *Philip*. In what seemed an incredibly short time, he was being rowed swiftly out to the *Helena.*

'What's the matter?' Brett was there to greet him as he came on board, pale and agitated.

'Bad news.' He wasted no time on greetings. 'The worst. It's Peter. I'll never forgive myself. But how could I have imagined it? My own people . . . How was I to know they felt so strongly about the Acropolis? I can still hardly believe it. Forgive me, *kyria*?' He had spoken, throughout, to Phyllida.

'But what is it, Alex? What's happened to him?'

'He was attacked, last night. There's a trap-door in the ceiling–we used to play there as boys, my brothers and I. How in the world was I to imagine anyone else would remember it; would want to use it? Oh, he defended himself gallantly, did my Brother Petros, but by the time I heard the tumult and came to the rescue, he had received wounds enough to finish an ordinary man. They ran, when they saw me, the cowards, but I'll be revenged on them, if it takes the rest of my life.'

'But Peter?'

'Alive. Just. And calling for you, *kyria.* I'd be wicked to give you much hope, but, with nursing, with care, I think he has a chance. It's loss of blood, mostly . . . surface wounds; they tried to fight quietly, you see, in the dark, with their yataghans. But I've nothing at the castle, nothing! No basilicum powder, no bandages, not even laudanum for his pain. I left my old nurse clotting the blood, as best she might, with spider's webs. You'll come quickly, *kyria*? Five minutes may make the whole difference.'

'Yes. Yes, of course.' No time for doubts. 'Jenny, will you tell Price what I'll need? Thank God, Dr. Howe made me keep some of the medical supplies I ordered from England.' And then, remembering. 'Brett?'

'He's calling for Phyllida?' Brett spoke across her to Alex.

'Constantly. As if he had something on his mind, something he needs to say to her. And, besides, there's the nursing. If he's left to my old nurse– Well, you know what they're like. I'd not give him three days.'

'But with Phyllida, you think there's a chance?' Brett was weighing pros and cons.

'He's asking for me, Brett. You must see I have to go?' But why did she have to? Because she loved Peter, or because, guiltily, she knew she did not?

'I suppose so.' His tone of qualified agreement enraged her. 'You've horses, Alex? Two hours ride, you said?'

'Yes. I left my companions behind, and did it in less this morning. But it will take us longer, going back. I brought a horse for you, too. I thought you'd want to come.'

Now the whole difficulty of the situation struck Phyllida. 'But, Brett . . . But, Jenny . . .'

'Nothing for it, love,' said Jenny. 'Aunt Cass and I will do well enough on board here, with Price and Barlow and Brown. Of course Brett must go with you.'

'But–'

'No time for "buts",' said Alex.

'Naturally I shall come,' said Brett.

Phyllida's preparations were quickly made. 'Three or four days should settle it, one way or other,' Alex had said, urging her once again to lose no time. 'I've a side-saddle for you–of sorts.'

She was wearing Turkish costume, as she and Jenny always did on board ship. Her other one and a change of linen she thrust hurriedly into the portmanteau Price produced . . . He was assembling bandages and medicines under her direction . . . It seemed no time at all before she was kissing Jenny and Cassandra good-bye.

'Take care of yourself, love.' Jenny held her tight for a moment.

'And you, Jenny.'

Brett had been busy giving orders to Barlow and Brown. 'You'll do exactly as Captain Barlow tells you, Jenny.' He joined them now. 'I've told him–you'll understand this, Phyllida, I know–that at the slightest sign of danger, he's to sail at once.'

'Leaving you behind?' Jenny protested.

'If necessary.'

'But it won't be,' said Alex. 'You're ready, *kyria*? Good.'

On shore, they found the rest of Alex's party awaiting them, three wild-looking shaggy-haired Greeks in sheepskin cloaks and dirty white kilts, and Phyllida felt a sudden spurt of fear. 'Brett?' She turned impulsively toward him, but Alex was between them.

'Here is your horse, *kyria*. It's something of a makeshift saddle, I'm afraid.'

It was indeed. The horses were tough little mountain-bred ponies, their saddles made of wood, with looped ropes for stirrups. It was a nice point, Phyllida thought, whether the roughly modified side-saddle into which Alex was helping her was more or less comfortable than Brett's, whose stirrups were so short that he had to ride with his knees close up to his chin.

'Leave it all to the horse.' Alex handed her the much knotted reins that might once have been leather. 'Keep close behind me.' He was leading the way already up the steep lane between terraced houses, and Phyllida forgot her growing anxiety in surprise at how crowded the village was. Old men sat in the sun at dark doorways and under the fig trees that seemed to find nourishment, by a miracle, among the bare bones of the rock. Two young women paused for a moment in their endless spinning to gaze at the little cortège . . . A ripple of salutations greeted Alex as he rode at its head.

As they passed the last house and the tiny whitewashed church, the lane widened slightly and Alex slackened speed to let her catch up with him. 'It will be single file from here onwards. You can manage, *kyria*?'

In the village, the lane had been roughly paved, now it was merely a faint line across jagged edges of grey and blue slate mixed here and there with limestone and quartz. The horses slipped and their hooves clinked and clattered on the bare rock, so that conversation would have been impossible even if Phyllida could have thought of anything but the immediate problem of balance. Impossible, too, to get more than the briefest glimpse, from time to time, of the towering mountain range running southward towards Taygetus. Petro Bey's castle had vanished now behind a buttress of the range. A turn of the path gave her a sudden view back to the shining water of the bay and, beyond it, the rocky promontory of Modon and then sea again . . . She strained her eyes, wondering if it might be possible to see as far as Zante. Her horse stumbled, she nearly lost her balance, recovered herself with an effort, was aware of Brett, closing anxiously up from behind and decided she would do no more sea-gazing.

The track was making its way steadily upwards over one rib after another of the mountain range. Once, they dipped sharply down to cross a stream-bed, dry now, with only the wide rocky bottom to suggest the torrent it must be in spring. Then they were climbing again, steadily now, up a spur of the mountain, and Phyllida, lurched and jolted by the hard wooden saddle, forgot everything in the mere effort of keeping upright, keeping balanced . . .

Ahead of her, Alex paused at the top of the long slope. 'There,' he pointed ahead. 'Not long now.'

The castle stood at the crest of the next spur, cliff dropping sharply in front and rising as steeply again behind it. Phyllida had one quick glimpse of it, silhouetted against the light: medieval turrets . . . a square Maniote tower . . . a little cluster of other buildings, clinging like moss to the rock.

'Half an hour more,' Alex called back over his shoulder. Did she dare turn and pass the encouragement back to Brett? She thought not. Bones and muscles she did not know she had were aching now. She set her teeth and forgot everything but the effort of hanging on.

She did not dare imagine what the climb up to that clifftop stronghold would be like, and was amazed when Alex pulled his horse to a halt on a narrow ledge of rock where the path seemed to come to a stop. 'There.' He turned to smile encouragement, then pursed his lips in a clear, high whistle.

It was answered from above. 'Good,' he said. 'I told them to be ready. I'm sure you've had enough, and the next bit is the worst of all.'

His three retainers had jumped down from their little horses. One of them was holding all three, while the other two stood in an elbow of the rock, and stared upwards. Phyllida steadied her own horse with one hand and turned to follow their gaze to where a huge osier-plaited basket was coming slowly down the sheer side of the cliff.

'It's quite safe.' Alex had dismounted and tethered his horse to a metal ring sunk in the crude rock. 'Will you go first, Phyllida, or shall we send milord?'

# 23

The huge basket swayed dizzily upwards. Fending herself off the wall of rock with her feet, Phyllida obeyed Alex's instructions not to look downwards, and wondered if she would ever have come had she known that this hazard awaited her. Of course she would. And after all it was not a great deal worse than being hauled on board ship in a bosun's chair. At least the rock was steady.

The basket swayed inwards. Firm hands caught and held it. Brett, who had gone first, helped her out. Behind him, she saw a group of the usual wild-looking Greeks, and beyond them the castle, very much more tumble-down and less romantic near to than it had seemed from a distance.

'What now?' She turned to Brett.

'We wait for Alex. He said he would come up by basket–quite a concession, I think. There's a steep flight of steps round the other side. I gather it's a matter of pride to use them.'

'But must we wait? Can I not go straight to Peter?' She turned to the Greek nearest her, and addressed him in his own language. 'My brother,' she said. 'The *Kyrie* Petros. You will take me to him?'

He shrugged. '*Den katalabaino*' (I don't understand).

'Best wait,' said Brett as she was about to rephrase the question. 'The basket's down already. Alex won't be a minute. And he's got your packet of medicines. Lord.' He moved to the edge of the plateau. 'What an extraordinary place. A dozen men could hold it against an army. And look at that for a view, Phyllida.'

Tears choked her throat at his return to the old friendly tone. Silently, she joined him near the sharp, unprotected edge and saw the same view that she had briefly glimpsed earlier, but wider now . . . sea, and hills and sea again, with every detail etched clear and strangely flat in the pure Greek light.

'I suppose the hills are between us and the fort at Navarino.' Brett had been looking northwards. 'Look! There's smoke up there–that must be near Kalamata surely. I wonder if Ibrahim is out again.'

'I do hope not. Ah! Here's Alex. Can I go to Peter at once?' she asked as Alex leapt, unaided, out of the imprisoning basket. 'Your people didn't seem to understand.'

'Very likely not. Some of them are Albanians. Their Greek is rudimentary, I'm afraid.' He turned and conducted a quick, unintelligible conversation with one of his followers. 'He says Peter's fallen into a deep sleep at last,' to Phyllida. 'Best not disturb him, don't you think? Besides, you're tired and hungry. I left orders for a meal to be ready the moment we arrived. You'll be better able to deal with what is going to be a difficult enough task when you've eaten. All Peter's wounds will need re-dressing, and, frankly, you're not going to find him an easy invalid.'

'I suppose not.' It was true. She was exhausted, and famished. 'Well, if he's really asleep?'

'Yes, thank God. It's the best news yet.' He turned to lead the way round the high, square tower that dominated the plateau, to a huddle of buildings clustered between it and the cliff. Some were fortified, others merely the usual flat-roofed little Greek houses, badly in need of a coat of whitewash. 'I told you we were in no state to entertain a lady.' He had read her thoughts. 'But I hope the food will make up for the primitive conditions. This way.'

A low, arched entrance led into a larger room than Phyllida had expected. Lit only by narrow slits, high up in the thick walls, it struck almost dark after the brilliant sunshine outside, and Alex shouted an order, 'Lights for my guests!' before seating them at a rough wooden table. 'I have no Turkish customs here,' he told

Phyllida. 'None of that luxurious lolling about on cushions. We're a Spartan society.' He was seating her, as he spoke, on the upright chair next to his own big one. Brett and the handful of Greeks who ate with them had to make do with stools.

Now men with torches filed into the room from a dark doorway at the far end and took their places behind the seats of the chief members of the party. By the flickering light, Phyllida could see that the rough walls were decorated with arms of every kind: guns, pistols, yataghans and swords, while a few broad-headed lances stood in the corner.

The peasants in Kitries might have been pale and bent for lack of food, but there seemed no shortage of it here. A delicious, if greasy, vegetable soup was followed by freshly grilled fish. 'Caught in the bay this morning,' Alex told her. 'And none the worse for the ride up. You'll take some more, *kyria*?'

'No, thank you.' Impatience to see Peter was burning in her. This endless, ceremonial meal seemed a mockery of the morning's hasty journey. She longed to break it up, but caught Brett's eye fixed on her across Alex, surely in warning. He was right, of course. They must not insult their host. 'It's delicious,' she went on. 'But I'm rather tired.'

'Of course.' He clapped his hands and servants hurried in with a huge wooden platter piled high with fresh fruit and a dish of the cakes of nut and honey she knew so well. More wine was poured, though she had already had quite as much as she wanted. 'You must try this.' Alex ignored her protests. 'It's something quite special of our own.' His eyes glittered in the torch-light. Jenny would say this was a scene straight out of Sir Walter Scott. What a world away Jenny seemed . . .

There was coffee at last, and tiny glasses of ouzo, which Phyllida managed to refuse. 'Alex–' She did not like the note of uncertainty in her own voice. 'Don't you think Peter might have waked by now?'

'Ah, Peter.' He nodded to the group of men who had sat a little away from them at the big table, and they rose and left the room. 'My Brother Peter.' She felt Brett, beyond him, tense at something strange in his tone.

'Yes. It's time I went to him.'

'A devoted sister.' Stranger and stranger. 'He wasn't sure you'd come. I knew you would. And you, milord. You've won me a pair of pistols, the two of you.'

'Where *is* Peter?' Phyllida knew that quiet tone of Brett's.

'That's the question, isn't it? Let me think. Four hours—more like five since we left the harbour. I should think they're well out to sea by now.'

'What in the world do you mean?' She was afraid to understand.

'I wonder if the others will have been as easily fooled as you.' He drank, and smiled at her over the glass. 'Such a good sister. But so is Jenny. I'm sure, when Peter arrived with his tale of treachery, she will have been quite as quick to act as you.'

'Treachery,' said Brett.

It felt cold in the hall, and darker. 'Peter's not here,' said Phyllida. 'He's not hurt at all.'

'Of course not. Aren't you relieved, *kyria*?'

Shock and anger held her dumb. Yes, and fear. Fear admitted at last, that secret dread of hers that had haunted her ever since they left Nauplia. It all came, horribly, clear now. The night Peter proposed to Jenny: she had thought, oddly, that Alex was pleased at the result. No wonder! It had ensured Peter's co-operation in his plans against the *Helena* . . . Plans, she saw now, that went further back, the further she looked. He had saved them, that day at Spetsai, because he wanted the *Helena* himself. But then, she felt herself redden with rage and shame, he had thought he might get her and her fortune as well, and had held his hand. When she refused him, he had begun to plot again, had suggested that they leave Nauplia and hide in his 'safe' anchorage under Sounion. She had saved them, for the moment, when she refused to go, but now . . .

'Kidnapped.' Something wonderfully steadying about Brett's tone as he summed it up. And then, across Alex, to her: 'At least, Phyllida, we were both fooled equally.' He turned back to Alex. 'So. You've got us here. No need to discuss the means. What we need to know is the end.'

The calm tone that steadied Phyllida was acting as an irritant on Alex. In his imagination, this scene had played itself quite differently. He poured more ouzo with a hand that was not quite steady. 'The end? Why, two marriages; two splendid settlements, and, from you, milord, a ransom that will enable me to make this castle fit for my American wife.'

'But–'

Brett's glance silenced Phyllida. If Alex thought him rich enough to pay an immense ransom, should he be disillusioned? 'Let me understand you,' he went on, still in that tone of dangerous quiet. 'Peter has boarded the *Helena*, you're telling us, with one of your lying stories–and done what?'

'Taken her to a place of safety, of course. Down by Matapan, to await my instructions about your ransom and our double wedding. He'll have told them, you see, that unless they do as he bids, you two will be killed.'

'Ingenious,' said Brett. Pure nightmare, this matter-of-fact conversation. 'And will we?'

'Oh, I don't think that will be necessary. A few weeks as my guests–I hope you won't mind the upper stories of the tower?–while we make the arrangements. Peter will need your power of attorney, *kyria*; a letter to that man of business of yours on Zante. And you, milord, will have to write your friends in England. That will take rather longer, of course, but once Phyllida and I are safely married, I think we will be able to accept your word of honour and treat you as our guest.'

Once again, Brett's glance silenced Phyllida. 'And Jenny?'

'I told you.' Impatiently. 'A double wedding. I have Peter's promise that he'll wait. Well, of course . . . He needs his fortune–and hers.'

'And you trust him?'

'We're brothers.' His tone betrayed him. This was his weak point. 'Besides'–he turned a travesty of the old smile on Phyllida–'he knows that he is entirely dependent on my wife's goodwill. And therefore on mine. You need have no fear for your sister, milord.'

'No?' Once again, Brett's calmly ironic tone forestalled an outburst from Phyllida. He was trying to convey something to her, now that Alex had turned half away from him to speak directly to her. 'Time.' Was that the word his lips were forming. Play for time?

Why? Well, why not? Lost in a sea of emotion, of rage with herself, with Alex . . . black anxiety for Jenny . . . feelings beyond endurance about Peter . . . she was in no state to think. If Brett had some idea, some shred of a plan, she would be only too glad to go along with it.

'Alex.' It hurt her to use his name. 'I can't believe it. I can't take it in.' Behind him, Brett's look was approving. 'I'm ill.' She put a shaking hand to her head. It was nearly enough true. 'That ride . . . and now this . . . I don't understand–anything . . . I think I'm going to faint–' At what point in the incredible conversation had they all risen to their feet? She swayed now, and made herself clutch Alex for support.

He was suddenly, horribly, all solicitude, a tender arm round her. And beyond him, Brett's glance, approving, supporting her. 'So you're human after all, *kyria.*' Alex, too, sounded approving. 'I confess, I'd wondered. I'm glad it's a woman I'm to marry, not a goddess. I've always thought they'd be awkward company in–' He stopped, changed the phrase. 'In the home. And, that reminds me.' He turned and shouted an order to one of the torchbearers. 'Don't think I've not made my preparations for you. Jenny has your aunt for chaperone.' He laughed, quickly, strangely. 'Ah, here she is. Oenone, the *Kyria* Phyllida is not well. Take her to her room. Look after her.'

The short, dark-haired, dark-clad young woman who had appeared in the doorway spat something at him in quick, unintelligible Albanian. 'Take her to her room, Oenone,' he said again, his voice a threat. 'And speak Greek, so we can all understand you.'

'I bid you welcome.' The hate in the woman's voice was like a blow. 'Come with me, *kyria.*'

Passionately, horribly, Phyllida feared being separated from Brett. But again his glance was encouraging. Extraordinary, how they seemed to be able to communicate without words. He wanted her to go with this furious young Greek woman. Here (was he telling her?) was another weak link in the chain Alex had forged for them. She made herself stagger towards the glowering young woman. 'I'm not well. Help me?'

Some rudimentary preparations had been made in the upper tower room. Sheepskins on the raised bed-place, a table, a chair and, Phyllida was glad to see, the small bag of necessities Price had packed for her—it seemed a lifetime ago. 'You'll be safe enough here.' Oenone spoke at last and her words showed the same uncompromising dislike as her silence. 'Milord has the room below. There is to be a guard at the bottom, night and day.'

'Milord below?' This was wonderful news. She had been horribly afraid, back there when she left him, that she might never see Brett again.

'Yes.' The woman's smile was cruel. 'Locked in, like you. So think now, quick, before I leave you, if there is anything you must have—that I can give you.'

'Some water.' It was a request no Greek would ever refuse. 'If you please?' At all costs, she must break through the hatred she felt like a wall between them.

'Of course.' Oenone went to the doorway and shouted a command down the steep stair.

'There's a spring then?' Anything to get Oenone talking.

'The best in the Morea. You'll not die of thirst here.' Her tone suggested all kinds of other possibilities, none of them pleasant.

'No. Oenone—may I call you that?' She felt the girl's recoil, but went on as if she had not. 'I'm Phyllida. Tell me, are we the only women up here?'

'The only ones of any account.'

'I see. And you?' How in the world could she phrase the question.

But Oenone had been waiting for it. 'I am Alexandros Mavromikhalis' wife.' She spat it out like a challenge. 'In the eyes of God. We were betrothed in our cradles. I warn you, *kyria,* nothing but disaster will come of your marriage with him. Blood on the hearth and blood in the bed . . . Nights of misery and days of anguish. Death would be better.' She looked about her, wildly, and Phyllida was actually afraid, for a moment, that she was going to produce a dagger from the black folds of her dress and suit the action to the word. At all costs, she must get the conversation down to a lower key.

'You can't for a moment imagine I want to marry him?' she asked.

'Who wouldn't?'

'Not I, for one. Do you understand what he has done to me?'

'No. Nor do I care. Only that you are here, the priest is ready, all Alexandros' promises to me broken, poured out like water on the ground. What does it matter what you think or say?'

'But, Oenone, believe me: I *would* rather die than marry Alex.'

'You think so now?' The girl looked at her strangely. 'Well, you may get the choice yet. Ah, here's the water.' She took it from a man at the door. 'I'll leave you to rest.' Savage irony in her tone.

'You're going to lock me in?' Phyllida was aware of the man waiting outside.

'Of course. Fear nothing. Alexandros wants you alive. I have orders that your meals be brought you here, except when you eat with him. You will have plenty of time for rest.' And with that she withdrew, slammed the door and turned the key from outside.

Left alone, Phyllida hurried to one of the slit windows that pierced the four sides of the square room. The one where the light shone brightest, it commanded a thin strip of the view she and Brett had gazed at from the plateau. Far off, towards Zante, the sun was setting and the two narrow strips of sea were crimson with its light. Zante! The *Helena*. Where was she tonight? Had Peter really been able to take command?

And now, at last, she must think about Peter, whose treachery was so infinitely worse than Alex's. She sat down, shivering suddenly, on the bed-place. Peter and Jenny. Jenny and Peter. It was worse, infinitely worse than what had happened, what might happen to her. She was old, she felt now, a thousand years old in failure and despair. It hardly mattered what became of her. But Jenny, young, bright Jenny, so gay and therefore so vulnerable. Suddenly, her head was down among the sheepskins and she was crying as if her heart would break.

Or had it, long ago? Vaguely considering this, she settled herself, without realising it, more comfortably among the warm, smelly sheepskins and fell fast asleep.

When she woke, it was pitch dark and she could not think, for a moment, where she was. Then, with the sound of a low, steady knocking on the door, it all came horribly back. But she made her voice steady as she called 'Come in,' in Greek. To show panic would be to feel it.

Oenone entered carrying a lamp, and once again Phyllida was aware of a man, half seen in the shadows at the door. Listening?

'Alexandros sent me.' Oenone's voice still held the note of hatred. 'To ask whether you would prefer to sup with him and Milord Renshaw, or by yourself here.'

'Oh, here, please.' Even to see Brett, she could not face another confrontation with Alex tonight. As soon as she had spoken, impulsively, she realised that it was the right answer so far as Oenone was concerned.

'Very well.' Was there the slightest possible softening in that uncompromising voice? 'I will give the order.'

'Oenone!' Phyllida's voice stopped her at the door. 'Won't you join me?' What plea to use? What line to take? She took none, but left it there.

Oenone put the lamp down on the table and paused to look at her, surprised. 'You wish that?' She shrugged. 'I'll ask Alexandros.'

Twenty minutes later, she was back, ushering in a man with a loaded tray. 'Alexandros says he is glad you and I are to be friends.' Irony vied with hatred in her voice, but Phyllida made herself ignore all but the words.

'I'm glad too.' She moved forward to help unload the tray. 'Oenone–' The man had retreated to his old place outside the door. 'Must we have him listening?'

'Yes. Those are Alexandros' orders.'

Phyllida almost despaired at the lifeless, acquiescent tone. Then she remembered Brett's last glance, his unspoken command. Here was one of the weak links in the chain that bound them. Here was her chance. No use wondering what he and Alex were saying to each other, down in that gloomy dining hall. Her chance was here, with Oenone, who had so much to gain, so much to lose . . .

She began very slowly and carefully, with general subjects, with the state of Greece, the fighting in Nauplia. Inevitably, Oenone was starved for news of the course of the war and listened eagerly when Phyllida talked of the hopes that were building up of intervention by the Allied Powers.

'Peace?' She tasted the word, wondering. 'I hardly remember what it was like. And as for freedom . . . I've never known it. Not really . . .'

'Tell me.' Phyllida was quick to take advantage of this change of mood. 'Where are you from, Oenone?' It was the nearest she dared get to a more personal question.

'Tripolitsa. We had a big house there. I used to play in the orange groves–' She had forgotten Phyllida, gazing back into that vanished past. 'I remember the day it all started.' Her eyes sparkled. 'How they screamed and ran, those wretched Turks, and a Greek vengeance waiting for them at every turning. There was a child I used to play with, up and down the terraces, Fatima, her name was, the daughter of the Aga. How she wept! How she prayed and clung to my dress! She, who used to call me her little slave. I wonder where she is now.'

'She wasn't killed then?' Phyllida managed to keep her tone merely enquiring.

'Oh, no. Not many of the women and children were. Just sold into slavery. I'd have liked to have kept her myself, but mother didn't want her. Mother–' Her iron-hard composure was cracking at last.

'What happened to them? Your parents?' She thought Oenone had forgotten who was listening, in the relief of talking about it at all.

'What do you think? They were killed, both of them, when the Turks retook Tripolitsa. At least, I hope my mother was killed.'

'And you?' Dared she ask it.

'I was lucky, I suppose. I had gone to the mountains with our flocks. It was the spring, you see. When Ibrahim came, my mother sent word I must stay. My cousin would come for me. Alexandros.' The word brought her back to the present. 'Why am I telling you this? You, of all people!'

'Because we're two women in a houseful of men? Because it's good to talk about these things. The Turks killed my father.' Algerian Pirates, Turks, what was the difference . . .

'They did?' Oenone's interest was caught.

'Yes. And took me prisoner.' Briefly, not to lose Oenone's hard-won attention, she told the story of her captivity and escape.

'Now I see.' Oenone seized on it. 'It is the milord you love, the strange, stiff Englishman who will let nothing move him.'

'Yes.' Why deny it?

'And he?'

'Loves an Englishwoman, who would not have him.' Was it still true? How right Oenone was about Brett: he would indeed let nothing move him.

'So!' Oenone's eyes had that strange half-mad sparkle again. 'You will marry Alexandros to make the Englishman sorry.'

'*No!*' It came out almost as a shout. 'I told you. I'd rather die. Alex and I are of different worlds. It would be a disaster. I'll tell you the truth, Oenone. I did accept him. I was mad. I knew it almost at once, and told him so. I'm guilty towards you, both of you. Though of course he did not tell me he was engaged to you.'

'I see.' At last, Oenone was thinking as well as feeling. 'I could not understand why he was in such a passion about it. He doesn't love you. How could he? It's his pride. How did you dare treat him so?'

'I don't know. But you must understand, we look on things differently in America.'

'You must indeed. To dare treat a man so. And Alexandros, of all men!'

'I have never regretted anything so bitterly in my life,' said Phyllida. It was true, but how extraordinary to be actually apologising to this furious Greek child. For as the strange conversation continued, she had realised how young Oenone was. Her dark, shapeless dress, the lines of pain in her face, and her present state of tension had all combined to hide the fact that she was probably younger even than Jenny.

Jenny! It brought her back, horribly, to the present. But Oenone was on her feet now, collecting dishes on the tray. She thought she had gone far enough for tonight, and was increasingly aware of the silent listener at the door. She made no effort to detain Oenone. Play for time, Brett had urged her, in that extraordinary silent communion. But time, after all, was what they had. Or was it? Would Alex insist, tomorrow, that she write to Biddock, that Brett write to his 'family' in England. Or would he wait until he had heard that Peter had succeeded in taking over the *Helena*?

At least Oenone had left the lamp. Phyllida prowled about the room, fighting anxiety, fighting despair. Then she stopped, motionless, at the sound of a commotion on the stairs outside. Brett's voice, raised: 'I must say good night to the lady!' A man's voice, refusing, a scuffle, the slam of a door . . . Brett had let her know that he was down there, now, in the room below her. And the guard? She was at her own door, head close to the hinge, listening. Yes. Footsteps echoed away down the long stair. The guard would stay comfortably in the room at the bottom of the tower.

So? Now she was prowling about the room with a purpose, anxiety and despair alike forgotten. An old tower, roughly built, the walls huge blocks of stone, the floor heavy planks, but securely nailed down, as if, no doubt, this room had been used as a prison before. And Brett, below there . . .

She picked up the lamp and began a minute inspection of the floor. Nothing. Not a crack. Not a chink. And if the ceiling of Brett's room was as high as hers, not a hope of communication between them. But she had the lamp. Burn a hole in the floor? No, she told herself; not yet. And, finally, slept.

# 24

Phyllida waked to broad daylight and the sound of shouting. Extraordinary to have slept so soundly, and yet to wake feeling exhausted. She put an instinctive hand to her forehead, felt it sticky, and told herself, dismissing a quick spurt of anxiety, that she had merely slept too heavily among that tangle of odorous sheepskins. But she wrapped one round her, against the dank morning air of the tower, before hurrying across the room to the slit window that commanded the plateau.

Maddening to be able to see so little, but something was obviously going on down there. Alex's voice came up to her, shouting a series of orders, unintelligible at this distance. She saw him for a moment, moving across her narrow line of vision, then he disappeared among a shouting crowd of his followers. Something was certainly happening, but what?

No sound from the room below. But then, why should there be? Or how should she hear it? Brett might have been killed in the night, and she not know. She would not think like that: absurd, cowardly thinking. Alex had no intention of killing them, so long as there was a chance of making money by them alive.

Horrible to think she had let him fool her so, had actually agreed to marry him. And by doing so, had started all this? His pride, Oenone had said. He would marry her to prove something to himself. All her fault . . .

No. She moved away from the window and made herself go through the best morning toilet she could. A jug of cold water; a visit to the sordid corner of the room Oenone had indicated . . . All the time she was arguing with herself, discussing every episode in her fatal relationship with Alex. What a frightening, patient, waiting game he had played. When she had accepted him, he must have thought he could have it all, legitimately. Changing her mind, she had signed what might well be all their death warrants. Her teeth were chattering. She would not admit to herself how ill she felt, or how frightened.

Someone knocked on the door. 'Come in.' She expected Oenone, felt a craving for hot coffee, took an involuntary step backward when Alex appeared.

Thank God she was up and dressed. 'This is a very early visit.' She made her voice cold and steady.

'Yes.' He made no pretence at apology. 'I've come to say good-bye. For a while. Ibrahim is out from Navarino. He threatens Kalamata once again. I'm sending every man I can spare.'

'You're not going yourself?'

He turned on her furiously. 'Your brother has betrayed me. There's been no word from the *Helena*.'

'Where is she?' Relief and happiness sang in her.

'I don't know.' It infuriated him to have to admit it. 'She must have sailed in the night. God knows how.'

'And Peter?'

'Gone with her, for all I know.' He was angry beyond thought. 'To Zante, no doubt, to announce your death and claim your estate.'

'Oh?'

'He'll regret it till the day he dies. Which may not be far off. The wind's in the right quarter today. It will take more than the *Helena*'s engines to save him from my vengeance.'

'You're going after them? To Zante?'

'What else? You can be composing your letter to your agent while I am gone. I have told Milord Brett to do the same. They will have to wait till I return. I dare not lose a minute now, but would not leave without saying farewell to my wife.'

He cares nothing for me, she thought, compared with the *Helena*. Hard to tell whether this was cheering or not. But—something she must say: 'Alex!'

'Yes.' He turned back, impatiently, at the door.

'I'll write you a letter now, if you wish. In five minutes. Giving you everything; my whole estate; if you'll only let us go, Mr. Renshaw and I.'

He paused for a moment, his hand on the door. 'And

who would believe it? Not your Mr. Biddock, that's certain. Only our marriage makes the whole thing possible. So, be ready, when I return–'

'But, Alex, Oenone–'

'God damn Oenone!' He was gone, the door slamming behind him. And then, a scuffling on the stairs; the sound of something crashing to the floor; silence.

Five minutes later, Oenone appeared, very pale, very composed, with coffee and two slices of hard, black Greek bread.

Drinking eagerly, Phyllida found that the coffee was little more than lukewarm. Her throat hurt, and she could not make herself eat the dry bread. Should she have tried to make Oenone stay? She thought not. There had been something about her this morning that forbade talk. Had she, in fact, been on the stairs and heard what Alex said about her? Was this cool coffee the second breakfast tray she had brought? Phyllida thought she must hope so.

Her head ached, but she was full of hope. The *Helena* had vanished, without a word from Peter. Surely it must mean that Jenny and Cassandra–yes, and Barlow and Brown–had refused to be fooled. Had they gone for help? Might the *Cambrian* steam suddenly into Kitries harbour?

And what good would that be? It was two hours hard riding over the mountains to this impregnable fortress. Could Captain Hamilton be expected to waste his time on such a rescue when the whole of Greece cried out for his help? And, yes, she reminded herself. There had been Trelawny, that wild young follower of Byron's, who had attached himself to the rebel, Odysseus, and been rescued by Hamilton from a cave on Mount Olympus–a place, by all reports, even wilder and more remote than this one. Thinking of this, she thought she was glad that Alex had refused her offer this morning–gladder still that he had not stayed a moment longer. If he had, might she not have promised to marry him, anything, if he would only let Brett go?

The plateau was quiet now. The distant, narrow view of sea, and hill, and sea again was serene. Only a few small clouds, scudding across the brilliant sky, told of Alex's following wind. But he thought Peter had taken over the *Helena* and was bound for

Zante. Suppose, just suppose he was wrong . . . She did not know what instructions Brett had left, but knew him well enough to be sure they had been full of good sense. Suppose Peter, intending surprise, had been himself surprised. Suppose the *Helena* was off, under steam, to fetch help. Then she would be going in the other direction, back round Cape Matapan, for Nauplia, and Captain Hamilton.

No good hoping too much, or fearing too much either. She remembered Brett's half-spoken instruction the night before. He had wanted time. Well, miraculously, it had been granted to them. And her task, obviously, was Oenone. If she had really heard Alex's ruthless dismissal of her that morning, might it not have made that task a little easier?

It was a bitter disappointment when her frugal luncheon was brought by an old, old Greek woman, who hardly seemed strong enough to carry it. Thanking her, Phyllida resisted the temptation to ask for Oenone. The hot vegetable soup and a glass of wine made her feel better. She had merely been imagining things, this morning, when she thought she was ill. She was tired, that was all, and glad to pass some of the endless afternoon in sleep.

Once more, she woke with a headache, but forgot it when Oenone appeared with her supper.

'Please stay with me?' She had noticed at once that the rough wickerwork tray held food only for one. 'It's so lonely up here.' And then, as Oenone hesitated, 'And with nothing to do . . . Isn't there something useful I could be doing? Sewing perhaps? For you?'

Oenone's eyes were swollen as if she had been crying all day. She looked at Phyllida sombrely. 'Do you not understand anything? You are in my power, now Alexandros has gone. You should be on your knees, begging me not to kill you. And instead, you offer to sew for me! What, pray? My bride-linen?'

'If you like. I tell you, Oenone, talk of killing means nothing to me. I would gladly die rather than marry your Alexandros.' She had noticed how Oenone disliked her use of the diminutive, 'Alex.'

'You really mean that.' Oenone turned to give an order to the man on duty at the door. 'You're not even afraid to be locked in with me?' She said it almost in amazement, as the man locked the door on them and went to fetch the wine she had asked for.

'Of course not.' But she was, a little. 'Oenone,' she went on quickly. This moment alone together was too good to be wasted. 'I am sure we can help each other, you and I.'

'How?' It was uncompromising enough. 'Don't think, *kyria,* that you can blandish me into betraying Alexandros. In the eyes of God, he is my husband. It is my duty to do his will in all things.'

'Even in this, which is flouting the will of God?' And then, seeing that this was too complicated an argument for the girl to grasp: 'Oenone, I must tell you. This morning, I offered Alexandros all my fortune if he would only let us go, Milord Renshaw and I. Would not that be better? You know, as well as I do, that I am no wife for him. He must know it, himself, in his heart. It's only his pride–'

'Yes,' said Oenone. 'But his pride *is* Alexandros.'

'Then we must think of some way of satisfying it. Oenone, think! Suppose I was to give all my money to you, freely, as your dowry?'

'And why should you do that?'

'For letting–' But Oenone's finger was on her lips.

'Hush!' she said. 'The man is coming back.'

As the key grated in the lock, Phyllida thought his arrival could hardly have been more timely. She had managed to put the idea of conniving at their escape into Oenone's head without actually saying the words. Besides, was there not encouragement in the way Oenone had silenced her? Already, to some small extent, they were fellow conspirators.

'You took long enough!' Encouragement, too, in the way Oenone scolded the man as he appeared with a bottle of wine and two glasses. 'I've eaten already,' she explained to Phyllida. 'But I will keep you company while you eat.' And then, suddenly eager, like the child she really was, 'Tell me about your country. About America. Alexandros says it is full of miracles. Are there really boats, there, that go without wind?'

'Why, yes. Did you not know? Milord Renshaw owns one of them, the *Helena*. I believe that is what Alexandros really wants, more than anything else.' Both of them, now, were aware of the man at the door, listening.

'Without any wind?'

'Yes. By machinery.' The word meant nothing to Oenone, but what did that matter? 'That is why Alexandros left in such haste,' she went on. 'Because he heard that the *Helena* had left Kitries harbour.'

'I see.' Oenone was puzzling it out. 'I thought it strange, when the news came that Ibrahim was out, and Alexandros did not march north himself. He sent every man he could spare.' She was making excuses for him.

'Yes, but, don't you see–' This was inspiration. 'The *Helena* would be worth any number of men to the Greek cause. Imagine what she can do. Come up against the wind. Tow a fire-ship into the enemy fleet in the teeth of it. There's another one already, up in the Gulf of Aegina, the *Karteria*; she did wonders in the defence of Athens. I can understand why your cousin wants the *Helena*.'

'Yes.' Oenone drank the strong, retsinated wine. 'But why should Milord Renshaw understand?'

Another opportunity. But how to use it? So many questions she wanted to ask. And always she must remember the man at the door, listening. 'I sometimes think he hates the *Helena*,' she said at last. 'He built her for the lady who should have been his wife. The one who jilted him.' Had she got the Greek word right? Yes, clearly Oenone had understood her.

'She was called Helena? Yes, I see. So in exchange for his freedom?' She, too, was thinking of the man at the door, and spoke fast and low.

'Most certainly.' That was enough for now. She raised her voice a little. 'How is Milord Renshaw? I can hear nothing from down there.'

'Of course not.' Oenone laughed. 'These towers are not built of firewood. They are built to last, to be held against the enemy. You'll not hear a sound from Milord Renshaw, but he's there right enough.' She laughed again. 'And behaving like a milord too. Do you know, he managed to make old Anastasia fetch him paper and pen. He's writing a book, she says. Can it be true? A real book?'

'Indeed it's true.' Oh, splendid, capable Brett! 'He's writing a book about Greece. One that should make the whole world sympathise with your cause.'

'Like Milord Byron?' Oenone was no fool. She proved it again in what she said next. 'But if Alexandros lets him go, and he writes about this?'

'It will depend how he writes. Suppose Alexandros had captured us [careful, don't use the word kidnapped], not for personal reasons, but because he knew what the *Helena* could do for the cause of Greece. And then, suppose Milord Renshaw wrote how well we were treated, as captives here, given the best of everything, sharing your joys and sorrows, protected from the Turk–'

'We have talked long enough.' Oenone was on her feet. 'The wine is finished. I will see you tomorrow, *kyria*. Sleep well.'

Phyllida fell asleep, among the sheepskins, whose stink hardly bothered her any more, with a prayer on her lips. Time . . . with enough time, she thought she could talk Oenone into freeing them. If only she knew where the *Helena* was, and what had happened to Jenny . . .

Nightmares, of course, and in the morning the familiar headache, a little worse today, but yielding, at last, to hot coffee, brought by the old crone, Anastasia, who had found paper and pen for Brett. And that must have been something of an achievement, Phyllida thought. Where in the world, in this barbaric stronghold, would one find pen, and, still more unlikely, the amount of paper Brett would need?

Oenone did not appear until suppertime, but when she did, there was food for two on the tray, carried by a Greek Phyllida had not seen before. Was this a good sign? Impossible to tell. But, surely encouraging, was a new look about Oenone, a brightness, a sparkle in her eye . . .

'You look better today.' Phyllida had waited until the simple meal was set out on her table and the man had withdrawn to the doorway.

'You can see it?' Oenone poured wine for them both. 'There's news today, splendid news. Alexandros sent a messenger back from the harbour. There's an Allied Fleet assembling off

Navarino. They mean to make the Turks see reason, he says. Think, *kyria,* it may mean freedom for Greece at last.'

'Freedom for us, too, I hope. Milord Renshaw and me.'

'What do you mean?' Obviously, in her excitement, she had not stopped to think of the implications of this news.

Phyllida answered her with a question. 'Alexandros hopes to be one of the men who will govern free Greece, does he not?'

'Yes?' Puzzled.

'Think, Oenone. If the Allies do give freedom to Greece, they will have a considerable say in its new government. It stands to reason. Well! What hope will Alexandros have if he is known to have kidnapped an English milord and held him to ransom. It will be the end of everything, so far as he is concerned.'

'But if you were his wife, you would not speak against him.'

'I tell you, I will never be his wife. Besides, even if I was forced to marry him, there would still be Milord Renshaw, whose voice carries infinitely more weight than mine. But Alex must have thought of this. What did his message say? Did it not mention us?'

'I don't know exactly,' Oenone admitted. 'It came to my uncle, who is in command here in Alexandros' absence. When he told me about the Allied Fleet he said nothing about you. But then'–she thought about it for a moment–'he cares nothing about politics. He thinks only of life here in the Mani. He's never been further away than Kalamata. He would rather Alexandros stayed home . . .'

'And lived by brigandage.' Phyllida finished the sentence for her. And then, remembering, flashed an anxious glance at the man on duty in the doorway.

'No need,' Oenone smiled, her face astonishingly young for a moment. 'He speaks only Albanian. He might understand a word here or there, but that's all.'

Phyllida concealed the leap of excitement this news gave her. Oenone had intended tonight's conversation to be private. 'Your uncle's in command here?' she asked.

'Of course.'

'And might not let us go even if Alexandros told him to?' Was this pushing her luck too far?

But at least Oenone was giving it serious thought. 'I don't know,' she said at last. 'Alexandros' word is usually law, but it's true, now he's away . . . My uncle is already planning to buy the finest set of arms in Kalamata.'

'With his share of the booty? I see. Oenone, can you get a message of your own to Alexandros?'

'Not possible. No one can. The *Philip* sailed yesterday.'

'In pursuit of the *Helena*?'

'I suppose so. Alexandros will catch her. There's nothing to be done until he gets back.'

'Oenone, you're wrong. For all our sakes, you must believe me. You saw how angry Alexandros was when he left yesterday?'

'Yes.'

'Did he tell you why?'

'No. Alexandros does not explain things to me.'

'It was because he thought he'd been betrayed.' God, how difficult this was. 'He had arranged, with my brother, that he would take over the *Helena*.'

'With Petros, yes.'

'You know him?'

'I have seen him.'

'Alexandros thinks Petros betrayed him. There was no message, you see. He thinks my brother has seized the *Helena* and taken her to Zante, to claim I am dead and take possession of my estate. But he's wrong. I'm sure of it. My brother is a fool—' Extraordinary to say it so calmly. 'But he's not a scoundrel. You've met him. What do you think?'

'I think you are probably right, *kyria*.' It pleased Oenone to be consulted. Phyllida could see her putting brains to work that she had hardly known she possessed. 'But in that case—' She thought it through. 'What happened on the *Helena*?'

'What you'd expect, if you knew anything of Milord Renshaw. He would have left instructions with his captain. Careful ones. Covering everything. I think when Petros went aboard they must have been very surprised—and very cautious.'

'So?'

'I think they have probably kidnapped Peter in their turn and gone to seek help. They won't know about the Allied Fleet off Navarino. They will have gone the other way, round Cape Matapan, to Nauplia, to look for Captain Hamilton and the *Cambrian*. So don't you see, Alexandros will go all the way to Zante and find nothing . . . Worse still, by the time he gets back, he may find that Hamilton has come to Kitries and rescued us . . . In that case, he's a disgraced man. There will be nothing left for him, but brigandage here in the Mani.'

There was a long silence. Then: 'Why should I believe you, *kyria*?'

They had come a long way in two days. 'I don't know.' Phyllida took it as carefully as possible. 'Because it's true? Because we are two women, and understand each other?' And then, seeing Oenone still mute and unconvinced: 'One thing you could do. You could go and ask Milord Renshaw what instructions he left on the *Helena*. No need to tell him why. No reason why he should lie to you. Besides, he's a man of honour. Tell him I ask him to tell you the truth. He will.'

'Yes.' Oenone thought about it. 'He will.' She had said 'will', not 'would'. 'And if he confirms what you say,' she went on. 'What then? Do you really think Captain Hamilton would rescue you?'

'He rescued Milord Trelawny after Odysseus was killed.' Would Oenone have heard of this?

Mercifully, it seemed that she had. 'It's true,' she said. 'They're capable of anything, those English sailors. And it would be the end for Alexandros?'

'Believe me, Oenone, it would.'

'Then I had better go and talk to Milord Renshaw. You've finished, *kyria*?'

'Yes.' What had they been eating? 'You'll tell him—' What could she ask Oenone to tell Brett? 'Tell him I'm well, and that I beg him to answer your questions.' Dared she ask Oenone to come back and tell her the result? No, there was the uncle to be considered. If things went as she began to hope they might, it would be fatal to have aroused his suspicions of Oenone.

Time crawled, yet raced by. How long would it take Alex to reach Zante and return? Her narrow view, next morning, showed her clouds still moving swiftly across the azure sky. The wind that helped Alex to Zante might delay his return. Unless he had in fact caught the *Helena*, and came back under steam. But that she would not believe. There was more smoke, today, visible above the hills to the north. Ibrahim was still at his murderous work. Which meant, surely, that the tiny garrison of the fortress would not be increased by the return of the party who had gone north to fight him. If Hamilton should come, or if she could persuade Oenone to help them escape, there would be so many fewer men on the plateau to be dealt with.

When Oenone arrived with her lunch tray, her heart gave an almost sickening lurch of hope. The man on duty at the door was the Albanian again.

The vegetable soup was thin and tasteless today. 'Alexandros did not send the provisions he promised.' Oenone said it almost in excuse. And then: 'My uncle says he'll have to send a couple of men down the valley tomorrow.'

'Oh?' Careful, she warned herself. Don't assume Oenone is telling you, on purpose, that the small garrison is to be diminished by two more. 'How long will it take them?' Surely a natural enough question to ask?

'Two days. Maybe more. Certainly one night away, since their families are down there. I think we can count on two days.' And then, quickly. 'Say nothing. Careful, *kyria,* don't forget the man at the door. Tone, he will understand, if not words.'

'Yes.' Phyllida made herself pause, drink wine, take a bit of bread softened in the watery soup. Then: 'You are going to help us? You talked to Milord Renshaw?'

'He's a man, that one. He understood me almost before I understood myself. You're right, *kyria,* he'd never have left the *Helena* unprotected. Alexandros might have taken her, perhaps, but never that brother of yours.'

Poor Peter! But, 'That's what I thought.'

'So. I have decided.' There was something extraordinary

about Oenone this morning. In her new decisiveness, she reminded Phyllida of some fierce young woman from Greek legend: Electra, perhaps? 'Milord Renshaw has given me his promise,' she went on. 'Now, I must have yours, *kyria.*'

'Yes? What has Milord Renshaw promised?'

'To say nothing, ever, that will harm Alexandros. To write good of him in his book. He tells me it will have many readers, all over the world, and I believe him. I do not know much, but I know when a man speaks truth to me. He tells me he is a poor man, with nothing in the world but the *Helena*, and I believe him in that, too. So the money must come from you.' Her voice was as calmly practical as ever. 'You said, the other day, that you would give me a dowry. You meant it?'

'Of course.'

'Yes. Milord Renshaw says I can trust you, and I believe him in that too. So: you will promise me the half of your fortune. And you will promise, as milord has done, never, so help you God, to speak of how you escaped.'

'I promise. All you ask.' It was extraordinary; it was too good to be true. Dared she believe it?

'Milord is writing a paper for you to sign.' Oenone had taken Phyllida's consent for granted. 'He says he will make it simple, so I can understand. I do not read your English writing very well.' She laughed. 'I have told my uncle I visit you because you help me with my reading. Remember that, if he should come to see you. At supper time, milord will make a scene about the wine. The man will go and fetch new—we have our laws of hospitality, we Greeks—while he is gone, milord will give me the paper. Later, you will give me a reading lesson, and sign it.'

'And then?'

'Leave all to me. I must manage as best I can. But, if the men go down to the valley tomorrow, it will be tomorrow night. You will be ready to do whatever I say, without question. I am trusting you, *kyria,* with more than my life. You will trust me in return?'

'I will indeed, Oenone.'

Oenone emptied her glass. 'You are amazing, you Franks. You ask me nothing? And promise me all this? Wealth, to make Alexandros glad to have me . . .' She seemed to be battling with herself. At last: 'I must tell you,' she said. 'It is not much I will be able to do for you. I shall get you, before first light, out of the castle and down to where they send the baskets. After that, you must find your own way, and God go with you. I have told Milord Renshaw where the paths lead, and told him not to tell me which he plans to take. So, whatever happens, I cannot betray you.'

'Yes.' There was something wonderfully comforting about Oenone's complete confidence in Brett. 'But, Oenone. One other thing. These clothes. I look like a Turkish woman.' She had not missed the hostile reaction of the peasants at Kitries, the covert spitting, the looks that would have killed . . . Turkish costume was all very well in Nauplia, but might mean death, here in the Mani.

'You're right.' Oenone considered her for a moment, thoughtfully. 'No hope of clothes like a Frankish woman's. But—you're thin and tall.' It was not a compliment. 'In one of the fustanellas Alexandros wears for night work, you could pass well enough as a boy. It will be black with dirt, of course. You'll not mind that? They smear them with lambs' grease, you know, so they'll get black quickly, for safety at night.'

'I'll not mind.'

'Good. Then, if we cut your hair and blacken your face, you will pass for milord's Greek guide.' She stood up. 'It's time I went.'

'But you, Oenone? Will it be safe for you? What will your uncle do, when he finds us gone?'

'You think of that? So did milord. In the face of your own danger. I shall never understand you Franks. But we worked it out, milord and I. He's clever enough to put both feet in the same shoe, is Milord Renshaw.' She laughed, and seemed for a moment almost human. 'Do you know what he has found? The paper old Anastasia brought him is a poem, he says, a splendid poem all about the Mani that will make us famous. I am helping him to read it—it's in our Greek characters, of course, and he finds it difficult. Was it not a fortunate thing that Alexandros gave strict orders to our uncle that you two should be treated with every kindness your imprisonment allowed?' Using her brain at last, she seemed to be coming alive, becoming a person, before Phyllida's delighted eyes. Now she was making a business of clattering the dishes on to the wickerwork tray. 'He will ask me to help him tomorrow night,' she went on. 'Uncle is always drunk at night. He won't notice. He's a very stupid man.' She had only discovered it this minute. 'When he finds me, unconscious, in milord's cell, and you gone, it won't occur to him to wonder how you found your way. Besides–' She said it with pleasure. 'He would never imagine a woman could do it.'

'And Alexandros?' Idiotic to raise this doubt, but somehow she could not help herself. 'Should you not come with us, Oenone, for your own safety?'

'No. I shall stay here. Next day, I shall go to Kitries, to wait for Alexandros. I must be the first to tell him, don't you see?'

'Yes. You're a brave girl, Oenone.'

'Oh, courage.' She dismissed it. 'What is that? We all have it, we Greeks. I would like to be wise, like Milord Renshaw.' She was at the doorway, and turned. 'Sleep well, *kyria*, and rest well, too, tomorrow.'

# 25

'There!' Oenone stood back to survey her handiwork. 'You'll do. I'm sorry about your hair.' She had cut it jaggedly and smeared it with grease, so that it hung lankly round Phyllida's blackened face. 'You must walk with the longest stride you can manage,' she went on. 'And see to it that the fustanella swings.'

'Lucky I've been wearing trousers so much.' Her throat hurt and her head had not stopped aching all day. It was hard to pay attention to what Oenone was saying.

'The men on guard should be fast asleep by now,' Oenone went on. 'I told them milord had refused his wine, and they had better finish it. That way, if my uncle should enquire, he will think it was milord who drugged it.'

'Clever.' She found Oenone almost frighteningly so.

What was that book of Mrs. Shelley's. *Frankenstein*? About a monster who came alive? The sight of Oenone suddenly using her excellent brain suggested it, and Phyllida thought, through the pounding of her head, what a surprise she would be to Alex as a wife.

'Time to go,' Oenone said. 'A pity there's no glass to show you what a fine boy you make . . . But it's too dark, anyway. Come, *kyria,* milord will be waiting.' She blew out the lamp. 'Lucky there's a moon. We don't want someone looking over from the other buildings and seeing lights moving about here. They should all be drunk asleep by now, but you can't count on it. Follow me down the stairs. Careful: your hand on my shoulder.'

The door below, Brett's door, was locked, with a thin line of light showing round it. 'Wait here a moment.' Oenone breathed the words. 'I must make sure of the guard.' She seemed to be away an age, while Phyllida stood shivering in her strange clothes. How much colder it was up here than down on sea level; no wonder if her throat hurt and her teeth chattered.

'Good.' Oenone appeared, soundlessly, beside her. 'Dead to the world, both of them.' She was feeling for the keyhole in the darkness of the door.

'Both?'

'There's always one on duty outside. There.' The key grated in the lock, and the door swung inwards with a scream of hinges that made Phyllida realise just how wise Oenone had been to make sure of the guards first.

But here was Brett coming forward to greet them, lamp in hand. Extraordinary to have feared never to see him again and now to be greeted as casually as if they had been parted by the merest trivialities. It was almost satisfactory to see his expression change to one of amazement as she moved forward into the lamplight. 'Good God,' he said. 'I'd not have known you. I congratulate you, *kyria.*' To Oenone.

'Yes. I think she'll pass in the daylight. We must at least hope so. You're ready? We're committed now. The sooner the better.'

'Of course.' He picked up a small bundle like the one Oenone had helped Phyllida pack. 'You promised me a weapon, *kyria.*'

'You shall have your choice. Now, blow out the lamp, and follow me. And, not a sound.'

For a moment, before he blew out the lamp, his eyes met Phyllida's. This was a leap in the dark, they said: anything might happen. And, as silently, she answered him: anything was better than what they were escaping.

Down the black stairway. Phyllida's hand on Oenone's shoulder, Brett's on hers sending a convulsive shiver through her. At the bottom, a glimpse of a lighted room, two Greeks snoringly asleep on the hard earth floor. One quick glance at them and Oenone led the way out on to the moonlit plateau and straight across towards the lighted hall where Alex had entertained them.

Instinctively, Phyllida hesitated, and felt Brett, behind her, do the same. Then his hand, still on her shoulder for guidance, closed harder with a message of comfort. They were committed to this wild venture, to trusting Oenone. They must go through with it. A quick, impatient twitch from Oenone, in front, set them in motion again, feeling horribly exposed among the strange shadows of the moonlit plateau. Phyllida thought she had never felt so complete a silence. The only sound, their footsteps, soft-shod on quiet rock, echoed like drumbeats in her head, vying with the pulse that had been beating heavily there all day.

Now they were at the door of the big hall. Oenone's hand told Phyllida to stay where she was, and Brett took the message, wordlessly, from her. They stood, his hand still reassuring on her shoulder, and watched Oenone open the door of the hall, letting out a blaze of light, and no sound at all. She vanished for an endless moment, then reappeared, silhouetted against the light, and beckoned them forward.

The hall was lit by a huge fire, blazing dangerously on the untended hearth. In front of it, a grey-haired Greek lay fast asleep, half on, half off the chair Alex had used. 'My uncle.' Oenone mouthed the words. 'Nothing would rouse him.' Her hand swept the weapon-hung hall. 'Choose what you need. But, quietly.'

There were fewer weapons than before. Phyllida watched Brett as he lifted two straight, short daggers from their places. Without ammunition, the few remaining muskets would be useless, not worth carrying as a bluff. She turned, at his warning touch, and saw Oenone on the far side of the fireplace, beckoning. Beside her yawned a dark hole that had not been there before. She felt Brett catch his breath in surprise, and followed him as he picked his way silently round the big table.

Still in silence, they followed Oenone into the pitch blackness of the hole, turned instinctively to look back towards the firelight, felt her moving beside them, and saw darkness close across it.

'There,' said Oenone clearly. 'No one can say that I showed you the secret way. You could search for a thousand years and still not find it. And still less the way back.'

'Secret or sacred?' asked Brett, surprisingly.

'Both, I have no doubt.' She understood him perfectly. 'And safe, which is more to the point. It leads down, inside the rock, to the lower plateau. No need for a light. They built well, our ancestors, it's smooth going every inch of the way. So, follow me.' Her hand found Phyllida's in the darkness and placed it once more on her shoulder. 'And you, milord, behind the *kyria.*'

'But.' Surprisingly, Brett hesitated. 'If it's a sacred way, what does it lead to? Up here?'

'Milord!' No mistaking the threat in Oenone's voice. 'This is no time to be thinking of antiquities for your book. Follow me, and watch yourselves.'

It was good advice. The paving was smooth and well-laid, but there were still occasional joins that might trip the unwary in that heavy, total darkness. Several times Phyllida had to pause, holding Oenone back, while Brett seemed to trip and recover himself.

'Don't dally!' Oenone's voice came back to them angrily. 'We're dead, all three of us, if you're not away from the lower plateau before first light.'

After that, they moved forward more swiftly, in concentrated silence. But it seemed an age before they saw pale light ahead and emerged through what seemed to be a crack in the rock-face on to the plateau. Away and below, moonlight glimmered on the sea. It looked terrifyingly far off, across a wild chequerboard of black and grey shadow, with here and there a lighter gleam where the moon caught a shining patch of flint.

Oenone was looking up at the stars. 'We've not done too badly after all. You've an hour or so before the dawn. Do you remember where the path to Kitries begins?'

'I think so.' Brett pointed. 'Over there. And the other way?'

'I'll show you. The one to Kitries is easy to find. It's used all the time. The other's just a goat track, hardly that. You'll need your wits about you, if you decide to take it.' She was leading the way along the edge of the plateau, and went on before there was time for them to speak. 'For God's sake don't tell me which you mean to take.'

'I haven't decided,' said Brett.

'Good. There.' She paused where the cliff came down to cut off the plateau. 'You see?'

'Yes.' It was more than Phyllida could. 'And you say, this way, it's two hours to the nearest house.'

'Yes. About the same distance as to Kitries. But, as I told you, the people that way are no friends of ours. Now, I must leave you. If I'm not back before my uncle wakes, nothing can save me. God go with you, my friends.' Surprisingly, she kissed Phyllida on both cheeks.

'And with you.' Brett bent to kiss her hand. 'If I can be of service to you, ever, I am yours to command.'

'The best thing you can do for me is get clear away. Good-bye.' She vanished into the dark cleft of the rock.

'Well,' said Brett. 'Here we are.'

'Yes.' They had moved back with Oenone and stood now at the centre of the pleateau. 'Did you mean it when you said you hadn't decided which way to go?'

'Of course not.' He had turned, already, and was moving away from the Kitries path. 'You heard her say that the people this way are their enemies. It's our only hope.'

'But, Brett!' There was so much they had not had a chance to discuss. 'Suppose they've gone for help, on the *Helena*, they'll come to Kitries.'

'Yes.' He was at the edge of the plateau now. 'But not by tomorrow–not by today, I should say. Phyllida, there's no time for discussion. I'm going this way. Are you coming?'

'What else can I do?' She swallowed a helpless sob. The path up from Kitries had been bad enough, but by Oenone's own admission, this one was worse. The throbbing in her head was louder than ever; she was almost surprised that Brett did not hear it. To look down, now, was agony.

'Good.' He had expected nothing else. 'Keep close behind me, and for God's sake watch your feet. A twisted ankle, and we're lost.'

'Yes.' Tell him about her head? Tell him she could not do it? But, already, she was doing it. They were on the goat track, which was just enough of an indentation on the steep hillside to show as a shadow on the bare, moonlit rock. There was no vegetation up here, except an occasional huge cactus glittering like a sheaf of silver spears. Don't look at them, don't look anywhere but at Brett's back. When had he taken her bundle and added it to his own? What would he do if she was to sit down on the path and tell him, simply, that she could not go on?

A thousand hammers were beating out a rhythm in her head. 'He'd go on,' they said. 'He'd go on and leave you.' It was easier, a little, if she kept her head bent downwards, watching the darker shadows that meant loose stones on the path. For an endless while it went on, sideways and a little downwards, along the edge of the steep slope. Then, gradually, it turned upwards again. It made the walking a little easier, with less chance of a fall, but Phyllida's breath came harder and harder. If she opened her mouth, her throat hurt worse. The hammers in her head were beating faster now. At each step she took, she thought she was going to stop and tell Brett she could go no further, but each time, somehow, the other foot dragged itself forward and she went on. At last, half an hour, a million years later, Brett stopped. She had lagged a little behind him and it took her a gasping moment to catch up. Each breath hurt now, all through her.

Brett was looking back, not at her, but beyond. 'Thank God,' he said. 'At last we're out of sight of the plateau. If the alarm should be raised, they won't know which way we've gone.'

'No.' It came out as a croak and he looked at her quickly, then away.

'Heartless,' said the hammers in her head. 'Quite heartless.' But already he had turned and moved on, downward again now, so that she understood, through an increasingly dizzy pain, that they had rounded an escarpment of the mountain. Surely, now, if they were out of sight, they could stop for a moment and rest?

'Brett!' It hurt so much that it came out merely as a whisper and apparently he did not hear, but went steadily on ahead. 'Brett!' No use. She could hardly hear it herself, the whisper of a lost soul, out there on the cold mountain. She thought she had told her feet to stop, to give up and let her lie down and die there, on the bare rock, but if she had, they ignored her, and went plodding on, after Brett.

Up again. Down again. Up. Down. Slipping; sliding; stumbling. 'Brett!' She stopped. 'I can't.'

This time he heard her, turned, his face a blank in the moonlight. 'You must.'

'I can't, I tell you.' She was leaning, heavily, against an outcrop of rock that jutted up by the path. 'Couldn't we rest, just a little?'

'No.' Ruthless. 'If you stop, you won't get started again. You know it as well as I do.'

'I don't care. Just leave me then. No one would hurt me, a woman.'

'No?' He looked upwards. 'I never heard that vultures respected the sex.' He had moved back towards her as he spoke, now pulled her upright. 'Come on.' Not an iota of sympathy in his tone. 'You must see that I can't leave you. It's half an hour till dawn. There were horses, back on the plateau. How long do you think it will take them to find us, once they start to search? It's not only your own life you're risking, but mine and Oenone's.' He was pulling her forward, awkwardly in the narrow path.

She stumbled. 'I hate you.' Recovering herself, she found she was moving forward again. He had had to let go of her hand, and was plodding ahead once more as if nothing had happened. 'Hate you . . . hate you . . . hate you,' rang the beat in her head. 'Not only your own life . . . mine and Oenone's.' Cruel . . . cruel . . . Alex would be better . .. Anything would be better . . . She slipped again, recovered herself and heard, above them on the mountain, an owl cry. Vultures, Brett had said. She imagined them, picking at living flesh, then bones bleaching to eternity on this bare rock. Another owl, and then, almost a miracle, the bleat of a goat, ahead and below, and not very far. And something else. Lifting her head for a moment, with an effort that hurt so much as to make even pain unreal, she saw, above them on the right, the ragged mountain edged with a thin line of brightness. Somewhere, far to the east (over Nauplia? over Jerusalem?) the sun was rising.

And, almost another miracle, ahead of her Brett had stopped. 'The path's wider now. I can help you a little.' His voice was matter-of-fact. She almost pulled away, but his arm round her was too comforting. 'Easier now,' said his voice, and the hammers in her head took it up. 'Easier now . . . easier now . . . easier now.' Her feet kept time with his, slipping and stumbling among the loose rocks of the path, because, now that she had him for guide, she need not make herself look down, but kept beside him, passively, putting one foot in front of another.

'Easier now . . . easier now . . . easier now . . .' When had she shut her eyes? Opening them, she was seared by pain, but saw, in the flash before they closed again, that the sun was up. Rosy-fingered dawn . . . rosy fingered . . . The hammers beat more and more slowly. She did not know that her steps were slowing to match them, that Brett, now supporting her almost entirely with his left arm, had turned to glance down at her anxiously.

Then, for a moment, she was conscious again, aware of figures all round them and voices, hostile . . . challenging . . . And above them Brett's. '*Philhellenoi*,' he said. '*Angloi* . . .'

She was sliding down, down, a thousand miles down, into a blackness where only the drumbeat of pain spelt life.

She was warm. She was lying down. Above her, voices echoed strangely, speaking Greek, incomprehensible to her exhausted brain. One of them Brett's? She opened her eyes. 'I hate you,' she said, and slept again.

Someone was making her drink a warm, vile brew. Brett, of course. 'Sage berries,' said a voice. She could understand the Greek now. 'The best sudorific. Make her drink it all.'

She opened her eyes. Yes, it was Brett's hand that held

the unspeakable brew to her lips. 'No!' Feebly, she tried to turn her head away.

'Drink,' said Brett's voice. 'They risked their lives for you, gathering the berries.'

She drank like an angry, obedient child and instantly fell asleep again. Now she was not just warm, she was burning, sweating . . . Dying? Poisoned? She pushed away heavy coverings and felt them tucked firmly back round her. A hand felt her hot forehead. 'Sweating like a pig.' Brett's voice of course.

'Thank God.' A Greek. Praying? It sounded like it.

Sweating like a pig. 'I hate . . .' She was asleep again, dreaming now, the wild dreams of fever . . . Blood . . . and fire . . . the weapon-hung hall, the old Greek, not asleep, but lying by the fire, his throat cut, bleeding horribly . . . like a pig . . .

'Drink it!' Brett's voice, pulling her into reluctant consciousness, the same odious concoction held to her lips. What had he said? She knew she must drink, did so and sank fathoms down into a real sleep.

'Much better,' said a voice. The one she had heard praying? 'Get some rest now, milord, we can look after her.'

'No,' said Brett. 'I must be here when she wakes.'

Phyllida opened heavy eyes. 'I am awake.'

'Speak Greek if you can.' Brett was sitting on the floor beside her, and spoke, himself, in Greek. 'It's more courteous to our hosts, who have saved your life.'

'So practical,' said Phyllida, and then, in Greek: 'I'm sorry . . . Thank you.' She was asleep again.

Next time she woke, she was hungry. When had her throat stopped hurting? No voices. Nothing. She opened her eyes . . . The other times, surely, it had been dark, there had been lamplight, shadows . . . Now it was twilight. Morning? Evening? Impossible to tell, still more so to imagine how long she had lain here.

Lain where? A pile of sheepskins on a floor of beaten earth . . . A very odd-shaped room; shadows looming down on her . . . an attic? Suddenly, terrifyingly, she imagined herself back in the tower of the Mavromikhalis . . . on the very top storey now

. . . left there to die? 'Brett!' Had it all been a dream? No. 'Sweating like a pig,' he had said. How could she have imagined that?

She must have spoken Brett's name aloud. A figure detached itself from the shadowed corner of the strange room and came forward, lamp in hand, to stand over her as she lay, helpless and terrified, on the ground. Black skirts . . . black . . . a long white beard . . . Was she going mad? No. Suddenly the foreshortened figure made sense. A Greek priest.

'You are better, my daughter.' The other voice, the one that had prayed over her.

'Yes, Father. Thanks to you.'

'And to the milord, who has nursed you night and day. He is sleeping now. I made him, when I saw you were better. No sense having him ill too.'

'No.' The effort of understanding his peasant Greek had exhausted her already.

He must have seen it. 'Rest,' he said. 'When you wake, there will be food. We have a chicken, saved for your recovery. I'll tell them to kill it and start making the soup.'

Soup. The idea was delicious. This time she slept lightly, in and out of dreams, and waked again to that strange twilight. And Brett, beside her, automatically leaning forward, as she stirred, to tuck the sheepskins back round her. A little light filtered in from one of the corners of the odd-shaped room. It showed him exhausted, the mark of sleepless nights heavy on his thin face . . . 'Nursed you night and day,' the priest had said. Brett.

'How tedious for you.' She opened her eyes wide in the half-light to gaze up at him.

'Tedious?' This time he spoke English, like her. His voice was exhausted, like his face, but just the same there was a new note in it, one she had never heard before.

'Having to nurse me all this time. How long?' She began to raise herself on an elbow, to face him, was aware of sheepskins slipping in all directions, and thought better of it.

'It's all right.' Could there be laughter in Brett's voice? 'You're perfectly respectable, you know.'

'Respectable!' She was taking it all in now. 'You've been nursing me!'

'I have indeed. Do you still hate me, love?'

' "Sweating like a pig",' she quoted. And then, 'What did you call me?'

He *was* laughing. 'You did hear that. I rather thought you had. You started hating me all over again about then. *Isn't* it a lucky thing none of our hosts speak English?'

'I don't understand.' But did it matter whether she understood or not, so long as he spoke to her thus, in this voice he had never used before?

'It's not fair to tease you.' He had taken both her hands, somehow, in one of his. 'Darling Phyllida, I should break it to you that you have been delirious for over a week.'

'A week! And you've been nursing me?'

'And you've been talking. How you talked! You hated me like poison for the first few days, and, frankly, I don't blame you. But admit, love, if I'd so much as hesitated, back there on the mountain, you'd just have lain down and died.'

It was perfectly true. Sympathy would have been the end of her. 'But, Brett, you keep calling me–' She stopped.

' "Love".' He supplied it. 'Well, so I should, since when you stopped saying you hated me, you proposed marriage to me.'

'What?'

'Several times. And as if you meant it, too, so don't start trying to talk your way out of it. You're well and truly committed, my love.'

'But–'

'Yes?' He was bending over her, dizzily close.

'Did you accept me, Brett?'

'Ah, that's asking, isn't it?' His smile smoothed out troughs of fatigue from his face. 'After all that talk about hating me, I might well have said no, mightn't I? And then where would we be? But you put it to me so pressingly, love, I was afraid it might make you worse if I refused. So, very much against my better judgment, yes, I accepted you, my darling. Look.' He lifted her left hand and she saw that she was wearing his signet ring. 'It's a bit big,

I'm afraid. But you see, I was taking no chances. You're not going to be allowed to change your mind this time.' The loving tone deprived the words of their sting.

'Brett, I'm going to cry.'

'No you're not. You're going to eat some soup. And here it is.' He turned to thank the woman who had come soft-footed out of the shadows. And then, still in Greek. 'They saved their last cockerel for you, Phyl.'

'I don't know how to thank you.' Phyllida smiled shakily up at the woman. 'And—something I remember your saying, Brett. Someone risked their life gathering—' She had forgotten the word.

'Sage berries.' He supplied it for her. 'Yes, that was Sophia here, and her grandson. Lucky for you Sophia knows her herbs. She thinks you must have had the fever ever since we left Nauplia. It comes and goes, she says, getting worse and worse.'

'Yes. I did feel strange sometimes. And that night, coming here, I don't know how you managed to make me . . .'

'It was touch and go,' he said soberly. 'If I'd known, before we started, how ill you were, I don't think I'd have chanced it, but thank God I did.' He had taken a steaming bowl from the woman. 'What a fuss you made about that medicine. That's right.' She had taken a sip of the hot, strong-flavoured broth. 'Sophia says you'll recover fast, now the fever's left you.'

'She's gone.' It was still difficult to take things in.

'Yes.' He was speaking English again. 'I told them, by the way, when they first captured us—do you remember any of that?—that we were engaged. Isn't it a fortunate thing it turns out to be true?'

'But, Brett, are you sure?'

'Surer than I've ever been of anything.' He silenced her with a mouthful of soup. 'And happier than I ever imagined I would be.'

'Again?' Instantly, she wished it unsaid.

'No. And if you weren't my patient, I'd shake you for that, Phyl. I said "ever" and you know I meant it. You're thinking of Helena. Naturally.' Another hot, delicious spoonful of soup. 'Do you know, I hardly remember what she looked like? And as for what I felt about her! Nonsense! A boy's nonsense. I've known that —oh, for ages. I've just not admitted it to myself. I'm not very proud of it, but I think a broken heart seemed a more respectable subject for gloom than a lost fortune. And then, when I saw you with Alex, found you had engaged yourself to him—then I knew. Too late.'

'So that's why you were so horrid to me!'

'Well, of course.' Another spoonful of soup. 'I was so angry with myself. What else could I do but take it out on you?'

She laughed, and choked a little. 'What a cheerful outlook for our married life.' And then, on a totally different note, 'Brett!'

'Yes, love?' At once, he was as serious as she.

'You're sure that's not what it is? You aren't "making an honest woman of me"? Because of all this . . . the kind of thing Cissie Biddock would say?' She had just remembered something he had said. He had begun by telling the Greeks they were engaged. Before . . . Before, in her delirium, she had given herself away so completely. What if he was merely making the best of it now . . . making things easy for her. It would be like him. Her eyes filled with tears. 'I was such a fool about Alex,' she explained pitifully.

'Yes, weren't you, love?' Today, nothing could shake him. 'Almost as big a one as I was about Helena. Just think: if it had not been for your arrival, that night at Constantinople, I really might have drunk poison for her sake.'

'And, Lord, how cross you were at the time.' She was smiling, but then, again: 'Brett, you're quite, quite sure?'

'Idiot.' Very deliberately, he put down the empty soup bowl. 'I can see I'll have to show you.'

Very much later, 'Brett,' she asked. 'What exactly did I say? When I was delirious?'

'Enough.' He was settling her back among her sheepskins. 'I've never had a more satisfactory proposal. And as for Alex—you should have heard yourself. I'll certainly never be jealous of him again.' He bent to kiss her once more. 'Now sleep, love, and if you dream, mind it's of me.'

# 26

'But, Brett, where are we?' Phyllida waked to happiness, and a question. 'What is this place?'

'A cave, love. We were lucky, that night we escaped. The Turks had raided Kalamata, and further. The Greeks from along the shore had taken refuge in the mountains. This cave is above the path we were on. I doubt if I could have got you as far as the village.' He thought it over. 'I would have, of course, but it would have meant carrying you. And you're not a bit of thistledown like Helena, thank God. Though you're pretty close to it, right now. I wonder how long it will be before we can move you down.'

'Down?'

'Back to the village. The Turks have done their worst, and gone again. Most of the Greeks have gone back to pick up the pieces, but Sophia and Father Gennaios stayed to help me nurse you, God bless them.'

'Brett, what are we going to do?'

'You are better.' The arm round her gave her an approving squeeze. 'I wondered when you'd ask that. But it's hard to plan until we can get down to the village and learn the news. There's been none of Alex, by the way. Father Gennaios says he would have heard if he was back. So that's something.'

'Yes. And the *Helena*?'

'No news of her either, I'm afraid.'

'She didn't come to Kitries? With help?'

'No. But it's not much more than a week. Don't look so anxious, Phyl. Think! Everything's at sixes and sevens. There's a British squadron, under Codrington, somewhere near Navarino; that we do know; and a French one, under De Rigny, off Cythera. Not to mention some Austrians, who seem to be favouring the Turks. And the Turks themselves. None of them would have harmed the *Helena*, but, God knows, they've got their own problems. It may not have been easy to persuade them to drop everything and sail gallantly to our rescue.'

'But you really think they're safe? That Peter hasn't–' How could she ask it?

'My darling, I don't in the least want to speak ill of my future brother-in-law, but do you seriously think that Peter would have been able to outwit Barlow, and Brown, and Jenny, and Cassandra?'

'No.' She had thought about it so much. 'Thank God, Brett, I don't.'

'Well, there you are. They haven't come to our help, but that doesn't mean they're not safe. I hope,' he added honestly.

'Oh God, so do I. Because if they're not, Brett, it's all my fault. If anything's happened to Jenny, I'll never forgive myself.'

'Hush!' The arm that was not round her touched her forehead, lightly, in reassurance. 'Don't excite yourself, love, it's bad for you. Besides, remember, we both decided that day at Kitries that we must go to Peter's help–both believed he needed it. In fact, we both let Alex fool us. Much more excuse for you than for me. After all–'

'I had engaged myself to him! As if that was any excuse. What a fool, what a blind, besotted fool–'

'Hush,' he said again. 'It makes a pair of us, remember. You and your Alex, I and my Helena. We'll have more sense from now on, won't we, love?'

'Yes.' She brushed her cheek lightly against his supporting shoulder. Extraordinary to feel so safe at last, so easy, so free to talk to him. Safe. 'Brett?'

'Yes?'

'What do you think has happened to Oenone?'

'I wish to God I knew. There's been no sign of search parties in this direction, that's one good thing. I hope it means that uncle of theirs is waiting for Alex to return. By which time I also hope you'll be strong enough to move on.'

'But where? What in the world are we going to do?'

'As soon as you're up to it, we're going across country to Navarino. It's the only thing we can do.' He had felt her start of amazement. 'The one thing we really know is that Codrington is there with a British squadron. He's got the combined Turkish and Egyptian fleets bottled up in the Bay of Navarino. If we can only get in touch with him, we'll be safe. Or, failing that, if we can manage to surrender to Ibrahim Pasha himself. I can't say I'd much like to encounter one of his marauding parties of Turks. It's terrible, what they're doing. I'm afraid they're in a state to kill first and question afterwards. But Ibrahim's something else again. He rather fancies himself as an enlightened prince. Besides, he's no fool. He'll know that to harm us, at this crucial point in the war, might bring the Allies in against him.'

'But aren't they already? If Codrington's on guard over the Turkish fleet?'

'You might almost think so. But, no, as I understand it, it's merely a question of enforcing the armistice the Allies have proposed. The Greeks have agreed to it; the Turks have not—yet. Until they do—or don't—it's a stonewalling game. De Rigny, the French admiral, is waiting off Cythera in case the Turks manage to slip out and attack Hydra. But I don't think Codrington will let that happen. Comic, isn't it, to think of that old sea-lion and his handful of ships bottling up the whole Turco-Egyptian fleet.'

'Yes.' He made it all seem so reasonable. 'But, Brett, how do we get to Navarino?'

'We walk, I'm afraid. And by night. I wish I knew just how long it would take, or how soon you'll be strong enough to start. With horses, of course, and by daylight, it's only two or three days' journey from here. But in the dark, and on foot— It's all right, love.' He had felt her shudder. 'We won't start unless you are fit for it. After all, the wisest thing we could do might turn out to be, simply, to wait it out here until the armistice is either agreed or enforced.'

'But, Alex—'

'Well, yes, that is the difficulty. That's why I hope old Sophia is right and you recover quickly. Because in that case I think we must try the journey across to Navarino. Father Gennaios tells me there is a regular underground route. That's how he knows so much about what is going on up there. If we go, he'll find a guide for the first night who will get us to a safe house this side of

Kalamata, where we can lie up for the day. Then, with luck, there will be someone to take us on.'

'Yes, I see. Brett–' What had she meant to ask him? She was tired, too tired to think, too tired to worry.

Waking, what seemed like centuries later, Phyllida stretched luxuriously on her hard bed. She was tired still, so tired that each movement was a conscious effort, but her head was clear, that ominous hammer-beat gone, and she was not just hungry, but ravenous.

She had thought she was alone, but her movement brought old Sophia forward out of the far shadows of the cave. 'Good.' A toothless, benevolent smile. 'You are really better. I shall bring you food; you will eat and grow strong.'

'Thank you.' It was still hard to muster the Greek words. 'And milord?'

'Has slept the sun round too. He needed it, poor man. You're a lucky woman, *kyria*. He nursed you like a mother.' Again that toothless grin. 'Or a lover. Father Gennaios wants to marry you two, before you go. He's a good man, the holy father, but easily shocked.' It was not a Greek word Phyllida knew, but it was easy enough to see what the old woman meant. 'Think about it, *kyria*, while I get your food.'

Marry? Here? In a cave in the Greek mountains? To avoid shocking an old Greek priest. Crazy. But rather pleasantly crazy. Smiling a little, Phyllida drifted off into a light doze, from which she was roused by Sophia, with, inevitably, more chicken broth, this time with pieces of meat floating in it, and hard black bread to be soaked to edibility. 'You can manage?' The old woman set down the bowl on the ground beside Phyllida. 'Good. There is a man with urgent news from the village. Eat, *kyria*, and may God make it healthful for you.'

'Thank you.' Delicious to be able to eat without her throat hurting. It was only as she dried up the last drop of soup with the last softened morsel of strange-tasting bread that she had time to notice the bowl. Not at all the rough earthenware she would have expected, but an elegant, open shape, with around it–she lifted it up with hands that still shook a little—a design of little figures. A chariot . . . Greek warriors . . .

'Yes.' Brett had appeared while she stared at it. 'They find them in these caves, and, being practical, use them to replace what the Turks have destroyed. Just think, that may well be a picture of Telemachus and the son of Nestor driving their chariot from Pylos to Menelaus' home in Sparta. Quite impossible, of course, to do it in a day, if Homer's Pylos is really Navarino, as the scholars claim. But I like to believe that we may be doing part of their journey in reverse.'

She could not help laughing. 'Brett! You're not really thinking about your book?'

'Of course I am. And a good thing too, now I've a wife to support. Don't forget, you've given half your fortune to Oenone, and, if I know you, half the rest will go to Peter. Murray had better like my book!'

'Brett, you don't mind?' Delicious to have him read her thoughts like this.

'Mind? I'll be glad of it. Look, my darling, if you think I'm marrying you for your money, think again. And, by the way, did I hear old Sophia say something about Father Gennaios to you?'

'Yes.' Was she ready for this?

'I'm sorry. I had not meant to put it to you so soon. But you do look remarkably better.'

'I feel it.' He looked better too, she thought.

'There's nothing like happiness.' Once again, he seemed to be thinking her thoughts. 'But, since the subject has come up, what about Father Gennaios and his plan? I found him, just now, on his knees in the far cave, asking forgiveness for conniving at sin.' He saw her puzzled look. 'Our sin, you understand. No use telling him I've been much too busy looking after you to nourish what he would consider wicked thoughts.' His smile melted the very marrow of her bones. 'I have, of course: hosts of them. But it's not just that, love, though, mind you, the sight of you, with your ragged hair and your dirty shirt, brings out the satyr in me, I don't know why. Would you mind being ravished, love?'

'I don't know.' She thought it over. And then, 'Is it really so dirty? What a fright I must look. What's so funny, Brett?'

He stopped laughing with an effort. 'I make an improper suggestion to you and all that worries you is the dirtiness of your shirt! And, yes, since you ask, it's filthy, and I must ask Sophia if she can't find you another one. She's a miracle, that woman. They'd like to see us married, you know, she and Father Gennaios, but that's not all I'm thinking of. There's your aunt, too. Can you imagine how she'll feel when she learns we've been gallivanting about the countryside, without even Alex for chaperon?'

'Oh dear, yes. She'll be appalled, poor Aunt Cass.'

'And it's not entirely nonsense, though I can see you think so, little revolutionary that you are. Imagine the handle for gossip it will give the Cissie Biddocks of this world. And do you know, my darling, I find I no longer like the idea of a scandal—not when it's connected with you. So if the idea is not too unpleasant to you, shall we let Father Gennaios make an honest couple of us? We can always do it again, properly, with white lace, and orange blossom, and Jenny for bridesmaid, as soon as we get back to civilisation. Frankly, I don't mind how often I marry you.'

'I love you.' She said it as if it answered everything, as indeed it did. 'Only, please, darling Brett, if I'm to be married, get me a clean shirt?'

'Asked like that, I'd get you the moon.' A long, shaking kiss, from which he pulled away. 'I'd better see about that clean shirt, love. Quickly.'

He was gone longer than she expected, and returned with a grave face. 'Bad news, I'm afraid. There's a messenger up from the village. The Turks are out from Modon again. No one knows, yet, which way they're going, but I think we can expect the villagers back up here soon. At least we won't lack witnesses for our wedding, though I confess I had hoped that we might celebrate it in the chapel down in the village, even if it has got no roof.'

'You mean we'll have to be married in here?' Her heart sank at the idea.

'No, no. Not so bad as that. Though, mind, I'd marry you under water, instead of under ground, if it was the only way. But, you'll see, when you're strong enough. This is only one in a whole chain of caves. Father Gennaios has made himself a chapel in the largest of them. And not the first to do it either. I think we're going to be married by Greek Orthodox rites in a pagan temple. Do you mind?'

'Not if you don't.'

'That's my girl. Now, try and rest a little.'

She woke to the sound of quiet commotion echoing strangely along the line of caves. Old Sophia was standing over her. 'I thought they'd wake you, *kyria.* The Turks are at Kalamata again, God roast their souls in hell. But look what my grandson brought me, the clever boy. He could find water in the desert, that one, or roses on Taygetus, if he wanted them.' She laid a vine-leaf-wrapped bundle in Phyllida's lap. 'They're for you, of course. Better than any medicine.'

'Figs!'

'And some grapes,' said the old woman proudly. 'Eat all you can, *kyria,* they will do you good. And you must be strong for your wedding night. Oh! That reminds me.' She was enjoying this. 'You're not to imagine I'll let you get married dressed as a man. I've sent my grandson down to the village again for my bridal outfit. I've kept it hidden all these years, for my daughter to wear, but never had anything but sons and grandsons.' Naturally, she was delighted about this. 'You won't mind wearing it, *kyria*?'

'I shall be proud to.'

'Good. And I'll tell Yannis to bring a shirt for you, too, if he can find one. Your trousseau!' Once again, it was a Greek word Phyllida did not know, but the meaning was obvious. 'He's fetching the crowns from their hiding place. He's a safe boy, my Yannis. Father Gennaios doesn't mind telling him where they are.'

Crowns? Of course, a Greek wedding. 'You're all so kind,' said Phyllida.

'Nothing of the sort. You are our guests.'

Phyllida gained strength rapidly, but it was three days before Sophia pronounced her well enough to leave the cave. And even then, it was only possible to go out at night, since the Turks were still on the rampage in the valley below. 'It's horrible, my Yannis says,' reported old Sophia. 'In the old days, they spared the olives and the fig trees, hoping they'd soon be harvesting them again. Now, thank God, they know they never will. So they're destroying whatever they can. It will take us a lifetime–Yannis's, not mine–to make good the damage they're doing.'

'Yes, it's unspeakable,' Brett confirmed the grim story later. 'But I still think, the moment you're strong enough, that we should try and get to Navarino. There's a rumour that Alex is back.'

'Oh!'

'Yes. In a way, we should be grateful for the Turkish atrocities, since it means these caves are full of refugees. And all of them blood enemies of Alex's. Even if he should learn we are here, I doubt if he would risk an attack. Of course, we must hope that Oenone will have made him see sense.'

'My God, yes. For her sake . . .'

'I know. It depends so much on what he has learned of the *Helena*'s whereabouts, and the state of affairs in general. But no use looking so anxious, love. There's nothing we can do about it. Try and forget it, and get on with your studies.'

'Yes.' Father Gennaios, though delighted that they wished to be married, had insisted that they make a serious attempt at understanding the Greek Orthodox service, before he would perform it. 'How are you getting on, Brett?'

'I like it. But I keep wondering if the Father will suddenly insist we promise to bring up our children as members of his church.' He was suddenly holding her hands in a grip that hurt. 'There's one thing I must tell you, Phyllida.'

'Yes?' When he used her full name she knew it was serious.

'I know Sophia is going round smirking like the old earth mother she is, and talking about blessing the bride-bed, and I don't know how many other pagan customs, but nothing is going to happen between us, love, till we're safe out of this. Suppose everything should go wrong . . . it's not likely, but it could happen, and we must face it. Suppose I'm killed, and you're captured. It doesn't much matter whether it's by Alex or the Turks. It will be bad enough without the possibility that you're carrying my child.'

'But if you should be killed, Brett, your child would be my only consolation.'

'Bless you, love. But I still say, no. Be realistic, Phyl. Suppose it takes us several months to get out of here. And then we have to make the dangerous journey across to Navarino. And you have to keep stopping because of morning-sickness. I remember my mother before Jenny was born. It won't do, you know; we can't risk it. Besides, I want my son to be born, where he should be, in England.'

'Or my daughter?'

He laughed, and kissed her. 'Just like you, I hope.'

The days dragged by, with food increasingly short among the refugees in the caves. The men went down to the valley every night to see what they could salvage from the shambles the Turks were making. Father Gennaios invariably greeted them when they returned and saw to it that everything they brought was shared equally. Sometimes there would be a whole sheep, or even a pig, superstitiously butchered by the Turks, and then there would be merry-making as it roasted in the early hours of the dawn, and a quiet day as everyone slept off the unwonted meal. But equally often they came home empty-handed, or with only a few pot herbs and, with luck, a little dirty flour from one of the village hiding places.

As soon as she was well enough to move about a little and realised that the others were often getting nothing all day but thin soup made, sometimes literally out of grass, Phyllida refused to be treated differently from the rest, and Brett could only respect her for it, though, inevitably, it slowed her recovery. She got used to being almost always hungry and ignored an occasional dizzy spell as Brett took her at first and last light every day for a slightly longer walk down the narrow track that led from the caves. 'It's a risk,' he admitted, 'but it's one we've got to take. You must be able to keep up with the guide when the time comes.'

The walks did her good, but made her hungrier still, and the dizzy fits came more often. A week had passed without the raiding parties bringing back so much as a quail. Supplies of flour were running low too. Brett watched Phyllida finish her inadequate meal and went off to find Father Gennaios.

That night he went out with the raiding party. They returned at dawn, triumphant, laden down with sides of home-cured bacon and sacks of flour.

'Enough for several weeks.' Father Gannaios summed

it up. 'God bless you, my son. It was a lucky day for us when we took you in.'

'But you won't forget your promise, Father, nor the men theirs?'

'Fear not. We have sworn it by bread. If we break it, we are men accursed.'

'What promise, Brett?' Phyllida waited to ask the question until they were alone.

'That whatever the temptation, they will never go back. In fact, I doubt if any of them could find the entrance, without me to show it them, and I hope to God we took little enough out of all that plenty so it won't be noticed.'

'What plenty? Where did you go, Brett?'

'To the secret way up to Alex's fortress. Do you remember how I hung back the night Oenone brought us down, and how angry she got?'

'Yes?'

'I was feeling about in the dark. It seemed so odd that she should not use a light, there in the heart of the rock. She didn't want us to see that the sides of that causeway were stacked with pirates' loot. You never saw anything like it. We had lights last night, of course. It was like Ali Baba's cave. Bales of silk, arms, bundles of hides and sheepskins, and, best of all, food . . . We took nothing else. That was the understanding on which I showed them the way; that and their solemn promise never to go back.'

'But will they keep it?'

'I think so. They swore "by bread". It's a solemn oath. Besides, I led them about the plateau so many times, I don't think they'd ever find the entrance again. Father Gennaios chose them, at my request, for courage and stupidity. It will be a nine-days' wonder to them, that treasure cave.' He laughed. 'And I told them it was guarded by an evil spirit only I could tame. After that, there was no more talk of helping themselves to anything but the food I allowed.'

'But, Brett, Oenone—'

'I know, love, but I promise you I was deadly careful. We took only a little here and there. There is so much, it will never be noticed. I understand now why those wretched villagers at Kitries looked so much worse than our friends here. Gennaios tells me that Alex levies a tenth or more of all they grow.'

'Wicked!'

'Yes. And as for Oenone: don't forget that you have paid and overpaid her for all we took.'

'Why, so I have. I'd quite forgotten!'

He laughed. 'Money doesn't seem real up here, does it?'

It was October now. The nights were getting colder, but the Turks were still out on the plain, and the villagers remained in the caves, where life was pleasanter on a steady diet of bread, bacon and soup. Phyllida walked for an hour each morning and evening and felt better every day. The cold mountain air, and Brett's constant company acted as a tonic; happiness bubbled up in her. 'Now,' said old Sophia. 'Now you begin to look like a bride.'

'Just as well,' said Brett. 'Since tomorrow's the day.'

'Tomorrow?' Phyllida caught her breath. 'So soon?'

'Yes. Father Gennaios has asked me to get a message through to Lord Codrington: to try and make him understand the full dreadfulness of what the Turks are doing, here in the Morea. The sooner the better, and, of course, it means we will be helped by the underground chain. You must see how much safer we will be if we are actually working for them.' And then, 'You haven't changed your mind, love? About marrying me?'

'What do you think?' She leaned up, to give him a butterfly kiss. 'It's just—I've been so happy here. I was beginning to hope we could stay . . .'

'You must see we can't. It's not only a question of Alex. Have you noticed how much colder the nights are growing? Soon life will be impossible in these caves. If the Turks still hold the valley, God help our friends here. There's snow on Taygetus already. How long do you think it will be before it falls here? No, Phyl, this is our chance, and we must pray God, and take it. So sleep well, love. No walk tomorrow morning. Rest all you can. Father Gennaios insists on marrying us exactly at midday. At dusk, we leave. The moon's just right—enough light to follow a guide, but not enough to betray us. The word has gone out, tonight, ahead of us. We will be expected all the way. Who knows, a week from today we may be being entertained by Lord Codrington.'

Strange to be wearing women's clothes again. Strange, too, to think of plump old Sophia as a young girl in this heavily embroidered robe and flowing veil. 'There.' The old woman leaned forward to kiss her. 'May it be as lucky to you as it has been to me, *kyria*. Now, come with me. You must not see milord until you meet before the altar.'

Strange? It was beyond strangeness that she should be threading her way through this maze of twilit passages to meet Brett before a Greek priest and a pagan altar. Now the old woman paused, crossed herself, curtsied, and Phyllida, following into the light, did the same.

An astonishing place, all adazzle with light. Where did it come from? She looked up, way up to the centre of a naturally domed roof, and, amazingly, to a patch of vivid blue sky. 'Our church is lit by God himself.' Sophia had been watching her. 'Come, *kyria*.'

Following obediently to the centre of the huge, domed cave, Phyllida was aware of the friendly crowd of Greeks, muttering prayers and good wishes all round her. Sophia paused and motioned to her to go on alone into the circle of light under the high opening, where Brett and Father Gennaios awaited her beside a huge round rock that looked strangely smooth, as if it had lain under the wash of the tide for centuries. Sunlight made a halo of Father Gennaios' white hair and picked out lines of anxiety in Brett's face. It glinted, too, on the crowns carefully held by the boy, Yannis, and a girl about his age. A Greek she had never seen before stepped forward out of the shadows.

'This is my friend Dimitrakis,' said Brett. 'He has agreed to give you away. Come, love—' She had hesitated, just a little. 'It's close to noon. It's lucky then, Father Gennaios says. Not that I need luck, marrying you.' He led her forward into the circle of light. Dimitrakis took her hand and the children closed in behind with the crowns. Father Gennaios was standing directly in front of the round rock. As he began to intone the words of the first prayer a great beam of light from above seemed to concentrate itself on the stone, which glowed like an opal, like fire . . .

It lasted throughout the service, the crowning, the exchange of rings—Brett's signet, the plain gold one she had inherited from her mother, just fitting on his little finger—Father Gennaios blessing them . . . Above him, the light was dwindling, and as he said the last prayer, the rock turned dark again.

Sophia was kissing her. They were both crying a little. Behind her, Brett was explaining. 'It's good luck if the ceremony is concluded while the rock shines thus. Extraordinary, isn't it? I wish I knew what it was, but Father Gennaios won't let me examine it. This cavern is only used for solemn occasions.' He looked upwards. 'They must have to hurry in midwinter, when the sun's not overhead. But, come, Mrs. Renshaw, they want to feast us, bless them. Not the best preparation for a night journey, but it can't be helped. We owe them too much.'

'We do indeed.' Extraordinary to feel the warmth of goodwill that flowed around them. 'Brett.' She smiled up at him, still through a mist of tears.

'Yes, love?'

'We'll never have a nicer wedding.'

# 27

The wedding party was held in another large cave opening off the 'chapel'. This, too, was saved for ceremonial occasions and had its own small opening to the sky, which served as a chimney for the huge fire that blazed in the centre of the stone floor. Women who had not attended the service were busy round it, and a delicious smell of roast mutton greeted the bridal party. At the far end of the cave there was a slight natural rise and Phyllida saw that three seats had been carved out of the rock.

'Today, you are queen.' Father Gennaios motioned her to the central one. 'And we your subjects.' He seated Brett on her right and himself on her left. Dimitrakis sat down on the ground beside them and the rest of the Greeks arranged themselves in a loose circle round the fire. Phyllida was the only woman to be seated. The others were busy serving out lavish portions of roast mutton to the men.

'It doesn't seem right.' Phyllida voiced her protest, low and in English, to Brett as she accepted a slightly charred chop.

'It's the custom.' Spoken in Greek, it was at once explanation and warning. 'Eat well, love. You'll need it tonight. Besides, think of the sacrifices they must have made to give us this feast. It's the least we can do to enjoy it.'

'Yes. And the risks they must have run!' Someone must have pawned his life, down in the valley, for this young sheep that tasted so deliciously of the rosemary branches that had cooked it. She turned to Dimitrakis. 'Who found the lamb?'

'I, *kyria.*' He smiled. 'For our friends, Milord Renshaw, and his lady, who would not gladly risk his life?'

Her eyes filled with tears. How horribly she had misjudged the Greeks, basing her verdict, of course, on Alex.

Alex. She turned to Brett. 'I wish Oenone could have been here. I wish we knew she was safe.'

'So do I, love. And the others. But, look! The *Romaika*'s beginning, and you must lead. For a little while.' He produced, amazingly, a clean white handkerchief from the pocket of the faded canvas trousers that made him look so unlike his kilted hosts. 'Here! Take one end.' He held the other. 'Just lead round the fire for a little while. That will be enough.' Somewhere, beyond the now dwindling fire, someone was plucking at some kind of mandolin.

A curious shuffling step. She had watched it many times and thought the dance uninteresting. Now, with Brett's hand holding the other end of the handkerchief, with firelight shadow dancing on the roof of the cave, she found it quite different. The music was the beat of the blood, of the heart . . . The curious hesitating step, forward, pause, forward again, was the pulse-beat of happiness. She felt life coursing through her, to Brett, and, beyond him, to their friends, these homeless Greeks who were joining in, one after another, some holding handkerchiefs, some holding hands, to take their pace from her.

At last the music changed, quickened. Dimitrakis broke out of line to perform a vigorous *pas seul.* Brett dropped the handkerchief and took Phyllida's hand. 'Now! Change as fast as you can. Sophia will show you the way to your own cave. The light's fading fast, and we are to be twilight walkers from now on.'

'But Father Gennaios. We must thank him.'

The old priest had dozed off lightly on his rock throne, but woke at once to bless them in rolling Greek phrases. Their thanks he brushed aside. 'We have done for you only what the law of hospitality dictates. And, now, you are my children. Come back, one day, and show me yours.'

'Cry at your wedding, happy for ever,' said old Sophia cheerfully as she led Phyllida down a maze of twilit passages to her own cave. 'An odd sort of marriage,' she went on, helping her out of her bridal garb. 'But no odder than mine. I was married at twelve –for fear of the Turks, you understand. My husband went back to his village immediately, and I was working in the fields again by evening. But not dressed as a man!' This still scandalised her, and it was with many a disapproving '*Po, po, po*' that she helped Phyllida into the fustanella and closely fitted black jacket Oenone had provided. 'Not but what it suits you,' she admitted at last. 'You make a good enough boy, if you keep the jacket buttoned. No need for Yannis to be ashamed of you.'

'Yannis?'

'He is to be your guide for the first part of the journey. It's the roughest, too, I'm afraid. Down to the village. But Yannis knows every rock of the path–and no need to fear he'll have had a glass too much ouzo either. Not my Yannis. There, the bundle, and you're ready.'

'Sophia; I don't know how to thank you.' Impossible, insulting to give her money. What had she packed in the bundle–a lifetime ago, urgent in her anxiety for Peter? Nothing of the slightest use. The only precious thing she had, her ring, she had given to Brett in exchange for his.

'Are you ready?' His voice from the low entrance made her start and turn. 'Look what Father Gennaios has given us as a farewell present.' He was holding two of the sheepskin cloaks that were coat, bed and everything else to the Greeks.

'God bless him! But, Brett, Sophia. I've nothing–'

Brett was feeling deep in his trousers' pocket. 'The first time I've paid your debts, love, but not, I hope, the last.' He produced a sovereign. '*Kyria* Sophia, this has been my lucky piece for many years. I need it no longer, since my wife is my luck. May it bring you good fortune, as it has me. See! It has the picture of the King of England on it.' He bent to kiss her, first on one cheek, then on the other. Phyllida did the same, crying a little, trying to say 'thank you', but Brett was urging her away, out into the gathering dusk, where Yannis was waiting.

The first bit of the path was easy, since it was where she and Brett had taken their daily exercise, and she knew every boulder, every illogical twist, every outcrop of sharp flint that might cut through their silent pigskin shoes. They walked steadily for nearly an hour; then Yannis, a little ahead, turned to let them catch up with him.

'The next bit's difficult,' he said. 'I think we had best wait till the moon rises.' He looked up to the five-fingered silhouette of Taygetus, outlined, now, against the faintest hint of light. 'Not long to wait. Sit.' His gesture made the cold, bare rock seem the most luxurious of divans. 'Rest.' With instinctive tact he perched himself on a boulder a little away from them so they could speak English without seeming to exclude him.

If the sheepskin cloak had seemed heavy and awkward to carry at first, it proved itself now, acting both as protection from the cold rock and from a new bite in the air. 'A strange wedding night, love.' Brett had settled himself so that Phyllida could lean against him as comfortably as the harsh outlines of the rock permitted.

'Yes.' She leaned luxuriously back. 'Won't this be a story to tell our grandchildren!' And then, 'What's that?' It came again, a wild unearthly keening. From all around? From behind? 'Dogs?' Her voice shook a little.

Ahead of them Yannis was on his feet.

'Wolves,' said Brett. 'Where are they, Yannis?'

'Behind us,' said the boy. 'Near the entrance to the caves. They smell the food. We'd hoped they'd not come down from the heights so soon.' He looked at the pale band of light, a little broader now, above the mountaintops. 'With your consent, *kyria,* I think we should start now. The ladder is difficult in the dark, but at least they cannot follow us down it.'

The howling came again, nearer, echoing from cliff to cliff. 'So long as it's not impossible,' said Brett.

'Nothing's impossible. It is but for the *kyria* to put her feet, at each step, where I show her. We will have to go ahead a little way, *kyrie,* to a place where she can wait. Then I will come back for you. You trust me, *kyrie*?'

'Of course.'

'If they come too close, shout at them, throw something, anything to hold them off for a moment. But, whatever you do, *kyrie,* don't try to come down the ladder alone. It's death. Come, *kyria,* no time to lose. Do exactly as I show you, and there is nothing to fear.'

Nothing to fear? With Brett waiting up there, and the howling of the wolves perceptibly nearer? But at least no time to waste in fear of this 'ladder', whatever it might be. A foot, downward, to the resting-place where Yannis put it. A hand, obediently following his. Another foot; another hand. Thank God for the soft, gripping pigskin shoes. What was below? Better not think of that. Think, rather, of Brett, above, waiting . . .

Once, her right foot slipped from the resting-place Yannis had found for it, and she hung for an endless moment, supported by her left hand and one insecurely placed toe. But Yannis was there, his hand over hers, steadying her, helping her find her foothold again. If she panicked, if she fell, she would take him with her. And Brett? She would not panic.

It seemed to go on for ever. Hand, foot; hand, foot. 'This way, *kyria,* that's it.' Yannis encouraging, helping. Yannis . . . a boy of, what? Fourteen?

Suddenly, there was light. 'The moon's up,' said Yannis. And then, quickly: 'Don't look down!'

Good advice. Better not know. Foot, hand. The wolves again, very near now. Oh, Brett . . .

'There.' Yannis' voice, low, triumphant. 'Sit there, *kyria.* Don't move an inch. Wait.' Already his voice came from above her, as he climbed like a monkey back up the 'ladder'.

She could see it now, almost perpendicular in the moonlight, and Yannis' dark figure moving now this way, now that, up what must be an incredibly intricate route. No wonder their hosts felt safe in their caves.

The wolves again, directly above her, Brett's voice, shouting, and the sound of rock on rock. He had thrown something at them, and, so doing, had started a small landslide.

'Lie down, *kyria*! Hold tight!' Yannis' voice came anxiously from above, but she had already done so. Rocks rattled harmlessly past her. It was over. Peering up, she could see nothing now but the loom of the cliff. Then, far, far above–could she really have come down so far?–voices, Brett's and Yannis', indistinguishable, drowned by the renewed howling of the wolves.

The air bit cold. She wrapped herself more tightly in her sheepskin cloak. If they are killed, she thought, what shall I do? When the Suliot women were surrounded by the Turks, they danced on their mountaintop, and gradually, as they approached the edge, each one threw herself over, carrying her child with her. But I? She shivered. Her money. The great burden of her money. Peter and Jenny, Oenone . . . Whatever happens, she thought, I shall try to live.

'Phyllida!' Brett's voice. 'Can you hear me? Are you safe?'

'Of course I'm safe.' Her voice was tart with relief. 'If you think you're going to get rid of a perfectly good new wife by dropping rocks on her, you're mistaken. You didn't even hit me.'

'Thank God.'

She could hear them, now, above her, moving, pausing, moving again as she and Yannis had done. 'And the wolves?' she called up to them in Greek, and was rewarded by Yannis' laugh. 'They have never learned to climb the ladder, *kyria.* Fortunately. Neither up nor down. They're stupid, like the Turks. There!' The two of them joined her on her narrow ledge. 'Five minutes' rest, *kyrie,* if you wish.'

'No need. If you're ready, love?'

'Of course.' She was on her feet, carefully keeping her eyes away from the dizzy drop below. 'Which way?'

'It's easier now.' Yannis edged past her to take the lead. 'We follow the ledge. Keep close behind me, *kyria,* and don't look down.'

She had no time to look anywhere but at her own feet, carefully finding their way along the rough path. Downwards and to the left it took them, round a long spur of the mountain. 'The village is just below us,' Yannis said. 'Spit from here, and it should land on the dome of the church. A pity we can't fly.'

No need to elaborate on the point as they followed the curve of the mountainside further and further from their destination. But at least the moon was well up now, and the going easier. They stopped once, to adjust Phyllida's bundle, which had slipped on her back, where Yannis had made her tie it, under the sheepskin cloak. 'Just as well it didn't slip up there on the ladder,' he said as Brett made it safe for her.

She shivered at the thought, but already they were moving forward again, steeply downwards, into a deep gorge. She could smell rosemary now, and from time to time felt the softness of growing things under her feet instead of the bare rock. Here and there, a darker shadow was a tree.

Then, quite suddenly, they were in thick woods, pine by the smell of them, and, perhaps—Phyllida slipped and caught a branch to steady herself—the stubby little valonia oak. No moonlight here to help them. They had to find the path with their feet, moving forward at a snail's-pace. 'I see now why you said it would take all night.' Brett spoke from behind her.

'Yes.' Yannis spoke without turning round. 'But we're not doing too badly. Soon we'll reach the halfway point and rest a while.'

Only halfway. But the rest did her good, with the handful of dried fruit and a sip from the flask of ouzo Yannis produced. And after that, the going was steadily easier as the path broadened towards the village. At last, 'Wait here,' said Yannis, 'while I make sure that all's safe.'

'Exhausted, my poor love?' Again, Brett had settled

himself so as to provide the most comfortable possible resting place for her.

'Tired,' she admitted. 'I'd just as soon not have to climb that "ladder" again.'

'Good God, nor I. And when you think that they do it carrying whole sheep and pigs!'

'And Yannis made a special trip for the bridal crowns,' she said sleepily.

'And that ravishing outfit of yours.' He bent to kiss her. 'Our first night together as man and wife, and look at us.'

But she had fallen asleep.

She did not hear Yannis return, or their quick, anxious conversation, and only roused, reluctantly, at Brett's gentle, insistent shaking.

'Time to be moving, love.' He helped her to her feet. 'We've had to change our plans. The Turks were here yesterday. I'm afraid they found the hut where we were to have spent the day. Yannis thinks the church is the best place . . . Not much chance that the Turks will come back again so soon.'

'No, God damn them.' Yannis did not sound like a boy. 'What else is there for them to do here?'

'Were there people in the hut?' Phyllida made herself ask it, as they set forward again, walking side by side now.

'Yes.' Brett said no more, and she did not ask. She was beginning to notice a new smell, mingling with the fresh dawn scents of pine and herb, the smell of burning.

'They hadn't come this far for years. Not since they burned the chapel.' It was a shock to realise that Yannis was crying. 'The old ones did not think they would. They said the ladder was too steep; they'd stay at home, where they were comfortable. They're comfortable now, God rest their souls.'

The smell of fire was much stronger. They had left the forest behind and instead of slippery pine needles, Phyllida's feet felt firm, well-trodden earth as they walked between high hedges that she thought were prickly pear. It was darker, the moon must be setting, but ahead of them she could see a red glow.

'The village,' said Yannnis. 'Lucky for us they didn't bother with the chapel. Here.'

The building loomed up, dark against the further glow. 'Don't look.' Brett had her inside.

The central dome of the little church gaped open to show paling sky and a last star, but one corner of the entrance was still roofed, and the three of them settled there, after Yannis had said a quick prayer.

More dried fruit, Brett making her take a burning sip of ouzo, Yannis' voice: 'The old ones had saved a cockerel for you, since it was your wedding.'

And Brett's: 'Don't think about it. Or rather remember that I shall tell Milord Codrington everything I have seen.'

'Yes,' said Yannis, 'but that won't help the old ones.'

When Phyllida woke, it was twilight. Still? Again? And what in the world was that rushing noise? She stirred, was aware of Brett's sheepskin covering her as well as her own, and sat up. Suddenly, lightning flashed across the open roof of the church, showing the altar, drenched and desecrated, faded frescoes on the crumbling walls, emptiness . . . And rain pouring steadily down through the gaping roof; pools gathering here and there on the uneven floor; a trickle of water advancing steadily on the dry corner where she had slept. And Brett and Yannis? No sign of them. Had the Turks come back and found them?

The church door hung crazily on broken hinges. She peered cautiously out round it, but could see little through the torrential rain, hear nothing but the sound of its falling. Lightning again, and the crash of thunder, nearer this time. Primitive terror surged up in her. In a moment she would be screaming, rushing out into the storm to look for Brett.

Nothing of the kind. She turned back into the church and went busily to work damming the little stream that threatened to drown their one dry patch.

'I knew I could count on you.' Brett's voice made her start. 'Yannis was afraid you might panic if you woke and found yourself alone, but I told him he didn't know what American ladies were made of.'

'I nearly did. Oh, Brett, you're soaking!'

'Aren't I just? Don't kiss me, love. Someone in our party had better stay dry. Yannis not back yet?'

'No. Where have you been?' She managed not to make it a reproach.

'Doing my duty by Father Gennaios. Open my bundle for me, love, and get out my notebook. I must write it all down, while I remember.' He unfastened his travelling pen-and-ink stand from his belt and set it down on a flat rock. 'Thank goodness Father Gennaios made me some new ink. Pretty odd, I suspect, but it should last till we get to Navarino.'

She had unwrapped his bundle and found it to contain one clean shirt, a bundle of manuscript thickly covered on one side with Greek characters and on the other with Brett's fine, clear hand, and the invaluable notebook. 'But, Brett, if the Turks should catch us?'

'I know.' He faced her over it. 'But, think, love, what they are doing here is unspeakable. If they catch us, we're witnesses. We haven't a chance. My writing it down can make no difference. At least'—honestly—'I don't think it can. And I do think I owe it to Father Gennaios, for all they've done for us.'

'It's so very bad?'

'Yes.' He was writing away busily now. 'A day-to-day record will be infinitely more convincing than anything we can remember.'

'But, Brett, in that case, should I not see too? To act as another witness?'

He looked at her sombrely. 'You'll see enough, I'm afraid, before we get to Navarino.'

Yannis appeared some time later, shaking the water from his thick hair and triumphantly holding out a pair of quails. 'At least we can eat.' He handed them to Phyllida. 'I'll light a fire while you pluck them.'

'A fire? You think it's safe?' Brett looked up from his writing.

Yannis laughed scornfully. 'You don't think the Turks will be out in this! God has sent the rain as a protection for us, *kyrie.*' And then, thoughtfully, 'And, that being the case, do you think He will mind if I light a fire in His church?'

'I'm sure He won't,' said Brett. 'But how will you manage?'

Yannis laughed. 'My grandmother says I could light a fire at the bottom of the ocean.'

'Yes.' Phyllida looked up among a shower of feathers. 'And find roses on Taygetus if you wanted them.'

'Why in the world should I want them?' But he was right about the fire, and the quail, slightly scorched on the outside, rather raw along the bone, was the best meat Phyllida had ever tasted.

When they had finished, Yannis meticulously cleared away the traces of their meal, dousing the fire with the rain-water that still came down in torrents. 'A bad night for walking, I'm afraid.'

It was indeed. The rain sluiced down. The darkness was absolute and they had to walk in single file along a path that was rapidly turning into a stream. 'At least no one else will be out,' said Yannis, leading the way. 'And the path lies through the fields for the first few hours. It should be easy enough. If the worse comes to the worst, and it hasn't cleared by the time we get there, we'll have to shelter in the ruins at Mandinia. But I think it will clear. These storms don't usually last long.'

A flash of lightning seemed to contradict his words, and showed Phyllida, for an instant, the pitiful ruins of the village street, and ahead of them black shapes, swinging slightly in the drenching rain. Yannis crossed himself. 'God rest their souls.'

After that, they did not try to talk, but plodded forward, with water seeping up through their shoes, and down through every gap left by the rough sheepskin cloaks. An occasional flash of lightning showed a desolate landscape of scorched fields with here and there the leafless skeleton of a savaged olive or mulberry tree. From time to time, Phyllida heard Yannis mutter a curse under his breath. These must be the fields where he had played, or, more likely, worked as a child. Fantastic to remember that he was still little more than one.

After what seemed an age of this silent, water-logged walking, Phyllida thought she felt a slight slackening in the rain . . . There had been no lightning for a while and, above them, pale gaps were appearing among the clouds and at last, for a moment, she saw the half-moon before a flurry of clouds hid it again.

'I told you God was with us.' Yannis stopped to let them catch up with him. 'This is Old Mandinia. The ruins are just up there.' He pointed into the darkness. 'The new village is on the hill, but we don't go there. Our way lies along the shore, and, if you agree, *kyrie,* I think we should go on. The clouds are breaking up by the minute. By the smell of it, I'm sure it is clearing. There will be moonlight, when we need it.'

'Good,' said Brett. 'Better to walk ourselves dry anyway. Don't you think, love?'

'Yes, indeed.' Standing still, she began to feel clammy coldness shiver through her.

'This way then.' The path led gradually downwards between dark hedges that Phyllida thought were reed rather than the usual prickly pear. Then, suddenly, ahead of them a great arc of pale light.

'The sea,' said Yannis. 'Carefully, now, *kyria,* over the stones.'

They were large, smooth pebbles, worn by centuries of Mediterranean storms, and though the going was slow, it was not impossibly difficult. Besides, the rain had stopped; the clouds were breaking up and at last the moon shone out, turning the sea to silver and showing up a black mass looming beyond it. 'Navarino's beyond there.' Yannis stopped for a moment to point. 'A pity you can't swim it.'

'Yes.' Brett's arm was under Phyllida's to let her lean against him for a moment and rest. 'We could do with a couple of devoted mythical dolphins right now.'

Phyllida laughed. 'We certainly couldn't be much wetter.' But already Yannis had turned to plough forward again over the sliding stones. 'We mustn't waste this light,' he called back over the rough sound of the gravel. 'We'll need it along the cliff edge.'

The moon was almost overhead now and Phyllida was able to see that the ground was gradually rising to their right, and the strip of pebble beach narrowing. 'Lucky there are no tides here.' Brett spoke from behind her.

'Yes.' It was extraordinarily hard work walking through

the slipping, sliding shingle, and Phyllida breathed a sigh of relief when Yannis paused for a moment ahead of her, as if getting his bearings, then turned suddenly inland. Catching up with him, she saw that the way ahead was barred by a stream, rushing darkly between high banks.

'Nearly there now.' Once again, Yannis stopped to let them catch up with him. 'The mill at Armyro is your next halting place. Your new guide will meet you there. I hope.' He moved forward cautiously and they followed, their feet blessedly silent now, on beaten earth.

The first sight of the mill was daunting enough. All its superstructure was gone, and it was nothing but a black lump, huddled over the noisy stream. No light showed anywhere. But, 'It's been like this for years,' said Yannis, his whisper almost drowned by the rush of water. 'Wait.' He moved nearer the dark building and gave the unmistakable eery hoot of a hunting owl.

After a moment, another owl answered him, twice.

'Good,' said Yannis. 'We wait.'

A light showed in the building, a man appeared, and Yannis went forward for a quick, unintelligible exchange in the local dialect. 'All's well,' he told them at last. 'Petrakis expects you. He will send you on tomorrow night. God go with you, my friends.' He turned on his heel before they could answer, and was gone, at a steady jog-trot, down the dark path toward the sea.

'Dear God,' said Phyllida. 'He's not going back tonight?'

'Not all the way, I hope.' Brett turned to return the greeting of their new host, Petrakis, a silent man who led them without more ado into the desolate ground floor of the mill, fed them a curious meal of dried bean porridge flavoured with garlic, and left them to sleep. 'Don't stir out until I come for you. I must see where the Turks have gone now. The next part of your journey will be the most dangerous; they're everywhere round Kalamata. A pity we can't get you across by ship.' He spat. 'There are no ships. They've burned the lot. Sleep well, friends, and God guard you.'

'I forgot to tell you.' Brett was arranging his bundle as a pillow for her. 'From now on, our hosts know of you merely as a boy.'

'Well,' said Phyllida as he bent to kiss her, 'I might just as well be one.' And fell asleep.

She woke to the familiar, soothing sound of Brett's pen scratching on paper. It was full light in the mill, sunshine pouring in from various holes in the roof, and she lay for a moment simply enjoying it after all their twilight living. And enjoying too the sight of Brett, hunched over a rough trestle table, hard at work.

Had she moved, or was it simply her gaze that brought his eyes round to her? 'You're awake?' He dropped his pen and came to stand over her, so that she could see the tide-marks the rain had left on his shabby canvas trousers.

'Yes.' She smiled up at him. 'A fine figure of a husband you are, love! I wish your cousin the Duke could see you now.'

'Lord, how he'd envy me.' He bent to kiss her. 'But you've not met his wife. What a delicious word "husband" is, by the way. Did you sleep, love?' His arms were round her, hard.

'Yes, my darling.' She pushed him away, lovingly, with both arms. 'There's someone coming. And I'm supposed to be a boy, remember?'

'Well.' He gave way, laughing, rueful. 'It's in the best Greek tradition, after all.'

# 28

Petrakis reported that the Turks were still active on the plain round Kalamata. 'They're not leaving two stones standing together; the olive groves are burning, the orange trees cut down, and God help the people who didn't get into the mountains in time.'

'Can we get through, do you think?' asked Brett.

'If you're lucky. Anyway, it's as dangerous to stay here as to go on. They were at Mandinia last night. Lucky for you you came by way of the beach. I'm to take you as far as Nisi. We should be there in two nights, God willing.'

They crossed the stream on the ruins of a bridge, made their way down to the sea again and started once more the slow plod along the stones. By midnight, their feet found sand, the cliffs fell away on the right, they had reached the Messenian plain.

'Not a word from now on.' But Petrakis had hardly spoken throughout the walk, except, once, to urge Phyllida to walk faster, impatiently. 'Hurry up there, boy!'

They spent next day huddled close together in a kind of wigwam woven of branches hidden deep in a little wood, close to a stream. 'It will be better at Nisi,' Petrakis said as they finished the slabs of bean porridge they had brought with them, and made ready to start off again in the twilight. 'I hope.'

The walking was easier that night, along field paths, but the smell of fire haunted them, and once they had to make a long detour through a reed-bed to avoid a camping party of Turks. It was hard going and Petrakis kept looking anxiously at the paling sky. 'Hurry, can't you?' he whispered to Phyllida. 'There's no safe house this side of Nisi.'

'The boy's tired.' Brett caught up and gave a supporting arm to Phyllida as they rejoined the path.

'Tired!' Petrakis spat. 'At his age, I'd killed twenty Turks.' But he stopped for a moment, not so much to let Phyllida rest, as to sniff the air, carefully. 'No fire this way,' he decided at last. 'I think we're in luck. We'll need it, too; it will be daylight before we're there. Be ready to hide in the reeds if you hear anything.'

Rosy-fingered dawn, indeed. Phyllida was too tired to care, too tired to notice the chorus of frogs that greeted the splendidly growing light. But not too tired to imitate Petrakis and throw herself into the spiky reeds at the sound of noise ahead. It was only a small party of Greeks, late refugees, no doubt, from Nisi, but Petrakis let them go by in silence. 'What they don't know,' he whispered as they emerged stiffly from their hiding-place, 'they can't tell.'

It was full daylight when they reached the safe house at Nisi, a hovel on an island set in the middle of a swampy stream, which they had to ford, knee-deep in icy water.

As Yannis had done, Petrakis made them wait while

he gave the owl-hoot signal, conferred briefly with their new host, then turned, without giving them time to thank him, and was gone.

'But what will he do now it's daylight?' asked Brett.

'He won't go far.' Their new host was on old, old man with white hair and about three very black teeth. 'He thinks he'll be safer on his own. He's probably right. Come, then, I've food for you.'

It was actually hot, fresh-caught fish cooked on a smokeless fire of charcoal, and Phyllida would have eaten it bones and all if Brett had not filletted it for her, as for a child. Then, instantly, she was asleep, and, almost as soon, it seemed, being roused again.

'Only two more days.' Brett did his best to encourage her as they ate a quick meal of cold fish. 'Andreas here says he knows an old shepherds' track that should keep us well away from the Turks. They're out from Modon, anyway, not Navarino, so when we've crossed their trail we should be safe enough.' He and Andreas were busy packing up the rest of the fish in vine leaves. 'A night in a deserted shepherds' hut, I'm afraid. But he'll see us all the way.'

'And when we get there?' As always, they were talking Greek, and it was Andreas who answered her.

'There will be a Frankish boat waiting for you by Nestor's cave,' he said. 'Under Palaeokastron. The Turks are on top, of course, but they've never found the inlet. The Franks are to wait, each night, until you come. I hope the message you bear is worth their trouble, and mine.'

If it was intended as a question, Brett did not choose to answer it. 'So do I,' he said.

Inevitably, the night's walk began by the cold plunge through the stream, but the pace Andreas set soon had them dry and warm again. As they came up out of the marsh, they were greeted with the familiar, horrible smell of burning.

'There was a hamlet over there.' Andreas paused for an instant to point and whisper. 'They had submitted to the Turks. They thought they were safe. They burned them in their houses. Can you smell it, *kyrie*?'

Brett's hand was comforting on Phyllida's. She thought

he was going to say something, but it was only: 'God rest their souls.'

They crossed the broad path to Modon somewhere in the cold ebb-time after midnight. 'No need for the Turks to travel at night,' said Andreas, leading the way swiftly across. 'And not far, now, to our resting-place.' He had seen that Phyllida was beginning to flag.

The shepherds' hut was a crazy structure of wicker-work, concealed in a thicket of oaks on the rising ground of the promontory they must cross to reach Navarino.

'It will be downhill all the way tomorrow night,' said Andreas as they made their simple preparations for the day's sleep. 'The boy will find it easier.'

'Just think.' Brett leaned over Phyllida as they settled themselves, side by side, in their sheepskins. 'Tomorrow, we may be on the *Cambrian*.'

'It's too good to be true. Brett—' But his glance, quickly, over his shoulder to where Andreas seemed already fast asleep, was a warning. Anyway, she was too tired to formulate the odd uneasiness that had plagued her all day. Trying to understand it, she slept.

'Downhill all the way.' Andreas repeated it cheerfully as they finished the rather battered remnants of the cold fish. 'And a short stage at that.'

'Short?' Brett sounded surprised. 'But won't we have to make quite a detour, if we are to reach the north side of Palaeokastron?'

'You're well informed, milord.' Was he slightly taken aback? 'But, in fact, the Turks keep such poor guard, up there at the north end of the bay, that we can go in, most of the way, quite safely, on the old causeway.'

For some time their tiny path, little more than a goat track, led through low scrub. Judging by the scratches she received, Phyllida thought there must be holly bushes among it, and they had to walk well strung out to avoid lashing each other with backward-springing branches. At last they emerged, suddenly, into an open space with a broad view of leaden sea ahead, and a great semicircle of lights showing.

'Good God,' said Brett as Andreas paused to let them catch up with him, 'it's the Turkish fleet.'

'Yes. That's the Bay of Navarino,' said Andreas. 'The dark patch beyond the lights is the island of Sphacteria, and there'—he pointed south—'is the main Turkish camp at Neokastron.'

'And I suppose that's Palaeokastron, where we're going?' Brett had turned to look at the few lights scattered on what seemed to be a headland at the north end of the great bay.

'Yes, but there's a lagoon between us and it,' explained Andreas. 'We have to go down this way, to the causeway. It's rocky going for a while I'm afraid. Keep close behind me.'

As they stood, Brett's hand had found Phyllida's on the far side from Andreas. It was telling her something. She looked at him sideways, puzzled.

'I'm going ahead for a while,' he told her now, his voice impatient. 'Make sure you keep up. I'm tired of lagging along at your pace.'

For a moment she was furious, then understood the message his hand had given. 'I'm sorry,' she said meekly, falling in behind him.

Though steep, the rock path was nothing compared to the 'ladder' they had negotiated with Yannis, and Phyllida was grateful both for this and for the fact that it was now Brett who turned back to help her over the difficult bits. She did not like Andreas. Why?

Puzzling over this, she slipped and nearly fell, to be caught and angrily reprimanded by Brett. He seemed to be making a special point, tonight, of treating her roughly, like the boy she was supposed to be. 'Keep your mind on the path,' he said now, crossly, and she recognised it as good advice. Time enough to think about Andreas when they were safe on the *Cambrian*.

Were there really British ships, out there beyond the dark patch that was Sphacteria? Suppose they had sailed away, gone to Zante for food and water, or, simply, been scattered by the storm that had drenched them, how many nights ago? She had heard Brett say what a difficult station it was for a squadron to keep, exposed there on the squally coast. 'All very well for the Turks in the Bay of Navarino.'

What would they do if they got to Nestor's cave and found no boat awaiting them? So far, on this twilight journey that began to seem as if it would never end, she had thought merely about each stage as she toiled through it. Now, nearing the end, she had time to think about that, and found herself, illogically, terrified. Why? she asked herself again, and, puzzling over it, fell a little behind on a smooth bit of path and was surprised by Brett's voice, genuinely angry now, she recognised, with anxiety. 'Keep close, for God's sake.'

They must be nearly down to sea level. The rock had given way to what felt like well-trodden sand, and the path was winding among high reeds so that she could see nothing but Brett's back, moving steadily ahead. Impossible, on this twisting path, to be sure of direction, but (she looked up at the stars) surely they were still going south as well as west?

'Brett?'

'Hush!' How had he known what she was going to say, and why was she so sure that he had? 'Keep close,' he said again, urgently, and she knew she had been right to be afraid.

Somewhere, a frog croaked. But surely it must be hours, still, before dawn? They had not stopped yet for their halfway rest. It had looked a long way up to the headland of Palaeokastron, and if they had to circle it, to the north, in order to get to Nestor's cave . . .

Another frog. And Brett's hand, hard on her own. 'Whatever happens.' He had let them get a little behind Andreas. 'Keep close to me.' For the first time, he spoke in English.

Ahead of them, Andreas paused impatiently to let them catch up. 'The boy's tired,' said Brett, in irritable explanation.

'We'll rest at the causeway.' Andreas turned again to lead on through rustling reeds. And now, extraordinary after all these nights of walking with only an occasional owl for company, Phyllida could hear the sounds of humanity. A ship's bell echoed hollowly across the water, another and another, sounding, she thought, erratically from here and there in that great semicircle they had seen from above. And–hard to tell about direction–but, surely, nearer, a horse whinnied . . . Could they really be so near to the Turkish camp?

Brett had heard it too, had paused, instantaneously, ahead of her, was now going steadily forward as if nothing were the matter. She made herself do likewise. Forward. To what?

Something dark, looming ahead, solider than the reeds. Andreas' voice from ahead, oddly loud: 'The causeway at last.'

And, instantly, pandemonium all round them, turbaned figures, a scimitar flashing, Andreas' voice, loud and terrified: 'The Turks!'

And Brett's, pitched over the din, cool as if he were shouting above a storm; in Turkish: 'We are Franks. I bring greetings from Reshid Pasha to your leader, Ibrahim.'

'Franks?' The savage hands that had grabbed her out of the shadows were suddenly more gentle.

'Yes.' Brett, too, was held between two turbaned soldiers. 'I demand that you take us, at once, to Ibrahim Pasha. If you'll show a light, you'll see we're Franks. After all, the need for surprise has passed. Why stand round in the dark, croaking like frogs, when you've got what you came out for? Only'—his voice was stone calm—'if you hurt us, you'll regret it to your dying day. Which won't be far off. Do what you will with the traitor.' A rustle among the reeds suggested that Andreas had made a dive for it, and been caught.

'You speak boldly.' As before, their captor's voice came from above. 'Bring them up on to the causeway, and strike a light.'

She was dragged forward and up, out of the reeds into dwindling moonlight that was instantly drowned in the flare of torches. Ahead of her, Brett was facing the enemy leader. He had thrown off his sheepskin coat, and torch-light showed him straight and slim in jacket and trousers, as different as possible from his shaggy guards. 'Do you speak English?' he asked.

'No. But it's true, I can see you are a Frank. And you have messages, you say, from Reshid Pasha for my master? Tell me, then, what does he look like? Reshid?'

'Short. Wiry and active as ten goats. And a bad man to anger. I saw him outside Athens just before the garrison yielded.

He gave me his word for their safety. And kept it. I won't vouch for yours if you harm us.'

'But the boy.' By now Phyllida, too, was standing, closely held by her captors, in the blaze of torch-light. 'The boy is Greek.'

'Nonsense,' said Brett. 'Look closer. He is my brother. We are cousins of the Frankish Duke of Sarum, and if you touch one hair of our heads, our King himself, the great George the Fourth, will wreak a hideous vengeance on you.'

'Bring them in.' The Egyptian leader had made up his mind. 'We must think more of this.'

Nightmare. Disaster. But at least she and Brett were still together as they started down the badly paved causeway that led south to Neokastron. His story that they were brothers had been accepted, for the time being. But what chance was there that Ibrahim Pasha would believe them to be messengers from Reshid in Attica? Everyone knew that there was no love lost between the two Pashas. Just the same, she told herself, they did both serve the Sultan; there must be some communication between them.

Brett must have been thinking on the same lines. 'We've bought ourselves some time,' he said quietly. 'And, don't forget, these are Egyptians.'

'Yes.' Surrounded by the savage, turbaned figures, it seemed cold enough comfort. Not much chance of her being recognised as a fugitive from Mahmoud's harem. But if they found she was a woman? Shivering at the very thought, she made herself keep up the brisk pace set by their guards, though every muscle screamed with exhaustion. So far, hope had kept her going. From now on, fear must.

She was cold with fear, her mind numb with it, and grateful that Brett had obviously decided they had better not talk. Somewhere behind them, she heard Andreas begin a protest, and heard the crunch of the blow that silenced him. After that, no one spoke.

It was still dark when they reached the gates of Neokastron and were challenged and passed through by the sentries.

Inside, the Egyptian army was asleep. Well, why not? They were as safe, here in Greece, as if they were at home in Alexandria.

Their party had paused in the thicker darkness among buildings. 'I insist on seeing Ibrahim Pasha.' Brett advanced a step to confront the leader.

'He's not here.' Brett's tone of command had its effect. 'You'll have to wait, all three of you, till he returns. I've had no orders about Franks, but Ibrahim usually likes to see them himself. We're short of space," he went on. 'You're a milord. If I put the Greek in with you, will you spare his life? Ibrahim will want to hear all your stories.'

'Of course. You have my word.' Increasingly, Brett seemed in control of the situation. 'We Franks don't hurt the old. Not even traitors. Besides, Andreas here has served my purpose well enough, since I wanted to meet your master. But we all need food and drink.'

'You shall be fed. Ibrahim returns tomorrow. He shall hear at once of your arrival.'

The cell door slammed behind them. Andreas crouched, terrified, in a corner, but Brett took no notice of him as he made a quick, thorough search of the cell and its adjoining, noisome closet. 'It could be much worse.' He spoke cheerfully, in English, to Phyllida, who had sunk down on the pile of brushwood that passed for a divan. 'We're still together.'

'Yes, thank God. But what will you say to Ibrahim?'

Amazingly, he laughed. 'Let's cross one bridge at a time, shall we, love? After all, we're alive; they've not even searched us.'

She had actually forgotten those damning notes of his, wrapped up in the innocent-looking bundle. 'What will you do?'

'Wait.' He turned, almost with sympathy, to the snivelling, grovelling old man in the corner. 'Don't be afraid. It's true, what I said. We won't hurt you. Why should we?'

'But why?' The question had been burning in Phyllida ever since she had begun to suspect Andreas.

'They burned my village.' He was actually glad to explain. 'Kolokotronis and his gang of thugs. They said we had helped the Turks. Well, what else could we do, living where we did? I wasn't there that night. When I came back–do you remember that smell, *kyrie*? The smell of burning?'

'Yes.' Brett seemed to have expected this.

'All of them,' said the old man. 'My daughter and her husband. All their children. And I, watching the fire from the mountain, smelling it. If you want to kill me, *kyrie,* do. I don't much want to live.'

'I thought it was that. No, I don't intend to hurt you, but you must tell me just how much you have betrayed.'

'Very little, since that was all I knew. Just that a messenger was coming. I did not think you would be a Frank, *kyrie.'*

'Lucky for us all that I was. Well, if you want to live, and I expect, in your heart, you do, you will tell a true tale when you are questioned. Say you expected a messenger, and were surprised that it was a Frank. That way, we may all survive.'

'Yes, *kyrie.'* The old man came forward to kiss Brett's hand. 'I am your slave.'

'Nothing of the kind.' Brett leaned forward to blow out the lamp. 'Look! It's morning.' And then, 'Good God, look at that.' He had moved to one of the two slit windows that pierced one side of the cell, and Phyllida hurried to the other.

It opened straight out on to the Bay of Navarino and the Turkish fleet, at anchor, a forest of masts and spars, curving away and then round again, far off, at the northern end of the bay below the promontory with the other fort.

'A splendid defensive position,' said Brett thoughtfully. 'I imagine they have their French advisers to thank for that.'

'French?' Phyllida was finding it hard to keep her eyes open.

'Yes. The Egyptians learned by the experience of being conquered by Napoleon. They've had French advisers ever since. Ah.' A key grated in the lock. 'I was beginning to be afraid our friend had forgotten us.' He made Phyllida eat a little of the greasy rice dish they were brought, then settled her on the brushwood divan. 'Sleep, love; you've all the time in the world.'

She smiled up at him. 'And then our great King George the Fourth will come riding to my rescue on his white charger?'

'Precisely.' And then. 'Don't look at me like that, love, or I shall kiss you, and what would our friend there think?'

'What indeed?' She smiled again, sleepily. 'You and your cousin the Duke!'

'Yours too, Mrs. Renshaw.'

'Good gracious!' Still smiling, she plunged, fathoms down into sleep.

Waking, she thought, insanely, for a moment that she must be in hell. Red light flickered on the ceiling; the whole building was shaking, and noise, echoing through her brain, made thought almost impossible.

'Brett!' Now she saw him, over by one of the slit windows, gazing out. Andreas was at the other one. Quite impossible that they should hear her over the din that shook the walls. She rose, shakily, to her feet, exhaustion still like lead in all her limbs.

'Brett?' She joined him in his window and he turned to put a reassuring arm round her. 'Dear God!' Now she saw what he did. The whole bay seemed ablaze, and a pall of smoke hung heavy overhead, as ship after ship fired off its broadsides. Then, as it had before, their own building shook to its foundations.

'There must be a battery above us,' said Brett coolly. 'For once, I rather hope the British aim's not too good.'

'British? But, Brett.' She had to shout above the noise. 'What's happening?'

'It's the most extraordinary thing I ever saw. But for you, love, I wouldn't have missed it for anything.' A gust of wind shifted the curtain of smoke momentarily, and she saw that where, before, there had been a single semicircle of Turkish ships, it was now doubled. Other ships, flying British, French and Russian colours, had anchored close beside the Turks and were exchanging a devastating fire with them.

'They came in as cool as you please.' The battery above them must be reloading, and it was easier to hear what he said. 'The *Asia*–old Codrington's flagship–was in the lead of one column and De Rigny's *Sirène* of the other. There was just enough wind to bring them in, and the most extraordinary silence. You could hear the rigging creak; the orders shouted . . .'

'And the Turks?'

'Did nothing. Leaned on their guns in the batteries across there, and watched, as if it was a naval display.' He pointed to the battery on the southern tip of Sphacteria that was now belching out fire and death. 'I imagine the same thing must have been going on above us here. It was beautiful sailing, too. They came in, perfectly, in line, and moored, each in turn, close to a Turkish ship.'

'And then?' The battery had opened fire again above them, and she had to mouth the question.

'The Turks opened fire on one of our boats. It looked to me as if she was carrying a flag of truce; taking some message or other. It was hard to tell from here. But I could see the flag of truce. And this is the result.'

'But we're not at war!'

'We may not have been. I should say we are now, wouldn't you?' As he spoke, a well-aimed ball from the battery above them brought the sails of a French 74 down to make a shambles of her deck.

Phyllida was trying to count. 'But, Brett, there must be twice as many Turkish ships!'

'More than that, love.' He sounded amazingly cheerful about it. 'But it's discipline that counts in a sea battle. If you'd seen the way our ships came in, you'd know they'd take a lot of beating.'

'And, my God, they are!' Horrible to think that with each flash and crash of artillery, more blood was running on the sanded decks, more lives pouring away down the scuppers.

Near them a Turkish ship blew up, the noise of its explosion making the pandemonium before seem mere commonplace. Bodies, a mast, pieces of flaming timber were tossed into the air like a child's handful of toys.

'Don't look, love.' Brett moved over to the cell door. 'I wish we could block it somehow.'

'A wedge.' Andreas joined him from the other window. 'They left me my knife.' It had been tucked inside his leather boot. 'I could have killed you while you slept, *kyrie*.'

'And you take credit for not having done so?' Brett

merely laughed. 'Well, by all means cut some wedges and make the door as secure as you can. They aren't going to feel kindly towards us Franks while this day's work lasts.'

'And if we're beaten?' Phyllida asked. 'Out there?'

'We're as good as dead in here. I think we must face that, don't you? But we're not going to be beaten. British, French and Russians beaten by a set of barbarians! Nonsense.' He did not like the white, still look of her. Andreas was busy cutting the wedges for the door. 'Whatever happens, love'—he spoke urgently—'remember to act the boy. He's betrayed us once—' A quick jerk of his head indicated Andreas. 'He would again.'

'Yes. But, Brett.' She was silenced by the roar of gunfire from the bay, then went on, painfully. 'If they're beaten, out there, nothing can save us. You said so yourself. So—before they come . . . Promise you'll kill me?'

'I'll do nothing of the kind.' His angry tone was more bracing than any amount of sympathy. 'And I'm ashamed of you for asking it. We're going to fight for our lives to the last ditch, just like those gallant sailors out there.'

'Well,' she said, 'hardly ditch.'

'No.' A quick, relieved glance for her calmer tone. 'We've so much to live for, you and I.'

'And so much to lose.'

'Don't think like that! I'm surprised at you, Phyl. Remember how you jerked me out of despair, back at Zante, that night. My God!' He was back at the window. 'There goes another Turkish ship.'

'Poor creatures.' She shuddered. 'Look, there's one swimming, quite close in.'

'And being picked up by a British boat. Have you noticed, love, that not one of the Allied ships has blown up, or struck her colours. At least, not that I can see. And, remember, there's something else on our side. That fleet out there is half Turkish, half Egyptian. And there's no love lost between them. I doubt if they'll work together as well as ours.'

'You mean the British and French, who last met at Trafalgar?'

'You're no fool, are you, love?' He was delighted to

see reason taking over from panic in her. 'But I still think I'm right. You should have seen the way they came in together, British, French and Russians. And the moment the Turks opened fire on that British boat, De Rigny was at it hammer-and-tongs from the *Sirène*. I can't see the Russians so well, but it looks as if they must be giving a good account of themselves too.'

'It's horrible.' She was shaking again. 'And don't say, "don't look", because how can I help it?' An anguished face, floating close under their window, an arm thrown up, then sinking, gave point to her words.

'Because I order you to. Come here, Phyl.' He pulled a stool towards the rough table. 'Sit down. Write what I tell you. It won't be pleasant, but it will be better than watching. And much more useful. Had it occurred to you, love, what an admirable last chapter this will make for my book?'

'Oh, you're impossible.' She was somewhere between laughter and tears, but she sat down as he had commanded.

'Nothing of the kind. I have a living to make, remember, for us and our son.'

'Daughter.' Her voice was almost steady as she picked up the pen. 'Very well, my lord, dictate.'

# 29

All the long day, the battle raged, and all day long, Phyllida sat at the table, writing to Brett's dictation, steadied by the need to listen for his voice against the thunder of gunfire from outside and from above.

'One good thing.' Brett paused in his dictation to come and put a gentle hand on her shoulder. 'I think the Egyptians must have forgotten all about us.'

'As well they might.' Her voice was almost drowned by a ragged burst of firing from the battery above them.

'I don't think they're doing a bit of damage from up there.' He had felt her fear. 'Not now. Their chance was when the Allied Fleet sailed in, and they let it go. Our ships won't think them worth powder and shot, not now. Luckily for us.'

'I do so hope you are right.'

Hard to tell when the glow of many fires in the bay merged with that of sunset. In his corner, Andreas was praying. Brett turned, wearily, from his window. 'I think it's almost over.'

'You mean?' She rose, stiffly, to join him.

'I think–' He stopped as a Turkish ship blew up in a blaze of horrible light that revealed, for a moment, the whole sweep of the bay. 'You see? It's the Allied ships that are still there.'

'They've taken a terrible pounding.' Silent tears streamed down Phyllida's cheeks.

'Yes, but they're all firing still, which is more than the Turks are.'

Darkness came suddenly, emphasising the red glow of the burning ships, the occasional shower of sparks as one blew up. The firing had slackened now, and the battery above them was silent. Lights began to show on the Allied ships, still anchored in formation. 'They'll keep close watch tonight,' said Brett. 'And so must we. I can trust you, Andreas?'

'I swear it, by bread and by the deaths of my children.'

'Then you and I will take watch about. We must be ready for the Egyptians if they should decide to break down the door.'

In fact, none of them slept much. The red glow persisted all night, and from time to time there was another explosion as a Turkish ship blew up. 'They must be destroying them on purpose,' said Brett. 'It's like them.'

Worst of all, now that the firing had ceased they could hear the screams of the wounded, some drifting on spars in the bay, white faces caught for a moment in the light of a burning ship, others doubtless on the orlop decks of the surviving ships, where the surgeons would be about their dreadful business.

Towards dawn, Phyllida slept a little, restlessly, and woke to see Brett and Andreas back at the windows. It was quiet at last and only daylight filtered into the dismal little room.

'It's all over.' Brett turned as she stirred on the brushwood divan. 'A classic victory. I think it may mean the beginning of freedom for Greece.'

'Yes.' Andreas looked a thousand years old this morning. 'And what does it mean for me, a traitor?'

'Nothing of the kind,' said Brett. 'We were ambushed, don't you remember, by pure chance? And a lucky one, I begin to think, for my brother and me. Think, man, if you'd taken us to Nestor's cave as was arranged, what chance would we have had of being picked up by a British boat, with that battle raging?'

'I hadn't thought of that.' Hope dawned on his ravaged face. 'You'll tell that story for me, *kyrie*, you and the boy?'

'I don't see why not.' He turned back to the window, the subject finished. 'Ah! There's a Turkish boat going out to the *Asia*. I hope to God old Codrington's survived.'

'Yes.' Phyllida was up now, moving stiffly about the cell. 'Brett, do you know we're almost out of water?'

'Yes. If they don't remember us fairly soon, we'll have to call attention to ourselves, but, frankly, I think the longer we leave it the better. Just don't wash your face this morning, love. It looks charming as it is.'

'I doubt that.' She made a face at him.

He laughed. 'To me, you'll always look beautiful. But God knows what your aunt's going to say. It's not just your dirty face, it's that hair of yours!'

'Is it terrible?'

'Just as well we've no glass. I only hope I still look enough of an English milord to convince Ibrahim.' He looked ruefully down at his shabby blue surtout and stained canvas trousers.

'The extraordinary thing is, that you do. I can't think how you manage it. Here I am, a complete slut, and you're still a perfect English gentleman. Even without a shave!'

'I'm not absolutely sure I like your tone. I've half a mind to give you a brotherly beating, strictly for the benefit of our friend there.'

'Pray don't! But are you really going to let him off?'

'Why not? If we get out of this ourselves.'

'Yes.' Had she let herself take it too much for granted, this morning, that they would?

Time dragged. Out in the bay, the Allied ships were scenes of frenzied activity as sailors swarmed over them, repairing the damage of the day before. 'Most of them will be fit to sail by tomorrow,' said Brett. 'And probably will. There's nothing more for them to do here. I hope Ibrahim gets back before then.'

'You're waiting for that?'

'Partly. Besides, it's important not to lose face. I'd rather they came to fetch us. If you can hold out a while longer?'

'Of course.' She was starving, and parched with thirst. They had shared the last mouthful of warm, brackish water a couple of hours earlier and the heat in the little room made thirst even harder to bear than hunger. But if Brett and Andreas could bear it, so could she.

It was afternoon, and the activity on the Allied ships had diminished somewhat when they heard the sound of trumpets on the landward side of their prison. 'That sounds like Ibrahim,' said Brett with satisfaction. 'I just hope, among all the bad news, someone remembers to tell him about us. Take the wedges out of the door, Andreas. We don't want to seem to have been afraid.'

'Yes, *kyrie*.'

Phyllida watched with amusement as Andreas obeyed the casual order. 'Will you bully *me*?' she asked in English.

'Bully? Oh—I see.' He smiled at her. 'It's good for him, don't you see. It makes him feel safe.'

'I wish I did.'

'Maybe I'd better bully you too. Ah, here they come. You're my tiresome little brother, remember. And'—in Greek—'Andreas, you will say as I say.'

'Yes, *kyrie*. Though it mean death.'

'I hope it won't.' He turned to face the door as it was thrown open to reveal an Armenian interpreter, unmistakable in his strange-shaped cap and fur-trimmed pelisse.

'At last!' Brett's voice was angry. 'I come with messages for your master, and you leave me here for twenty-four hours, without food or water.'

'Ibrahim himself has sent me.' The man looked frightened. 'You are to come at once.'

'Without food?' Brett appeared to think it over, then conceded the point. 'Very well. I can understand that Ibrahim has much on his mind today. We will come.'

'He said nothing about the other two. It is only you he wants.'

'I do not move without them.'

This time it was the Armenian who yielded.

Ibrahim Pasha was a short, stout, vulgar-looking man with a face badly marked by smallpox. Plainly, almost shabbily dressed, he still stood out unmistakably the leader, among a group of richly furred two- and three-tailed pashas.

Brett approached him without hesitation, the Armenian protesting at his side. 'We don't need this man. I speak your language.' Brett was half a head taller than the Egyptian, but the two pairs of eyes met and held steadily.

At last, Ibrahim smiled. 'You are a brave man, milord. Yesterday, your ships destroyed ours, and today you dare speak to me thus?'

'Not only *your* ships,' said Brett. 'The Turks seemed to me to suffer even more than the Egyptians.'

Something flashed in Ibrahim's grey eyes. 'You bring me a message from Reshid in the North?'

'So I said.' There was the slightest possible emphasis on the last word. 'What I have to say to you, Your Excellency, is not for all ears.'

Once again, Ibrahim's lips parted in the cruellest smile Phyllida had ever seen. 'Very well. Stand apart, all of you. But I warn you, Englishman, this is not a good day with me. If you are wasting my time, you and your friends will not live long to regret it. Nor will your death be easy.'

Phyllida and Andreas were dragged away by their guards before they could hear more. Brett was speaking fast, and with conviction, but what in the world could he be saying? He seemed very far away, the whole thing hopeless. 'Andreas,' Phyllida whispered in Greek, 'if the worst happens, will you kill me, quickly?' She could see the outline of the dagger still in his boot.

'Yes, *kyria*. I promise. It will hardly hurt.'

*Kyria*. How long had he known? But a movement in the crowd brought her eyes back to Brett and Ibrahim. It was over. Ibrahim was laughing and clapping Brett on the shoulder. 'You shall have Tahir Pasha for your escort,' he said as they moved nearer. 'You will tell Milord Codrington from me that he may be all-powerful at sea but I remain master here on land. You shall see my army before you go.'

'I shall be honoured,' said Brett. 'We would also be glad, my companions and I, of food and drink. We have had nothing for twenty-four hours.'

'Companions? Oh–' He glanced at Phyllida and Andreas. 'Your bother, of course. The Greek is mine.'

'No,' said Brett, very quietly. 'I gave him my word.'

There was a little pause. Then Ibrahim laughed. 'You're a man, Englishman. You would not consider staying to advise me? I need men like you, now that those rats of Frenchmen have shown their true colours by abandoning my fleet in its hour of need.'

'They put it in very good order first,' said Brett.

Phyllida sometimes thought that the meal that followed was the worst of all she had been through. 'If I seemed too eager,' Brett explained to her afterwards, 'I was afraid he might think again.'

The greasy Turkish food choked her and in this strictly Muslim camp there was no wine to wash it down. Beside her, Brett was talking easily to Ibrahim about life in Paris and London. How had he realised that the Egyptian longed to be thought a man of the world? As time dragged on, she began to think that Brett was being too successful. Would they ever get away?

The light outside the tent was dwindling. Brett looked up. 'Your Excellency, it will be dark soon. I do not in the least wish to be mistaken for a boarding party by the British. We know too well what good shots they are.' His tone managed to make it a compliment, implying that only heroes could have defeated the Egyptians.

'You're right.' Ibrahim was on his feet. 'But I am sad to part with you, Englishman. Come back some day, in happier times, when I am master here in Greece, and we will talk again.' And then, looking beyond Brett to Phyllida, 'Your brother is very quiet.'

'He knows his place,' said Brett. 'Make your bow to the Pasha, Phyl. We must be going.'

She managed a passable bow, acutely aware of her Greek costume and the absurdity of it all. Greek. What had happened to Andreas?

'Well, boy,' said Ibrahim. 'What is your name, pray?'

'Philip Renshaw, Your Excellency.' Her voice came out a nervous squeak.

'So he can speak. But younger than I thought. I'm surprised you risked him here in Greece, milord. Well, Philip Renshaw, I like you none the less for having accompanied your brother into danger. Ask a boon, and I will grant it.'

Goodness, she thought, he thinks he's something out of the *Arabian Nights*. And spoke up quickly. 'Your Excellency, our man, Andreas, he comes with us?'

'Oh, the Greek!' Ibrahim looked round in feigned surprise. 'What happened to him? Fetch him, someone. He goes with his masters.'

Andreas joined them down at the quay, bleeding horribly from a network of light sabre-cuts. 'It's nothing,' he answered Brett's exclamation. 'They were only beginning. God bless you, *kyrie,* for remembering me.'

'You have my brother to thank.' But Tahir Pasha had already boarded the Turkish version of an admiral's barge, the slaves, some of them Greek, were bending to their oars, there was no time for thanks. Only, as they climbed on board: 'I didn't tell them, *kyria,*' whispered Andreas.

As they approached, it was possible to see the full extent of the damage the *Asia* had suffered the day before, but discipline on board was as precise as ever; the decks were already white again, with only a sinister stain, here and there in the scuppers, as a reminder of all the blood that had poured across them yesterday. Best of all was the sight of Lord Codrington, waiting to receive them, imposing in his full-dress uniform as Admiral of the Fleet. If he felt any surprise at the sight of Brett and Phyllida following in Tahir Pasha's wake, he did not show it. His interpreter was ready to join Tahir's, and Phyllida listened in a daze of relief as the first formal exchanges took place. The pasha had brought Ibrahim's assurances that no further hostilities would take place–at sea. 'On land is another matter, but the milord here is empowered to speak to you about that.' A Turk, Tahir did not seem to like this much, and Codrington favoured Brett with a quick, considering glance, then turned to settle the armistice terms with the pasha.

At last it was over, the Turks had gone and the Guard of Honour been dismissed. Codrington turned a long, hard stare on Brett. 'Well, young man, you had better tell me all about it.'

'Yes, my lord. But, first, allow me to present my wife, Mrs. Renshaw.'

'Mrs.!' He looked her up and down, then surprised and touched her by a courtly bow. 'Accept my congratulations, ma'am, on a lucky escape.' And, to Brett, 'You're that cousin of Sarum's, of course. The *Helena*'s owner.'

'Yes–' Eagerly.

'All's well.' Codrington anticipated his question. 'She came in a few days ago, in company with De Rigny. We sent her off to Zante, to be safe.'

'Thank God for that.'

The admiral actually laughed. 'A proper spitfire you have for a sister, by what De Rigny says. He had to talk of mutiny, and irons, before he could dissuade her from sailing, single-handed to Kitries to your rescue. You must understand that we've had affairs of our own to attend to.'

'I do indeed. We saw it all, from over there.' Brett pointed to Neokastron.

'You did? Then you saw who started it.'

'The Turks. They fired on a flag of truce. But I've more to tell you than that, sir, when you have the time.'

'Yes. Tomorrow, perhaps. For the moment, we must think what's best for Mrs. Renshaw.' His glance was friendly. 'This is no place for a lady, even such an intrepid one as you must be, ma'am.' And then, with a look, surely, of amusement, 'I have it: the *Redstart*. She arrived a little late for the battle and suffered no damage. Captain Froxe has his wife at Zante. What could be more suitable?' He turned away to give a rapid series of orders. 'You and I will talk tomorrow, Mr. Renshaw. I take it whatever you have to say will keep till then?'

There was something indescribably glum about the atmosphere of the *Redstart*. Here were no sinister stains in the scuppers, no groans from below-decks, and no cheerful skylarking of sailors as they repaired damaged spars and rigging above. Captain Froxe had made the mistake of setting his wife safe ashore on Zante before he followed the rest of the fleet into Navarino Bay, had lost the wind, and missed the battle. He received them with the dull civility of a man who sees his career in ruins, and showed obvious relief when Brett pleaded exhaustion on both their parts. Captain Froxe did not want to hear about the battle he had missed. He was glad to ring for his man and have Phyllida shown to the slip of a cabin that normally belonged to his wife's maid. Brett would have to share with a group of officers. Andreas presented a slight puzzle, which he solved by settling down outside Phyllida's door. Froxe shrugged. 'It will save putting a marine on duty.'

When Phyllida waked, it was broad daylight. She had fallen asleep, as for so many nights before, in all her dirt, snugly wrapped in the filthy sheepskin capote. Now, listening to the civilised sounds of shipboard living all round her, she could not bear herself a moment longer. She opened the cabin door a crack, and Andreas started up to greet her with his broad, black-toothed smile. 'At your service, *kyria*!'

'Andreas, do you think you could find me hot water—much much'—She pantomimed a large vessel—'and—' What in the world was the Greek for a looking-glass? Once again, she had recourse to pantomime, and suddenly the old man grinned again to show he understood and trotted off down the long corridor.

He returned, after a considerable interval, with Captain Froxe's own man, carrying a jug of hot water, and a small hand mirror. 'Captain's compliments, ma'am, and he thought maybe you'd not mind helping yourself to one of Miss Mincheon's outfits.' His tone was apologetic.

'Miss? Oh—the maid.' Phyllida laughed. 'It couldn't be worse than this.' Looking as she did, she could hardly blame the captain for not offering her the run of his wife's clothes.

'We sail as soon as Mr. Renshaw returns,' the man went on. 'He's been with the admiral all morning.' And then, suddenly confidential, 'I hope he gets back soon. We're due to dine on Zante today. At Mrs. Biddock's, where Mrs. Froxe is staying. The master says he hopes you and Mr. Renshaw will give him the pleasure of your company.'

Phyllida had been looking with horror into the glass. 'In that case,' she said, 'I had better get to work.'

With Andreas back on duty outside, she began by washing her hair. Probably as well, she thought, that Oenone had cut it so ruthlessly short. Though she had been eaten alive by fleas and doubtless worse, she did not seem to have acquired any permanent infestation. Her hair was soon curling in rather wild ringlets round her face, a testimony to Oenone's erratic shearing. Nothing she could do about that.

Delicious to peel off the Greek costume at last, to use up the rest of the cooling water, and then dress from top to toe in Miss Mincheon's clean linen, which smelt, blessedly, of lavender from little bags tucked here and there among it. Miss Mincheon's best dress was a pale grey muslin, cut high, with a daring little frill round the neck. It actually fitted, though several inches too short, but after wearing gaiters for so long, Phyllida found it hard to take this very seriously. She slipped Brett's signet ring back on to the hand that still looked brown rather than clean and opened the cabin door again.

'*Kyria*!' Something heartening about Andreas' surprise.

Captain Froxe's man appeared behind him. 'The captain would be honoured if you would take coffee with him in his cabin, ma'am.' He was too well trained to permit himself anything but the slightest blink at her transformation.

She could have been wearing chain mail for all the notice Captain Froxe took of her. He was in an anguish of anxiety.

'We shall be late.' He gazed past her at the chronometer on the wall. 'We shall be worse than late. She'll never forgive me.'

This seemed to be a far more serious matter than simply being late for a battle. Hen-pecked, no doubt. Phyllida spared a moment to be sorry for him, then moved forward, with an apology, to pour herself a cup of coffee.

'What? Oh, yes, yes, of course. But where can he be–' He stopped, thought about it for a moment. 'Mr. Renshaw.'

She was beginning to see just how wise Brett had been to insist on that Greek wedding. 'My husband, you mean?' Strange to be using the word, for the first time, almost as a matter of defensive strategy. 'I imagine he had a great deal to tell Lord Codrington. We saw the whole battle, you know.'

'Yes, yes,' said Captain Froxe. 'But we shall be late for dinner.'

Brett arrived, cheerfully apologetic, ten minutes later, and the anchor was already coming up as he climbed on board. By the time he joined them in the captain's cabin, they could feel the ship begin to respond to a following wind. 'I'm sorry if I've made you late, Captain–' And then, seeing Phyllida smiling at him from the other side of the table, 'Good God, love, what are you playing at now?'

'I'm an abigail,' said Phyllida cheerfully, 'but at least, thank God, I'm clean.'

'You're beautiful.' He ignored Captain Froxe to come round the table and kiss her lightly. 'I'd forgotten what your hair was like.'

'At least it's not infested!' And then, 'But we're shocking Captain Froxe.'

'Too late. We've shocked him.' The captain had murmured something incomprehensible and left the cabin. 'Tell me, love.' He settled close beside her, one arm round her waist, while he poured cool coffee for them both with the other. 'What's the matter with the poor man? Aside from missing the battle, I mean.'

'He's got a termagant of a wife on Zante,' explained Phyllida. 'No, Brett! Think if someone should come in! They're doubtful enough about us already!'

'And if they found me making shameless advances to

you, they'd know we weren't married?' He laughed and let her go. 'And we're going to be late for dinner? At the Biddocks!' He was enjoying every minute of it. 'Do you think it too much to hope that Jenny and your aunt will be there too?'

'I've been wondering. And–Peter?'

'If Barlow and Brown have obeyed orders, your Brother Peter is confined to his cabin at least; in chains if he's been difficult.'

'Oh, Brett! But, surely, you never imagined–'

'No, frankly, I didn't. But I did give orders that any emissary from Alex must be treated with the greatest suspicion. The rest follows from that.'

'And their safety. Thank God. I only wish we knew that Oenone was safe! But, Brett, I've been longing for a chance to ask. How in the world did you persuade Ibrahim to let us go?'

His arm was round her again. 'A bad moment, that one. I was afraid he might be too angry for reason, but he's no fool, Ibrahim Pasha. When I put it to him that this defeat might be the beginning of independence for Egypt as well as for Greece, he was only too happy to have me go, as his emissary, to Codrington. I've told you before, love, there's no love lost between the Egyptians and the Turks.'

'But you told them, before, you had come from Reshid Pasha.'

'Yes.' Cheerfully. 'It saved our lives for the moment. I'm afraid you've a hardened liar for a husband, love.'

'I shall never believe another word you say.'

'Not even when I say, "I love you," love?' He shook her a little, gently, and let her go. 'It's time we were up on deck. We must be nearly there, and Captain Froxe will be in agony, lest we delay him still further.' And then, as she stood up, 'I never saw an abigail with skirts as short as that!'

She laughed and looked ruefully at her exposed ankles. 'I know. Do you think there's any hope we could stop at the *Helena* on our way to this dinner party?'

'Not the least in the world, my darling, so if I were you, I would resign myself to the knowledge that you've the prettiest pair of ankles I ever hope to see.'

'You're a great comfort!' Her tone was so cross that Captain Froxe, joining them at that moment, began to think they must be married after all. He agreed at once to Brett's request that a message be sent to the *Helena*. 'Though I shall be surprised if we do not meet your sister at Mrs. Biddock's.' An anxious glance at the chronometer decided Phyllida not even to mention the question of her dress. She was afraid she was problem enough to Captain Froxe as it was. Where Codrington had accepted their marriage as the most natural thing in the world, Froxe seemed perpetually to be looking at it nervously, sideways.

'Mr. Biddock is your man of business, I understand?' They were in the captain's gig now, being rowed swiftly ashore.

'Yes.' She was looking at the *Helena*, safely moored some way away along the jetty, with a sudden mist of tears in her eyes.

'He must be delighted to see you.' Was the captain anxious about arriving with two uninvited guests, and such dubious ones at that? 'His wife and mine are the greatest of friends.' It gave the last touch to Phyllida's picture of his domestic tyrant and her eyes met Brett's with a suspicion of a twinkle.

'English soil—or as near as makes no difference.' Brett helped her ashore, and she paused for a moment to look round her at the well-remembered quayside, the tumble of houses up the hill, to enjoy the sight of a dark-leaved orange tree above a garden wall, and persimmons golden as the apples of the Hesperides beside it. She took a deep breath, compounded of harbour, and garden, and, somewhere, the smell of baking.

'Freedom,' she said.

'Yes, yes.' Captain Froxe had sent a man running ahead to announce them. 'This way, my dear'—he paused—'lady. We're most deplorably late for dinner.'

Brett had taken her arm. 'Lucky you're so rich,' he said *sotto voce* as Froxe hurried on ahead. 'I somehow don't feel he much approves of us, do you?'

'Approves!' She could not help laughing. 'He can't even

bring himself to call me by my name. What will he do when it comes to presenting me to his wife?'

'I look forward to finding out. You don't mind, do you, love?'

'Mind? Now I've seen the *Helena* safe? If only we knew about Oenone.'

'We'll find out.' But they had arrived at the Biddocks' house.

Coming in out of the bright sunlight, it was hard, for a moment, to distinguish faces among the group that awaited them in the Biddocks' saloon. Captain Froxe was bending over Cissie Biddock's hand, unnecessarily profuse in his apologies. Beside her, Biddock was in a visible anguish of embarrassment.

He bowed rather stiffly to Phyllida. 'My dear Miss Vannick–'

'Mrs. Renshaw.' Brett's correction was made in tones of steel.

'N . . n . . no.' Could he actually be contradicting him? It seemed he was. Brett's hand tightened on her arm as Biddock began again. 'Some form of ceremony gone through on the mainland I collect?' He got it out with difficulty. 'Under normal circumstances, perhaps.' He looked from one to the other. 'Miss Vannick, Your Grace; try to understand my position.'

'What did you call me?'

'Y . . . Y . . . Your Grace.' And then with a wretched attempt at humour, 'You must see that whatever she may be, Miss Vannick is quite certainly not Mrs. Renshaw.'

'But my cousin? The child?'

'Tragic,' said Biddock. 'Quite tragic. The smallpox.'

'I don't understand,' said Phyllida.

'No.' Amazingly Brett was laughing. 'Why should you? I do apologise, my love, I seem to have made you a Duchess without knowing it.'

'A–Good God! Me?'

'I'm afraid so. That's why Mr. Biddock is in such distress. Peers of the realm usually marry in more state. Will it make you feel better, sir, if I tell you that our first intention, my wife's and mine, is to get married again with all the ceremony you can contrive. And that reminds me, where's Jenny?'

He was answered by a commotion in the doorway as Jenny burst in and threw herself into his arms. 'B., my darling B., you're safe!'

'If you call it safe! I'm married!'

'I'm so happy I could cry.' Jenny was kissing Phyllida. 'Will you very much mind being a Duchess, love?'

'I shall hate it,' said Phyllida uncompromisingly, then turned to fling her arms round Cassandra's neck. 'Aunt Cass, you're all right?'

'And why not?' asked Cassandra. 'But, dear child, what in the world are you doing in that rig? Your ankles!'

'Oh!' She had forgotten all about Miss Mincheon's dress. 'It's something I borrowed. Dear Aunt, don't you think, as a Duchess, I may perhaps carry it off?' She turned back to Brett. 'Darling, must I be a Duchess?'

'If you dislike it so much, my love, we'll just have to live in America.'

'Do you know, I have the most lowering feeling that it might be worse there. But'—Thoughts of Miss Mincheon had reminded her—'where is Mrs. Froxe?'

'She don't much like her entrances spoiled,' said Jenny naughtily. 'I collect Mrs. Biddock has gone to tell her we are all met.' Suddenly, she was looking past Phyllida at the little group of officers who had accompanied Captain Froxe from the *Redstart*. She turned so white that Phyllida put out an instinctive hand to support her.

'What is it?' Phyllida paused at sight of a young lieutenant making his determined way towards them.

'Miss Renshaw.' He bowed punctiliously, then took her hand. 'It's been a very long time.'

'Too long,' said Jenny.

'Well!' began Aunt Cassandra as the nameless young officer drew Jenny ruthlessly into a corner, but Phyllida was not listening. She had seen Brett's eyes fix, in horror, on the curving stairway that swept down into the room.

Mrs. Froxe was making her entrance. A beauty. Well,

Phyllida corrected herself, an ex-beauty. Perhaps a mistake to pause for that moment at the head of the stairs, collecting eyes, since the angle from which they saw her served unkindly to emphasise a slight softening of the clear line of the chin, a corresponding thickening of the elegant waist. Now she moved forward again, as Captain Froxe came up to meet her, babbling his apologies.

She frowned down at him, and aged another five years. 'It's all of a piece. My convenience, your duty to my hosts, are to be as nothing compared with the affairs of a couple of draggle-tailed refugees.' She was looking past him now, and let out a sudden gasp as her eyes met Brett's.

Cissie Biddock had fluttered down the stairs behind her. 'My dear.' She broke a queer little silence. 'I should have explained. It's the Duke of Sarum, and'—she paused—'Miss Vannick.'

Brett's hand closed like iron on Phyllida's elbow as he moved her forward to the foot of the stairs. Ignoring Mrs. Biddock, he gazed down for a moment into Mrs. Froxe's angry blue eyes. Then, 'Well, Helena,' he said, 'how do you do?' And, without giving her time to answer, 'May I have the pleasure of making you known to my wife, the Duchess?'

He was a Duke. He could behave like that. And this, incredibly, was Helena. Was this the face that launched a thousand ships, or, more to the point, brought Brett to the point of suicide? Curtsying solemnly, Phyllida was aware of Helena's eyes on her ankles, and badly wanted to laugh. Instead, she smiled sweetly and thanked her in dulcet tones for the loan of her maid's dress.

Mercifully, Cissie Biddock was marshalling the company in to dinner. Phyllida seized her chance to turn on Brett. 'If that's the way Dukes behave, I'm against it.'

'I know.' Meekly. 'It was very bad of me. But admit I was provoked?' They were parted by Cissie Biddock before she could answer him.

Who had arranged the table? Helena was sitting on Biddock's right, with Brett beside her. Phyllida was aware of Brett's angry reaction and grateful to him when he controlled it. This was no moment to be fussing over precedence. Besides, she immensely enjoyed watching Helena play off her beauty's armoury on Brett, and then felt guilty when she was aware of Captain Froxe, beside her, watching it too. Further down the table, Jenny had contrived to sit beside her lieutenant, and Phyllida found a safe subject by asking Captain Froxe his name.

It meant nothing to her, but Froxe appeared to think well of the young man, for what that was worth. Jenny's look of happiness was infinitely more important. And Peter? The minute this interminable meal was over she must get Jenny, or, more likely, Aunt Cassandra into a corner and find out what had really happened. But, over coffee, she found herself buttonholed by Mr. Biddock. 'If I might have a private word with you, Miss'—he stopped, compromised—'Ma'am?' He was shepherding her, as he spoke, into his downstairs office.

'If you wish.' She must break it to him about her gift to Oenone. 'But, first.' This she must ask. 'My brother?'

'Safe on the *Helena*.' His tone held deep disapproval. 'No one has told me anything about it, and I do not in the least wish to know. I only thank God your father had the good sense to leave things as he did. But we have more important things to discuss.'

'Yes?' Was he finding this more difficult than he had expected?

'I rely on your good sense.' He stopped, started again in a rush. 'You must see it's impossible, ma'am. The story of a wedding in some hole or corner of mainland Greece might do well enough for ordinary people, but for a Duke! Imagine the scandal! I rely on your good sense, Miss Vannick,' he said again. 'You will do the right thing, I am convinced of it.'

'And that is?' She would not let him see, yet, just how angry his use of her maiden name had made her.

'Vanish, ma'am. Go back to America, at once. There's a packet sails tonight. I've made all the arrangements. I did it the minute I heard.'

'Did you consult my aunt?' She noticed with detached interest that she was trembling a little.

'I had no opportunity. But she'll see the sense of it. I booked a passage for her, too, of course. Don't you see, it's the only way. Then if the Duke wishes, he can come over, after a decent interval, and woo you in form.'

'I have never heard so much nonsense in my life.' And then, while he gaped his surprise, 'Did you, Mr. Biddock, have the effrontery to book the passage in my name?'

'Well, of course.'

'Then I would be grateful if you would get together the papers relating to my estate. I am transferring my business to Mr. Barff. Today. Your last action on my behalf will be cancelling that passage.'

'Passage?' Brett joined them. 'I was wondering where you had got to, love. But what's the matter?' He put an arm round her and felt her tremble.

'Mr. Biddock wants me to "vanish." So as not to disgrace you, My Lord Duke. He's been so good as to book passages on tonight's packet for my aunt and me. He suggests that—if you should happen to feel like it—you might come to America in a year or so and woo me decently. Brett!'

He had burst into a fit of laughter. 'And you let him make you so angry? My poor darling, where's your sense of humour? He hadn't, I take it, consulted your aunt? I can hardly see her lending herself to such a scheme.'

'No. I'm taking my affairs away from him, Brett.'

'Oh, I wouldn't do that.' His fingers found her ribs in something between a pinch and a caress. 'Such a palaver. We've enough to do as it is, love.' He turned to Biddock. 'The Duchess will forgive you, this once, Biddock. See to the cancelling of the passages, and explain that it was your mistake. Then come back to me, here. We've a great deal to attend to.'

'Yes, Your Grace. Thank you, Your Grace.' It was hard to tell which of them he was addressing.

'You don't mind my taking the law into my own hands?' Brett turned to her smiling, as Biddock left the room.

'Do you know, I find I rather like it. Do you think I'm going to dwindle into a dependent "yes-my-love" wife?'

'I very much doubt it.' He took her in his arms. 'Alone at last!'

'Oh no we're not,' said Phyllida crossly. 'What is it, Jenny?'

'The *Philip*!' Jenny threw open the shutters. 'Look! I'd know her anywhere.'

'And Alex handling her,' Phyllida agreed. 'Lord! Look at that for a landing.'

'Damned risky,' said Brett, 'like all his behaviour. But you have to give him credit for courage. Besides, he provides us with an admirable excuse to leave this appalling party. If I have to endure five minutes' more conversation with Mrs. Froxe I shall say something to her we'll both regret.'

Jenny could not help laughing. 'Oh, B., you horror, and when you think how you pined over her!'

'Yes,' said Phyllida. 'How glad I am I didn't accept that place on the packet. I'm not going to give you the chance to forget *me*, love.'

'You're right about that. But, come, we don't want Alex getting to the *Helena* before we do. You've got Peter safely locked up, I trust?'

'Yes,' said Jenny, 'in your cabin. I don't know where you and Phyllida are going to sleep, B.'

There was only time for the briefest exchange of news before they were boarding the *Helena*, to an enthusiastic welcome, and the sight of the *Philip*'s boat, rapidly approaching.

'You'll let me handle this?' Brett asked Phyllida.

'Gladly.' She was aware of Jenny's amused eye on her. Had she used to be so self-willed? 'But you won't be hard on Peter?'

'I propose to be very good to Peter. I hope. But I think we'd best see Alex first, if you don't mind?'

'Of course not.' She was not even sure that she wanted to see her brother. What in the world, after all that had happened, could they say to each other?

Alex, on the other hand, climbing lightly on board, showed no sense of shame whatever, and that was really rather a relief. He greeted them all, just as usual, with his ravishing smile, and went on to congratulate Brett and Phyllida on a happy escape. 'And on your marriage?' He made it just a question.

'You are well informed. Yes, Father Gennaios married us.' Brett said it, deliberately, as a challenge.

'So I heard. And you led his people on a raid of my stores! If I'd not been so pleased with Oenone otherwise, I'd have been angry with her about that.'

'She did not know I had seen them,' said Brett. 'She took the greatest possible care to prevent it. I'm glad you recognise the debt you owe her. She saved you from a very difficult situation.'

Alex threw back his head and laughed. 'Yes, as things have turned out, I really think she did. A girl in a thousand. And'—he turned to Phyllida—'you intend to keep your word to her, *kyria*?'

'My wife always keeps her word.' For the first time, Brett allowed anger to show. 'You are come, I take it, to collect Oenone's dowry. I warn you, I am going to see it tied up for her and her children. That's why we need Mr. Biddock, love.' He turned to explain to Phyllida. 'He will do what we tell him, without asking questions. But there's one other condition I am going to make.'

'Oh?' Alex's bright eye was suspicious now.

'Yes. We've got Peter Vannick shut up in my cabin, which I happen to want for myself, and my wife. I think you had better take him home with you. By his behaviour he's much more a Greek than an American. You agree, Phyl?'

She suppressed a pang. But, almost certainly, Brett was right. 'If he does, yes.'

'Then we had better have him up here. Barlow, would you?'

Peter looked so haggard that Phyllida forgot everything in pity for him. 'Oh, Peter!' For a moment he was her little brother again.

'Don't "oh Peter" me!' He rejected her advance angrily. 'It's your fault; all of this. If you'd not persuaded our father to make that unjust will, none of it would have happened.'

'That settles it,' said Brett. 'I've two things to break to you, Mr. Vannick. One is that your sister has promised your half of her fortune to Alex's wife, in exchange for our freedom. So much for your dreams of wealth.'

Peter managed a sneer. 'And I take it I am to languish

in prison? A shade embarrassing for you, surely, My Lord Duke?'

'That's just what I thought,' said Brett. 'So I am hoping to persuade Alex here to take you away with him. I'–he emphasised the pronoun–'shall arrange to have an annuity paid to you through him. While you live with him, it continues. Agreed, Alex?'

'Agreed,' said Alex. 'Come, *koumbaros*, it's time we were going. As for the money'–he smiled his heart-stirring smile for the last time–'I trust you implicitly, milord.'

'You can,' said Brett.

They were gone. Phyllida, leaning against the rail, watched their boat pull away towards the *Philip* and tried not to cry too obviously. 'Don't.' Brett's comforting arm went round her. 'You did your best by him. Now, I really hope, he's ready to learn a little sense.'

'Oh, do you think so?' She smiled up at him, shakily.

'Yes. There's nothing like making a real fool of oneself. I should know. Lord, I wonder you didn't take that passage on the packet after one glimpse of my Helena.'

Her smile broadened. 'Depressed you, did she? Brett, how soon can we leave here?'

'Just as soon as we've done our business with Biddock. You'll let me handle it for you?'

'Gladly. If he will.'

Now his smile was a little grim. 'Of course he will. There's something, I think, that hasn't occurred to you, my love. I'm afraid when you married me you made me master of your fortune. I'm ashamed not to have pointed it out at the time, but there were more important things to think of. Will you mind very much?'

'Mind? You mean the whole burden is yours now?'

'If you want to put it that way, and as soon as Biddock accepts the fact of our marriage, yes.' Could he really be looking at her nervously?

'Delicious!' she said. 'You'll make me an allowance–a paltry one, of course–and I'll run up bills, and you'll scold me. Do you realise, Brett, that I've been managing money since I was seventeen? Oh what a plague I'm going to be to you.'

'Aren't you just! But I shall have my redress. I shall

shut you up, love, in a turret at Sarum Hall and feed you on bread and water until you behave yourself.'

'Oh, well.' Cheerfully. 'After some of the things we've eaten, you and I, bread and water will be quite a treat. But tell me, love, is there really a Sarum Hall?'

'Well, of course. A Gothic ruin in the middle of Salisbury Plain so inconvenient that none of my relatives has lived there for years. And no money to keep it up. My cousin the Duke left nothing but debts, Biddock tells me. And my uncle is dead, so Helena is a rich woman.'

'Good,' said Phyllida. 'Then we don't need to trouble ourselves about her. I should think, shouldn't you, that with what remains of my fortune we might make ourselves quite a snug corner in your Gothic ruin? If you approve, of course. Oh, *won't* Aunt Cassandra be pleased?'

'And you, love?'

'Dear Brett, if I can be happy with you in an Egyptian dungeon, don't you think I'll manage in a Gothic ruin? Oh, look, there's Price!' She held out her hands warmly as Price approached, closely followed by Cassandra, with Jenny and her lieutenant ('Now where the deuce did *he* spring from?' said Brett beside her.) 'Price,' said Phyllida, 'I am so delighted to see you. You can see how I've missed you.' An expressive hand drew his attention to her unusual garb.

'Thank you, Your Grace.' He was holding a bouquet of orange blossom. 'They're from us all, Your Grace. To wish you both as happy as we know you'll be.'

'Oh, thank you.' She took the fragrant bouquet, her eyes suddenly full of tears. 'But where in the world did you find them, so late in the season?'

He smiled suddenly. 'Perhaps best not to ask, miss–I beg your pardon–Your Grace.'

She sighed, 'I shall never get used to it.' And then, eagerly, 'Price, my things?'

'I've taken the liberty of laying out a dress in your cabin. I've moved everything back there, now Mr. Vannick's gone. That's why I wasn't here to greet you sooner.' He looked, she thought, for once in his life, a little self-conscious, and she understood why when she hurried down to the cabin she had shared, for so long, with Cassandra, and found her own things and Brett's neatly arranged there, and her best white muslin, exquisitely pressed, ready on the bed.

When she returned to the deck, Brett had vanished. 'He's gone to see old Biddock,' Jenny explained. 'To arrange your second wedding, I expect. Just think of having two!' And then, as a logical connection, 'May I present Lieutenant Chalmers of the *Redstart*?'

Brett did not return till suppertime. 'All's fixed,' he said. 'Have you decided what you're to wear at your second wedding, love?'

'Good God, no. I never thought.'

'There's a Duchess for you,' he said lovingly. 'What a fortunate thing someone in our family has some sense. We don't want to shock the natives by any lack of ceremony, do we? So I have arranged for the best dressmaker on the island to visit you first thing tomorrow with several miles of valenciennes and all the seamstresses she can find. I expect, among you, you can produce something that won't actually shame me by three o'clock in the afternoon?'

'I expect so,' she said meekly. 'But, Brett!'

'Yes, love?'

'Price has put all your things into my cabin.'

He looked down at her, a smile in his eyes. 'You're sure you don't mean that Price has put all *your* things in *my* cabin?'

'Well.' She coloured. 'You could put it that way. But the thing is . . .' She took a deep breath. 'We're being married tomorrow. So–what about tonight?'

'What do you think?' he said.



5

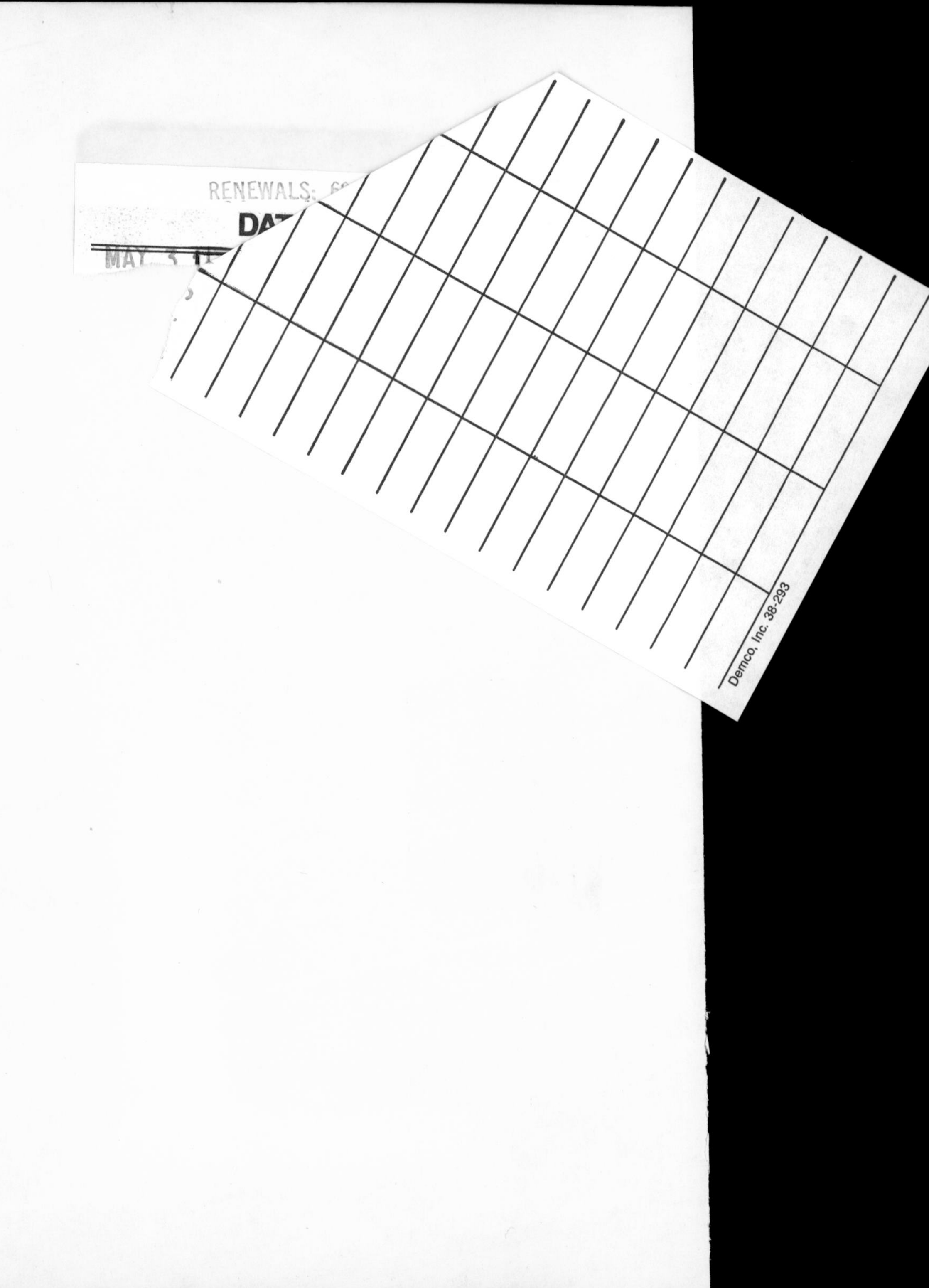
RENEWALS
DAT
MAY 3
Demco, Inc. 38-293